Separation of Church and State

A Thriller

JOSEPH MAX LEWIS

SEPARATION OF CHURCH AND STATE

Copyright © 2014 Joseph Max Lewis

Published by 4 Pine Publishing

eBook 978-1-7338456-2-5
Print Book 978-1-7338456-3-2

This book is a work of fiction. The names, characters, places, and incidents are products of the writer's imagination or have been used fictitiously and are not to be construed as real. Any resemblance to persons, living or dead, actual events, locales or organizations is entirely coincidental.

All rights reserved. Except for any review, the reproduction or utilization of this work in whole or in part in any form by any electronic, mechanical or other means, now known or hereinafter invented, including xerography, photocopying and recording, or in any information storage or retrieval system is forbidden without the written permission of the author.

Printed in the USA.

Cover Design and Interior Format

Also by Joseph Max Lewis

The Diaries of Pontius Pilate
Separation of Church and State
Baghdad Burning
Hell Rises
Final Warning
Aftermath

Short Stories
Just Verdicts
John Hancock – July 4, 1776
John Hancock – The Final Chapter
Black Site

LEARN MORE AT:
www.josephmaxlewis.com

CHAPTER 1

IN THE FUTURE

"IF WHAT YOU SAY IS true, American elections are a hoax," Cardinal Thomas Guzetti said. "Why bother to vote? Congress and the Presidency? Nothing more than advisory boards, a pretty facade to placate the citizenry."

The hot glare of stage lights chased away every shadow and illuminated the handsome face of guest moderator Tim Lewis. Tim tried to decide if he should interrupt Guzetti. He wanted to be fair, but knew his own performance had to be perfect. New York City's flu epidemic had knocked out the regular host of Real Reliable News' Network's award winning "Law for Lunch" public affairs broadcast, giving Tim, fresh out of journalism school, an opportunity most of his peers would literally kill for. Before Tim decided, Guzetti's debate opponent intervened.

Harvard Law Professor Morris Liebowitz faced the camera with a dismissive smile before responding. "I've come to expect that kind of fear mongering from the Christian Right, Cardinal, but you're a Harvard educated lawyer." Liebowitz shook his head. "We've always had a living constitution."

"Cardinal Guzetti," Tim said, "doesn't Professor Liebowitz have a point? It does seem a bit extreme to suggest our democratic process is a sham because we have a Supreme Court." Tim felt a twinge of guilt for "sculpting" Guzetti's words, but it was a part of the job. The R.R.N. management and newsroom had little tolerance for Christian viewpoints. If the Cardinal didn't lose the debate, and look out of touch while doing so, Tim's career would suffer.

"Hardly extreme, Mr. Lewis," Guzetti replied with a smile. With his plain black suit and Roman collar, he looked like everyone's favorite neighborhood Priest. "It's a matter of simple logic," Guzetti said, "not because of the Supreme Court as an institution, but because some are claiming we have a "Living Constitution."

"Of course we have a Living Constitution," Liebowitz said.

"Please Professor Liebowitz," Guzetti continued, "let me make my case."

It was the moderator's decision and a tricky one. Guzetti wasn't what Tim expected. He found himself liking the Cardinal and that was dangerous. Mishandling Guzetti could ruin his career. Tim decided to let Guzetti speak, trusting Liebowitz to trip him up. Few people were a match for the brilliant Harvard Law Professor. Tim could feel the sweat beading up underneath his thick TV makeup.

"As many people know," Guzetti said, "if Congress or a State passes a law that violates the Constitution, the Court can and should declare the law null and void. It's 'Unconstitutional,' we say. So let's think this through, a 'living' Constitution means the Constitution changes when five Justices decide it changes, isn't that correct Professor Liebowitz?"

"No it's not." Liebowitz' bushy eyebrows quivered. "As community standards evolve, the Constitution evolves. Do you think America still allows people to be placed in stocks for petty offenses?"

"I stand corrected. The Constitution evolves when community standards change. But who decides whether our standards have changed? Not our citizens. Five Justices make that decision, don't they? No one else gets a vote. Therefore anytime the American people want a change in the law and elect Congressmen who pass a law making the change, if five Justices don't like it, all they have to do is say it's 'unconstitutional' because we've 'evolved'."

"Extremist nonsense," Liebowitz said.

The Law Professor looked delighted, but for some reason Tim felt uneasy.

"Our country has had judicial review since its inception, since Marbury vs. Madison," Liebowitz said. "Any two hundred year-old document, no matter how brilliantly drafted, must be interpreted in light of subsequent developments. Since the ratification of our Constitution we've developed automobiles, wiretaps, contraception and the internet. Surely Cardinal, even the Catholic Church has heard of these things."

The Cardinal smiled, allowing Tim and Liebowitz a laugh at his and his Church's expense. Tim felt better, Liebowitz looked smug.

"Of course judicial review has always existed and the Court does have the power to strike down laws," the Cardinal said. "But only if they're unconstitutional. That's why judicial power must be dependent upon what's actually written in the Constitution. Otherwise, the Court can do whatever it wants. As I said, all five Justices on the Supreme Court have to do is declare a law unconstitutional, when really they just don't like the law and think they're smarter than the rest of us."

"Cardinal, really," Liebowitz said. "As we already proved, interpretation must occur to accommodate changes in society. Where does it say 'telephone' in the Constitution? It doesn't, but do we want the Government listening in on our phone calls just because telephones weren't invented at the time of the Constitution and you Christians are paranoid?"

"Did you really prove interpretation is what's at issue here?" The Cardinal took a moment, steepled his fingers, and then continued. "I'm afraid I'm not convinced and an old joke helps to explain why." Guzetti looked over at Tim. "I am afraid it's a bit risqué though."

Tim couldn't resist the potential for controversy. If the Cardinal actually told an off color joke on national television . . . He gestured permission to Guzetti.

"An old Priest from New York always wanted to go to Paris," Guzetti said. "When the day finally arrived, he decided to take along an interpreter. After they landed in Paris and checked into their hotel, he told the interpreter to ask for directions to a famous cathedral. In turn, the interpreter approached a local citizen and seemed to relay the Priest's request by interpreting it into French."

CHAPTER 2

FIVE BLOCKS AWAY FROM "Law for Lunch's" Manhattan studio, Law Professor Fred Stueben fought flu symptoms while holding court at a trendy midtown watering hole called "The Warehouse." He sat facing three admiring students, his back to the bar's television. He was thus unaware of the disaster unfolding behind him.

A nearby table of young, successful looking businessmen kept their eyes on the television while they talked.

"I like this Catholic guy," one of them said, "but you never see him on TV anymore. Hey Tony, turn it up," he said in a voice loud enough to be heard over the clatter of plates and buzz of conversation.

Stueben was in the middle of his third cocktail, but he immediately recognized the voice of Cardinal Thomas Guzetti. You don't see him, Stueben thought, twisting around, because he's effective. We don't allow him on the air.

"What's he doing on Law for Lunch?" he said out loud.

Stueben suspected he was slurring his words. The students swallowed their laughter and looked from the Professor to the large screen television mounted above the bar.

"Professor, what's wrong?" a leggy, third-year law student said.

What's wrong? Stueben ignored her. There's no way that idiot Liebowitz should be allowed in the same building as Thomas Guzetti, he thought, especially with Judge Quintin Anders, a "Living Constitution" Supreme Court Nominee before the Senate for confirmation. Did this woman know just how many Senate staffers watched "Law for Lunch"? Did she wonder what might happen if a couple staffers convinced their Senators that Guzetti had a point about the whole "Living Constitution" thing? That's what was wrong. It was like turning on the television news just in time to see your own house burning down.

"Cut him off," Stueben yelled at the television.

"They can't hear you," a young businesswoman yelled back.

Everyone in the bar laughed and clapped. A stunned Stueben slumped into his chair. He knew he should get up, call Merkel and get Guzetti off the air, but he couldn't seem to get to his feet.

"So," Cardinal Guzetti continued, "our Priest is in Paris, asking to see a cathedral. His interpreter seems to pass on the request to a local citizen. The worthy Parisian responds in French, gestures with his hands and points down the street. The interpreter nods, replies, and then leads the Priest away. Now, the Priest asked to see a cathedral. If he ends up in front of a Cathedral, a Church or even a Synagogue or Mosque, fine, the interpreter was interpreting. But . . ."

Guzetti scratched his cheek, looked from the moderator back to Liebowitz and then into the camera with practiced ease.

". . . if the Priest ends up in front of a whorehouse, maybe the interpreter is not really an interpreter, maybe he's a United States Supreme Court Justice."

The bar erupted with laughter. Even the show's moderator seemed to be fighting back a smile. Liebowitz sputtered, his famous eyebrows twitching spasmodically. The Cardinal managed to look perplexed by the reaction. It reminded Stueben of a chattering Liebowitz mouse and a Guzetti boa constrictor. Meanwhile, the lunch crowd took in the dignified looking Cardinal in his collar and burst into renewed laughter.

"A ridiculous analogy," Liebowitz managed. "No one on any Court is engaged in such an endeavor."

"Really? Why is the establishment clause of First Amendment, despite the free exercise of religion clause, being used to suppress religious expression when it was designed to protect religious expression?"

"Of course that's because of the constitutional separation of church and state. The wall of separation actually protects religion."

"With protection like that, who needs danger?"

"And there, Cardinal, is a perfect example," Liebowitz said, beaming. "Like it or not, the Constitution is the highest law in the land."

"And there, Professor, is our whorehouse. This is the Constitution," Guzetti said, holding up and then handing over a pamphlet copy of the U.S. Constitution. "Please, show me, not just in the First Amendment, but anywhere in this document where it says, quote, separation of church and state unquote."

"Of course it's not written down, but that doesn't mean it's not a constitutional principle."

Stueben slid out his cell phone, then glanced up. "The Warehouse" was a reconditioned building notorious for bad cell phone reception. Its ceiling, embedded with pipes and wiring, suspended a heavy steel track for the still operational overhead crane. He stuck the phone back in his pocket, sighed and tried to decide what to do.

Conversation at the other tables began to die down as more people looked up at the TV screen.

"I see, even though the Founders said Cathedral, they really meant whorehouse," Guzetti said.

A second table of young professionals burst into laughter. Stueben ground his teeth. Evidently the moderator hadn't recovered from the whorehouse joke. His two guests continued, un-moderated.

"This is outrageous and demonstrates the danger of permitting religion in the public square," Liebowitz said. "History teaches us, or should have by now, that wars caused by religion and especially Christianity, have killed more people than all other causes, combined."

"I'm afraid that's not accurate. Communists like Stalin, Mao and Pol Pot each killed millions, and they were all confirmed atheists. Remember China's Great Peoples Cultural Revolution? At least twenty million people died before it was over. The killing fields in Cambodia claimed the lives of unknown millions, but some estimates suggest twenty five percent of the country's population died at the hands of the Khmer Rouge. Joseph Stalin starved ten to twelve million Russian peasant farmers to death and killed another two million building the great Canal outside of Moscow. All three of these monsters were confirmed atheists."

The moderator, who the screen identified as Tim Lewis, grimaced like he'd sipped sour milk.

"Wait a minute Cardinal Guzetti," Tim said. "The Catholic Church during the Inquisition killed a lot of people. How many people were burned at the stake because your Church claimed they were heretics? Here in our country Protestant extremists tried women for witchcraft in Salem. You can't deny that."

"Deny these events occurred? Of course not. Tragedies. Probably five thousand people were killed during the Inquisition. In America, thirteen were put on trial during the Salem witch trials. Horrible and indefensible, no doubt. But millions of human beings were slaughtered by Stalin, Pol Pot and Mao. I'm afraid we Christians are amateurs compared to you atheists."

"A good time for a break, gentlemen," Tim said. "This is Tim Lewis, sitting in for Tony Brown. More constitutional debate when we return with Cardinal Thomas Guzetti and Professor Morris Liebowitz on 'Law for Lunch.'"

The commercial break jolted Stueben out of his stupor. Guzetti, not surprisingly, destroyed Liebowitz and his clichéd arguments, no doubt setting the movement back by years.

"I'm leaving," Stueben said. He jumped to his feet, almost surprised his legs worked. "Here, take care of this." Stueben sniffled, tossed a Gold Card on the table and set off. Tray-laden waiters glared at him but moved to one side. At coat check a line of well-dressed men and women shuffled toward the counter. Stueben walked past them and flashed a twenty dollar bill at one of the attendants.

"Hey pal!"

"Quickly, quickly," Stueben said, tossing the twenty on the counter and pointing at his overcoat. "Richard," he said to the maître de, "a cab. It's an emergency, man. Move."

"Of course, Mr. Stueben."

Stueben collected his coat, pushed through the bronze and glass doors and punched in the direct dial number for "Law for Lunch's" creator. While he climbed into the cab, Anthony Merkel's voice-mail picked up.

"Today is Friday, October 7 and like everybody else in New York, I've come down with this three day flu. Hopefully I'll be in on Monday. I'm still checking in, so if it's an emergency, leave a message. Thanks."

BEEP.

"Anthony, its Fred." Stueben sneezed. "Someone's put Thomas Guzetti on Law for Lunch's air with that idiot Liebowitz. Cancel this bloodbath before Guzetti can cause any more damage. The last thing we need right now is something like this." Stueben hung up and stabbed another number into his cell phone.

"R.R.N. news division."

"Law for Lunch," Stueben said.

"One moment."

"Law for Lunch, Ellen."

"Ellen, its Fred Stueben. Where's Anthony and who's that young idiot moderating?"

"Mr. Stueben, I, Mr. Merkel . . . is down with the flu, Mr. Brown is down with the flu and he assigned Tim to do the-"

"Why's Thomas Guzetti participating? You scheduled that Professor from Dartmouth, what's her name? Liebowitz is supposed to win these debates. He's brilliant, remember?"

"Ms. Hart canceled because she caught the flu, so Tim-"

"Tim who?"

"Tim Lewis, he invited Cardinal Guzetti. Ms. Hart cancelled late in the morning and we only had an hour before-"

"Get them off the air."

"I can't do that. I'm the receptionist."

"I want the control room."

"I'll get you the control room."

Stueben waited while the phone rang and rang. Finally, someone picked it up.

"Jeffers. We're live, who the hell is this?"

"Stueben."

"Uh, Hi Professor. We're pretty busy right-"

"Get them off the air."

"What?"

"I said get them off the air."

"Just shut down 'Law for Lunch?' Sorry Professor. I know you and Mr. Merkel are friends but Mr. Merkel's the only one who can-"

"Call him."

"I can't just call him."

"Call Merkel on his private line and tell him some kid reporter booked Cardinal Thomas Guzetti opposite Morrie Liebowitz."

"Okay, for you I'll do it."

The producer hung up. Stueben leaned over the front seat.

"Get me to the R.R.N. headquarters on 15th St."

A few moments later Stueben's cell phone rang.

"Stueben."

"It's Merkel," the executive producer of Law for Lunch croaked over the phone.

"Did you see the bloodbath that just took place on your show?" Stueben lowered his voice. "Now, when we're two confirmation hearings away?"

"I didn't see; I heard. Tim Lewis is a good kid, not a true believer yet, but absolutely opposed to the hypocrisy. Relax. I pulled the plug on the show. We'll finish with part of a lecture from the Attorney General on the same issues."

"Good, but a lot of damage's been done. We'd better hope this-"

"Don't be dramatic. Its' way too late for one debate to make any difference," Merkel said.

"Don't underestimate Guzetti. I'm on my way to your studio. Someone needs to have a talk with that young man."

"Fred, he works for me, not you."

"Then straighten him out, now. You might think it doesn't matter, but a lot of us do. We're friends and allies and I'll back you up, but I want my way on this. You can't coddle that kid, just because he's cute. It's a weakness Anthony."

"It's not a weakness; I'm grooming him for recruitment into the Society."

"How long will it take you to get to the studio?"

I'm calling from the car. We're about ten blocks away."

"You can't ignore this. Either straighten him out or fire him."

"I said I'll deal with it."

"I want to sit in."

"Agreed."

CHAPTER 3

Guzetti's strong performance caught Tim off guard. Usually, Christians relied upon fuzzy, Biblically based arguments during public policy debates. Not Guzetti. He'd proven to be a capable debater.

Capable?

Okay, a lot better than capable. Some might even say he was winning, but Tim told himself it was close. Nothing that couldn't be fixed. In the final two segments he'd intervene more aggressively during Guzetti's time. It wasn't fair, but Tim wanted, he needed, Liebowitz to finish strong. Just in case. The first indication of how badly he misjudged the show came from Producer Tom Jeffers.

"Change of plans, gentlemen," Jeffers said. "We're going to finish up the show with tape from the Attorney General's speech on the First Amendment last week at Georgetown Law School. It'll be a perfect finish to the great debate you guys put on."

"We're not changing anything," Tim said, half out of his seat. "Tom, this is my call." Tim liked Jeffers, he liked everyone at R.R.N., but no way was he getting his air time cut. "Sorry Tom. At least for today I'm your boss. We go live in twelve seconds. Do it. Gentlemen, have a seat."

Tim hated embarrassing Jeffers, but planned on making it up to him. The Producer fiddled with his headset, glanced around like he wished he were somewhere else, then told him.

"Tim, Anthony Merkel called and told me to cut your mike. We're running the video of the Attorney General."

Everyone in the studio knew how much Tim admired Merkel. He could see sympathy in Jeffers eyes, so he tried to shrug it off.

"Well, that's it then," Tim said, his voice cracking.

Separation of Church and State   15

"Mr. Merkel wants you to go back to twenty and wait for him to call," Jeffers said.

In other words, slink back to your small cubicle on the twentieth floor and wait for a phone call from the Boss. Then it got worse.

"I guess he's coming in," Jeffers said. He looked down at the floor and fiddled with his headset.

Liebowitz threw his lapel mike onto his seat, ignored the Cardinal's outstretched hand and stomped over.

"I wasn't prepared for this," Liebowitz said. He glared down at Tim, bushy eyebrows dancing. "You set me up. I'm telling Merkel, either you go or I do."

Liebowitz stormed off, leaving Tim blinking like a punch drunk boxer. He took Cardinal Guzetti outstretched hand without really thinking.

"The truth isn't very popular these days, son," Guzetti said. "Neither are those who give it a fair chance. If I can ever help you, call me," he said in a soft voice.

The Cardinal handed Tim a plain white business card with his name, title and what appeared to be a private direct dial number, then left. Jeffers came over and put his hand on Tim's shoulder.

"Tim, Merkel likes you. We all make mistakes. He knows that."

"Thanks. Sorry. I snapped at you. Tom. Sorry."

Tim unclipped his lapel mike and left the set. When he reached the make-up room door he held his breath, but the room was mercifully empty. He chose one of the four prep stations and went to work scraping off the clay like make up. His face stared back at him from a lighted, chrome-framed mirror.

On the way in several members of the stage crew had mumbled encouragement as he'd passed them. Don't sweat it, they said. Mr. Merkel knows everyone makes mistakes.

"You know the truth, though, don't' you," Tim whispered to his reflection. Yes, Anthony Merkel might know everyone made mistakes, but that didn't mean he tolerated them. Merkel didn't tolerate mistakes, he fired them.

Anthony Merkel arrived at the R.R.N. building in the back of a network owned limousine. The limo entered via a private entrance to an underground parking lot. As an Executive Producer and Real Reliable News Network's Director of Special Reporting, Merkel possessed a restricted access key to a special set of VIP elevators. The limo dropped him off and Merkel took the elevator straight to the Fiftieth Floor. He waved a greeting to his Secretary and entered a spacious, window lined corner office. The view of Manhattan traffic crawling along hundreds of feet below was a daily reminder of Merkel's position and place in the world. Before he sat down, his intercom buzzed.

"What is it Sharon?"

"Mr. Stueben just checked in downstairs and is on his way up."

"Send him in when he arrives. Oh, after you let Stueben in, call young Tim Lewis and ask him to come up here. You might as well make it sound ominous."

Merkel made himself a Scotch and soda at a walnut shuttered wet bar, picked up Tim Lewis' personnel file and took everything over to a gleaming mahogany conference table. His throat burned and his joints ached, but he felt optimistic. The situation with Tim was the opportunity he'd been waiting for. Merkel set his tumbler down just as the office intercom buzzed.

Fred Stueben charged through the door and slammed it behind him.

"Where's he at," Stueben demanded between coughs. Merkel sneezed in response and popped another antihistamine.

"He's on his way up."

"Did you see what happened?"

"I watched the tape on the way over." Merkel took another slug of scotch, coughed, then shook his tumbler back and forth so the ice cubes clinked against the glass. "Not pretty."

"Not pretty is an understatement," Stueben said. "What do you think everyone's going to be talking about? Right now, when we're so close. Something like this will sink into the public culture. Forget about all the Senate staffers who watch the show. Law for Lunch is one of the nation's most influential public affairs shows. We can't afford to have people questioning the Living Constitution, let alone the Separation of Church and State. Now? Are you kidding me?"

Merkel laughed and polished off the last of his double scotch in one long pull. He thought about Tim Lewis' handsome face and form. Such a sincere boy, and so concerned about his career. Who knew what wonderful things might happen?

"You're over reacting," Merkel said. "It's too late for anything like this to make a difference. Here," he said holding out his glass. "Make one for yourself and make me another."

"I think you're over confident."

"Fred, for the last 40 years we've been using every outlet at our disposal, which in recent decades is almost all of them, to demonize Christians of every denomination and stripe. We use movies, cartoons, television shows, books, everything."

Merkel's intercom buzzed.

Tim found himself checking the Eastern Standard Time wall clock in the R.R.N. newsroom every few minutes. A skeleton news staff still bustled about, phones rang and reporters, associate producers and staff shouted across the room at each other. But word traveled fast, even in the flu ravaged newsroom. It left Tim, like any potential pariah, isolated by the ambitious careerists who knew disfavor could be contagious.

So he waited it out in his cubicle, transferring his Law for Lunch notes, Liebowitz's and Guzetti's business cards, his legal pad, and other research materials into an open mouthed leather satchel. He removed an expensive digital micro recorder from the satchel and fiddled with its settings for a few moments.

Looks like this is your last chance, Pal, Tim thought to himself.

For over fourteen months he'd been secretly recording not only his meetings with Anthony Merkel, but also any off the cuff comment the great man made. The recordings would serve as the basis for a Pulitzer prize-winning account of modern journalism, focusing on his hero, Anthony Merkel, a legend in advocacy journalism.

Tim's desk phone rang and his Pulitzer fantasies evaporated. It was Merkel's secretary, Sharon Moore. She was a nice woman and since Tim had once helped her, he hoped she'd give him an idea of what he'd be walking into.

"How bad is it, Sharon?"

"I think you'd better just come up, Tim."

Tim's stomach knotted. He shoved the recorder into his front pocket, picked up a tablet and pencil and forced himself to walk to the elevator. When the doors opened he went in with his head down, pre-playing his responses to Merkel's likely questions. When he looked up he was face to face with one of R.R.N.'s in house security staff, a guy by the name of Carl Hardesty. Hardesty stood six foot four inches tall with a barrel chest and close cropped white hair. Although he was physically intimidating, that's not why everyone called him "Creepy Carl." It was because of the way he looked at you, that, and his eyes. Carnival glass green. Tim pulled up short under Hardesty's cold stare, like a buffalo calf looking into crocodile eyes.

"What floor, Mr. Lewis?" Hardesty said.

"Uh, Fifty please."

"Of course, Fifty," he said, managing to sound displeased.

Tim watched each floor number light up and fade. He tried to ignore the feeling the other man was staring at him. Hardesty got off the elevator at twenty-two, but the ride seemed to take forever.

Forget about "Creepy Carl," Tim thought. Get ready.

While the elevator climbed to Fifty Tim concentrated on catching his breath, straightening his tie and arranging his clothing. By the time the elevator shuddered to a stop he was mentally and emotionally prepared for a difficult interview.

Normally, Tim loved his first glance at the Fiftieth Floor lobby. The doors clacked open to reveal large gold letters mounted on a blue wall. "R.R.N. - Special Reporting Unit." Today, he barely noticed. He stepped into the reception area with his game face, a neutral look that gave away nothing. On either side of the lettering two matching receptionists, beautiful and blond, sat behind two identical reception stations. On most week days the area bustled, but today the offices were dark and empty.

Tim approached Merkel's secretary-receptionist on Mediterranean Blue carpet so thick it was like walking on a particularly firm mattress. Sharon Moore glanced up and a flash of sympathy crossed her delicate features.

"Just go in, Tim," she said. "They're waiting for you."

Tim walked down the hall and into Merkel's office. Merkel was on the far side of the conference table, seated alongside R.R.N. legal contributor Fred Stueben.

"So this is the idiot," Stueben said.

"Enough, Fred," Merkel said. "Sit," he said to Tim, pointing at one of the chairs on the opposite side of the conference table.

"Mr. Merkel, I understand you wanted to see me."

"What did you think you were doing?" Merkel said.

Tim slid his chair to the table and caught a glimpse of his future. Doing the weather for some small market TV station in Central Ohio or, even worse, Pittsburgh. Merkel was going to send him home with his tail between his legs. Not good enough for the big time, everyone would whisper. Then he remembered his recorder and slid his right hand underneath the conference table. Merkel and Stueben both stared at him, seemingly oblivious to his hands, so he took a chance, pulled out the recorder and turned it on. If nothing else, he'd at least get to write his book.

"You put Cardinal Thomas Guzetti on Law for Lunch, in a debate, with Morrie Liebowitz of all people," Merkel said.

"Mr. Merkel that's because–"

"Did I ask you to speak, Tim?" Merkel waited and let him sweat. "Where'd you even get his name?"

"His office called our junior producers on four or five occasions and offered his services. He seemed qualified and–"

"And," Merkel said, "we ignored his offers because we don't want Guzetti or anyone like him appearing on television. Especially on Law for Lunch. Despite that fact you felt free to call him up and give him access to our audience. What's the purpose of modern journalism, Mr. Lewis?"

"To educate the public and provide them with an information flow that enables them to reach proper conclusions and make wise decisions. We're change agents."

"This isn't Journalism School," Stueben said. "You don't get patted on the head just because you can parrot back the right answer. What you do is what counts and what did you just do? You let both sides of the argument be heard, you idiot. It's the kind of mistake that kills careers. And you just made one."

Tim was still hunched forward with both hands underneath the table. When he realized his hands were shaking he slid the micro recorder onto the seat of the next chair and leaned back. He kept his face neutral.

"I'm afraid Fred's right, Tim," Merkel said, shaking his head.

Merkel and Stueben stared at him. After a long minute, Merkel finally gave him permission to speak.

"Anything to say for yourself?"

"He's a Christian theologian, Catholic, a Cardinal." Tim fought down butterflies and kept his voice even. "I know he has a law degree but, Mr. Merkel, you never expect these guys to be intellectuals. How many times have we laughed while watching Christians during debates? All they ever do is quote the Bible, I mean, if their opponents believed in the Bible they wouldn't be debating them anyway. This guy, Guzetti, knew the law, he made arguments I've never heard before and hardly even mentioned the Bible in his argument. How was I supposed to know?"

"Not good enough," Stueben said.

If Stueben, a close confidant of Merkel's, said "not good enough," Tim didn't like his chances. There it was, his childhood dream, six years of school, all the hard work and making the right connections, gone. If that wasn't bad enough, his hero was going to be the one to destroy his career. He was suddenly hollow, like someone scooped part of his insides out and sewed him back together.

Then he received, if not a pardon, at least a reprieve.

"Tim you've exhibited extraordinarily bad judgment today. However your work up to this point has been exemplary. You've shown a great deal of promise. While my initial inclination is to agree with Fred, I want to take the weekend and consider your fate. Is this acceptable or do you insist upon a decision now?"

"Mr. Merkel, please, take the weekend and thank you for-"

"Enough. As I say, my inclination is to terminate you, so don't be too optimistic. Nevertheless I want to give this some thought before I make a final decision. Until then I want you to think about what I'm about to tell you. Are you listening, Tim?"

"Yes."

"These fundamentalist Christians are very intolerant and dangerous, but not all of them are stupid. Regardless of my decision next week, you will have a future in journalism. The question I must decide over the weekend is if you can operate at the level of R.R.N.'s Special Reporting Unit. In the meantime, let me explain this to you since it's obvious you can't figure it out for yourself.

As you said, the job of the modern journalist is to act as a change agent. The way we accomplish that is to control the information flow - what information gets to the public and what information doesn't get to the public. Remember, most members of the public, even the intelligent ones, do not follow current events on a day-to-day basis. Also, they evaluate information from a background of outmoded American nationalism and Judeo-Christian values."

"Plus, they're ignorant and stupid," said Stueben.

"Please, Fred. Because of these facts, limited attention span and a background of limited perspective, our job is to keep the public from being misled. If we expose them to all of the so-called facts out there, and the arguments of the reactionaries, the public will be confused and reach the wrong conclusions. We will have failed the public. Therefore, in the same way parents don't expose their children to certain types of adult drama and sexual depictions until they're mature enough, our job is to protect the public from confusing facts and arguments."

"Mr. Merkel I couldn't agree more. I've always tried-"

"What you did today is inexcusable. You know the viewer-ship of Law for Lunch. You know the audience size of Law for Lunch. You've not only confused the general public, you've also misinformed some of the more intelligent segments of our society who look to shows like Law for Lunch for guidance in selecting and providing context for information and news stories. I trusted you with the influence of Law for Lunch, and you were overwhelmed by your opponent."

"But the Cardinal was the interviewee and I-"

"Be quiet and listen Mr. Lewis. This is a lecture, not a discussion. I have no doubt you 'tried' but you're not catching on so I'm going to spell it out for you. We're change agents; we control the information flow, blah, blah, blah. That's journalism school gobley gook, pie in the sky. How do we accomplish our mission, for real, on the ground? You've no idea, do you?"

"We provide context to a story so the public-"

"No! First, interviewees, guests and experts aren't on news shows to educate or inform, they're on to accomplish the show's agenda or purpose. Before so-called conservative and Christian interviewees are allowed on the air, we put a choker collar around their neck and attach it to a leash. On-air disagreement with or correction of them by the moderator is the leash and air time is the choker. A conservative or Christian who forcefully presents the best arguments of their position is interrupted and corrected. That's a short yank on the leash. If they respond to the correction, drop the effective argument they're using for a less persuasive one and appear to be more uncertain about their position, we give the choker some slack. Let them learn and allow the progressive argument to gain the upper hand. If they restrain their objections, don't present their strongest arguments and do their job, which is to lose the debate, then we slackened the leash and they're allowed to appear thoughtful and respected. The conservative or Christian is permitted to breathe our air time, enjoy their fame, sell their books, do their speeches and live the good life. If they don't, we yank on the leash a couple times and if they don't respond to that, they're banned."

"That's why we never call Guzetti," Tim said, almost to himself. "He's not leash trained."

"Who needs him?" Stueben laughed. "It's not like there's any shortage of either conservatives or Christians more than willing to sell out for some air time and a few pats on the head. 'You've really grown since our last talk. You're so much more thoughtful than most Christians, not one issue, like those pro-lifers.'" Stueben looked disgusted. "I thought you said this kid's promising."

"Like Howard Teller, the former Presidential adviser," Tim said laughing and trying to join in. "Mr. Merkel calls him a professional conservative punching bag."

"You'd be well advised to listen, Tim," Merkel said. "It's obvious you're still learning. The question is can you still be taught. I'll decide that over the weekend. But, for the sake of your future, wherever it is, remember this. Our duty is to protect the public so they're not inflamed or prejudiced by bigoted, outmoded ideas."

"Yes sir."

"Take the weekend off and come back Monday, 7:45 a.m. and wait until I call you."

"Yes sir. I just want to say-"

"Now." Merkel yelled through the sore throat and congestion. "Get out of here before I change my mind."

Tim gathered his stuff and rushed out of the room.

CHAPTER 4

"SATISFIED? HE PRACTICALLY RAN OUT of here."

"It doesn't matter if *I'm* satisfied, Anthony." Stueben wondered if Merkel's lust for Lewis was clouding his judgment. "What matters is if the Board and senior membership of the Society are satisfied."

"I don't think the Board and senior membership appreciates the significance of our efforts," Merkel said.

"You'll get a chance to explain it, believe me." Ever since Pontius Pilate's Diaries were discovered and publicized, everyone was under heightened scrutiny. Society security services now investigated any incident involving a Member that was deemed "questionable."

"What'd you mean?"

"Expect an official visit," Stueben said. He looked toward Merkel's door. "We shouldn't even be talking about this."

"Relax." Merkel reached across the conference table and punched the phone's intercom button.

"Yes, Mr. Merkel."

"Sharon, pull the electronic cleaning logs please."

The two men watched each other and waited while Merkel's secretary shuffled some papers.

"Sir? I have a notation the sweeps were done this morning at the 7:15 a.m. In fact, the guys were just leaving when I came to my desk. That was a little before 8 a.m."

"Full electronic sweeps, right? Passive and active devices."

Merkel's Secretary didn't respond. It sounded like she was flipping over pages in a loose-leaf binder.

"Yes Sir."

"Thanks, Sharon."

Merkel hung up.

"Good enough?"

"I guess. I'm telling you, you can't be too careful."

"I sweep my apartment, car and offices for bugs every day. You don't think I'm careful?"

"I'm just saying everyone's on edge right now."

Merkel went to the wet bar and refilled their glasses.

"Have you ever been to Israel?" Merkel said.

"I avoid Jews like the plague." Israel? Stueben wondered if Merkel was becoming a liability. What did Israel have to do with anything? "Sometimes it's inevitable," he said, "like with Liebowitz, but other than that, why would I go to Israel?"

"What a politically correct answer. You maneuvering for board membership? Liebowitz." Merkel laughed again, his breath heavy with the odor a cherry and menthol cough drop. He handed Stueben a fresh drink, then then took a sip of his own. "The only place Jews have been safe for the last three centuries is the United States. The only consistent friends they and Israel have are American Evangelicals. But, we've managed to convince some of them they'll be much safer if they destroy Evangelical political strength and undermine the public's confidence in their country." Merkel shook his head.

"Is this going somewhere? I'm not Lewis and I'm in no mood to be lectured."

"I'm explaining to you why you're over reacting to Tim's little slip up this afternoon."

"Slip up?"

"Listen to me, Fred. The Holocaust Museum is in Israel. Talk about a work of art, the Nazi campaign against the Jews was flawless. The first part of the Museum is a long hallway of exhibits and you'll not find a single instance of actual persecution. It starts with framed reproductions of newspaper articles caricaturing Jews and blaming them for Germany's problems. A little further down you'll find displays of cartoon depictions and examples of plays, movies, music, books, and billboards ridiculing Jews and their beliefs. The government run, I mean public, schools began teaching children the Jews had a history of trouble making and betrayal."

"Everyone hates the Jews and we're all proud of the Holocaust,"

Stueben said. "So what? We're talking about here and now, the Project."

"So am I. Your business is the law. My business is information and the formation of perception. You want to hear this or not?"

"I want – yes."

"The Nazi propaganda campaign used every medium of communications to present a negative, well accurate, but nevertheless negative depiction of Jews. The first step was public ridicule, fashionable bigotry. The next step had more teeth and initiated the process of isolating Jews from the larger society. For example, the Nazis passed laws, ordinances and rules excluding Jews from most professions, trades and even sports clubs."

"Like using a Doctor's or Catholic hospital's opposition to abortion to exclude them from either practicing medicine or participation in government programs and subsidies."

"Exactly. Same thing with certain small colleges and the military with the abolition of 'don't ask don't tell.' In the next step the government clandestinely encouraged certain elements of their political party apparatus and labor union allies to launch attacks against individual Jews, Jewish business, even entire neighborhoods. They blamed the Jews for most of the violence. At the same time, the government restricted the rights of Jews to vote in elections or participate in political life. The government responded to the violence it created by establishing 'Jews only' neighborhoods. The Nazis claimed it was the only way they could protect Jewish citizens from violence."

"Sure, they wanted to destroy the personal connections between average citizens and their Jewish neighbors."

"Indeed, but why? Because by the time they initiated the neighborhood relocation of Jews 'for their own safety' few ordinary Germans were affected. It wasn't as though the victims were friends and neighbors. Jews were strangers. Odd, trouble making, perhaps even treacherous strangers."

"You're making my point, Anthony. Nazis isolated the Jews by using Hitler's emergency powers. We don't have emergency powers. We need to mold public opinion if the Project is to succeed. So, I'm still waiting to find out how this little history lesson helps your friend Tim Lewis."

"What'd you think we've been doing to Christians for the last thirty years?" Merkel blurted out. "We've constantly stereotyped Christians, casting them in the most negative light possible. News reports, stand-up comedy routines, movies, TV shows. When's the last time you've seen a Christian portrayed in a positive way on a TV show or movie? How about in a best-selling novel? National news broadcast? I guarantee you two things. Tens of thousands of cases of abuse and crime occur every year and we ignore them because they're not newsworthy. But I tell you this, if a Christian is involved, we'll cover it, over and over, until the idea of Christian and abuse, Christian and extreme, Christian and dangerous, Christian and crime, Christian and weird or intolerant or stupid sinks into the public consciousness."

"The Catholic priesthood project made your job a lot easier," Stueben said. "Mix pedophile homosexual Catholic Priests with teenage altar boys from troubled backgrounds. It's the gift that keeps giving."

"You've got a right to be proud of your participation in that."

"It surprised me how easy it was Anthony." Stueben was regaining confidence in his ally. "We just targeted seminaries got the door open and that's all it took. The rest of the Church had no idea what happened until it was too late."

"If we stopped everything we're doing right now, these stereotypes would still last at least a generation. We didn't and don't need to create separate neighborhoods, people don't even know their neighbors anymore. Public perception's been molded; it's too late for a couple of lost debates to change that."

"Like I've been telling you, the Board's obsessed with Pilate's Diaries, but I've got to admit, I'm surprised how successful we've been at discrediting them."

"That's a perfect example." Merkel ticked off each point on a finger. "Twenty copper scrolls. Discovered by a respected archaeologist. Translated by a gifted linguist. Their authenticity attested to by a well-respected physicist after state of the art carbon dating. The Diaries of Pontius Pilate - discovered. But, they don't tell us what we want to hear. We want to hear there are many different paths to God. Pilate proved Jesus Christ rose from the dead and then claimed he was the Son of God. Oops."

"You think this is funny?" Stueben said.

"Every study ever conducted proves an early program of indoctrination influences all but the most independent minded of people for their entire life. People interpret information so it fits what they've been told. They filter out information that contradicts their world-view. The Society raised questions about the Diaries' authenticity, but most people dismissed the Diaries because they contradicted what we've taught them – there are many paths to heaven. The fact is, people didn't *want* to believe the Diaries. We just gave them a reasonable sounding excuse to believe what they want to believe."

Merkel suffered through a sixty-second coughing binge, then sipped his Scotch. Finally, he looked over at Stueben.

"Your turn," Merkel said. "I know you received an invitation to Amsterdam so tell me, what's the status of the project?"

Stueben knew he and Merkel were sick, medicated, and maybe a little drunk. It occurred to him an invitation-only update on the progress of a Society project fifty years in the making wasn't the best topic for an informal discussion. However it was Friday, the offices were secure, and Merkel was one of his best friends and closest allies. His earlier concerns about Merkel had been dispelled.

In fact, the R.R.N. chief's tutorial on the Society's anti-Christian propaganda program was a valuable new tool in his quest for Board membership. In future discussions with senior members, Stueben would not only hint at powerful allies, he would also display an appreciation of Society operations beyond his area of expertise. Allies and sophistication were the building blocks of Board membership. Merkel was worth keeping, and Stueben decided to remind the Producer he was a useful man to be allied with.

Stueben told Merkel what he'd learned in Amsterdam. The completion of a project both men always thought lay decades in the future was now only months away. The Society was about to settle a two millennium old blood feud in a nationwide paroxysm of violence that would change America forever. Stueben answered a few of Merkel's questions and celebrated with him.

"Of course the old hypocrite Guzetti was right," Stueben said, concluding his explanation. "Once we created the idea of a living constitution we could do anything we wanted, given the right Judge."

"Why wasn't there more resistance from the lawyers?"

"Never underestimate the human desire for power. A Living Constitution puts Judges and Lawyers in charge of the country. Do you remember Justice Allen? He's the one that retired right after the last election."

"Yeah. We did a two-hour special, "America out of Touch." Allen said American Courts would soon adopt foreign law; it was inevitable."

"I'll bet he did. Think about it this way. Today, when Judges decide they want to do something contrary to the law, they need precedent, an old case saying what the law is. If there is no old case, or if all the old cases say the law is the exact opposite of what they want to do, Judges end up quoting statistics, medical opinions, social worker digest's and other non-law related publications. Even the general public understands how contrived this is. But, once foreign law is accepted in U.S. Courts, Judges can truly do whatever they want and cite legal precedent. All they have to do is send out their law clerks or have so-called public interest law firms scour the world for a tribal Judge in Papua New Guinea who decided the way they wanted to. Then, they cite a tribal Judge. If they can't find one, they go to a poor Third World country, bribe a plaintiff and defendant to file a lawsuit, write the legal opinion they want, then bribe the Judge to say he wrote it. By the time the American lawsuit reaches the Supreme Court, there's a ready-made foreign law precedent to support the decision."

"Didn't Allen say well-reasoned rulings by a 'wise Indonesian Judge' could be binding on the United States Supreme Court?"

"Right. That's why mainstream lawyers called him 'Indonesian Allen.' Of course we branded them extremists, but they saw what we were trying to do."

Merkel finished the last of his watered down Scotch. After the rush of excitement, he looked weary.

"Fred, thanks for the update, but I've got to call it a day."

"I'd better go too."

Merkel reached over and pressed the intercom button.

"Sharon please call a cab for Mr. Stueben."

The two men stood up. Without warning Merkel rounded the desk and embraced Stueben for the briefest moment. They stood back from each other, their eyes glinting. Merkel held out his hand.

"Soon."

"Soon," Stueben replied.

CHAPTER 5

TIM LEWIS LEFT THE RARIFIED atmosphere of the Special Reporting Unit and returned to his cubicle in the newsroom's honeycomb. R.R.N. kept a 24 hour news crew on the sixth floor, but the main newsroom had been deserted by the flu ravaged staff. The only activity was flickering overhead lights, leaving the cavernous room un-naturally quiet. Tim began loading his briefcase with take-home work for the weekend. He refused to consider any outcome other than continuing his career at R.R.N. Once he stashed the last pack of documents into the satchel, it hit him.

My digital recorder.

If Merkel discovered Tim had taped their conversations, not only would his career at R.R.N. be over, his career in television would be over. Merkel was famous for pursuing an enemy until he was destroyed. To Merkel, the digital recorder would be considered an act of war. Tim's desire to use the material for a fawning biography wouldn't matter.

Tim grabbed his phone and punched in Merkel's extension.

"Good afternoon, Anthony Merkel's office."

"Sharon, it's Tim."

"Good afternoon."

"I know, I shouldn't be calling but I'm in a serious jam."

"How may I help you Sir?"

"Merkel's giving me a chance; he's thinking about keeping me on and will decide over the weekend."

"Yes sir."

"Someone else is there, the other receptionist."

"Yes sir."

"Problem is when I went up for my meeting, I brought along

some files and I'm afraid I left one of the most sensitive ones in his office."

Sharon didn't say anything for a long moment. Tim listened to the hum of the newsroom's overhead fluorescents and held his breath.

"All I can do is take a message, sir," she said in her normal voice. "Stay there, Tim" she whispered.

"Thank you."

Sharon Moore covered Tim's call by jotting down the name and number of an office supply vender on a spiral bound phone memo tablet. You could never be too careful when dealing with Anthony Merkel, she thought. The guy seemed to know everything. She glanced at the other receptionist.

"Amy, can you cover me for a bathroom break?"

"Sure thing, Sharon."

"Thanks. I'm having some gastro problems today. I know, more than you want to know," Sharon said as she grabbed her purse. "I'll just be a moment."

Sharon dashed down the hall and ducked into the restroom. A woman she didn't know was leaning over one of the sinks, touching up her makeup. The room smelled like ammonia and pine.

"Hi."

"Hi," the other woman said. She snapped her compact closed, gave Sharon a brief smile and left. No one else was in the room.

Sharon went into a stall and called the R.R.N. switchboard on her cell. No way was she sitting on the toilet. She never used public bathrooms, ever. When the voice mail system answered she punched in Tim Lewis' extension number.

"Tim Lewis."

"Tim it's Sharon. What's going on?"

"I left one of our investigative files up there."

"Up where?"

"In Merkel's office."

"Tim–"

"I was scared. I just bolted out of there, you know? Look, are Stueben or Merkel still there?"

"Stueben's gone, but Merkel's still here."

"Can you help me? I know it's a lot to ask but–"

"Tim."

Sharon thought back to when her nephew was awaiting surgery. Bobby was a great kid plagued with health problems that had demoralized him. Tim barely knew Sharon at the time, but he heard about Bobby and found out the kid loved Jet's quarterback Tyrone Jackson. Though only an intern, Tim had already developed a network of contacts. He spent over a week calling in favors and let Jackson know not only about her nephew's health problems, but also of his near worship of the Jet's QB. A week later Tyrone Jackson roared up to her sister's house in a red Corvette convertible and motioned to her nephew.

"Come on Dog, we're bustin outta here."

Sharon smiled at the memory. Jackson spent the entire day with Bobby. She could still see the looked of gratitude in her sister's eyes and the smile on her nephew's face as he climbed into the Vet.

"Tell me what I should be looking for," she said.

"You won't recognize it. It's in with a stack of papers on the conference table."

"If I can't recognize it, I don't know how I can help."

"Get me into his office."

"He's still here."

"I talked with them, remember? Merkel's sick and he's guzzling Scotch. He won't last the day."

"I can't let you in his office."

"Sharon, please. Make up some excuse to work late and call me when he leaves. I'll bring up more files and go straight back to his office. No one will notice if I've got an extra file. I'll be in and out."

"And what happens if–" Someone opened the bathroom door. "I'll call." Sharon snapped the phone shut, washed her hands and returned to her station.

"Thanks girl."

"You're welcome," Amy said.

Sharon tried to work, but caught herself staring at the computer screen, lost in thought. How far was she willing to go? She could, no would, lose her job if they were caught. It was a good job. But if Merkel discovered Tim left sensitive files lying around, on top of the Law for Lunch fiasco? He'd fire Tim, no question.

Sharon decided she'd help, but only if Merkel left early. Fortunately, Merkel didn't permit security cameras on the fiftieth floor because confidential sources were interviewed there. If Merkel left early, Sharon would volunteer to cover for Amy Gerard, the other receptionist, so she could leave early. She was certain Amy would accept. The R.R.N. elevator stopped at every floor at the end of the day and it took a maddening amount of time to get to the lobby. Amy often missed her bus as a result and had to wait forty minutes for the next one to arrive. Sometimes Amy ran the stairs and sometimes she gritted her teeth at every stop as they rode down together. Either way, by the time Amy hit the side walk she was forced to run to catch her bus.

"Sharon? Sharon?"

"I'm sorry?"

"Talk about concentrating on your work."

It was Amy.

"Can you cover a bathroom break for me?" Amy said.

Before Amy could take her bathroom break Anthony Merkel walked through the reception area to the private elevator.

"Call my driver Sharon. Ladies, enjoy a great weekend."

"Have a good weekend Mr. Merkel," the two women sang out.

Sharon notified the garage as the elevator doors slid shut behind him. Her hands started shaking, but just a little, hardly at all. If Merkel caught her helping Tim he would not only fire her, he'd make sure she never worked in network or cable television again. She flashed a beautiful porcelain veneer smile at the other woman. It was a good plan and Tim was a good kid.

"Not only will I cover your break," Sharon said, "I'm thinking since Mr. Merkel left early, you can leave early and I'll cover for you."

"Sharon, on Friday? Catching the five bus! You're the best."

Once the indicator light showed the cab had descended a couple floors the two women shared a soft laugh across the reception area.

"You are out of here early girl," Sharon said with a smile she hoped didn't look fake. Amy came from around her station, ran over to Sharon in heels and high fived her.

"Thanks to you," she said pointing. "Back in a flash, I'm changing shoes."

While Amy disappeared down the hallway, Sharon watched

the elevator light as it dropped past "L" and stopped at "B". She checked her watch: 4:18. She decided to let Amy go at 4:45 and bring Tim up at the same time. She called Tim via the switchboard.

"Hello?"

"Tim?"

"Yeah, it's me. Merkel told me to leave and I'm afraid to let anyone know I'm still here."

"He's gone and I've arranged for Amy, the other Receptionist, to leave around a quarter till. Get ready. As soon as the elevator door closes on her, I'm calling you. You get five minutes in his office Tim, that's it."

"Sharon if my job wasn't at stake I would never ask you to-."

"Be quiet. Give me your cell phone number." Sharon wrote it on the palm of her hand. "As soon as Amy leaves I'll call you. Be ready and come straight up. Unless you see someone else in reception, walk over to my station. I'll go to the bathroom. I have an extra office key for Mr. Merkel's office. I'll put it on top of my counter, behind the frame of last year's excellence in journalism award. Get the key and go. When you're done, walk straight back, replace the key and get on the elevator. I don't want to see you after I leave my station. Understand?"

"Yes."

Sharon closed her phone and checked her watch. It was 4:30. Amy returned wearing tennis shoes and carrying her high heels. She shoved the heels into a carry bag along with the rest of her stuff. The two women smiled at each other and went back to work.

Sharon returned to a list of junior producer assignments for Special Reporting. While Amy clicked and clacked away at her keyboard, Sharon managed to type in part of one name before zoning off, envisioning her and Tim caught. There would be a horrible exit interview, she'd be fired, they'd take her badge and electronic door key and then security would drag her out of the building by the arm. She sat back in her chair. In front of her was part of a producer's name, somehow scheduled with the project of a different producer.

"Great," Sharon said under her breath. She deleted the name and typed in the correct one, but knew she'd re-check everything for accuracy before e-mailing it to Merkel. She made a determined effort at maintaining her concentration and managed to type three more appointment dates, matched to the correct name and project title.

"Sharon."

It was Amy wearing a big grin, holding up her left arm and tapping the face of her wrist watch with her finger. Sharon managed a smile she hoped wasn't too phony and made a back handed "scat" motion with her hand. Time to call Tim.

CHAPTER 6

CARL HARDESTY EXITED ON TWENTY-TWO and waited, watching the floor indicator climb upward. The elevator took Lewis straight to Fifty.

Too bad, Hardesty thought. He would've loved an excuse to harass that pretty boy. Hardesty didn't like anyone, but in particular he didn't like Lewis. He hated his good looks. He hated the way he smelled. He wished he could inflict pain upon Lewis, but that was an indulgence he'd put behind him.

After the light stopped at Fifty, Hardesty returned to R.R.N.'s basement security suite. Seeing Lewis in the elevator put him in a mood. He ignored the dispatcher's greeting, frowned at the squawking radio checks from the other guards and scanned the bank of security monitors. Once he concluded there was no one in the building he could legitimately harass, he dropped into a black naugahyde swivel chair and fantasized about his last free-lance murder.

Carl Hardesty was by any reasonable definition an animal and by any technical definition a serial killer. Since the time he was a twelve year old boy he'd barely managed to hide his contempt for everyone around him, especially those smaller and weaker. One day he found himself fantasizing about specific children and how he'd like to kill them. Each one was different. He tortured animals. When he first heard of Charles Darwin's "Origin of the Species" from a deranged comedian on late night television, it was like a religious epiphany. The comedian explained certain select people were evolving into higher beings with great mental powers, but were being held back by the human sub-species, like Christians, whose thoughts interfered with the convergence of higher evolved mankind's mental power.

Hardesty finally realized why he wanted to kill. He now understood his desires weren't crimes or anything to be ashamed of. He was a mechanism of natural selection, a servant of mankind. The more of the subspecies he could eliminate, the quicker evolution would take place. He met his first victim in a bar. When the guy laughed at his evolution theory and told him the comedian was a drunk, deranged, and a pedophile, Hardesty learned inflicting pain advanced his own evolutionary condition.

After that he was careful. For years he killed on his own, first targeting drifters, hitch hikers and runaways, then working his way up. The only reason they caught him was he deviated from his usual stalking ritual. He lashed out at what he called a "target of opportunity" and left physical evidence that lead the police right to him. He still remembered the despair he felt locked in a police interview room with two hardened homicide detectives. That's when his life changed, forever.

One of the detectives left the interview table, reached up and unplugged the video camera recording their conversations. The room smelled of sweat and urine.

"Now we can talk," the Detective said.

"I told you, I got nothing to say," Hardesty replied.

"Quit acting like an idiot. Why'd ya think we waited till two forty a.m. to bring you in? No one's here but us. This," the detective said, holding up a cardboard banker's box, "is the evidence we have. The video tape from the security camera, the DNA material and the souvenir you took from your victim."

"Someone planted that."

"Sure. Here's the deal. We work for people who can use your services, for the rest of your life. You agree, the evidence disappears and you're released, tonight. Someone'll get in touch, give you a straight job where you can be useful and give you plenty of opportunity to kill people."

"You guys're nuts."

"Shut up," said the other Detective. "This is the deal. You get away with murder. You get to kill again, which we know you like. Alot. You get a job and protection. In exchange, you don't kill without permission. You do as you're told. You never talk."

"I'm gonna walk you outta here right now," the first detective said. "I'm gonna give you your belongings and then spring you. I'll wait thirty minutes before I check the lobby. If you're still there, I'm taking you back in custody. I'll arrest you, interrogate you - on camera this time - and you can take your chances with a jury. If you're gone when I come out, you've accepted the offer. Forever. What you did to the teenager from New Haven?"

"What?" How did they know about that? His face must have given him away because the cop merely shrugged.

"Our employers know everything. In fact, it's kind of scary what they know. What's important is you understand your most ambitious homicidal fantasy will seem like a spa treatment compared to what our employers will do to you if you betray them."

The men all looked at each other for several seconds.

"I was there one time, someone got a big mouth and they made him into an example. Even an animal shouldn't suffer like that."

What had impressed Hardesty, scared him in fact, was the Detective looked scared.

"Your choice. Let's go."

Hardesty walked. Later that week he was contacted by a slender young man with a facial mole who turned out to be his contact. The evidence against Hardesty disappeared. His contact arranged an interview for a well-paying job at R.R.N. and over the last three years he killed often, but only on command.

Carl Hardesty didn't know it, but he was a creature of The Society for Human Enlightenment and its cruel master.

Now he sat facing bank upon bank of video screens monitoring every floor, elevator, and hallway at R.R.N. Hardesty didn't see the monitor screens, his eyes were unfocused. He was sequentially reliving the last seven of his independent murders. However, in one of his favorite pastimes, he substituted Tim Lewis' face and voice for those of the victims. He didn't know it, but he made a sound, half growl and half moan, low in his throat.

"What the heck's that about?"

Hardesty forced himself out of the fantasy, but it took a few seconds. His self-control could only stand so much. He struggled to push the blood stained images away from his eyes. When his vision cleared, the other guard was ignoring his monitors and watching Hardesty with a quizzical look.

"Throat thing, can't seem to shake it," Hardesty said.

"Better see a Doctor," the guy replied. He didn't sound convinced and Hardesty thought about killing him where he sat. Instead he looked up at a circular, black on white, wall mounted clock.

"Think I'm going to do an irregular on Fifty," the killer said. He was referring to the random, irregular patrols Security did of the Fiftieth Floor by order of Special Reporting boss Anthony Merkel. At times like these he had to keep busy. Hardesty left his chair and headed toward the elevators. The time was 4:50 p.m.

CHAPTER 7

A MY GRINNED, GRABBED HER BAG and dashed toward the elevator. First she hit the down arrow button, then turned and pointed at Sharon.

"You are b-a-a-a-d news, girl. Rebellious."

The elevator doors opened, Amy waved and step into the car. Sharon waited until the doors closed.

"Yeah, rebellious," she said.

Sharon looked down at her sweaty hands. The elevator car was already moving, so she pushed the re-dial button on her cell phone. It occurred to her she'd used her personal phone more today than she had in the last two years. Big violation of company policy, she thought. Unauthorized cell phone use.

You ain't seen nothing yet.

"It's Tim."

"Come up now and don't forget what I told you," Sharon said, hanging up on him.

She stashed her phone and leaned back, waiting. The floor light indicator for the closest bank of elevators began moving. After a brief stop on twelve, it crept up to twenty and stopped again.

"Tim's floor," she thought.

The light resumed a steady climb toward the 50th floor. Sharon waited, feeling like a condemned woman watching as the firing squad rifles were leveled. The cab arrived and the doors bounced open with a ring.

Tim walked out of the elevator looking every bit as nervous as Sharon felt. It gave her a grim sense of satisfaction. He headed toward her station with a stiff smile on his face. She didn't smile back. Before he could say a word, she pointed her finger at him.

Cold.

"Take a seat Mr. Lewis. I'll be back in a moment."

Tim looked confused but took a seat in the waiting area. Sharon left the station, ignored his quizzical look and marched down the hallway.

If he can't follow instructions he deserves to be fired, she thought.

As soon as Sharon left the reception area Tim jumped out of his chair and ran over to the chest high counter top surrounding her workstation. Sure enough, an office key card was stashed behind one of R.R.N.'s framed journalism awards. The second elevator bank showed its car moving upward, past the tenth floor.

Merkel doesn't use those elevators, Tim thought.

He returned to Merkel's office, swiped the key card and the lock flashed green. He peeked into the office, glanced down the hall and then stepped inside, pulling the door closed behind him. He went straight to the gleaming conference table. There were two empty glasses surrounded by water rings, but no file folders. Tim felt guilty about lying to a friend, but knew didn't have a choice. Sharon liked him, but if she discovered he'd been recording Merkel's conversations without permission she wouldn't have helped him.

He couldn't remember which chair he'd sat in or which chair he'd put the recorder on, so he pulled out the two in the middle. The recorder tumbled off one of the chair seats and rolled underneath the table.

Great. What if Merkel forgot something and comes back for it?

Tim went to his knees, squeezed between the chairs and snatched the recorder. Then he straightened the chairs, backed toward the door and surveyed the room. Last chance. Everything looked in place. Tim was just reaching for the door knob when it rattled. He yanked his hand back like it'd been scorched.

"Sharon?" After several seconds, Tim reached for the knob, then stopped. "Sharon?"

He couldn't make up his mind, so he waited. And waited. Once he put his hand on the knob, but pulled it back. After ten minutes he decided whoever was outside was either gone or never going to leave. He yanked open the door.

Carl Hardesty left the elevator and raised an eyebrow at the empty reception stations. He decided to check the west hallway first and unknowingly trailed Sharon toward the women's bathroom. The west wing of offices had been deserted all day, their occupants the victims of some sort of flu bug. Hardesty shrugged. Because of his evolved state, he enjoyed great health and never got sick.

Before reaching the end of the hallway he stopped, tilted his head up and sniffed, like a bloodhound, or maybe a wolf. Something troubled him, but he couldn't decide what it was. He tried a few doors, then made his way back to the reception area and walked down the east hallway. Again, all the doors were closed and Hardesty tried doorknobs at random, just to make sure they were secured. Some instinct made him stop at Anthony Merkel's office and walk to the door.

Hardesty furrowed his brow. He couldn't take his eyes off of the doorknob, it seemed like it was about to turn. When nothing happened he meant to turn away, but found he hadn't moved. He tried the door, but it was locked. He tried it again. The back of his neck tingled. He thought he could hear someone on the other side of the door whispering "share" or "Sheraton," but that was impossible. While there is no such thing as a truly sound proof office door, Hardesty knew Merkel's was about as close as you could get outside of a CIA interrogation room.

"Mr. Hardesty?"

He straightened and glared toward the reception area. The delectable Sharon Moore. Over the months he'd enjoyed more than one fantasy featuring Sharon, rope and sharp objects, but never before had his desire been so intense. Hardesty despised anyone ever surprising him.

I'll make her pay, he promised himself.

"Mr. Merkel's gone for the day."

"I know that Ms. Moore," he said. He made it sound like someone saying "ashes to ashes" at a beloved parent's funeral and thought he could detect the slightest quiver in her voice when she answered. It made him feel better.

"Well then, why wait at his door?"

"You weren't at your station," Hardesty said. Dust to dust.

"I've, um, been having stomach problems," she said. "Sorry I missed you on the way up."

That quiver again, like a dove he'd once held in his fist. Hardesty returned to the reception area, moving as though he intended to walk up to her. She smelled faintly of lilacs. Once her eyes widened he angled back toward the elevators and hit the call button. Rather than face the door, he watched her while the elevator worked its way upward. She didn't even waste time trying to stare him down, but turned to her computer as though engrossed. Finally the elevator bell rang her reprieve.

"Best of weekends to you, Ms. Moore."

She looked up. Hardesty was in exactly the same position, with the same expressionless face, waiting and watching. The elevator doors didn't dare close behind him. They stayed open while he waited.

"Uh, sure, thanks."

He nodded and turned to the elevator. After it closed and the car began its descent, he allowed himself a smile.

Tim opened the door expecting the worst, or at least a furious Sharon, but the hall was empty. He stuck his head out far enough to see the reception station. It was still abandoned. He stepped into the hall, but stopped before closing the door.

Slow down, Tim, maintain control.

He went back in and looked around, unable to recall how the chairs had been arranged at the conference table. He took an extra minute and rearranged them. When he returned to the door and looked back something seemed wrong but he couldn't decide what it was.

If Merkel memorized the position of every item in his office I'm screwed anyway, he thought.

Tim pulled the door closed and walked down the hallway, waiting for someone to jump out from behind one of the closed doors. It seemed to take forever to get the elevator. The reception area was still empty. He punched the "up" or "call" button, then checked his watch. 5:05 p.m. He hoped for luck and in an encouraging development the elevator responded to the call by rocketing up the shaft. Still no sign of Sharon.

Then he noticed her purse sticking up from behind the counter of her station. It hadn't been there when he arrived, so she'd returned and then left again. In a hurry. His stomach did a flip flop. He couldn't think of what might have happened, maybe another R.R.N. executive had returned. Whatever happened, it couldn't be good. Both halls were clear, but the elevator light now climbed upward in slow motion.

When he checked again Sharon was coming out of the bathroom. She was in her stocking feet and even with her makeup looked gray.

"Sharon, is everything-"

"It's all right."

Her voice was shaky and it looked like she might have been crying. The elevator light moved from forty-eight to forty-nine.

"Just go," she said. "Carl Hardesty was here and I-"

"Hardesty? What did he-"

"He's gone. Please leave."

The elevator dinged and the doors opened behind him. Tim didn't know how he was going to make it up to her, but he'd think of something.

"Okay, Sharon. Sure."

On the way down Tim thought to check the recorder. It was still running, although its indicator showed it low on battery power. A concealed security camera recorded the image of Tim checking out his voice recorder and transferred it onto a silver dollar sized compact disk in R.R.N.'s security office.

Tim returned to the twentieth floor to pick up his jacket and briefcase. The usually bustling building was deserted, adding to the sense of the surreal. He grabbed his stuff, then rode an empty elevator to the ground floor. As always he waved to the night guard across an empty lobby and went straight to Henry's.

Normally, Henry's was Tim's sort of place. The establishment was old New York: a long horseshoe bar; brass rails; hanging potted plants and varnished tables. As soon as you walked in you could smell the roasted peanuts set out on the bar and on every table. In addition to a huge selection of domestic and imported beers, it had great pub food. It didn't hurt that most of the media's young up-and-coming talent hung out there after hours.

On this night, Tim wasn't there to enjoy the atmosphere, the beer or the food. In fact he didn't even notice when the women began pouring in. On a typical day he left the office no earlier than six or seven, even on a Friday. Today, he'd arrived at Henry's early and started drinking early. Unlike most Friday nights he wasn't drinking beer, except as a chaser. He drank Crown Royal, quickly, savoring the burn as it ran down his throat.

"Lewis! I saw your interview with Liebowitz and that Catholic guy." It was another journalist from a competing news channel. "What the heck was that all about? I thought those guys were too busy molesting kids to do anything else," he said, laughing.

"Hi, Bill."

Bill erupted with a coughing binge lasting a full sixty seconds. Tim watched him, with his head cocked to one side and drained the last of his whiskey.

"Hey," Bill yelled at a waitress. "Bring me a Scotch and water and my friend whatever he's drinking." He pulled up a stool perched on it.

"Thanks, man." Tim said. "It's been a tough day."

"Tough? You don't know no tough over at R.R.N. Here's to the fair-haired boy," Bill said, raising his glass. "At my place the ratings are crashing and they're looking for someone to blame."

That started a three-hour conversation fueled by self-pity and alcohol. Both men eventually decided modern journalism was in deep trouble and they were just the two to fix it. They were friends forever. By the time the two men walked out of the bar it was dark and Tim had to hold onto Bill's handshake for an extra moment.

"Thanks, Dude," he said. Bill helped him get a cab and put him into it. "At least one other person besides me gets it," Tim said.

"Next Friday, here at 6:00 p.m., man," Bill said.

"You know it."

He didn't remember exactly how he got home, but somehow the cab was pulling up outside of his building. Tim handed the driver a twenty on a fifteen fifty fare.

"Keep it."

"Thanks," the driver said. The cabbie sounded surprised and pulled off immediately, leaving Tim to wonder if maybe the bill was bigger than a twenty.

Who the heck cares?

He caught his foot on the curb and almost did a header, saving himself only at the last moment. It took effort, but he made it up the apartment steps and found his keys. The next thing he knew he was closing his apartment door and pawing at the door chain. He was pretty sure he'd secured it, so he staggered toward the living room. He didn't remember stopping at the bathroom, but knew he must have because the pressure in his bladder was gone. The recliner surprised him by sliding all the way back, throwing him into a near prone position. There was his briefcase, right on his lap. Somehow, he'd managed to keep it.

Cool.

Tim tried to sit up, then decided it wasn't worth fighting the chair. Besides, the TV remote and cordless phone were on an end table within easy reach. He turned on R.R.N. news and decided to order a pizza.

When his eyes snapped open he wasn't sure if he'd blinked, been dosing, or had passed out. The briefcase was still on his lap. After some digging he found the recorder and switched off the table light. He woke up with a start, feeling like he did when that choir chanted in the movie "The Exorcist." Some details faded, but Tim retained a clear image of hundreds, maybe thousands of people out in a snowstorm, crowded together behind a barbed wire fence. Few of them had jackets, many were in short sleeve shirts and all were freezing to death. For some reason the scene made him think of Angela Baker.

Except for the dull glow of the television, darkness surrounded him. Somehow he knew it was only moments after midnight. Tim couldn't remember the last time he'd been as creeped out. He felt the presence of someone behind him, but couldn't get turned around.

Don't be stupid.

The digital recorder was in his left hand, playing nothing but static. He didn't remember turning it on, he couldn't remember what it played and he wasn't sure why he was afraid. The smell of cigarette smoke, fried food and stale beer was overpowering. Tim pushed the reset button and checked the LED readout to make sure it was set at Zero.

He was thirsty, but not thirsty enough to get up, so he tried to sleep. His eyes wouldn't stay shut, but it wasn't the headache and bed spins that kept him awake. The truth was he was scared, the "all you can do is run" kind of scared. He closed his eyes, waited, and finally gave in. His DVR's clock told him it was 12:45 a.m. The furnace kicked on about the same time Tim thought he heard movement in his home office.

Enough.

He kicked out of the chair and managed to stagger toward the bathroom. The darkened hallway was empty, devoid of any evil presence. He made it to the sink, got the medicine cabinet open and found his sleeping pills. Most of them ended up clattering off the ceramic tile floor, but he got two tablets into his palm and dry swallowed them. Like everything else, you weren't supposed to mix the pills with alcohol. Tim remembered something about people walking into traffic, trying to drive cars and even sending emails, all while asleep.

Who cares. Let me go to sleep. Please, God.

He found the aspirin bottle and choked down a couple of those. Before he started the long trip back to his chair, he paused outside the bathroom and stared at his office door. It was a bit further down the darken hallway. A bit too far down the darkened hallway, he thought. He turned toward the living room and made it back by leaning his shoulder against the wall and sliding along it for support.

In this dream he and Fred Stueben were standing just outside the barb wire, watching as thuggish looking men drug people toward crosses, real, honest-to-God crosses. Tim saw their faces. He saw Angela Baker. She was crying. Stueben tried to tell him something, but couldn't stop laughing. Finally he looked Tim in the eye and grinned.

"This is why we murdered Benjamin Kahn. All right, you got me," he said, laughing. "It was because of this *and* because Kahn's a Jew."

Stueben grew a tail and horns. His eyes flashed red. Tim backed up, but couldn't seem to catch his breath. He kept watching, afraid Stueben would chase him, but the horned law professor just laughed. When Tim saw Anthony Merkel he ran toward him and tried to tell him someone had killed Supreme Court Justice Benjamin Kahn. Merkel ignored him and kept repeating some stupid phrase over and over again. Tim woke up covered in goose bumps and sweat. The "Exorcist" choir was chanting again. He managed to glance at his watch. Three a.m.

The witching hour, he thought.

The TV was still on, turned to an R.R.N. re-run of its special on the American genocide against Native Americans. Tim remembered an interview with one historian who disputed the claim of "genocide" and pointed out more American Indians were alive today than when the first settlers landed. Merkel cut the interview because it wasn't consistent with the special's theme.

Stueben's right; I am stupid.

Tim thought about turning the television off, but he was afraid of the silence. And the dark. Eventually, the alcohol and sleeping pills counteracted the adrenaline. Tim's eyes slid shut. He fell asleep thinking about Angela Baker.

CHAPTER 8

CASHMERE OR "CASH" MANN WAITED at a varnished oak table in the fourth floor reading room of the United States Supreme Court Building. She was armed with a hermetically sealed plastic pouch filled with one ounce of a clear, odorless liquid.

If you have to bide your time, this is a nice place to do it, Cash thought.

The walls were lined with row upon row of bound treatises and Court Reporters. The floor space was dotted with heavy oak tables. Overhead, large chandeliers hung below a beautiful molded tin ceiling, illuminating the pages of a legal decision she was too excited to read. The room smelled like leather and history.

Cash leaned back, not the least bit upset to be working through the weekend. Her mentor in the Society for Human Enlightenment had told her the name of the liquid and that, technically, it wasn't poison. But, if she mixed it into the tea of someone with as weak a heart as say, Supreme Court Justice Benjamin Kahn, it might as well *be* poison. Cashmere didn't care as long as it did its job.

The building was not as quiet as an outsider might expect for a Saturday. When the Supreme Court was in session, law clerk work required keeping long hours. Cash knew she was lucky. Some "Living Constitution" Justices had famously told their law clerks how they wanted a case to come out, no matter what the law, then left the clerk to research and write an opinion attempting to justify it.

The Court's current leftists were more subtle. They understood the need to clothe their decisions in case law or statutory authority. But, until they were able to search the world for "foreign law" allowing them to do what they wanted, finding American precedent for their decisions was often impossible. That didn't deter them. They and their clerks spent hours searching, twisting, stretching, cutting and pasting American law, law review articles, and even letters from Presidents written years after the Constitution was ratified to give their opinions some semblance of legitimacy.

The Constitutionalist Justices expended just as much effort as their far left colleagues. Much of their clerks' work consisted of devising strategies to either discredit each scheme the leftists used in their draft opinions or to at least convince the one or two undecided Justices to join with the Constitutionalists. Cashmere's Justice was one of the Constitutionalists on the Court, but while he followed the law to where it led him, he did not join with the other Constitutionalists in trying to thwart the leftists. So, Cash usually had a lot more time on her hands than the other law clerks.

On the other side of the room fellow law clerk Amy Wu was leaning against one of the walnut columns, chatting with a law clerk named Arnold Epstein. Epstein was officially Cashmere's boyfriend and she was feigning an interest in converting to Judaism. Claiming a make-believe sexual trauma, she was making him "wait" for an intimacy that would never come. Unknown to Epstein, she was intimate with his best friend and fellow law clerk, Bob Harmon.

At first, Cashmere hadn't been sure she'd be able to seduce Harmon. He knew she was dating his best friend. But Cash was beautiful and skilled at a hobby she'd been practicing since she was twelve years old. When Harmon walked into the reading room, Cashmere let her eyes remain on him for just an extra second, not long enough to be really blatant, just long enough to give Epstein a creepy feeling in the pit of his stomach. Then she looked over at Epstein and gave him her hundred-watt smile. Epstein's confused looked disappeared and he smiled back. Wu glared at her before looking away.

Uppity Christian girl, Cashmere thought. It was too bad. Wu was very pretty. Between the two of them they could have had every man in the place at each other's throats. Cashmere sighed with regret and glanced at her watch. Almost lunchtime.

Though she was about to murder Benjamin Kahn, she wasn't

afraid, or even nervous. If anything, she was aroused. She'd already decided that tonight she would be "too upset" over Kahn's death to spend the evening with Epstein. When he took her home, she planned to tell him she needed "some space to grieve," and wanted to turn in early. A few hours later she'd call Harmon and let him in the back entrance to her apartment.

Cashmere got up and walked toward the library exit. As she passed near Harmon, Wu and Epstein, she stopped long enough to squeeze Epstein's arm.

"Justice Kahn and I are having lunch in his chambers," Cashmere said with a smile.

"That guy loves you," Epstein said.

"I'm just lucky I can learn from him."

Her relationship with Kahn *was* unusually close, even for the Clerk-Justice relationships that developed at the Supreme Court. However, luck had nothing to do with it. Cashmere had spent hours studying not only Kahn's biography, but also his psychological profile. Then she consulted with Society psychologists so she could use what she'd learned to establish a father-daughter type relationship with him. Cash hated Kahn and his pathetic ramblings about protecting the rights of America's citizens, "the greatest country ever," as he said over and over. For thirteen months Cashmere gritted her teeth and played along. She was rewarded by gaining unprecedented friendship with and access to Kahn. Today all of her misery and hard work would be rewarded. She'd been given the great honor of killing the filthy Jew on behalf of her master.

"Is anyone else going to the dining room? I'm picking up the Justice's lunch."

The other clerks were staying, so Cashmere said goodbye, then turned her head just far enough to one side so she could wink at Harmon before leaving. He didn't know it, but he was in for the time of his life later that night.

The dining room staff was expecting her and had a tray with Kahn's chicken salad sandwich and a small pot of tea waiting. Cash grabbed a Diet Coke and salad. She slid the tray off the dining table and took one of the spiral staircases down to the second floor. She passed through the Great Hall and walked past the courtroom, her heels clicking on and echoing off of the buffed slabs of

Alabama marble lining the floor and walls. Cash arrived at Kahn's chambers just as his secretary was leaving.

"See you at 1:30, Cash. Do *not* let him eat anything except that chicken salad," she said with a smile.

"Cashmere," Justice Kahn yelled, "don't listen to that spoil sport. We'll order pizza!"

"Let me get the door, Justice," Cashmere yelled back.

She set her tray on the secretary's desk, closed the door, then made sure Kahn's couldn't see the tray. She tore open the liquid packet's perforated corner and squeezed the solution onto the croissant. The liquid seeped into the salad and disappeared. She emptied the rest of the solution into Kahn's tea and stuck the empty packet into her pocket.

Cashmere carried the tray into Justice Kahn's office, a forty-foot by forty-foot walnut paneled room lined with bookcases and filed with expensive furniture. A maroon carpet with embroidered silver stars covered the floor. The Justice had ordered and installed a cut glass top for his cherry desk. He loved eating there while looking out the window and talking about baseball with his clerks.

Cashmere hated sports, except for ultimate fighting, but nevertheless knew every piece of minutia about the Seattle Mariners, a team she had picked at random. She was also well steeped in the history of baseball. Often times she and Kahn would engage in lighthearted disputations over the finer points of the game. She knew Kahn loved her like a daughter.

"I've been looking into the commerce clause precedent you asked me about."

"No, no, no," Kahn said, before picking up the sandwich. "Let's talk about that new kid, Jones, the left hander who just came up to the Oriels from the minors. Did you see him pitch last night?"

Cashmere smiled at the old man with genuine pleasure. He was already halfway through his poisoned sandwich and stopped chewing only long enough to gulp his tea. Cash crunched down on some lettuce covered with her favorite vinaigrette. She made a mental note to remember to ask where the cafeteria got it.

"I missed it on TV, but read about it this morning on the way in," she replied. "Five innings in relief and seven strikeouts. Not bad for his first start in the major leagues."

"Not bad? I told you there's still great homegrown pitching talent out there. He's from Kansas," Kahn said, beaming.

"I never said there was no homegrown pitching talent."

"Cuban defectors and guys from Puerto Rico are not homegrown!"

"Justice? Is everything okay?"

"I'm feeling . . . Cash, my pills!" The old man began to rub his chest.

"Where?"

Kahn pointed to a lightweight jacket hanging in the corner. Cashmere went to the jacket, found the bottle of heart medication and walked back, un-screwing the cap. In that brief time, the Justice had turned alarmingly ill. He gasped for air while clutching at his chest. He'd turned purple from the neck up. Cashmere was fascinated. When she neared his chair she leaned over the corner of the desk and held out the pills. As the old man reached for them, she turned the bottle upside-down with her right hand and swept her left arm across the desktop, scattering the pills, sandwich, and tea all onto the floor. The carpet absorbed the noise. Kahn looked confused and stared into her eyes for a fleeting second before sliding off his chair and tumbling onto the floor.

Cash watched him, then knelt down. She bent down so her mouth was near his ear, but so she could still look into his eyes. She wanted to see the fear, not for himself, but for what was next.

"I put something into your food you ugly Jew. I want you to know we're going to replace you with someone on the Court who'll help us kill all of you, once and for all. Another holocaust, all because you trusted me. I'll deal with those grandchildren of yours myself, personally and slowly. It will all be your fault."

Kahn was no longer capable of even gasping, so Cashmere picked up his phone and called the Security Office. A policeman answered on the first ring. She started screaming and crying, doing her best to sow confusion.

"It's the Justice, it's the Justice, help, help."

Cash had thought it through in advance. The policeman would know from his read out where the call came from. He'd alarm the security detail and two men would race toward Kahn's chambers.

"An ambulance, he's dying, oh please."

She dropped the phone on Kahn's desk, ran out of the offices and into the hall, intent upon slowing the initial response.

"He's dying; send an ambulance."

Supreme Court Justices tended toward the geriatric. Their Police force, trained to protect senior citizens, were all qualified paramedics. Knowing the importance of time the policemen rushed down the hall, pushed Cash to one side and ran into Kahn's office.

Every second helps, Cash thought.

She followed the police into Kahn's chambers. One officer administered CPR while the second rattled off symptoms into his shoulder microphone. As he was receiving instructions and passing them along to his partner, Cash put her finger in her mouth.

Authenticity is everything, she thought.

She watched the men work and bit down on her finger hard enough to draw blood. Her eyes teared up. Kahn went from purple to pale to ocean blue, from warm to cool. A physician and medical team rushed into the office carrying a defibulator.

"Open his shirt," the Doctor shouted.

Man, did that hurt, Cash thought, hoping she didn't overdo it with the finger.

The officers ripped open Kahn's shirt and undershirt, exposing his white haired chest. The doctor slapped the paddles together and looked at the paramedic who flipped switches on the shoe-sized box. When it hummed, he nodded at the Doctor.

"Clear," the Doctor yelled, applying the paddles. Justice Benjamin Kahn's body jumped in response to a huge electrical shock. The Doctor bent over and placed a stethoscope above Kahn's heart.

"Again."

The box hummed and the paramedic nodded. The Doctor shocked and then re-examined Kahn. He looked at the police.

"How long before I got here?"

"Five, six minutes," one of the officers said.

"But they arrived seconds after I called," Cashmere said, sobbing. She had wrapped her bloody finger in a tissue. No pain, no gain, she decided. "Do it again; do it again!"

"Ms., I'm sorry but-"

"Do it again!"

The outer office filled with clerks, staff and a moment later, two other Supreme Court Justices. One of them whispered to a couple of his clerks. The two men each took one of a resistant, still sobbing Cashmere's arms and led her out of Kahn's chambers.

"I'm calling the time of death 12:37 p.m., Monday, Oct. 19," the Doctor said. "Preliminary determination of cause of death, natural, heart attack."

Satisfied, Cashmere allowed the clerks to lead her out of the office and down to the Supreme Court conference room. Moments later Justice William Hardy, a fellow member of the Society for Human Enlightenment, came in and sat alongside her.

"We all know how much you and Benjamin loved each other," Justice Hardy said. "I am sorry you had to witness this, but it gives me a great deal of comfort to know Benjamin's last moments were spent with you." Hardy smiled at her.

Cashmere smiled back at him through her tears.

"In a moment I'm going to allow the D.C. police investigator to take your statement." He looked at the two clerks. "Thank you both, but you'll have to wait outside." The Justice looked back at Cashmere. "Don't worry child, I'm staying for the interview. After all, we don't want you here without representation," he said, smiling.

When the clerks left, Hardy whispered to her.

"You were magnificent. All you have to remember is keep it as short as possible. Don't say anything more than is required. Paraphrase the conversation with Kahn. Say, 'I think,' often. If you screw up, just admit it and say, that's not what I meant, I was reliving it as I answered, I'm so sorry. Got it?"

"Got it," she said.

Hardy walked out and returned a moment later, followed by a neatly dressed bald man carrying a small notebook and a pencil. The Inspector sat across the table from Cashmere and twisted his pencil, exposing lead.

"Ms. Mann, I'm Inspector Tom Alexander, District of Columbia Police. I know how difficult this is for you. Justice Kahn's secretary just told me how close you two were, but I've got to asked what happened."

"Just don't drag it out, Inspector." Justice Hardy's tone wasn't friendly. It was the tone he used during oral arguments when trying to intimidate Counsel away from a line of reasoning he thought might convince one of the Court's fence sitters to decide the wrong way.

"Of course, Justice."

Neither Justice Hardy nor Cashmere needed to worry. Cashmere was magnificent. Not only did she convincingly cry and sob, she managed to inject just enough confusion into her statement to sound like a traumatized young woman, but not enough to raise any suspicions.

After fifteen minutes, the Inspector was satisfied. He stood and held out his hand.

"Ms. Mann, thank you. I'm truly sorry. Everyone around here I've ever known or talked to loved Justice Kahn." Cashmere took Alexander's hand, but looked away. Justice Hardy stood up.

"Thank you, Inspector. A thorough but humane interview. We are grateful."

"Thank you, Justice."

"Good day, Inspector. Please, close the door behind you." Hardy waited until the door clicked closed, then smiled at Cashmere. "Masterful," he said. "Will Mr. Epstein escort you home now?"

"No," Cashmere said. "I've decided I'm going to be just too traumatized to do anything but stay home alone tonight. Then, later, I'll call Mr. Harmon to come and comfort me. I'm planning quite a celebration."

Hardy choked back a laugh. Cash had let him know about her little dalliance earlier in the year.

"Every girl should have a hobby," he said.

Seconds later someone knocked on the door.

"Come in," Hardy said.

Epstein rushed over to Cashmere and knelt beside her. Bob Harmon joined them and stood alongside Hardy.

Cash pretended to be listening to Epstein, but strained to overhear Hardy's conversation with Harmon. The Justice had a mischievous look in his eye.

"Mr. Harmon," Hardy said.

"Yes sir."

"You, Epstein and Cashmere are all friends, are you not?"

"Yes, Justice."

"I thought so. Listen, I'm concerned. You know them better than I do, but everyone reacts differently to grief. I'm very concerned about Ms. Mann, especially that she not be alone, certainly not for the next few days. I hope you'll do what you can to prevent that."

"You have my word on that, Justice Hardy," Harmon said.

What a pair of snakes, Cash thought approvingly.

"Very well," Hardy said. "Take care."

"Thank you, Justice."

"Cashmere, words cannot express my feelings, so I'll leave you in the good hands of these fine friends of yours," Hardy said.

CHAPTER 9

A STILL CONGESTED ANTHONY MERKEL DIDN'T wake up Saturday until 10 a.m. He crawled out of bed, stopped long enough to sneeze, then padded barefoot into the kitchen. While the coffee maker gurgled and spit, he swallowed a couple cold tablets and retrieved his newspaper.

Let's see what I missed, he thought.

Merkel ate a piece of toast, then took the newspaper and a fresh cup of coffee into his home office. Ten minutes later he was satisfied the Times hadn't beaten his network to any significant news story and remembered his messages. He hadn't checked his voice mail since early Friday afternoon. Merkel sipped his coffee, dialed into the R.R.N. system and remote accessed his mailbox.

Six messages.

At the punch of a button the names and numbers flashed across his home ID system just as though he were at R.R.N. The first two calls were from confidential sources in the Justice Department. The third call was time stamped 2:14 a.m. The incoming number was blocked, but that didn't prevent Merkel from seeing it displayed. R.R.N. technology enabled the system to unscramble blocked numbers and reveal the caller's identity.

Tim Lewis. At 2:14 a.m. Merkel stopped and hit play, toying with the idea of a leisurely Saturday morning alone with Tim in his apartment.

"Soon, but not yet," he thought, waiting for the message to queue up.

"Miiissstherr Merkel this is Thim . . . Tim, uh, Benj . . . Benjamin Kahn is going to be killed. Justice Supreme, Kahn. Murdered. You know? I know you know, don't you? I dreamed it, but that doesn't mean it's true. But it doesn't mean it's not true. After him, then thousands and thousands of people, maybe more, behind fences with crosses. I mean crosses, real ones, like they hang people on, you know? It's the story of the century. Call me."

The message sucked the air out of Merkel's lungs. How could Tim Lewis know about Benjamin Kahn's pending assassination? Maybe he'd heard Tim wrong. The kid had been drunk, his words so slurred they were often incomprehensible. The 2:28 a.m. and 2:40 a.m. messages removed all doubt. Tim was drunk, but insistent. Kahn was about to be murdered. The last message was a hang up call from Tim only thirty minutes ago. Merkel checked his watch and confirmed it was past noon. It was too late. Kahn was already dead.

Merkel dreaded what came next. Society protocol mandated a member notify internal security whenever sensitive information was compromised.

Sensitive?

The project was beyond sensitive. No matter how he managed the damage control, his upward movement in the Society for Human Enlightenment was halted forever. The best he could hope for was to keep his membership, and his life. You lose one, you lose both.

There's got to be another way, he thought.

Merkel leaned back in his chair, searching for options and remedies that didn't exist. Maybe Tim heard about Kahn's death after the fact, called him and the phone record time stamp was inaccurate. He knew the stamps were accurate. He sat up, re-accessed the account and replayed the messages one last time. Murder and Crosses, two of the clearest words Tim uttered.

He called Alan Williams, New York Security Chief for Society Operations. As Security Chief, Williams would know all about the project.

"Williams."

"Mr. Williams, Anthony Merkel. I'm-"

"I know who you are."

"I just discovered a phone message left late last night. An employee of mine says he wants to talk about the murder of

Supreme Court Justice Kahn. He also mentioned camps with wire fences and crosses. The employee is not a member of our Society."

"Who is this person and what's your relationship?"

"His name is Tim Lewis, a young but prominent journalist here at R.R.N. He works directly for me in Special Reporting."

"Where would he get such ideas?"

"I've no idea."

"Speculate. When's the last time you saw him? Has he ever interviewed anyone from the Society? Has he ever interviewed anyone who works for someone who's a member of the Society? When did you last see him?"

"Yesterday, around two in the afternoon. He made an on air mess while hosting one of our programs."

Merkel was nervous. He and Stueben should never have discussed the project so openly. They must have been crazy. Merkel knew instinctively it was either him or Stueben.

"Mr. Merkel?"

"I'm afraid Fred Stueben may have been a bit indiscrete. He participated in my interview with Lewis and after Tim was dismissed, Stueben brought up Kahn."

"Did he?"

"Yes. I tried to dissuade him, but he knows I have my offices swept for listening devices on a daily basis. He laughed when I asked him to be quiet and not only bragged about our progress, he also, um, speculated on what the future may hold."

"Hmm."

"But there's no way Lewis could've heard any of that. He'd already been dismissed and, Stueben is quite right; our offices are very secure. They're swept on a daily basis. In fact, I confirmed they were swept that very day."

"Where are your offices located?"

"I have a corner office on the west side of the Fiftieth floor."

"Please stay on the line."

Williams put Merkel on hold and turned to his computer. Within moments he'd breached R.R.N.'s computer security system and accessed its corporate files, using a "back door" provided by a Society mole in R.R.N.'s Technology Department. Once in, he typed a search request for "Tim Lewis" with one hand and picked up his cell phone with the other. New York was one of the hubs of Society activity. They maintained three security reaction teams, each working staggered eight hour shifts. Williams called the on-duty team.

"Yes sir."

The Tim Lewis' information was on William's screen, so he forwarded part of it to the reaction team leader as he spoke.

"High priority pickup. The name, address and a photo are coming through now. Got it?"

"It's on my Blackberry, Sir. What type of handling?"

"Put it in storage. I want to examine this merchandise personally. Move now and call the other teams while you're in route. Tell them everyone's on twenty-four hour standby, as of this second."

"Yes sir."

"Let me know when the package's in storage."

Williams hung up and turned to the computer. He exited R.R.N.'s Human Resources records and breached its in-house security system. It took him only minutes to find the video archive and determine there were no cameras on the Fiftieth Floor. He sat back and closed his eyes. Then his fingers went back to the keyboard and pulled up an interior view of an elevator car. The time stamp said Friday, 9 a.m. Williams fast-forwarded the video through the day, found Lewis entering and leaving the fiftieth floor, saw a small, blonde receptionist leave at 4:30 p.m. and then saw Lewis re-enter the car at 4:42 p.m. At 4:50 p.m. an R.R.N. security guard went up to Fifty as well. Williams recognized him.

"Well," he said, releasing the fast forward control. The video slowed to normal speed.

Williams pursed his lips, watched, and then fast forwarded until Lewis reentered the car. Lewis pulled something out of his jacket pocket. Williams stopped, rewound and replayed.

No doubt about it, Williams thought. Lewis had a small, state of the art digital voice recorder.

"I see you, Mr. Lewis. Soon I'll see you again," he said.

Williams hung up, let the video run at normal speed and took Merkel off hold. He kept his eye on the screen.

"Mr. Merkel?"

"Yes."

"How many receptionists on the Fiftieth floor?"

"Two. Sharon Moore and Amy Gerad."

"Describe them, please."

"They're both very attractive women. Amy is short, maybe five foot five and blonde, while Sharon is a taller blonde, six foot, maybe even six one, with an unfortunate tendency to match fabrics that don't really-"

"That's enough, thank you. From now on, say nothing and do nothing until we know what we're dealing with," Williams said. "Where are you now?"

"My private office at home."

"Is that where Lewis called you?"

"No. He called the direct dial for my R.R.N. office."

"Go to the office and see if he calls again. Don't talk to anyone except Lewis or me. If Lewis calls, invite him over to your office. Tell him you want to discuss the story and his career. Then call me. I'll work on this and get back to you in a couple hours, maybe sooner."

"Mr. Williams, I-"

Williams hung up on him and re-accessed Human Resources. Once he had Sharon Moore's name, address and photo on his screen he called the back up security team.

"Yes."

"It's Williams. I want you to make a high priority pick up. The information's on the way, now," William said, hitting the send button.

"Got it, sir, photo, name and addresses."

"Secure the package and take it to the warehouse for inspection. Now."

"Yes sir."

"One more thing. Activate Carl Hardesty for this mission. His information is on the way."

"Yes sir."

Williams returned to his computer, this time to access The Society for Human Enlightenment's secured personnel data base. The process was laborious and Williams knew it triggered an automatic notification to the cyber security office.

Any inspection of the detailed biographies kept on Stueben and Merkel would invite scrutiny, earn him a phone call and probably result in a debriefing with his supervisor. He didn't care. The security breach gave him a perfectly valid reason to check the records. His official reason for accessing the files, to determine if either of the members had turned traitor or rogue, was unassailable. His real reason, to decide which of the two men would be more useful to his career, was undetectable.

The bios were long and detailed. They included family background, Society ranking and activities, and a series of psychological profiles, each conducted every five years in keeping with Society security protocol. Williams spent ten minutes scanning both bios and was about to dig into the Stueben file when his landline rang. Probably his supervisor.

That was quick, he thought as he grabbed the phone.

"Williams."

"Mr. Williams, its Hage, team one leader."

"What?"

"Lewis is gone."

"Activate the Red Stone detectives and make sure they have photographs. Tell them it's a corporate espionage investigation. They're to locate and maintain surveillance until our in-house people get there."

"Yes sir."

"This is high priority, Hage." Williams hung up and redialed the second team.

"Carney," the team leader said.

"It's Williams. Where are you?"

"Fifteen minutes out from the package pickup."

"Change of plans. I want you to take possession, but keep the package on site as long as the shippers don't object. When you've established that's acceptable, call me. I'll meet you at the pickup location."

"I'll let you know as soon as I've confirmed the package has arrived."

Williams slipped into his shoulder holster, put on a light jacket, then grabbed his cell phone and car keys. With any luck, team two would have the receptionist in custody and tell him if her apartment was suitable for an interrogation before he arrived.

CHAPTER 10

TIM WOKE UP IN THE recliner. His head ached. It took him a moment to sort out what really happened and what he'd dreamt. The disaster on Law for Lunch was real. He rubbed some kind of grit out of the corner of his eye. So was his interview with Merkel and his drinking with Bill. So was his dry mouth and headache. The rest was harder to pin down. He remembered sitting beside Angela in the dark, listening to rain drum off of a metal roof.

They were sitting in a van parked on a wooded hillside. The surrounding terrain was covered with thick foliage and trees, like a haunted forest. Angela wore a Pittsburgh Pirate's ball cap and there was just enough light to see black rain drops sliding off of the leaves. Suddenly they were holding hands and running in the dark, being chased but moving too slow, being cut off and then surrounded, voices ahead, voices behind. Tim thought a blow from behind had sent him plunging into blackness. His last memory was of a cry of pain and terror from Angela. That was a dream, for sure. He'd lost Angela Baker years earlier and hadn't seen her since.

"Ugg," Tim said, cotton mouthed.

He opened and closed his eyes, trying to bring back the rest of it and got a fleeting glimpse of barbed wire. Then a long row of wooden crosses, their bases concreted into the frozen ground. A fresh stab of brain pain broke his concentration and he lost the picture.

He wrestled the old recliner into an upright position and climbed out. When he reached the bathroom he turned on the faucet and slurped down the pooling water as quickly as his cupped hands re-filled. When he ran out of breath he took a break, but soon went back at it.

Eventually he returned to the living room on unsteady legs, stopping at the fridge just long enough to pick up two bottles of spring water. The couch beckoned. He stretched out on it, turned off the TV and closed his eyes, sick and tired. At least the room stopped spinning. Tim sighed, drifted off, then snapped his eyes open.

Was it possible he'd called Anthony Merkel in the middle of the night? Was it possible he claimed someone would murder Supreme Court Justice Ben Kahn? He closed his eyes, trying to convince himself he'd only dreamt the call to Merkel. Eventually, he drifted asleep.

When he woke, morning sunlight streamed through the living room window. His now crusty dress shirt, tie and dress pants smelled stale-booze sour. Tim slid up on the couch, swung his torso around and got his feet on the floor.

Not bad.

It was 10:00 a.m. The water and additional sleep tamed his headache, reducing it to a dull throb. He decided to risk standing. When that went well, he shuffled toward the refrigerator. Thank heaven, plenty of bottled water. Tim chugged one bottle dry, tossed it in the direction of the recycle bin, then grabbed at, missed and finally corralled a second bottle. He took it with him to the shower, drained the last of it and stripped off his clothes. The hot water and steam felt great, but what about Merkel? He showered the suds off and tried to remember.

"No way," is what his intellect told him. Granted, he'd been drunk. But there wasn't enough alcohol in the world to make him call Merkel in the middle of the night when his career was hanging in the balance. Tim toweled off, went into the bedroom and grabbed some sweats. Back in the kitchen he found a stale bagel in the fridge, popped it into the toaster and poured a glass of milk while it heated up. He returned to the recliner, turned on the T.V. and pushed the recorder and telephone back to make room for his plate.

Tim knew the R.R.N. weekend news crew well enough to say 'Hi' when they passed each other in the hall. He smiled to himself when he saw their grim countenances and chomped into his bagel. The poor guys were trying to make the best out of the weekend news.

Probably some old lady's cat's stuck in a tree. More details after the break, Tim thought, grinning. Wait. His grin disappeared. He stopped chewing.

He dreamed Fred Stueben helped murder Supreme Court Justice Benjamin Kahn. The details flooded back. In fact, he could still remember, as drunk as he was, being certain Kahn was dead. Then he remembered he'd fallen asleep with the television turned on. Maybe Kahn did die and he'd heard the report in his sleep.

That's got to be it.

He worked the remote's channel button, scanning the news channels. Nothing, the normal 'slow news' weekend news stories. Tim moved to his home computer, got online and looked at "top stories" on his home page. Nothing about Kahn. Then he typed in 'Benjamin Kahn.' A raft of "hits" displayed on the screen, but nothing about Kahn dying.

Tim laughed. Since Kahn obviously hadn't died, Tim obviously only dreamt Kahn was murdered, and since he dreamt the murder, his call to Merkel was obviously just part of the same dream.

You've got enough trouble already without looking for more, he thought.

Tim went to his bathroom and returned with the pharmacy disclosures and warnings for his sleeping pills. He took his time and found the part he was looking for.

"Canrient is not to be taken with Alcohol, especially in large quantities, due to the high incidence of sleep disruptions. Reported events include sleep walking, operating machinery and household appliances or unknowingly undertaking other activities while in a sleep or semi-sleep state. Canrient users are especially prone to suffer injury and even death in such a state."

He'd called Merkel so R.R.N. could break the story.

Tim knew it. Dream or not, he'd called Anthony Merkel in the middle of the night and told him Justice Benjamin Kahn had been murdered. When he'd tried to tell Merkel, Merkel just kept repeating the same phrase, over and over, like a broken record.

Or a voicemail recording.

The nervous twinge in Tim's chest turned to a chill.

Did I call Merkel? How long will it take me to get fired after he hears that message? If I really made the call in the first place.

He fished his cell phone out of the briefcase and scrolled through his list of calls. The ones at the top of the list were the calls he'd made to Sharon. Nothing to any of Merkel's numbers. Not even to R.R.N.'s switchboard. He was just about to breathe a sigh of relief when he remembered his land-line.

No.

Tim used his cell phone for all of his business calls. He used the land-line for personal business, ordering pizzas, credit card stuff, whatever, and paid a fee to the phone company to block his name and telephone number. He discovered his already high-profile on R.R.N. made him a celebrity and complicated something as simple as ordering a pizza.

When was the last time he used the phone?

Wednesday afternoon he came home and ordered Chinese take-out from a place around corner. Yep, that was the last call he'd made. Tim picked up the phone, hit redial, and listened to the electronic beeps as the phone punched out the last outbound number. When he saw the numbers displayed on the phone's readout he knew he was in trouble even before it rang through.

"You've reached Anthony Merkel, R.R.N. Special Reporting. I'm unavailable at this time. Please leave your name and number and purpose of your call. Thank you."

Tim hung up before the mailbox beeped.

He'd been holding his breath. Now, the air gushed out and back in. Game over, Tim said to himself. He jumped off the couch and paced back and forth.

"Game over," he said, out loud this time.

Merkel already had serious doubts about Tim's suitability for R.R.N. What would his reaction be when he played back a delusional phone call in the middle of the night from the same person?

Game over. As soon as Merkel hears that message, game over. Tim stopped pacing. What if he never hears it? He replaced the cordless phone, picked up the cell, chose recent calls and found Sharon's cell number. If Sharon had keys to Merkel's office in case of emergency, why wouldn't she have the access code to his voice mailbox as well?

Okay, maybe not, Tim thought, but it's all I've got.

"Hi, it's Sharon. I'm too busy living my exciting New York City life to take the time to stop and answer right now. Leave a message, and I'll hit you back as soon as I can." Tim waited for the beep.

"Sharon, it's Tim," he blurted. Realizing how he sounded, he slowed himself. "Sorry. Sharon, its Tim Lewis. We've got a big problem I've got to talk to you about. Um, about yesterday."

It was dishonest implying his late night call to Merkel involved Sharon. Dishonest. The thought popped into his mind: if she refuses to help, you could threaten to tell Merkel she let you into the office. No, it won't come to that, and even if it does, I just won't do it. No way.

"You'd better call me back right away. I'm sorry about this."

Tim snapped the phone closed, sat down and reviewed his strategy. First, he was probably screwed. Even if someone else had Merkel's voice mailbox code as a backup, it might not be Sharon. Even if he threatened her, she might call his bluff. Tim knew he would never rat out Sharon for helping him. Those things were out of his control. But, if someone did have Merkel's voice mailbox code, and if Sharon was the one who had it, and if she was willing to help, he needed to be ready.

Tim went into his bedroom and changed into a pair of khaki pants, a dress shirt and leather loafers. His normal weekend work wear. He found his wallet and keys in yesterday's dress pants, put his cell and recorder in the briefcase, and took one last look around before leaving.

Without thinking, Tim went down the hallway to the stairwell. City living and long hours had turned him into a habitual stair climber. It was his normal habit and sometimes the only exercise he got. On his way the elevator bell rang and the doors slid open. He kept moving.

"Yes, I know Tim Lewis."

Tim slowed. It was Mrs. Erickson, an elderly neighbor on the other end of his floor. She was a little hard of hearing and often shouted when she talked. He heard muffled male voices and then Mrs. Erickson again.

"He should be home, but if he's not you can just leave the package in front of his door. This is a very safe building and we all look out for each other. I don't think I've ever seen two deliverymen on the same drop off before, it must be a very big shipment."

Tim moved to the stairwell, slipped through the door and eased it shut. He descended with as little sound as possible. Moments later he left the building, moved down an alley and crossed an adjacent lot onto 16th Street. Familiar territory. Calling for a cab in New York was often fruitless, so Tim always cut behind to 16th Street. The heavier traffic made it lot easier to catch a cab driver's attention.

He had to talk to Sharon. Fortunately, he remembered the street she lived on from the time he set up Tyrone Jackson and her nephew. Tim got lucky with a cab and gave the driver her address. Then he called her again. Voice mail. He left a message asking her to call him. When they got to her street, Tim wasn't sure which building was hers. He got out at the end of the block, paid the driver and started walking. He spotted Sharon's building about half a block away and re-dialed her number.

"Sharon, this is Tim. I'm outside your apartment building and I've got to talk to you. If you get this let me in when I ring up. If you don't I'll just wait and come in when someone leaves."

Two big guys came out of the front of Sharon's building, squeezing a thick roll of carpet through the front door. Tim was about to sprint down, hoping to catch the door before it locked but something - intuition maybe - stopped him. Once the men muscled the carpet all the way out of the door, a third man emerged. Tim was glad he'd stayed put.

Some property management company installed a row of hedges along the sidewalk in a vain attempt to add warmth to a cold block of apartment buildings. Tim ducked behind the hedges. He didn't know why, but he crouched down. Then he peeked through a gap in the branches.

The first two men had already hustled down the street and shoved the carpet into a waiting van. The third man stopped and scanned the streets one hundred and eighty degrees. Something was familiar about him. Whatever it was made the hair stand up on the back of Tim's neck. He was dressed in the same blue coveralls as the first two movers, but wore a billed cap pulled low over his eyes, making it hard to see his face. The man turned back. Tim could only see part of his face in profile. He seemed to be squinting at the hedges where Tim was hiding. When he tilted his head upward Tim still couldn't see his face, but it looked like he was sniffing something. Then he stopped. Tim couldn't move. Finally the man turned away, walked down the street and got into the van.

Once the van turned the corner, Tim stepped onto the sidewalk, feeling foolish. A cool fall wind picked up and chased brown and gold leaves across the street. Everything was normal, a normal day in New York City, just like any other day except he was rattled over the thing with Merkel.

You can't afford to act like a kid, imagining goblins in your closet, apartment building, and now at Sharon's apartment.

If he wanted to salvage his career, he was going to need his wits. Step one was getting in to see Sharon and there was no guarantee she'd let him in.

It would have been a lot easier to just ask the movers to hold the door, huh, Tim?

He walked toward Sharon's building, reconstructing its interior layout based upon old memories. The door and entranceway were full-length security glass, situated across the lobby from the elevator. The building didn't employ an 'on duty' receptionist or security guard; however the outer door automatically locked. It could be opened by key or an occupant could buzz a visitor in.

Tim considered his options. He didn't have a key and didn't know how to pick locks so he could either try to fool someone into buzzing him in or wait until someone came out. He knew with his looks and clothes he shouldn't have a problem sliding in behind a tenant or deliveryman as they left. On the other hand standing at the door and pressing all the buttons only worked in movies or down scale apartment buildings. If he began ringing everyone's apartment, someone would get suspicious and call the police.

By the time he reached the building door he'd made his decision.

If Sharon didn't buzz him in, he'd find someplace with a view of the elevator bank and wait. He found her last name and initial and gave her buzzer a five second blast, then waited. After sixty seconds and hit the buzzer again, this time holding it down longer, just in case she'd been out late.

He was thinking about another try when the elevator light blinked at four, then at three, and headed toward the lobby. Tim pivoted and walked out to the sidewalk. The elevator doors opened and a pleasant looking middle aged lady paused long enough to bend over and put a small white dog on the floor. She didn't notice Tim until she was near the door and he timed it so she got there a couple seconds before he did. When they saw each other through the glass he looked down at her dog, flashed one of his best smiles and fiddled around in his pocket, like he couldn't find his keys. The woman pushed the door open, smiled back and gave a gentle tug on the leash.

"Cool dog," Tim said.

"Come on Alex; let's let this nice man get in."

He held the door for her, then slipped into the building and went straight to the elevator. On the third floor he followed a carpeted hallway lined with ceiling mounted sprinklers down to Sharon's 3C apartment and rang the doorbell. He could hear it ringing inside, but no Sharon. After a few minutes Tim laid on the button again, longer this time. He leaned back and scanned the hallway in both directions. So far he'd been lucky. The third floor was deserted and dead quiet. He decided to take a chance and pounded on the door.

"Sharon, it's me, open up."

No one answered and he was pushing it. This wasn't his apartment building. He wasn't a guest. If anyone called the police he'd have to explain why he was there. That would take time, a lot of time he didn't have, so he checked his watch and returned to the elevator. Sharon probably wasn't home anyway. After all, it was 12:30 on a Saturday. No doubt she'd met a friend for lunch, went shopping, or left to visit her sister.

Now that he'd decided to leave, it seemed to take forever to get back outside. Every apartment door potentially concealed an inquisitive neighbor. He waited for someone to fling open a door but his luck held. No one opened their door, the elevator was empty and he left the building without seeing anyone else. Tim spotted a small restaurant across the street with tables behind full-length windows facing Sharon's apartment building. He called again and got her voice mail.

"Sharon, its Tim. I'll wait for you across the street at," he cranked his head to get a clear view of the restaurant's name. "Bistro Seven. When you get this message meet me there or give me a call and I'll come to your apartment."

The restaurant, just a tad pretentious, was still busy with a late lunch crowd. Tipping the hostess got Tim a table next to the window. He liked the location. Not only did he have a clear view of Sharon's apartment building door, he was only three tables away from one of the bistro's televisions. It was turned to R.R.N. and ran a transcript at the bottom of the screen for the hearing impaired.

"Hi, I'm Sherry," the waitress said over the sounds of lunch conversations and bus boys clearing off tables. "Today's special is chicken salad and tomato basil soup."

"Hi, Sherry. Skip the menu, the special sounds good. I'll take both."

"That was easy. You look familiar, like someone I know." She pointed at his brief case. "I know, you're a lawyer, been on TV, maybe on some high profile case?"

Tim wasn't sure if she was serious or not, so he smiled but glanced up at the television. He didn't want to be recognized or to get into a flirtatious conversation with a waitress.

"A lot of people tell me that. A lawyer? Heaven forbid. I just push paper in an office, that's all. Besides water could I get a Coke?"

"Sure." Sherry lost her smile for a second, but recovered. If nothing else, she figured she'd work a tip out of him. "Coming right up."

Tim lingered over the soup and sandwich, which were quite good. Sherry checked on him twice and on her second trip he ordered coffee. He was about to call Sharon when the television caught his attention.

R.R.N.'s breaking news music played and the logo flashed on the screen.

"This is Andrew Gentry," a grim faced news anchor said after the camera cut away from the R.R.N. banner. "We're sad to report Supreme Court Justice Benjamin Kahn died today after suffering a massive heart attack in his chambers. The seventy-four year old Kahn had a history of heart disease, including two heart attacks in the last five years. However, according to a Supreme Court spokesman and Kahn's family, the Justice recently visited his cardiologist and received a clean bill of health. Therefore his death this morning came as a huge shock to the Supreme Court and Kahn families."

"That's right Andy," the female said, taking over. "President Harold expressed his deep sorrow to the Kahn family and said, quote, 'not only is this a huge loss for the Kahns, it's a huge loss for the country,' closed quote. The President refused to answer any questions regarding Kahn's replacement, which will be President Harold's second appointment to the Supreme Court. Already interest groups are issuing statements, encouraging the President to be either progressive or moderate in his choice of Kahn's successor. Although the President insists it's premature and disrespectful for any political discussion regarding Kahn's replacement, this will be a historic appointment because it could shift the balance on the Court."

"Okay, watch this cup, its fresh brewed and very hot," Sherry said as she sat down his coffee. "Anything else?"

"Uh un, no," Tim said, not really hearing her.

"Judge Anders, whose nomination is currently before the Senate will fill a liberal seat on the Court. Kahn however, while supporting civil rights and other traditionally liberal causes, was also very much a mainstream jurist in his judicial philosophy. Unlike Judge Anders and his predecessor, Justice Kahn rejected the use of foreign law in interpreting America's Constitution.

The Justice famously joked, 'not only is America's Constitution not a living one, most of the men and women who interpret it are so old, they're barely "living" themselves.'"

"Benjamin Kahn died today at 12:34 p.m. in his chambers at the Supreme Court building."

"We're going to take a break, but we'll be back with our continuing coverage of the historic life and sudden death of Benjamin Kahn, an American original."

The screen flicked to a commercial and Tim swallowed a mouthful of coffee without much thought. The scalding liquid hurt all the way down. He gulped his ice water and waited it out, gritting his teeth and blinking away tears. Finally the pain subsided.

Justice Benjamin Kahn died Saturday at noon. I called Merkel in the middle of the night, predicting his death hours before it occurred. He glanced at his bill and threw enough money on the table to cover the check and a decent tip. Instead of getting up he sat, staring at the bill with unfocused eyes.

CHAPTER 11

MERKEL WAITED IN HIS OFFICE at R.R.N. headquarters, gnawing on a hangnail. In the three hours since Williams hung up on him, no one called and nothing had happened. When he tried to replay Tim Lewis' phone calls, they'd been removed from the system. The Society, no doubt, busily cleaning up. He considered a trip to his wet bar, but decided against it.

Since he no longer had the ability to replay Lewis's actual messages, he replayed them in his mind. Then replayed his conversation with Williams and thought about his part in the security breech, over and over, hoping he'd handled it right. When he was done, he wondered if he'd missed something. He couldn't see any harm in reviewing everything one last time, but his phone rang first. The display identified the caller as Williams, so he picked up.

"Merkel."

"We've taken the liberty of accessing your security system," Williams said. "Yesterday at 5:03 p.m. Mr. Lewis was taped while in an elevator descending from the 50th floor. He was examining a small digital voice recorder."

"My interview with Lewis was at 1:35 p.m. He was out of my office before 2:30 and ordered to go home."

"He didn't listen. The security videos are electronically time stamped and the system's pretty good. I'm confident they're accurate and Lewis' face is visible and clear."

"A voice recorder?"

"There's no question."

"I locked my office when I left. Two receptionists were on duty until 5 p.m. The women are both reliable and the office door is steel, the lock an electronically coded key card. State of the art.

The recorder couldn't have come from my office."

"Only one woman was on duty when Mr. Lewis made his visit, Sharon Moore, and she was not reliable. She allowed the other woman, one Amy Delray, to leave work fifteen minutes early. After she left Mr. Lewis took the elevator up to Fifty, walked over to Moore's station after she abandoned it and took your spare office key."

"Is this second hand or did you talk to Sharon, in person?"

"We spoke in person and I will say, rather extensively. I should point out the technology involved with a recorder such as the one used by Mr. Lewis makes the recording a great deal more problematic than an old style taped recording. Moreover, this recording wasn't taken over a phone line, was it?"

"I-"

"I don't expect an answer. With a digital recording, there'll be no question as to the authenticity of your conversation or of the identity of the parties. They'll just compare Lewis' recording to an authenticated digital recording of your voice and Stueben's. Of course law enforcement wouldn't have any trouble obtaining such samples."

"What do we do," Merkel asked. "Whoever recruited Moore and Lewis may have other plants within R.R.N."

"Ah yes, the nefarious Christian conspiracy at work, eh? Moore wasn't a plant. It seems Mr. Lewis was quite kind to members of Moore's family and since the poor lad left a file in your office-"

"That's bull."

". . . and Ms. Moore didn't want him to lose his job, she allowed him to retrieve the file from your office and return the key while she was in the ladies room."

"How can you be sure she's telling the truth?"

"Believe me, not only did she tell the truth, if she knew anything else she would have told me that as well. The most challenging problem in these types of interrogations is making sure the subject doesn't know what you think. They'll say anything to please you. By the way, I'm borrowing Carl Hardesty for the duration of this operation. He's already proven valuable in helping with Ms. Moore. Very persuasive."

"Hardesty? Sure, I'll list him as security for an offsite investigation or something. Look, maybe she wasn't in on it, maybe Lewis-"

"Come now, Mr. Merkel. It's pretty clear, don't you think? No conspiracy. No forgotten file. Just you and Stueben spilling your guts on tape."

"What happened to Sharon?"

"I'm afraid R.R.N. is going to have to report on a tragic loss to the R.R.N. family."

"Dead."

"Just one more victim of the senseless violence that seems to occur on a daily basis in this city nowadays. The victim of some sick sexual predator I'm told. She mentioned to you she had an uneasy feeling someone was following her around, didn't she?"

"That's right," Merkel said. "I told her to call the police, but she thought it might be her imagination. I tried to convince her, but she wouldn't listen."

"Tragic. Let's not get too specific or creative when you mention this to the police."

"Right. What about Lewis?"

"He already left his apartment by the time our people arrived," Williams said.

"So what do we do now?"

Williams didn't answer him. Merkel heard a muffled conversation on the other end and what sounded like snapping sounds. Finally a distant voice that sounded like William's said, "Move on this now." He was just about to repeat his question when the Society operative came back on the line. "Well. There're new developments. It seems while we were having our little chat with Ms. Moore, young Mr. Lewis placed several calls to her which escaped our notice."

"How the heck did you miss that!"

"Of course you recognize we wouldn't even be in this position if it wasn't for your incredible stupidity."

"I already told you Stueben is responsible for this, not me."

"Really? Do you think Mr. Stueben will agree with your assessment?"

"He's going to try to cover his rear end at my expense! Mr. Williams I assure you-"

"I don't require your assurances Mr. Merkel. However, it would be most helpful if you keep your criticism to yourself and do exactly what I tell you to do."

"Of course. I meant no disrespect."

"I'll be the man who writes the security breach evaluation and I've yet to decide what my conclusions will be."

"Of course."

"Very well, then. The answer to your question is Ms. Moore's cell phone was on a vibrate setting. Since our conversation together was . . . intense, we failed to detect the incoming calls. Afterward we gathered any of her possessions that might be of use, removed all of her clothing and jewelry and discreetly disposed of her."

"Oh."

"Indeed. I understand this isn't your area of expertise but let me assure you it can be stressful. It requires a great deal of concentration. There's a rather significant downside risk should one can be discovered in the midst of such operation."

"As I said, I apologize, Mr. Williams. I know Stueben is more senior in membership than I am, but he doesn't have my value or influence. I'm grateful for your patience with me and my emotional response to the situation. I'm someone who knows how to express his gratitude."

"I'll remember that."

"What do we do now?"

"Mr. Lewis is waiting for Moore at a restaurant called Bistro Seven. It's across the street from her apartment building. Some of my employees are already on the way with instructions to convince Mr. Lewis to accompany them. This time we won't be quite so rushed, and I'll be able to take Lewis someplace remote. Then I'll have a little chat with him as well."

"If he hasn't already made the recording public."

"I heard no hint of anything like that on his messages to Moore. You've heard how he was last night. He sounded very drunk. He's probably sick and wishing this would all just go away. He may not even know Kahn's dead. I think he's still hoping to cover this up before you hear the messages. It's even possible he deleted the recording."

"We should be so lucky."

"Soon we'll know, just as we did with Moore. Just a moment."

Merkel waited on the line, listening to what sounded like a heated discussion between Williams and other men. Williams came back on.

"He wasn't there."

"Now what do we do?"

"What I'd like to do is trace Lewis' cell. Doesn't matter if it's on or not. Unfortunately I don't have the equipment on site and we don't have the time to set it up."

"Isn't there–"

"I'm thinking."

"Please, think fast Mr. Williams."

Williams didn't bother to put him on hold. Merkel waited through another maddening silence. Then he strained to overhear the muffled conversations in the background. Williams came back on.

"I'll try calling Lewis with Moore's cell. If he answers I'll tell him I'm a police officer investigating Moore's disappearance and try to get him to meet me. Barring that, I'll keep him on the line long enough to allow my men to do a conventional phone trace to his location."

"Great."

"We'll see. Maybe we'll get lucky," he said half aloud.

"What are you talking about? It sounds like you're working on a key board."

"Right," said Williams. "Perhaps young Mr. Lewis is short of cash after his night of carousing. He might need to visit an ATM."

"Can you do that? I thought only the government had the level of sophistication necessary for that sort of penetration."

"Banks are difficult, I'll grant you," Williams said over the clacking of the keyboard keys. "In fact they tend to be better protected than many departments of state and federal government, but . . . Yes."

"What?"

"The bank R.R.N. uses for its payroll is an institution where we have . . . friends or . . . members. So . . ." The computer clacking continued in the background. "The Society has its own private access into the electronic records of many U.S. banks and . . . Lewis recently used an ATM machine a short distance from Bistro 7 and Moore's apartment. Hold."

Merkel clenched the phone, waiting for what seemed like half an hour until the line clicked back on.

"There's a good chance Lewis is heading back to Moore's apartment or even Bistro 7 to wait. One of our teams is in the area.

We'll initiate grid searches at her apartment and work outward. If he's on the streets, in the restaurant or returns to the apartment, we'll have him. On the other hand, he may have left. I've already mobilized private detectives we employ on a contract basis to search for Lewis and call us when they locate him. If we can't find him, I may have you try calling him. I'll call you back."

"Wait, don't-"

Williams hung up on him again.

CHAPTER 12

TIM WONDERED IF THE ALCOHOL and sleeping pills hadn't given him some kind of temporary mental breakdown.

Last night he'd been certain a sitting Supreme Court Justice was dead. Murdered. He'd been so certain he called his boss in the middle of the night to tell him about it. When he checked in the morning, it turned out Kahn wasn't dead. Nope, Kahn wasn't dead, Tim was delusional and so . . . he devised a plot a break into his boss' office, assisted by a co-worker he'd decided to blackmail into helping him. Now it turned out Kahn was dead after all and what a relief, Tim wasn't delusional. No, he wasn't delusional, he was insane. He'd plotted to break in to his boss' office and blackmail a co-worker so he could erase a message reporting the news scoop of the decade.

So what's next, Sybil?

He'd been aware of only his thoughts and the sidewalk before he snapped out of it. Bistro 7 was blocks behind him. A couple of passersby glanced at him, but neither wanted to look him in the eye. He wondered if he'd been mumbling.

Just calm down. You're going to need money.

He wasn't carrying much cash and thought he might need some over the next few hours. There was an ATM across the street. He got there before anyone else, popped in his debit card and punched in his pin. He planned on withdrawing one hundred dollars, but his finger punched an extra zero, instructing the machine to withdraw the maximum. It cranked out a raft of twenties. Tim stuffed the bills and card back into his wallet and walked off in the same direction as before. He didn't know where he was going.

A branch of the New York public library system was on the corner ahead of him, a beautiful two story building of gray stone with intricate friezes along the roof line. The perfect place to hole up and think. He'd loved libraries since he was a kid and despite having access to R.R.N.'s extensive internet resources, he always kept and used a public library card. Every library branch maintained a number of computers with internet for public use.

Some guy yelled at him, opened his jacket and offered to sell him one of the twenty or so knock off Rolexes strapped inside his coat. Tim smiled, breathed in the crisp autumn air and waved a no thanks. He crossed the street, rounded the corner and went in through the front entrance. The checkout desk was reached by pushing through two sets of heavy glass doors.

Tim palmed his library card and waited behind an old lady wearing a red leotard and a white guy with a crew cut. His gaze drifted outside. Traffic was light, so he did a double take when a gleaming black Ford Expedition crept down the street. What attracted his interest was even though the vehicle's windows were heavily tinted, the front and rear windows were rolled down on both sides. Four grim faced men were inside scanning the streets like a bank of search lights sweeping the skies of wartime Berlin.

"Probably looking for a street address," Tim thought. Still, he was glad the sun's reflection prevented the men from seeing inside the library.

"Next!"

"Oh, sorry." Tim went to the counter and handed over his card. "I'd like to use the internet," he said, smiling at the bored looking library aid.

"Sorry," she said, not looking sorry at all. "They're all in use. I listed you, so you're next. Check back in ten minutes."

Tim wandered through the stacks until he found a small reading table tucked away in a corner. He sat and ran his fingernail along the tabletop. It was etched with a heart and arrow proclaiming 'Ed and Tammy forever.' The area smelled of old books and dust. It was a good place to wait.

When a computer became available Tim logged on using his library card identification. The Internet was loaded with wire service and Cable News WebSite stories reporting on Kahn's heart attack. The Justice had been at his desk in the Supreme Court building when it happened. That was not unusual, according to

R.R.N.'s reporting. He scanned the page, looking for something, he didn't know what, maybe just something out of the ordinary. He found it reading a statement from a Supreme Court spokesman.

"At approximately 12:30 the Justice was having lunch with his Law Clerk when the first symptoms-."

"Law clerk. Law clerk, there's something about a Law clerk." He tried but the dream's details eluded him. Like squeezing a handful of sand, the harder he concentrated, the less he recalled. He continued reading.

Cashmere Mann. When Kahn suffered his attack, Mann tried to get him to swallow his heart medication, but the Justice spasmed and knocked the pills to the floor. She placed a hysterical call to the Supreme Court police who rushed to Kahn's chambers. While the police administered CPR, a medical team was summoned and arrived moments later with a portable defibulator. They were unable to resuscitate the Justice and he was pronounced dead at 12:36 p.m. Saturday. Tim's phone started ringing, entitling every patron in the library to glare at him.

"Cell phones off," someone said in a stage whisper.

Tim stuck his hand into his briefcase and fished around. Everyone stared at him. When he found the phone it displayed Sharon Moore's Cell as the caller. He hesitated. There was no sense talking to Sharon until he had a better idea of what was happening. He turned the ringer off and let her call go to voice mail. Tim looked at the phone, then switched it off for the first time since he began working for R.R.N.

He returned to the computer screen thinking, 'law clerk, law clerk,' but couldn't come up with why the phrase was significant. He'd learned all he could from the internet so he logged off and stood up to leave. Some of the other patrons looked up at him. He mouthed the word 'sorry' in their direction, returned the computer card to the loan desk and left. He still didn't know where to go or what to do, so he just walked. Within a few blocks he entered a well-kept, working class neighborhood.

When he stepped off the curb to cross a side street he noticed an un-lit neon sign for Tony's Tavern. Tim veered left and headed down to Tony's. It was already 3:00 p.m. on a Saturday, so a beer in a neighborhood bar would do just fine. He was still ragged from the night before. Tim opened the door and smelled spilled beer and fried fish. He waited inside the door long enough for his eyes to adjust to the dim interior. A baseball game was being called from a tinny sounding television set mounted behind the bar. Tony's was what Tim hoped it was, a comfortable neighborhood hangout. There were no more than a dozen people in the entire bar, a few older guys sitting on bar stools with tall classes of draft beer and the rest either at tables or playing pool in the back. Tim got a draft and found an empty table next to a window.

"Hey, Pete," one of the pool players yelled, "put on Local Nine, ok? I've got twenty bucks on Bronx High over Southern."

"Yeah," another guy yelled. "I've got Southern and as soon as we get the score, Tommy's twenty's paying for everyone's beer."

The guys in the back began laughing and ribbing each other good-naturedly. Tim wasn't interested but he looked over anyway.

"Any of you guys care?" The bartender turned on a local York Metro station, Local Nine. After a few moments of commercials, the Local Nine newscasters came back on.

"This just in. In a Local Nine exclusive, City Police have discovered an unidentified woman's body floating in the Hudson River. Local Nine has a camera crew on the scene. Since the body was unclothed and there are no identifying marks, Police have asked Local Nine to broadcast the woman's photo and to ask anyone who can identify her to call police at 212-444-3212."

A photograph of a woman's face flashed onto the TV screen. Tim stared. It was Sharon Moore.

"The body was discovered by River Rescue during routine patrol around 1:30 p.m. As we just reported, the body wasn't clothed and appeared to have been secured to some type of weight but came free. Police are refusing to speculate as to . . ."

Tim turned away from the television and zoned out. Stay still, breath in, breath out, he thought. He felt like crying and didn't want to shake, but wasn't sure he could stop himself. He looked out the window and took more deep, slow breaths.

Sharon's body was discovered at 1:30 p.m., but someone called him on Sharon's cell phone around 2:15 p.m. He pulled out his phone, turned it on and set it to "vibrate." Then he checked his calls. Sharon called him twice since he left the library. Okay, it wasn't Sharon. Was it the Cops using her phone? They often withheld information so they could sort out people with valid information about a crime from the crazies. Is that what it was? Wait, she was found in the water, so no way did her phone still work. Unless her killer kept the phone and wanted Tim to . . .

He called into his voice mail system. As he suspected, the dead woman hadn't bothered to leave a message. He grabbed a handful of paper napkins, put the phone on top of them and waited.

Tim was sipping beer and staring out the window when the phone buzzed with vibration. It was Anthony Merkel, calling from his office in the R.R.N. building. Tim didn't touch the phone, he just put his elbows up on the table and watched it, like a poisonous snake. When it quit vibrating, he drained the last of his beer in one long chug.

At least it wasn't from Benjamin Kahn, he thought.

Tim put his glass down, picked up the cell phone and removed the back. Maybe the beer helped calm him because his heart stopped racing and his thinking cleared. A set of alkaline batteries powered the phone. He took them out and dropped them into the briefcase. Someone who knew what he was talking about told him cell phones could be tracked, physically tracked, by triangulating the cell towers if the phone was left turned on. You didn't even have to be using it.

"Law clerk," the thought popped into his mind again, as though of its own accord. Tim put the cell phone in his briefcase and took his glass to the bar.

"Refill pal?"

"Good idea."

The bartender drew his beer, made his change and nodded when Tim returned to his seat. It occurred to him that he had a recording of what Merkel and Stueben talked about after he left Merkel's office. That was the day before Justice Kahn died. Tim pulled the micro-recorder out of his brief case, turned the volume down and held it up to his ear. He hit "Play."

All he heard at first were shuffling sounds, then a door closing. He realized that was him, closing Merkel's office door on his way out after their meeting. Once the door closed, Merkel was the first to speak.

"Satisfied?" Merkel said. "He practically ran out of here."

"It doesn't matter if *I'm* satisfied, Anthony," Stueben said. "What matters is if the Board and senior membership of the Society are satisfied." The recorder chirped as Tim fast-forwarded. He let up and the voices continued.

"Because by the time they initiated the neighborhood relocation of Jews 'for their own safety' few ordinary Germans were affected."

What the heck's that about? Tim thought. Then he hit fast forward again and waited a few seconds before going back to "Play." It was Stueben, talking with a smile in his voice. "Okay, maybe there'll be a personnel change and someone else will find another reason to change their mind."

"Enough cat and mouse. Tell me what's going on."

"The Anders confirmation is in the bag."

Anders was President Harold's controversial pick to replace retiring Justice William Simpson on the United States Supreme Court.

"Before the Senate even takes a final vote, there's going to be another opening," Stueben said.

"Kahn?"

"That's right. Seems the old Jew's heart's going to give out on him."

"I hate that guy," Merkel's voice said. "Man, I feel like crap."

The recorder beeped into Tim's ear loudly enough for some of the other patrons to glance over. He turned it off, stunned.

How the heck did Stueben know Kahn would have a heart attack, Tim wondered. On some primitive, subconscious level, he was afraid he already knew why. He was also afraid he knew why Sharon was dead and who was next, but his mind told him there had to be some more reasonable explanation.

He eventually remembered the recorder, hit "rewind" and then watched the display numbers reverse themselves. The beeping from a few moments earlier warned the recorder was low on power, so Tim decided to preserve the batteries. He hit "stop," put the recorder down and took another sip of beer. He decided to give the bar patrons a few minutes to forget about him.

In addition to the triple A batteries used to run its functions, the recorder featured an internal watch battery and was capable of preserving the digitized information almost indefinitely. But if Tim wanted to listen to much more of the recording, he'd need to plug the recorder into an electrical outlet or replace the batteries. He checked along the side of the recorder, located the adapter receptacle and then searched through his brief case for the transformer and power cord. Nothing. He'd either left them at the office or at home.

The bar was back to normal so Tim decided to trust luck to skip him to an important part of the recording. He hit fast forward for a few more seconds, then went back to "Play" and adjusted the volume. It was Stueben again.

"... everything will be more straightforward as time goes by and the project picks up momentum."

"Smart," Merkel said. "What's going to happen to Kahn?"

"You know six of the Supreme Court law clerks belong to us, right?"

That was it, Tim thought, law clerks.

"No. That's fantastic."

"Keep it to yourself, but yeah. Our physicians recommended a certain compound, I can't even pronounce the name, but anyhow it goes into his afternoon tea and boom, massive heart attack."

"Murdering Benjamin Kahn." Merkel's voice sounded thoughtful. "We're taking one hell of a risk. Especially considering we still only have four votes."

Tim snapped off the recorder and got up to leave.

CHAPTER 13

TIM STEPPED OUT OF THE bar's gloom and squinted into the afternoon light, his mind filled with conflicting thoughts and images. The sun was still well above the horizon, but soon enough it would be dark. He'd need to get off the streets, but for now something told him to keep moving. The air was filled with the sound of horns from passing traffic and a cacophony of foreign voices and music.

He ran across another ATM partially hidden behind a stainless steel hot dog cart a few blocks from Tony's. Tim waited for the light, crossed over and by the time he reached it the vender moved his cart. A moment later a young woman finished withdrawing her cash. A tall white guy with Rastafarian hair and ear buds stepped up, bobbing his head to the music. Tim waited for him to make his withdrawal and tried to decide what to do.

He knew he couldn't return to his apartment and he didn't have any place else to go. His work schedule and ambition hadn't allowed him time for friends. He wasn't sure he would've gone to friends in any event. Not after what happened to Sharon, he thought with a pang of guilt. Whatever he decided to do, he'd need money, so when his turn came at the ATM he withdrew another thousand dollars.

By the time the last twenty rolled out of the machine, Tim had formulated a plan. He dashed across the street and into a chain drug store. He bought three pairs of sweat suits, a cheap nylon backpack, a tassel cap, beef jerky, bottled water, a disposable cell phone, a palm sized disposable flashlight, a pair of generic high topped tennis shoes and packages of crackers and power bars. Tim left the store and found an unoccupied park bench. There he spread out his supplies and loaded the food and clothing into the backpack, then swapped his dress shoes for the high-tops.

The only thing in his briefcase worth salvaging was the recorder and his pocket calendar address book. Satisfied nothing was left inside to identify him; he placed his old cell phone in the soft leather briefcase, put the briefcase on the ground and stomped on it until he felt a satisfying crunch. He glanced around, but no one seemed to notice. His conduct just wasn't odd enough to stand out, at not least in New York City. Something in the side pocket of the briefcase caught his eye.

Guzetti's business card.

Tim spotted a dumpster tucked down an alley serving the storefronts across the street. He picked up the briefcase, shouldered the loaded backpack and stuck the card in his pocket. Then he re-crossed the street and ducked down the narrow alley. No one was watching so he picked up the dumpster lid and checked inside. The top layer was an assortment of twist tied black bags and loose garbage, thick with the aroma of composting food debris. He held the lid open with one hand and bent down to pick up the briefcase.

He was at eye level with the crack between the lid and base of the dumpster when he saw them. Tim froze, still in a partial crouch. His position gave him a clear view of alley all the way down to the street. And of the gleaming black SUV prowling down it. It was the same SUV he'd seen in front of the public library. Tim held his breath and the lid, not daring to move. The SUV slowed to a stop in front of the alley. The driver turned and exchanged a brief word with the passenger, took one more look around, then drove off.

Tim jammed the briefcase containing the shattered remnants of his cell phone into the dumpster, eased the lid down and wondered if he should return to the street or wait. With boldness he didn't feel, he ran to the end of the alley, checked for suspicious vehicles and hailed a cab. His luck held, but there was no longer any doubt. He was being hunted.

"Where to, pal?" the turbaned driver asked in an Indian accent.

"1704 9th Street. Near N.Y.U.," Tim said.

"Okay."

Tim climbed in the back and the cabbie turned on the meter and his radio. Some sort of sing songy Asian music. A few blocks later Tim leaned over the front seat and pointed at an ATM. "Stop there. Just wait for one minute. I need some cash."

The cabbie looked at him but pulled over. Tim withdrew another thousand dollars, stuffed the bills into his pants pocket and jumped back into the cab.

"Thanks."

"You're paying."

Somehow, Merkel and Stueben were involved with a conspiracy that had murdered a United States Supreme Court Justice. He'd inadvertently recorded a conversation outlining their involvement, before the fact. Whatever questions or rationalizations Tim may have had or made, he wasn't making them now. Sharon was dead, murdered, and her body discarded. He considered the possibility she was the victim of random crime until someone called him, not once, but three times using her cell phone. When he didn't answer, Arnold Merkel called him. Initially, the conspirators may or may not have known he'd recorded their conversation, but before Sharon was murdered they'd forced her to tell them everything she knew.

The Merkel and Stueben conspiracy. A nationally known constitutional law expert. One of the most powerful figures in television news. Six elite clerkships with the United States Supreme Court. A group powerful enough to murder a Supreme Court Justice and get away with it. Powerful enough to discover how Tim got his information and then murder his accomplice, within hours. A group more than powerful enough to arrange his death.

He remembered that crazy archeologist who claimed Pontius Pilate was a Christian and some mysterious group was trying to kill him to prevent people from knowing about it. The internet nut jobs said the group all worshiped the Devil. That they'd infiltrated the highest levels of government, media and finance. The Committee for Enlightened Humans or something. No, not Committee. Society. The Society for Human Enlightenment. That was it. Society. The adrenalin shot through him like an electric current. That's what Stueben said, a Society. Suddenly, the archeologist's claim didn't seem so preposterous.

They'd be watching every bus station, train station, airport, bridge and port - every possible way to get off of the island. Maybe it was his imagination, but after the last few hours he wouldn't underestimate them again. He assumed they had access to his bank records, credit cards, cell phone records and anything else they wanted.

"1704 9th Street," the cabbie said.

Tim looked around. The streets were filled with cars and busses, the sidewalks lined with young NYU students hustling back and forth to apartments or classes on the sprawling campus. It didn't look like he'd have trouble catching another cab. He paid the cabbie, waited until the cab disappeared, then hopped on the city bus. A few blocks later he got off and hailed another cab.

"Brooklyn," Tim said to the cab driver. "VA Medical Center near Fort Hamilton."

This driver, a Korean, didn't say anything. He just nodded, flipped down the meter and switched on more sing songey Asian music. Tim decided to hop a train and the New York and Atlantic's 65th Street Train Yard was on the Brooklyn waterfront. The VA Medical Center was within walking distance.

During his second year in journalism school, Tim did an investigative project on modern HOBOs as part of an advanced seminar. During the entire semester he'd spent three nights a week hanging out with HOBOs, railroad employees and security personnel at the yard. Ever since the crash of 2016, America experienced a renaissance in train hopping and HOBOing. He learned sympathetic rail employees would often look the other way when someone tried to catch a ride. But security, the so-called John Bulls, would catch you if they could, detain you if they did and turn you over to local police for arrest and prosecution. Tim knew if he was arrested, he'd never face prosecution. He'd be murdered.

The cab pulled up to VA hospital and he paid the fare, careful to include a tip that was neither too small nor too large. He planned to get a sandwich at the hospital cafeteria, wait until nightfall and make his way to the yard.

A security guard was stationed just inside the hospital doors to keep out transients and the mentally ill. Tim let the bag run through the x-ray and stepped through the metal detector. The guard ran his eyes over Tim's clothing and demeanor and decided in a microsecond he passed muster. Tim hustled down a long hallway, turned the corner and slowed down. He looked for and found directions to the hospital's third-floor cafeteria. Sunset wasn't far off so after Tim after ate, he alternated his time between the cafeteria and family visiting rooms. He sipped coffee out of a Styrofoam cup, haunted by the police photo of Sharon.

They weren't close, but Tim considered Sharon a friend. She was beautiful, loved her family and didn't deserve to die. Right then he decided he wasn't going to feel guilty about her death. If they'd been caught and she'd lost her job, that would have been on him. Murder? That was on Merkel, Stueben and the rest of them, what Tim was beginning to call "The Society." He remembered Sharon's sister and nephew and promised himself he'd make The Society pay for Sharon's death.

The sun was low in the sky and he was leaving when he remembered to buy batteries. Tim stopped at the hospital gift shop, bought an eight pack of AAA's and replaced the old ones in his recorder. Then he walked outside and headed toward Lower New York Bay.

By the time he reached New York and Atlantic Railroad's 65th Street yard the sun was already dropping below the Brooklyn waterfront. Tim walked with a confident step, wasting no time. Like most freight yards, the 65th Street yard was in a rough area of town. The entire yard was bounded by an eight-foot high chain link fence topped with barbed wire. It was also well lit and railroad security, the Bulls or John Bull, patrolled the perimeter in pickup trucks or Broncos on a periodic basis.

Tim had the advantage of learning from the HOBOs what areas of the yard to avoid. He circled around the southern end of the yard and located a section of the fence someone cut and then reattached. You couldn't tell until you were a few feet away. He smiled, remembering the hobos who taught him how to "catch out," HOBO terminology for jumping trains. The "Bull Mobile" was nowhere in sight and the railroad police office was at the other end of the yard so he squeezed through. The yard smelled of grease, oil and diesel fumes. Tim crouched down and jogged toward two long strings of motionless rail cars. The nearby crash of cars coupling together caught his attention.

He hoped it was the sound of a yard crew putting together an outbound train. Yellowish vapor lights made it easy to avoid the tracks, but he still had to cross them from time to time. Since empty cars were often allowed to roll quietly through the yard, if you didn't pay attention you could get run over. Tim moved around the front of a string of cars and jogged toward the sound of crashing metal. When he got close he looked over the couplers of another idle string to find out what was being put together.

It was a train of mixed freight cars. A Union Pacific locomotive was backing up to couple to it. Tim rounded the front of his string and jogged down the train line, evaluating the cars as he went. No open boxcars, everyone's favorite, were to be found. He ran past three locked boxcars, a couple secure plug door cars and several tank cars. Tank cars were the worst. You never knew what kind of nasty stuff they might be carrying. Fuel oil. PCB. Toxic Waste. You never knew and they always leaked. Tim passed them by. Since everyone seemed to be on the other side of the train, he took a chance and jogged down the length of it, checking each car. He passed the final tank car, another locked boxcar and then found what he wanted, a so-called grainer or grain car.

Although there were different types, a grain car was nothing more than a flat steel platform on wheels with a large grain bin bolted and welded to the platform. However, there were hollow recesses between the grain bin, frame and platform. These areas provided decent concealment and shelter from the elements. Smiling to himself, Tim went to the end of the car, glanced around, then climbed onto its back platform.

He concealed himself as best he could and dug into his backpack for one of the sweat suits. Even though the temperature was still in the mid-50s, the wind chill from the open end of the grain car would cut through his clothing. He'd dehydrate in a little over an hour if he didn't take precautions. Veteran hobos and Tim's own experience convinced him layering clothing was the best way to survive a long ride on open cars. He pulled a sweatshirt and sweatpants over top of what he was already wearing, re-zipped the pack and tucked himself further into the framework of the car. The pack made a comfortable pillow. Tim settled in with the aroma of oil and lubricating grease in his nostrils and closed his eyes.

He was surprised awake from an unexpected nap by muffled voices, clanging cars and shouts in the distance. Inching, sliding and finally crawling out from his cubbyhole, he peeked around the end of the grainer platform. A few cars down, flashlight beams sliced through the night before moving off in another direction. He was returning to his cubbyhole when he heard rapid footfalls crunching on the cinders and gravel alongside the rails. The footfalls slowed and then stopped at the end of his car.

Someone tossed a bag onto the car platform and climbed up behind it. Tim froze. The figure was in shadows and looking toward the rear of the train. Tim hoped to hide in the darkness, but the Engineer decided it was time to pull out. The locomotive yanked on the cars behind it and jerked the grainer forward. Tim's head banged off the bin. In a flash the figure slid back, hissed at him and held a three-inch knife to his throat. The man leaned close. For a moment Tim stared into a brown face with yellow teeth and a mud caked mustache. Then he looked for the knife.

"Quiet esse," the man said in a Mexican accent. He wiggled the knife in front of Tim's face.

Tim tried to jerk his head. The man jammed his forearm under Tim's neck, forcing his head back against the metal. Tim struggled to breathe. His assailant pinned him with one hand and ran the other hand over Tim's clothing. He stopped when he reached the wad of cash in Tim's front pants pocket. The train picked up speed on its way out of the yard.

"AH! Soon we will be out of the city and you can show me."

"You can have the money," Tim said.

"The money and anything else I want, esse," the assailant said in broken English. "Maybe let gringo live, maybe not." Tim almost choked on the man's breath.

When the man turned his head to check on the train's progress, Tim realized even if the Mexican let him live, without money and supplies he couldn't survive. Since the tape recorder was in his backpack and the Mexican would take everything, he'd have no choice but to turn himself in. When Merkel's allies found him, they'd never believe the recorder had been stolen. And they'd never allow him to live. Without his money and supplies, he was a dead man. He couldn't think of a way out. Tim had been in more than a few scuffles, but the Mexican was strong and had a knife. He didn't like his chances.

When it happened he didn't even think about it. The train slowed as it cleared the yard, and then increased speed as the locomotive and first few cars cleared the fence line. Right then, someone alongside the track yelled. The assailant was startled and lurched back, whipping his head around. When he did he removed the knife and his forearm from Tim's windpipe. Tim pushed off the base of the grain bin with his forearms and threw his head forward just as the man turned back. Tim's forehead struck him like a sledgehammer, right between his eyes and at top of his nose. The man dropped the knife and fell backward, reaching for his face. Tim whipped his body around, drew up his knees and kicked out as hard as he could. The heels of his feet hit the man in the chest, rocketing him backward and sending him tumbling off the end of the car. Tim watched as his shrinking yellowish grimace, like some Satanic Cheshire Cat, disappeared into the black night.

CHAPTER 14

"**N**O SIGHTINGS, MR. WILLIAMS."

"Let's give the grid searches two more hours. If we don't get him or at least get a recent sightings report by then, we'll call it off."

"I can't imagine this guy's got the nerve to stay in the area and off the streets, can you?"

"No. However, there's still a chance, however slight, he doesn't know we're after him. If that's the case, he may be in the area, off the street and merely ignorant. Two more hours. In the meantime, I'm moving some of the Redstone people to the port, bus, air and Amtrak terminals."

"Bridges?"

"We've been watching them from the beginning. If there's a sighting, your team will need to move fast."

"Understood."

Williams hung up on the team leader, called the private detectives and ordered them to cover all departure points off Manhattan Island. His phone rang with the peculiar tone reserved for calls originating from Society headquarters in Manhattan.

"Williams here, sir." Whoever was calling was a "sir."

"Who gave you permission to access the biographical and personnel dossiers of two high level members of our Society?"

William felt a thrill of fear, yet knew his best course of action was to be respectful, but non-apologetic.

"No one sir, and under the circumstances, no one needed to. We have a security breach."

Williams waited out a long silence on the other end of the line.

"What kind of breach and why wasn't I informed?"

"The situation's dynamic."

"What does that mean?"

"There's still a chance we can contain the problem."

"What happened?"

"I think I should report in person."

"Very well. Be here in forty minutes."

"My recommendation is that you allow me to continue my efforts at remediation before I report."

"Why?"

"As I said, Sir, we may be able to contain this."

"What's the nature of the problem?"

"I don't think–."

"Mr. Williams, you've just accessed some of the most sensitive of personal information available on the two individuals in question. Both of them are senior members with friends. They'll insist upon knowing what your justification is."

"At least one of the individuals will be no position to insist upon anything."

"I'm giving you a direct order. What's the security breach?"

"A journalist has obtained the details of our current legal project."

"What!"

"Moreover, I'm convinced the individual in question has a voice recording of a conversation between the members discussing the actions of project participants, in advance."

Boom, Williams thought.

"A recording. There will be an inquiry into this matter, you know that?"

Williams had made his choice. He was going to throw Stueben to the masters and protect Merkel.

"Yes," Williams said. "But time really is of the essence here, Sir."

"Your recommendation is accepted. Take whatever steps are necessary. Did you arrange accommodations for the two individuals involved?"

"One's cooperating; the other doesn't realize there's a problem."

"Place both under surveillance and take no action until we know more. Williams, this is important."

"I know."

"Very well."

As soon as Williams hung up, the phone rang again. He snatched it out of the cradle.

"What?"

"This is Ed Hallon from Red Stone."

"Yes?"

"One of our contacts at Cedar Sinai is admitting an emergency room trauma case, someone I think you should talk to."

"Why?"

"He's an illegal alien. He hopped on a train out of New York, ran across another hobo and tried to rob him. The other guy pushed him off the train. The other guy's physical description matches our surveillance target. The illegal's injured, but he's conscious and coherent. Communicating with the fellow's difficult. He claims his English is limited and the head trauma has him confused. I think he wants money. He's demanding to see my boss."

"I want to speak to this man personally. Can you arrange that?"

"Yes sir."

"I'll be there."

By the time Williams arrived at the hospital emergency room, the illegal had been admitted. Hallon left a Red Stone detective to wait for him.

'Mr. Williams? I'm Brian Hughes, with Red Stone."

"Where's he at Hughes?"

"West Wing, Room 1542. We've people on the floor outside his room."

"Let's go."

Red Stone did have connections at Cedar Sinai. The private detective swiped a card key and pushed through an employee's only entrance into the triage area of the emergency room. Williams followed him. The hallway was lined with wheeled hospital beds and curtained cubicles sheltering patients in varying degrees of distress. They walked past the nurses' station.

"Hey!"

"Dr. Lamp cleared us," Hughes said over his shoulder.

Williams was impressed by the man's sense of direction. The first few twisting and turning minutes through the hallways left him disoriented. Hughes moved on, took an elevator up to the fifteenth floor and led Williams down a narrow hallway. Another detective was waiting outside the room.

"In here, sir."

It was a dimly lit room with a green tiled floor that smelled of disinfectant. The bed nearest the door was empty and someone left a portable toilet alongside it. The fellow in the window bed had the dark skin and calloused hands of someone who'd lived a hard life. When he saw Williams he looked away with half a smile. His head was wrapped in white bandages and an IV line led from his arm up to a clear plastic bag of dripping fluid.

Williams walked to the bed. The smell of ammonia grew stronger, and he looked down at the man with distaste. He decided the interview part of the meeting was going to be brief.

"Watch the door," he said pointing to the hall. The two detectives went outside and took up positions on either side of the doorway.

"I'll make this quick. Tell me what I want to know and I won't hurt you."

The illegal hadn't bothered to look into Williams eyes. Instead, he sneered.

"No habla, esse."

Williams sneered back at him. He always kept a small Swiss Army knife attached to his key ring and now pulled out the jingling wad of metal. The man looked up quizzically. Williams managed to look bored as he un-clipped the knife from the keys and folded out the cork screw, bored right up until the time he leaped onto the bed. Before he could cry out Williams cupped his left hand over the man's mouth, stuck one of his knees into the man's groin and held the cork screw an inch from the man's left eye socket. He ground down with his knee until the man gasped.

"Now you understand, don't you? 'Esse.' Don't waste my time acting as though you're a Mexican. You're either Yemini or Saudi, Hezbolla or Al Queada. I don't care which, but don't jerk me around with any more 'no habla' bunk. If you don't answer my questions I'll put out one of your eyes. I can't stand your putrid breath, so I'm going to stand up. If you don't answer my questions I'll gouge out one of your eyes. If you yell out, I'll gouge out both your eyes."

The illegal's liquid eyes widened, but he didn't seem afraid, only concerned. Williams removed his hand and stood up. Then he smiled a smile his victim had never before seen.

"In fact, I might eat one of those eyes before I leave."

The man had certainly lived a hard life among dangerous men. To Williams it looked like he recognized he was in trouble. He waited until the man recognized something else, something worse, something true. After the man swallowed, Williams nodded.

"Well then," the Society Man said, managing a somewhat human smile, "I think we're making progress." He snapped his knife closed and reattached it to his keys. "So tell me, what about this 'gringo' on the train?"

"What'd you want to know? I told your man, gringo, blue Devil eyes-"

Williams started laughing.

"What?"

He'd caught the Arab by surprise.

"Believe me, you have never seen blue Devil eyes. I have. Pray you never do." Despite his sense of urgency, Williams still laughed on for a moment. He hadn't intended this part, but the terrorist was now thoroughly intimidated.

"I said I'll tell you what you want to know. Ask me and leave."

"What?"

"Please, sir."

"Very well." Williams removed Lewis' picture from his jacket pocket and held in front of the man's face. "Is that him?"

"Yes."

"What train was he on and where was it going?"

"Norfolk Southern uses the Atlantic yard as a transit point. It was westbound, Indianapolis."

"What were the stops?"

The Arab hesitated. It looked as though he sensed it was dangerous to lie or mislead the apparition standing before him.

"I'm not sure because I was riding all the way to Indianapolis. Harrisburg for sure, I think Pittsburgh, and Marysville, Ohio."

"If you get yourself discharged and manage to leave the country before I find time to deal with you, you may live. If you stay or talk to anyone about this - I mean anyone including the police - I will eat your eyes. That will only be the beginning."

Williams put the photograph away and didn't bother with the knife. He bent close, establishing direct eye contact with the man.

"Understand?"

"Yes."

Williams straightened and was already punching numbers into his cell before he left the room.

"Come with me," he said to the Red Stone men. When they were out of earshot of the nurses' station, Williams turned to face the trailing detectives. "Gentlemen, thank you for your help, as always. Contact your project supervisor and tell him I'm shutting down this project. Ask Mr. Hamill to invoice my office and pass along my thanks."

"Do we have him, sir?"

Williams fought down his displeasure. "I'm afraid the poor fellow has made it off the island. We'll let the authorities deal with him," he said. "Now excuse me." Williams continued down the hallway, looking for an elevator bank and a way out of the hospital. He punched a phone number into his cell as he walked.

"Evans it's me." Williams checked for eaves droppers. "Pull the train schedules and routes for all Norfolk and Southern trains out of New York and Atlantic Railroad's 65th Street and Atlantic yard. You're looking for a westbound freight train headed toward Indianapolis . . . I don't know, that's your job. Move on this. I want the train's schedule, crew, and content, the number of cars and a list of every stop between the island and Indianapolis. I need the yards, contact numbers and locations for each stop. What assets are available in the area. As soon you have the train route send it to my Black Berry . . . No, that's it, but this has the highest priority."

His next call was to Society headquarters. "It's Williams sir. Our man managed to leave the island. I'm requesting permission to employ nationwide Society contacts and to mobilize teams."

"How did he get off of Manhattan Island?"

"He hopped a freight train."

"He hopped a freight train. Do you know where the subject is going?"

"We're pulling down freight routes and train schedules now."

"Very well, mobilize your team, but do it on the way to the Club House. The Board wants a report."

"Yes sir." The man on the other end hung up on him. Williams paused just long enough to savor the fact he was not Merkel or Stueben, and then dialed into a Society dispatch center.

"Exotic Travels, specializing in trips to the unexpected, how may

I help you?"

"I'm Alan Williams. If you'll use my name you'll find I have reservations."

Williams listened to the clacking of computer keys, and assumed the dispatcher discovered what he should've already suspected. Alan Williams was a Society operative. He should also discover the Society Board just authorized Williams to appropriate Society resources on an "as needed" basis.

"Of course sir, you have one of our deluxe packages. How can I help you?"

"How long will it take to make reservations for a flight for twelve to Harrisburg?"

"Will you be traveling with the party?"

"No."

"Have you selected your own tour guide?"

"I'll leave that to you."

"It so happens there's a private charter available and it can leave immediately. Your party could be in Harrisburg at 9:45 p.m."

"Book the flight now."

"Consider it done."

Williams' phone rang again just as he reached for his car door.

"Williams."

"I wanted to say thanks for arranging our flight to Harrisburg. We're leaving Norfolk in ten minutes."

The dispatcher tasked a twelve-man team out of Norfolk, Virginia instead of the northeast. Williams wanted to know why, but knew better than to ask. The most important concern was time.

"When are you scheduled to arrive?"

"We'll land at Harrisburg airport in forty three minutes. Ground transportation will be waiting outside the terminal."

"Visit the Harrisburg train yard as soon as you arrive."

Williams snapped on the car's map light and squinted at his Blackberry. Dispatch already remotely loaded the team's contact numbers. It took him under a minute to organize and then send the team a photo of Tim Lewis, his R.R.N. personnel file and a sanitized narrative of recent events. William also sent them contact information for a sympathizer in local law enforcement, the train schedule and route for Lewis' train as well as maps and contact information for the Harrisburg rail yard. Finally, he included handling instructions – "preserve for processing unless spoiled."

"It's coming now, Williams said.

"Got it."

"Call me as soon as he's in custody." Williams hit "end," sighed, and pulled out of the hospital lot, en route to the "clubhouse" of the Society for Human Enlightenment.

CHAPTER 15

TIM TRIED TO ESCAPE THE wind by curling deeper into a corner of the grain car. The train clack-clack, clack-clacked as its cars rode over the track. Though he'd prepared by double layering his clothes, the wind and cold temperature were taking their toll. His face was left exposed and paying a price for it. He opened his pack for yet another bottle of water and chugged it down, not only to help relieve his chapped lips, but to counteract the dehydration. He estimated another hour until he reached Harrisburg.

Meanwhile he shifted around, trying to get comfortable on the cold steel deck. The wind rushed by. A full moon illuminated the countryside and his thoughts drifted toward Angela. It'd been a long time, but he wasn't surprised by the sudden longing. Fear of it was why he hadn't allowed himself to think about her for two years. Once upon a time he'd planned on spending the rest of his life with her. Now, even though his life was at risk and even though he couldn't trust anyone else, he fought back her memory.

She made her decision, Tim thought, pressing his lips into a thin line.

He finished the bottle, tossed it over the side of the car and smiled at his "who the heck needs her" thoughts.

I guess me, he concluded.

Tim spent the next few minutes rearranging the contents of his pack. Job one was protecting the recorder. Without the recorder he had no options, no leverage, nothing. Using his extra clothing, he constructed a cocoon of padding around the voice recorder. Once he was satisfied with the wrap job, he situated other items in the bag so they, in turn, would cushion the cocoon. The train shed speed. Tim looked up and saw they were moving up a slight grade and around a curve of track hugging the cliff side. He was pretty sure the distant lights were from Harrisburg, but moved to the end of the deck for a better view. A sudden gust of wind pushed him, broke his concentration, and reminded him. If he lost his balance here, he'd topple off the grainer, head first.

He stretched out flat on the car deck, making less of a target for the wind, and looked toward the city. It didn't take long to find what he was really looking for, an island of mercury vapor lights glowing in a sea of darkness. The light island was a bit to the north and outside of the city proper and could only be the Harrisburg train yard. Tim was no expert at train hopping, but he'd spent a lot of time interviewing hobos who were. Riding the train all the way into the train yard, let alone into Harrisburg, was asking to be arrested. Train yards and cities had cops.

Show time.

Tim zipped the bag, grabbed it by a shoulder strap and slid his rear across the metal deck. The train didn't seem to be going very fast when he was looking at the train yard lights, but that view gave a false impression. A glance down at the gravel and railroad ties flying past his car left no doubt they were still moving too fast. He stretched out for a look. A quarter mile ahead the track gleamed in the moon light. It wrapped around another cliff side before beginning a steeper climb up to the top of a ridge. On the right side of the track the ground was grass covered and gently sloping.

Perfect.

Tim grabbed his backpack and perched at the end of the deck. The train lost speed as it climbed but the track was still flashing by below him. The old hobos told him to never watch the tracks. Watching an object in the distance gave you the impression the train's speed was slower than it actually was, and that was dangerous. But, looking at the track made you think the train was going faster than it was and you'd never jump if you did that. He tried to look away, but found his gaze pulled back to the tracks.

Jump now, he thought. His arms and legs wouldn't obey.

The train would pick up speed at the top of the ridge. Jumping then would be suicide. He'd be trapped on board until the train pulled into Harrisburg or the yard. In either place, anything could happen. He could be caught by railroad personnel and arrested by the police. What if the conspiracy was waiting for him? Okay, that's impossible, he thought, but still.

Jump now!

Tim did a half lurch forward, froze, and threw himself off balance. He teetered, then pin-wheeled off the edge of the car. At the last moment he managed to use his leg to push off with enough force to throw him, head first, clear of the tracks. He landed on his right shoulder and back, tumbling down a steepening slope. The impact knocked the breath out of his lungs with a whoosh. As he gasped for air, he rolled over his backpack. Something inside crunched when his weight bore down on it. Then he was separated from the pack, tumbling down the slope, bouncing off sticks, rocks and finally rolling over something that dazed him.

After what seemed like hours of flopping around like a fish on someone's boat deck, he managed to get his first gasp of clean, cool air. Tim lay there a long time, savoring each breath. Everything ached, but when he began testing his limbs they all worked. He rolled onto his back and swung around, gasping at the stab in his shoulder, but otherwise able to sit. The chill air from a breeze ruffled his hair. He'd lost his tassel cap.

Tim decided to inventory himself before getting up. He eased his arms back and forth, then around. The shoulder was stiff and sore, but it wasn't dislocated or separated. The center of his forehead was sore, but that was from head-butting the illegal off the train. Everything else seemed okay.

He climbed to his feet. With the benefit of a full moon he found his backpack, then started toward town. After a few moments he detected the yellowish glow of a campfire shining through a thicket of tree branches and underbrush. He kept walking until he came across a patch of ground that felt a little soggy under his feet. The odor of old motor oil burning in the camp fire wafted into his nostrils.

Tim found a place in the shadows, stowed his gear and scuffed up some of the grass with his foot. The soil underneath was perfect, moist but not soggy. He pulled up a handful of dirt and rubbed it into his shoes, then worked his way up, trying not to over-do it. Once he was satisfied his clothing looked travel stained, he did the same thing to his back pack. He made sure the soil was caked under his fingernails and finished up by rubbing both hands, hard, over his face. Another valuable lesson learned from the hobos was before someone like him entered a HOBO camp, he'd better dress down. He ran his fingers through his hair, picked up his pack and moved.

Tim let the fire guide him in and heard the camp long before he saw it. Men's voices rose and fell in volume, the conversations occasionally punctuated by bursts of harsh laughter. Finally the trees and brush thinned enough to make out the silhouette of figures. The fire exaggerated their forms and cast long shadows dancing along the tree limbs. Tim stopped about thirty feet from the camp's clearing and took a deep breath. He knew what to do, walk-in, mumble hello to everyone and no one, make eye contact for only the briefest of seconds and then find an empty space on the edge of the circle of light.

He knew what to do; he'd just never been alone before when he did it. He'd always been with one or more friendly hobos.

Tim took another deep breath and walked through the last few trees, into the light thrown by the burn barrel. He took in the camp at a glance: a discarded car seat pulled up and serving as a couch, some tattered packs bound together with hemp rope and a bulging plastic garbage bag holding some hobo's possessions. The air in the camp tasted like the trash, old newspapers and discarded motor oil burning in a rusted metal trash can. Worn men with weary, fearful or hostile faces looked him over as he approached. For a second everyone stopped talking and the yellow light flickered across one side of their faces. Tim mumbled hello and walked into the circle so everyone could see him. Then he slouched off to one side, found a clear patch of dirt and sat down.

He was surprised by the number of men in the camp. Usually you could expect six or seven hobos at any given time, waiting to catch out on trains whose destination they knew. Tonight well over a dozen men were visible and Tim sensed the movement of others beyond the firelight.

He pulled out a dirty bottle of water and sipped at it while staring into the flames. Other hobos were glancing at him and in some cases staring. Tim acted like he didn't notice. Eventually, after Tim didn't look back, say anything or take his gaze off the fire, the other hobos lost interest. Some of the men around the burn barrel resumed their conversation about travel conditions and train routes. Most of the other men followed the conversation intently. Tim found himself relaxing.

Then he remembered the crunching in his backpack as he rolled down the hillside. If the recorder was smashed, the audio was probably lost for good. It wasn't like a tape recorder where you could salvage the cassette tape. His recorder was an expensive digital model that electronically stored the conversations on a chip inside the plastic casing of the recorder. The audio of Merkel and Stueben was the only leverage he had. If it was destroyed . . . he wanted to check, but it was too much of a risk.

Instead he sipped his water and listened for tips on conditions along the rails. Tim was a fugitive and for information on travel useful to a fugitive, you couldn't find a better place than a HOBO camp. Before deciding his next step - how he'd get back to Angela and Pittsburgh undetected – he'd gather as much information on local conditions as possible.

The substance of the fireside conversations morphed into a hum and he caught himself. Instead of concentrating, he was drifting off. He was worried about the recorder, his desire to check on it like an itch he couldn't scratch. He had to know, one way or the other. Tim looked around without turning his head and it seemed pretty clear everyone had lost interest in him.

He took his time, slowly working himself backward. Eventually he was at the very edge of the light cast by the fire, half in shadow, half in light. No one seemed to care or even notice. He worked the zipper on his backpack until he had enough room to squeeze his hand inside. To his great relief the unit was intact. The crunch he heard was a pack of Ramen noodles. He kept his hand in the pack and looked around. Everyone had forgotten him. He withdrew the recorder, turned the volume level down and held it up to his ear. No one was watching, so he turned it on.

"Satisfied? He practically ran out of here." Merkel's voice again. When Tim reset the recorder, he'd reset it at the part where he'd left Merkel's office. This time he intended on listening to the entire conversation.

"It doesn't matter if *I'm* satisfied, Anthony." That was Stueben's voice, for sure. "What matters is if the Board and senior membership of the Society are satisfied."

"I don't think the Board and senior membership appreciates the significance of our efforts," Merkel said.

"You'll get a chance to explain it, believe me."

"What do you mean?"

"Expect an official visit," Stueben said. "We shouldn't even be talking about this."

"Relax." Tim heard a dragging sound, then a tinny female voice. It was Sharon.

"Yes, Mr. Merkel."

"Sharon, pull the electronic cleaning logs please."

"Sir? I have a notation the sweeps were done this morning at the 7:15 a.m. In fact, the guys were just leaving when I came to my desk. That was a little before 8 a.m."

"Full electronic sweeps, right? Passive and active devices."

It sounded like someone was flipping over pages in a loose-leaf binder.

"Yes Sir."

"Thanks, Sharon."

Tim turned off the recorder, stared at the dirt and relived the day Tyrone Jackson picked up Sharon's nephew. The kid was ecstatic, barely said thanks and jumped into the Vet with Tyrone. After they sped off, the two sisters stood with their arms around each other, crying. Tim didn't know what to do, but Sharon motioned with her free arm and the two women included him in their hug. Tim admired that, how close they were, and she'd still be alive if . . .

So much for not feeling guilty, he thought.

The wind must have shifted because Tim's eyes burned. He took a moment to rub them before turning the recorder back on.

"Good enough?"

"I guess. I'm telling you, you can't be too careful."

"I sweep my apartment, car and offices for bugs every day. You don't think I'm careful?"

"I'm just saying everyone's on edge right now."

"Have you ever been to Israel?" Merkel said.

"I avoid Jews like the plague. Sometimes it's inevitable," he said, "like with Liebowitz, but other than that, why would I go to Israel?"

"What a politically correct answer. You maneuvering for board membership? Liebowitz." Merkel laughed again. "The only place Jews have been safe for the last three centuries is the United

States. The only consistent friends they and Israel have are American Evangelicals. But, we've managed to convince some of them they'll be much safer if they destroy Evangelical political strength and undermine the public's confidence in their country."

"Is this going somewhere? I'm not Lewis and I'm in no mood to be lectured."

"I'm explaining to you why you're over reacting to Tim's little slip up this afternoon."

"Slip up?"

"Listen to me, Fred. The Holocaust Museum is in Israel. Talk about a work of art, the Nazi campaign against the Jews was flawless. The first part of the Museum is a long hallway of exhibits and you'll not find a single instance of actual persecution. It starts with framed reproductions of newspaper articles caricaturing Jews and blaming them for Germany's problems. A little further down you'll find displays of cartoon depictions and examples of plays, movies, music, books, and billboards ridiculing Jews and their beliefs. The government run, I mean public, schools began teaching children the Jews had a history of trouble making and betrayal."

"Everyone hates the Jews and we're all proud of the Holocaust," Stueben said. "So what? We're talking about here and now, the Project."

"So am I. Your business is the law. My business is information and the formation of perception. You want to hear this or not?"

"I want yes."

"The Nazi propaganda campaign used every medium of communications to present a negative, well accurate, but nevertheless negative depiction of Jews. The first step was public ridicule, fashionable bigotry. The next step had more teeth and initiated the process of isolating Jews from the larger society. For example, the Nazis passed laws, ordinances and rules excluding Jews from most professions, trades and even sports clubs."

"Like using a Doctor's or Catholic hospital's opposition to abortion to exclude them from either practicing medicine or participation in government programs and subsidies."

"Exactly. Same thing with certain small colleges and the military with the abolition of 'don't ask don't tell.' In the next step the government clandestinely encouraged certain elements of their political party apparatus and labor union allies to launch attacks against individual Jews, Jewish business, even entire neighborhoods. They blamed the Jews for most of the violence. At the same time, the government restricted the rights of Jews to vote in elections or participate in political life. The government responded to the violence it created by establishing 'Jews only' neighborhoods. The Nazis claimed it was the only way they could protect Jewish citizens from violence."

"Sure, they wanted to destroy the personal connections between average citizens and their Jewish neighbors."

"Indeed, but why? Because by the time they initiated the neighborhood relocation of Jews 'for their own safety' few ordinary Germans were affected. It wasn't as though the victims were friends and neighbors. Jews were strangers. Odd, trouble making, perhaps even treacherous strangers."

"You're making my point, Anthony. Nazis isolated the Jews by using Hitler's emergency powers. We don't have emergency powers. We need to mold public opinion if the Project is to succeed. So, I'm still waiting to find out how this little history lesson helps your friend Tim Lewis."

"What'd you think we've been doing to Christians for the last thirty years?" Merkel blurted out. "We've constantly stereotyped Christians, casting them in the most negative light possible. News reports, stand-up comedy routines, movies, TV shows. When's the last time you've seen a Christian portrayed in a positive way on a TV show or movie? How about in a best-selling novel? National news broadcast? I guarantee you two things. Tens of thousands of cases of abuse and crime occur every year and we ignore them because they're not newsworthy. But I tell you this, if a Christian is involved, we'll cover it, over and over, until the idea of Christian and abuse, Christian and extreme, Christian and dangerous, Christian and crime, Christian and weird or intolerant or stupid sinks into the public consciousness."

"The Catholic priesthood project made your job a lot easier," Stueben said. "Mix pedophile homosexual Catholic Priests with teenage altar boys from troubled backgrounds. It's the gift that keeps giving."

"You've got a right to be proud of your participation in that."

"It surprised me how easy it was Anthony. We just targeted two seminaries got the door open and that's all it took. The rest of the

Church had no idea what happened until it was too late."

"If we stopped everything we're doing right now, these stereotypes would still last at least a generation. We didn't and don't need to create separate neighborhoods, people don't even know their neighbors anymore. Public perception's been molded; it's too late for a couple of lost debates to change that."

"Like I've been telling you, the Board's obsessed with Pilate's Diaries, but I've got to admit, I'm surprised how successful we've been at discrediting them."

"That's a perfect example. Twenty copper scrolls. Discovered by a respected archaeologist. Translated by a gifted linguist. Their authenticity attested to by a well-respected physicist after state of the art carbon dating. The Diaries of Pontius Pilate - discovered. But, they don't tell us what we want to hear. We want to hear there are many different paths to God. Pilate proved Jesus Christ rose from the dead and then claimed he was the Son of God. Oops."

"You think this is funny?" Stueben said.

"Every study ever conducted proves an early program of indoctrination influences all but the most independent minded of people for their entire life. People interpret information so it fits what they've been told. They filter out information that contradicts their world-view. The Society raised questions about the Diaries' authenticity, but most people dismissed the Diaries because they contradicted what we've taught them – there are many paths to heaven. The fact is, people didn't *want* to believe the Diaries. We just gave them a reasonable sounding excuse to believe what they want to believe."

Merkel suffered through a sixty-second coughing binge.

"Your turn," Merkel finally said.

Tim was so immersed he only half intended for his thumb to click the recorder off. Merkel and Stueben were members of a powerful group, a "Society," that hated Jews, thought Hitler was a hero and were recreating his campaign of hate against the Jews, only this time it was directed against Christians. And Tim caught them talking about the whole thing, on tape. No wonder they wanted him. It was almost unbelievable, except for two things. Supreme Court Justice Benjamin Kahn and Sharon. Both dead. Something moved on the edges of his peripheral vision. He looked up.

"Nice recorder, boy."

"The Mail Man likes your back pack; give it to him."

Three hulking, grime encrusted hobos towered over him. The wind changed direction, blowing the smell of feces and garbage off the men and over Tim. Before he could move, they spread apart, circling him on three sides.

"I want the black voice box, we'll split the rest," the first man said. He was waving a handle less, chrome-colored steak knife blade back and forth. The edges were scored, as though the man sharpened it on a rock.

"I can't give you the recorder," Tim said. "Take the bag, just leave me the recorder," he said, thinking about the two thousand dollars stashed in his clothing.

"You'll give me the box or I'll cut you boy, bad, so it will hurt."

CHAPTER 16

THE SOCIETY TRAVEL OFFICE WAS mistaken. Thanks to a favorable tail wind, the flight from Norfolk to Harrisburg only took forty minutes. Response Team Leader Rich Bouman and his men deplaned onto the runway apron where a small charter bus waited. As soon as the last team member climbed on board, the accordion doors clacked shut behind him. Bouman dropped into a seat near the driver, who released the airbrakes with a hiss. The bus jerked forward and left the tarmac.

"We'll be at the Harrisburg train yard in ten minutes," the Driver said.

"We're leaving our luggage on the bus. You'll insure it's secure, correct?"

"I'm in the Club, Bouman," the driver said, signifying his membership in the Society for Human Enlightenment. "I'm a partner in a downtown lobbying firm. New York called and told me a team running a high priority mission would be arriving and I was responsible for transportation. Here I am."

"Good. The worker bees annoy me. Don't tell me we're riding around on a bus all night."

"I ordered rentals, but this was the only way I could be sure you wouldn't have to wait. The rental company will drop off two Ford Explorers at the train yard terminal. I'll take the bus back after you leave."

Bauman nodded his approval. "This is why I prefer working with our own, especially on a job like this."

"What do you mean a job like this?"

"Just so we're clear, this one came from the top. We didn't get a lot of notice. No prep time, but it's a high priority job. Any screw ups, we all pay."

The driver pulled out his cell phone. "I'll double check on those rentals."

Bouman nodded again, satisfied. He was a big believer in the motivating power of fear. He stood up, grabbed an overhead hand strap and turned to face his men.

"Listen up! Leave the automatic weapons in the carry-ons. Take the personal radios and your side arms in shoulder holsters. That's it. Everybody have carry permits? What about photos of the target?

A couple of the men checked their wallets to make sure they had their concealed carry permits. A couple others made sure Tim Lewis' photo was on their PDAs. Bouman waited until they were finished.

"Good. Here's what we've got. Very sensitive. The target's one young guy, unarmed as far as we know and not likely to do anything but run. He's on an inbound Norfolk and Southern freight train, hiding in or on one of the cars, ETA in about twenty minutes. We'll be met by a local law enforcement contact who'll liaison for us with Railroad Security. The railroad cops will identify the track and the train and assist us in apprehending the guy if necessary. Let's make it unnecessary."

A couple of the men nodded, others murmured their agreement. The security forces of the Society for Human Enlightenment were not team players.

"We want him alive. Don't shoot him unless he's escaping and there's no chance of capture. If you shoot him, put a drop gun on him and blame it on the cop. Questions?"

When no one spoke, Bouman continued. "I want group leaders only on the radios - unless someone spots him. You see him; call it out, name and location. Otherwise, no chatter. That's it for now."

While the bus sped toward the Harrisburg train yard, Bouman's team geared up. Men grabbed their bags, pulled out and slipped into identical nylon composite shoulder holsters. They checked their 9 mm Semi-automatic pistols for smooth function by snapping the receiver slides back and forth. After ensuring the magazines were loaded, they slammed them home, placed the weapons on 'safe' and secured them in their shoulder holsters. Finally they pulled on identical dark blue wind-breakers and stowed away their machine pistols and extra magazines. By the time the men armed themselves and re-stowed their luggage, the bus was pulling into Western and Southern's Harrisburg rail yard.

The yard bristled with forty foot high stainless-steel poles topped with mercury vapor lights. Train cars were crashing together in the distance. The overhead lights reflected off a layer of ground fog, shrouding the entire yard in a sinister yellow glow. The driver crept along the service road as a train whistle blew from some distant corner of the yard. A Western and Southern security cruiser came into view and parked on the North East corner of the yard, its emergency lights rotating.

"Over there," Bouman said to the Driver. "Let's find the yokel who turned on the 'we're setting up a trap for you' sign."

The driver followed a gravel road around the yard's security fence to the cruiser. Two other vehicles were parked nearby, a Pennsylvania State Police cruiser and a Ford Bronco with Western and Southern Rail Road Police decals. Four men leaned against the hood of the car, sipping steaming coffee from Styrofoam cups. The driver parked right beside the police vehicles. No one said anything as Rich Bouman approached.

"Why are the overheads on?" Bouman asked, pointing to the cruiser's emergency lights.

"So you could find us. I'm Dan Black, Western and Southern security." Black was burly, with graying hair, a small potbelly and wide shoulders.

"Officer Black, turn off the lights."

Bouman put a lot of sarcasm into the word 'Officer.' Black gave him a hard stare, then walked around the front of the cruiser, leaned in the window and turned the lights off.

"When does the train get here?" Bouman said.

"It's still about twenty minutes away," another guy said. "I'm Tony Kiefer, Pennsylvania State Police." Kiefer was slender, dark haired and wearing a smokey the bear cap and uniform.

"Nice to meet you," Bouman said, shaking his hand. Bouman was furious about the lights and didn't offer anyone else his hand. The response team climbed down from the bus and scattered out behind him.

"This guy's dangerous, Trooper Kiefer, but I think there's a good chance we can capture him without anybody getting hurt. Where's the train coming in?"

"Track 18 R," Black said, pointing toward a gap in the security fence, "is where the train comes in but I think–"

"Good. I want four of my men in concealed positions near the fence line and the others someplace close to where you'll stop the train."

"Sorry, I didn't get your name."

"That's because I didn't tell you."

"My office is extending every courtesy to you and–"

"You're not extending any courtesy. Officer." Bouman said Officer like the word was an insult. "You're doing as you're told. I want you to place my men in appropriate concealed positions and get out of the way. Trooper Kiefer?"

The State Police Trooper turned to Black.

"Look, get us situated and then we'll be out of your hair."

"No problem," Black said. "Al, Fred, take these boys and put four along the drainage ditch at the fence line and rest up near the turn around. You can probably get four or five in that maintenance shed."

"Right, boss." The younger railroad cops led Bouman's team away.

"You're Ditch Team, you're Round team," Bouman said to his men.

"Anything else?" Black kept his voice flat but the muscles along the side of his face were tensed.

Bouman turned to leave. Before he walked away a sudden squawk on the Western and Southern radios stopped him and confirmed how close a call it was.

"Chief Black, this is Central Dispatch Tower. Train 14 westbound from New York City is two miles out. Dale says he can see our lights. Also, a guy from Ajax rental agency dropped off two Ford Explorers, said the keys and paperwork are in the glove boxes."

"Dale is 14's Brakemen," one of Black's men said to no one.

"You've got your transportation," the bus driver said to Bouman. "I'll transfer the luggage, secure it and leave the keys with the Tower Guard. Then, I'm out of here."

Bouman looked at his second in command and shook his head in disgust.

"Officer Black, that's all we'll need from you right now. Move these vehicles to another part of the yard where . . . Don't run your emergency lights, please," Bouman said, as though talking to a child. "Move to another part of the yard where you'll not be noticed and remain available – do we have radio communications with Rail Road Security, Trooper Kiefer?"

"Chief Black was kind enough to give me a hand-held radio with their security frequency."

"Very well." Bouman looked at Black. "Once we have the target in custody, we'll call you pick up my men and drive them to the terminal. How much time do we have?"

"Ten to fifteen minutes," Black replied.

"Move your men," Bouman said. "Trooper Kiefer I'll stay with you in your patrol car if that's all right."

"Glad to help."

"Wind it up men," Black shouted.

Moments later car doors slammed, engines roared to life and the three railroad security vehicles disappeared from sight. Bouman and Kiefer drove a short distance away to a detached string of box cars sitting on a railroad spur. The location provided a concealed view of the train tracks as well as the ditch team's position. Kiefer maneuvered his cruiser behind the box cars.

"Okay?"

"Fine. This is Bouman calling ditch team, over."

"Ditch team here and in position. We've got a visual on the locomotive. It's probably a mile, mile-and-a-half, outside the yard, Sir."

"No one moves until the last car clears the fence line. When it does, follow along behind it, two men on each side. Keep two men in place at the end of the train. At all costs, do not allow him to escape from the yard. Round team, this is Bouman over."

"Round team here and in position."

"Stay concealed until the Ditch team advises us the train's inside the fence line and comes to a complete stop. Then split your team in half and move, half of them down one side of the train, half of them down the other. Keep one man in front of locomotive and work each car, car by car, including the locomotive. Remember we want him alive."

"Roger."

"Questions?"

"Ditch team here Sir, the stretch of track is deceptive. The locomotive's a lot closer, maybe five hundred yards from the fence line."

"All right people."

Kiefer and Bouman watched in silence. The locomotive neared the fence line, slowed, blew two long blasts on its horn and entered the yard.

Bouman couldn't see them but he knew the ditch team watched from the shadows. Car after car passed inside the fence line and disappeared into the yard. In time the train configuration changed from locked boxcars, to tanker cars, to grain cars. Finally a brightly lit caboose cleared the fence line. Someone opened the back door of the caboose, washing the rear platform in light until the door closed. Moments later a lighter flared and lit a cigarette. The small flame illuminated a man's face long enough to show it wasn't Tim Lewis.

"Stay calm, everyone." It was the ditch team leader, transmitting over the portable radio. "He's a railroader." After a pause, the leader spoke again. "That's it, train's stopped."

Bouman keyed his mike. "This is Bouman, deploy." He turned to Trooper Kiefer. "Let's go, but no lights. I don't want the target to know it's anything more than Railroad Security until it's too late to make any difference."

The Trooper drove out from behind the string of cars and accelerated. They crossed several sets of track fast enough to bounce both men up in their seats. When they reached the train Kiefer swung around the caboose and drove alongside the cars toward the locomotive.

"This is good," Bouman said.

They stopped in the middle of the train and got out. Men were shouting to each other as the team coordinated its movements. Flashlight beams flickered along the side of each car and then underneath it. Bouman's men worked from both ends, from the caboose forward and from the locomotive backward, checking each car.

They took their time, examining every corner and crevice of each car until the two teams finally met somewhere close to the middle of the train. Bouman walked over for a report.

"No sign of him. No discarded clothing, no trash, nothing. We checked the cars and underneath. Nothing."

"Do it again," Bouman said.

"Sir?"

"Move your teams to both ends of the train and do it again."

Some of the men mumbled under their breath, but everyone returned to their original positions. A couple guys lit cigarettes. Some talked among themselves. After a few moments several began laughing. Bouman rejoined Kiefer and found him with three other men he didn't recognize.

"These guys are the train crew brakemen," Kiefer said.

"I don't see how he could get out," Bouman said, ignoring the newcomers.

"I'm with you," Kiefer replied. "Looked to me like your boys did a pretty good job, at least the first time." He gestured toward the train where cigarette embers flared and then subsided as they bobbed up and down, marking the progress of the search teams.

Bouman's jaw tensed, but he didn't say anything.

"In fact, I don't think he did get past you," Kiefer said.

"Then he's got to be on the train or in the yard."

"What about the hobo camp?"

Bouman acknowledged the train crew standing with Kiefer for the first time. The speaker was one of three middle-aged men wearing jeans, light jackets and carrying metal lunch boxes. They looked back at him.

"What do you mean, the hobo camp?" Bouman said.

"Usually hobos don't ride trains all the way into the yard, especially here, because Chief Black runs a pretty tight ship. Some yards, the bulls just sit in their office, drink coffee and watch T.V. Maybe once in a while they'll take a drive around yard. That's the kind of yard where a hobo will ride all the way inside the fence. This yard-"

"So where do they get off?"

The trainmen looked him in the eye and said nothing. Bouman pushed down his impatience and backed off.

"Sorry."

"About a mile outside the north west fence line," the Brakeman replied, pointing back in the direction from which the train came. He took a moment, bent at the waist and spit out a stream of tobacco juice to one side. Then he looked back at Bouman.

"There's a grade increase and a thirty degree bend in the track. Near Manada Gap. We slow up pretty good there and that's where they jump. The Camp's about five hundred yards from the track. It's in a decent sized patch of woods, at least for this close to Harrisburg. Every now and then the local cops roost it. Surprised Chief Black didn't tell you about it."

"What Police Department's jurisdiction," Kiefer asked.

"Don't know, but I can show you where it's at on a map. In fact, there's supposed to be a dirt road you can drive right up to it on. That's how the cops roost it."

"Show Kiefer. Please," Bouman said. He pulled out his radio while Kiefer and the brakemen walked over to the cruiser. "This is Bouman, leave one man in a concealed position at the front of the train, just in case. Everyone else, get back here, we've got a new fix on our man."

Kiefer jogged toward Bouman with the map in one hand and a flashlight in the other.

"I know where this is. Used to patrol the area. We got a short access road to a pipeline maintenance road, then a trail that veers to the left. I can get you to within a couple hundred yards of the camp in about fifteen minutes."

"Then let's move. Call Black and get my men to the Explorers." Bouman sprinted alongside Kiefer and jumped into the passenger's seat of the patrol car. Minutes later they were pulling out of the terminal with the two Explorers in tow.

"Close up behind us," Bouman said into his radio. "We're moving with sirens. Don't fall behind." He looked over at Kiefer who nodded once, then spun the car around, throwing up dirt and gravel behind him. The patrol car led a high speed caravan bouncing across set after set of railroad tracks until it hit pavement, sped up a concrete ramp and then slid squealing onto the highway before straightening out and accelerating, minutes away from the hobo camp.

CHAPTER 17

TIM LOOKED AROUND THE CAMPFIRE, hoping to catch a sympathetic eye in its flickering light. Everyone ignored him. The knife-wielding hobo closed in and dropped to his knee, inches away. Tim tried crab scrambling backward but the man reached out and snagged his ankle.

"Let him go."

Two younger, tough looking hobos left their place near the fire and stood behind Tim's assailants. The one on the left was a head taller than his friend, but they were both well built.

"Don't get in the way of the Mail Man!"

The hobo on Tim's left, the Mail Man, rushed toward Tim's rescuers. The hobo with the butter knife released Tim, pivoted on his heel and stood. Meanwhile the Mail Man reached the taller of Tim's rescuers. He sidestepped the Mail Man's rush, hooked the Mail Man's ankle with his foot and sent him sprawling into the dirt. Before he could recover, the tall guy went to the fallen assailant and delivered a stunning kick to his head.

The butter knife man whipped his weapon back and forth in a wide arc. The shorter of the two rescuers backed up long enough to time the wild slashes, then darted close. He caught the hobo's wrist, punched him in the chest, then twisted his wrist backward until the hobo relinquished the knife. With a final twist, he sent the man sprawling onto the ground. The third hobo glanced back and forth at Tim's rescuers, then turned and ran into the darkness.

"Come on kid," the short one said, "this is not where you want to be."

Without hesitation Tim reached out and took the man's hand. The stranger pulled him to his feet.

"Wait," he said. He bent over for his backpack and rushed after the two men as they left the camp.

The men grabbed their own packs on the way and wasted no time. Neither appeared rushed, but they were at the edge of the light and crossing into the darkness before most of the hobos even knew what happened. Tim on the other hand jogged out of the camp while still trying to zip up his backpack. Every hobo in the camp looked like a serial killer. The two men turned and waited at the edge of the clearing. Tim caught up.

"I can't thank you guys enough."

"What were you doing in that camp? This is no college lark, kid. Those days are over. Half of the people catching out now are criminals or illegals, or both. Most of the rest are mentally ill."

"Who are you guys?" They talked like college professors.

"We're going to get you out of here and put you on a bus home. No games. You try this again you're likely to end up dead. Come on, we've got better things to do than baby sit juvenile thrill seekers."

The men led him down a narrow dirt path at a jog. Tim struggled to keep up despite the fact the path was illuminated by a full moon. Without warning, the tension and stress of the last thirty-six hours swept over him, leaving him weary and his limbs leaden. After a few moments his foot caught on a rock or tree root. He stumbled, almost fell, and saved it only at the last moment.

The taller of the rescuers turned with a look of disgust and was about to say something, but his partner hissed. The taller man twisted around, crouched, and then turned back toward Tim. He put his finger to his lips. Tim stopped and mirrored the gesture to signify he understood. Mosquitos buzzed past his face. He was just about to ask why they were waiting when the short guy made a 'down' motion with his hand. Tim went down on one knee and hunched down. The men whispered, but not in English. Tim recognized the language from his time in New York's Diamond District. It was modern Hebrew. They crept back to him and spoke in low voices.

"Three vehicles, moving without lights, just drove down an access road to a small clearing up ahead of us. One's a Police Cruiser but the other two are SUVs. Sometimes the cops use that road to break up the camp when it gets too big or if they get complaints from surrounding homeowners. Normally, they just drive down with their lights on and the hobos run away. Everyone's happy."

The guy said something to his partner in Hebrew, then looked back at Tim.

"This is something different. No lights, no talking – it's like they don't want anyone to hear them. Odd. From now on we move low and quiet. Okay?"

"Yes."

"Let's go."

It didn't take long before Tim lost all sense of direction. The short breather did him good, but they'd left the path and cut through the brush. It was tough going. Sweat rolled into his eyes. He stumbled again and the other men waited until he caught up. Finally they pushed through more underbrush and slid down a slope covered with wet leaves into a narrow ravine. The shorter of the two men turned and raised his finger to his lips.

"We're almost there," he whispered. "Keep low, so you can't be seen over the lip of the ravine."

He slapped Tim on the shoulder and took off, bent at the waist. Tim shuffled along behind him, following the streambed to a storm drain discharge pipe. The moon went behind some clouds, leaving just enough light for Tim to make out a concrete gray circle reflecting ambient light. The center of the circle was pitch black.

The taller guy produced a small flashlight and checked the interior of the drain with a dim red beam. He looked back at his partner, nodded and disappeared inside the pipe.

"Okay," the shorter one said, "follow him in and remember the concrete will amplify voices and movement. If you've got to talk, do it in a whisper." He looked at Tim's face and gave him an encouraging smile. "Don't worry," he said, "it's probably nothing." He slapped Tim on the shoulder again and gave him a gentle shove toward the drainage ditch.

Tim entered bent over. There wasn't much headroom to spare. After ten feet the darkness thickened until it was soon complete. He reached out with his left hand and allowed his fingers to trail along the rough textured concrete. It was really dark. He couldn't tell how long they'd been moving when the first man stopped.

"Here," he said in a whisper.

Tim stopped so quickly he almost lost his balance.

The man snapped on his red light, illuminating the drain about ten feet in either direction before it was swallowed by the darkness. The shorter rescuer joined them and positioned himself beside his partner, part way up the side of the concrete tube. Both men sat and drew up their knees.

"Right here, kid."

They made enough room for him to squeeze in between them. Tim stepped over one of the guy's legs and lowered himself onto the concrete. He kept his backpack between his knees. As soon as he was situated the taller man doused his light, plunging them into darkness.

"Only talk in whispers," the shorter man said.

"Okay," Tim said.

"Here's the plan. We'll wait for ten minutes, then I'll check to see if they've passed us by. Once we're clear we move quickly and quietly. Understand?"

"Yes. You're Israelis aren't you?"

Tim turned to the guy on his left and repeated his question.

"You're Israelis right?"

"Are you the least bit grateful to us for helping you?"

"You don't know how much I-"

"Then be quiet and don't assume anything. The best favor you can do for us is to forget you met us."

"They're looking for me."

"What?"

"Those guys are looking for me. Listen, I know you guys are Israeli spies; it's the only thing that makes sense. I heard stories while I was working at R.R.N., you know, that Israel was worried the Arabs were going to sneak some sort of weapon of mass destruction into the States and target Jews. Supposedly the Israelis thought terrorists already completed a dry run from Mexico, disguised as illegal aliens."

"R.R.N.?"

"Yeah, I'm Tim Lewis and I-"

The shorter guy spoke over him in Hebrew, then addressed Tim.

"You're reading too many spy novels kid. I'm from Cleveland."

"I've got a driver's license, press pass and R.R.N. id card in my wallet."

"Knock it off or we'll leave you. I'm going to check the far end of the-"

"I'm not kidding about this Society. They're every-"

"What, this what?"

"Society for Enlightened Humans . . . or something like that."

"The Society for Human Enlightenment," the tall one said slowly.

"That's it!"

"Shhhh."

"Sorry."

"Great." The two men began what sounded like a heated exchange in whispered Hebrew. It lasted for several minutes and didn't seem to solve anything.

"I'll go now," the shorter guy said in English.

"Sure, you go right ahead," the tall one replied.

"Wait, there's one more thing," Tim said. "I overheard them discussing the murder of one of our Supreme Court Justices, a guy named Kahn." Tim liked the men and trusted them, kind of. Still, he wasn't going to tell them about the recording. Not yet.

"Benjamin Kahn died of a heart attack," the short one whispered.

"Six of the Supreme Court Clerks belong to this Society and one of them, the one working for Kahn slipped something into his food. You asked if I was grateful to you guys for saving me. They're planning to kill Jews. I didn't understand all of it but I'm telling you this, they're out to kill Jews and Christians, big time."

"Big time?"

"Knock it off Yosi," the short one said. "I'll take a look at that driver's license and R.R.N. stuff now."

"Sure." Tim grabbed his bag and the tall guy, Yosi, turned his light back on. Tim felt around inside the bag, came out with his wallet and handed the cards to the shorter one.

The Israeli pulled a blanket out of his own pack, threw it over his head and turned on another red lensed flashlight. Yosi turned his off. After a short time, the light turned bright white under the blanket.

"What's he doing? Isn't that much light dangerous?"

"He's checking you out," Yosi said. "And yeah, it's dangerous. If you're lying or are some kind of nut job I'm going to cut off your-"

"He's not lying." The shorter guy snapped off his light and came out from under the blanket. Yosi snapped his red light on.

"Look," the short guy said, handing something to Yosi.

"That's a blackberry."

"And that's your face," Yosi said, looking at the blackberry screen. He handed the device back to his partner.

"Okay, Tim Lewis, R.R.N. Special Reporting Unit, what's the game?"

Tim knew he should be cautious, but he was tired, scared and needed help. Something told him to trust these guys. He wondered how much sleep he'd had in the last day and a half. You've got to trust someone, he thought. He decided to split the difference, he'd tell them what he heard, but hold back on revealing the recorder.

"Like I told you, I was working at R.R.N. and went up to talk to my boss. He was having a conversation with." Tim stopped and looked back and forth at the two Israelis. "Do you know who Fredrick Stueben is?"

The two men glanced at each other.

"Go on," the short one said.

"Merkel and Stueben were drinking and I think both had been taking a lot of cold medication. There's a vicious bad flu bug going around New York. Anyway, they were off guard and didn't know I could hear them. Merkel told Stueben a story about how great the Nazis were, how they killed off the Jews and now their Society was about to do the same thing, not only to the Jews but to Christians as well. This kind of sounds crazy-"

"Go on."

"So, Merkel asks Stueben how the project's going. Stueben says they have six clerks working for Supreme Court Justices. One of them works for Benjamin Kahn and he's going to poison Kahn's food. If I heard right, this will let them do some of the things they want to do."

"Stand up, Tim Lewis."

"What?"

"I said stand up." Yosi produced a small knife. He wasn't pointing it at Tim; he was just looking at it. When Tim stood up, Yosi reached out and snagged his backpack. Tim tried to grab it back, but the shorter Israeli grabbed a handful of his sweatshirt and pulled him away.

"There's hardly enough room to - hey!"

"Quiet!"

"Shut up. Shut up."

"Fine."

"If you're telling the truth, what're you worried about? Now stand back."

Tim remembered what two Israelis did to the big hobos and knew he didn't have a choice. Once he moved back, the shorter Israeli stood up and frisked him.

"Pull up your shirts."

"What?"

"I said pull up your shirts, Tim, all of them. I want to see your bare chest."

Tim struggled against the Israeli, who let him go and took a step back.

"Shut him up, Ari," Yosi said without looking up.

"You're making noise," Ari said. "If we leave you here, we can be down this storm drain and out the other side in minutes. Do you think you can get out of this by yourself?"

Tim stood motionless, sucking in the clammy, wet air. Then he reached down and pulled his two sweatshirts, shirt and undershirt up, exposing his bare chest.

"Now drop your pants."

"Move up a couple steps first," said Yosi who was still sitting behind Tim. A ghost of a smile crossed Ari's face. "Like he said, come on, you know what we're doing."

Tim reached under his sweat pants, unbuckled his pants and then pulled everything, including his underpants, down to his knees.

"No cameras down there, no microphones on my chest, nothing, okay?"

"Okay, Tim, sit down." Tim pulled up his pants and sat. The Israeli turned to his partner. "Yosi?"

"Digital audio recorder. The one he was listening to in the camp. State of the art."

"Wait," Tim said.

Yosi backhanded the knife in Tim's direction without pointing it at him. Tim sighed. The Israeli adjusted the volume button, held the unit to his ear and pushed play. He listened for what seemed like a long time before he turned it off. He looked at Tim, then his partner and barked out a couple of angry sounding sentences in Hebrew. No one said anything for a while.

"I'll be back," Ari said.

Yosi stuffed Tim's belongings into the backpack, zipped it closed and handed the bag back to Tim. As soon as Tim grabbed the bag, Yosi turned the light off.

"What about the recorder," Tim whispered.

"I'll keep it safe for you."

"You heard it, didn't you? I mean it's pretty spooky-"

"Tim."

"Yeah?" It was the first time Yosi called him by name.

"It's spooky. Now shut up and wait for Ari."

The men waited in the dark, alone with their own thoughts. Tim was of two minds. On the one hand, the recording was his only leverage and the Israelis just took it. On the other hand, he was glad they'd kept it because it showed they believed him. The part of Tim that wanted someone else to deal with the recording struggled with the part that wanted to maintain control of it. They fought to a draw. After what seemed like a very long time, Ari still hadn't returned. Meanwhile, the darkness and fatigue proved a powerful sedative. Tim leaned back against the cool concrete, rested his head and drifted off.

Ari woke him up when he returned. He said one word in Hebrew, probably to identify himself to Yosi. Tim already decided the two men were spies, so it made sense they would train themselves to speak only English while they were in the country. Ari reported to them in English.

"It's clear now but we'd better be careful. There's at least ten men moving through the woods and they definitely don't want to be heard. Only one of them's a cop. None of the rest are in uniform."

"Great," Yosi said.

"Let's go." Ari grabbed Tim's shoulder while Yosi gave them a brief flash of illumination. As soon as everyone was lined up he cut his light. They shuffled forward blindly. After a while, Ari turned and whispered.

"Wait."

Tim couldn't hear the man's movements but could sense he moved ahead of them and was already outside the culvert, checking to insure no one was near. Once again, Tim was surprised by a whisper.

"It's clear. Hold onto my shirt and follow me out. Remember there's a ledge at the end of the pipe. It's only about a four inch drop, but if you fall you'll make one heck of a racket."

Tim followed the two men he now thought of as Israelis out of the drain. They climbed up the side of a ravine on their hands and knees and moved in silence. But before long, a flare arced into the sky with a "pop" sound a short distance away. When it burst overhead it brightened the entire area, bathing the men's faces in the kind of harsh white light found in a morgue's autopsy room. They froze. Then someone began shouting in the distance. Other men shouted back.

"Great, just great," Yosi muttered.

"Let's move," Ari said.

CHAPTER 18

A SLIVER OF MOON PEEKED THROUGH an increasingly dense cloud cover, providing just enough light for Kiefer to maneuver his patrol car down a rugged dirt road. Bouman's SUVs followed close behind. They were all running with only their parking lights for illumination, limiting visibility, but also reducing the likelihood they'd be detected. It was late autumn cold outside. Kiefer reduced his speed even further. They'd entered a rutted portion of the road covered by overhead tree limbs.

"Crap," the Cop said, hunching over his steering wheel. "I don't remember the road being this bad, or this long. Maybe we made a wrong . . . nope." He straightened up and turned toward Bouman. "That's the clearing, dead ahead."

The cruiser emerged from under the tree canopy and entered a football field sized clearing.

"Stop at the end of the tree-line closest to the camp," Bouman said. "Turn your parking lights off."

Kiefer complied, as did the SUV's behind them. There was now enough moonlight to see by, so Kiefer allowed the cruiser to drift to the left and hugged the arc of the tree line. They weren't quite halfway around the circumference of the clearing when he stopped, put his car in Park and turned it off.

"Easy on the doors getting out," Bouman said. Behind them the team left the SUVs and formed two lines.

"Tell us what you remember," Bouman said, as he and the trooper approached the men. "Halvert, give me the ordinance bag."

One of the men unslung a small backpack and handed it to Bouman.

"The hobo camp's about a quarter-mile through those woods,

over top of a ridge line, there," Kiefer said. The Cop was pointing behind the tree line in front of the men. "There used to be a pretty good trail leading to the camp. I'll bet it's still there."

"What about the camp?"

"It's not really a camp. It's just a big clearing in the trees, maybe 45 foot by 45 foot. You've got a burn barrel, maybe four or five old car seats and some wooden boxes people got from somewhere. Men will sleep there, but most hangout, eat and trade information with other hobos coming from the opposite direction. Trains, yards and Bulls - that kind of thing. Remember it's been four or five years since I worked this area."

"What's the terrain like on the other side?"

"Same as this side. Woods and heavy underbrush for maybe a mile, maybe a little less. Then the ground slopes up pretty steep for about fifty or sixty yards. Right at the top it flattens out and that's where the train tracks are. Used to be a pretty busy East West line, I think it still is."

"Got it," Bouman said. "We'll encircle the camp before we hit it." He slipped into the backpack straps, then continued. "We can't afford to let anyone escape. Understood? We can't afford it."

If they allowed the target of such a high priority mission to escape, someone, probably Bouman, would answer for it at the Club House. He mentally shuddered, then looked around at each of his men, making eye contact and sending the message, "If I go down, you go down."

"Good. Two teams, five men each, follow me down the trail. Soon as we see the campfire, split up. Sam, your team goes left, circle around the camp about twenty five yards out from the perimeter, drop one-man off every twenty-five yards until you get between the camp and the tracks. Jim, same thing only to the right. You've got twenty minutes to get everyone in place because I want you moving slow and quiet. But I want you moving. After twenty minutes we're going in, so everybody better be in position. Shoot if you have to, but try not to. We do this right, each of us moves in slowly and by the time the twenty minutes are up we've got the dang thing encircled, right?"

The men nodded back at him.

"Questions?" No one said anything. Bouman pointed at the two team leaders. "Get your men lined up." He turned to Kiefer. "Anything else?"

"Nope."

"Then let's move."

Kiefer led them along the tree line, stopping every few minutes and ignoring Bouman's frustrated sighs. The crickets set aside their music as the men approached, then resumed it after they passed, a rolling wave of silence. Bouman saw it at about the same time as Kiefer did. Just inside the underbrush a well-worn path wound through the vegetation and disappeared into the deeper night. What Bouman could see was narrow, overgrown and shrouded in shadow. He tilted his head toward the microphone clipped to his shirt collar.

"Single file, watch your face; there are plenty of branches and vines."

Trooper Kiefer was already on the path and soon swallowed by the shadows. Bouman slowed down to keep an eye on his men. They made the transition from open field to forested trail quietly enough to satisfy him, so he turned to catch up with Kiefer. A branch lashed at his cheek and he grunted, but moved faster, amused to know at least some of the men following him were going to suffer the same fate.

He'd almost caught up with Kiefer when he got lashed again. Bouman took grim satisfaction in reaching up and breaking off a small, pliable branch jutting out over the trail, like it was hoping to inflict pain. When the green shoot wouldn't detach from the larger branch, he stopped. Using his fingers for guidance, he stripped the damaged twig back along the branch, pulling on it until it finally came free. He heard his men stop behind him and really didn't care. Although no one could see it, a smile played on his face as he discarded the branch and turned back. Kiefer waited twenty yards ahead. Bouman rushed forward, then slowed when he remembered the branches.

I hate trees, he thought as he joined Kiefer.

"That's it," the Trooper said.

A faint orange glow flickered through the trees and foliage. Some kind of bug buzzed Bouman's ear, returning again and again as he tried to swat it. He gritted his teeth and moved back toward his men.

"This is Bouman," he whispered into the mike. "We have visual sighting of the camp. Everyone make sure your watch is set for 9:17 p.m., right now." The men all wore cheap but dependable rubberized watches called, "trailblazers." He gave everyone a moment. "Twenty minutes, that's 9:37. Move."

At his command the teams left the trail. One moved to the left, the other to the right. They made some noise moving through the brush, but not much. Kiefer and Bouman stayed on the trail and approached the camp.

Herman Alexander was a freshly minted Society member who loved the opportunity his new membership granted and never thought about the cost. When Bouman ordered his group to split to the right, he was the next to last man in the line. The first guy dropped off a short distance later. Then the group stopped again, long enough for the team leader to signal him to stay put.

Alexander saw a patch of deep black under a tree and moved toward it to wait. That's when he saw it, outside the circle his team was setting up. He left the tree and looked down into an open ditch. Probably a stream or creek, he thought. Something drew him toward it. He glanced at his watch and decided to check it out. Alexander dropped into the channel, checking in both directions.

Was that movement?

He jerked his weapon up at the sound and almost squeezed off a round. A narrowly averted disaster. The intruder was a fat but athletic raccoon, clawing its way up and out of the ditch. Before Alexander caught his breath, the raccoon darted into the underbrush on the other side. He smiled with relief, before noticing a gray half-moon reflecting the light up ahead.

"Drainage culvert," he thought. He listened and waited, undecided. Time made up his mind for him. By now the last few men would be getting into place. His watch read 9:33. Just enough time. He climbed out of the ditch and worked his way toward the glowing campfire in front of him.

While Alexander peered into Tim's drainage ditch, Bouman and

Kiefer closed on the camp. When they could overhear snippets of conversation from the campfire Bouman signaled a stop. He knelt down, took off the backpack and set it beside his foot. He checked his watch, pulled out a foot long silver tube from the pack and twisted off the cap.

Flare?" Kiefer whispered.

"Parachute flare," Bouman said. He turned the cap upside down and slid it onto the bottom of the tube. He checked his watch, waited for less than a minute and checked again.

"Don't look up; it'll ruin your night vision."

Bouman held the tube up off the ground, pointed the open end of it toward the sky and then slammed it into the dirt. The cap acted as a detonator and fired off a small charge that sent the flare "whooshing" into the sky over top of the camp.

"Nice shot," Kiefer said.

Moments later the flare ignited with a pop, pop, searing the night sky with white light. Cries of alarm, wonder and warning rang out from the camp. Bouman waited long enough to ensure the small parachutes deployed and were floating gently earthward.

"Let's move."

Bouman jogged past the trooper yelling.

"No one move, stay in the camp or you'll be shot!"

Most of the hobos froze, trying to process the sudden assault. Two of the bolder ones reacted, dashing toward the welcoming darkness. For a moment it seemed like the rest of the camp would scatter too. Something changed their minds. The first of the fugitives ran into a Society assault team member who didn't bother shooting the hobo, but instead lashed out with a long handled metal flashlight. The aircraft aluminum tube struck the hobo's chest with an audible THUD. The man dropped to the ground and the second hobo stopped in his tracks, looking back and forth between his friend, gasping and choking on the ground, and his assailant.

The Society man holstered his pistol and pointed the head of the flashlight at the second hobo.

"Get your friend up and drag him back to the fire. If I pull the pistol out again, I'm shooting someone."

By now the rest of the security team were tightening their circle around the camp, herding the derelicts closer together and nearer to the flaming burn barrel. Bouman walked into the midst of the hobos, scrutinizing each man's face. In seconds he knew Tim wasn't among the dozen or so ragged men in front of him.

"Trooper Kiefer?"

"This man's a fugitive," Kiefer said, holding up Tim's photo. "I want everyone to take a close look at his face and tell me where he is."

Kiefer and Bouman stared at a circle of sullen faces. No one spoke.

"I guess I've got no choice then," Bouman said. "Harrisburg General's Psych wing is already set up for you guys. I wanted to cut you some slack, but . . . Let's move them back to the vehicles men."

"I'm not crazy."

"They'll dope us up and that ain't right."

"It ain't fair for you–"

"I told you, I tried to cut you some slack, but no, you want to help a known terrorist–"

"What?"

"We ain't helping no dang terrorists."

"Sir, Sir, this fellow just left minutes ago with the Dragons."

"What?" Kiefer said. "Shut up, the rest of you SHUT up."

One of the Security men knocked a mouthy hobo to the ground and the rest fell silent.

The man who spoke up moved closer and touched the photo. He was grimier than most, his pants precariously clinging to his hips thanks to a tattered piece of rope threaded through three of his belt loops. Kiefer glared at the hobo from under his Smokey the Bear hat. The man cringed and started mumbling.

"This fellow just left minutes ago with the Dragons, sir."

"You're going to the looney bin you–"

"It's true it's true, two Dragons whisked him away, it's true it's true."

"Shut up, Beatle," a second hobo said. "We tell you, you leave us alone, law man?"

Kiefer walked up to a short, solid looking man with mottled skin and missing teeth. He didn't stop until the top brim of his hat touched the forehead of the shorter man.

"Maybe. Now tell me."

"Fifteen, maybe twenty minutes ago that kid had a little problem with some of the fellas around here. Couple of big white guys rescued him. He followed them out of the camp."

"Hobos?"

"I guess. I seen 'em around but they're weird."

Bouman pushed up into the personal space of both men, fighting to keep his voice under control.

"Which way did they go?"

"Toward the road, a little north of the clearing."

"Let's move," Bouman said. "We've got him! I want the same teams, left and right, moving in a picket line from this end, up to the tracks, and this end down to the clearing."

"Sir?"

"This better be good."

"On the way in I ran across a storm water ditch ending with a drain mouth. It ran underground. I thought I heard movement, but an animal bolted out of the bushes and I thought that was it. Now, I'm not so sure."

"Tell me about it." Bouman kept his voice soft, making it sound all the more sinister. He pulled out a three-inch knife, slender and pointed, like a dagger. The hobo glanced over his shoulder, but there was nowhere to go. He shuddered and waited with his head bowed.

"Look at me. I said look up! Tell me what you know about the drain."

"It's where your man said. Seventy-five, maybe eighty yards long, comes out just on the other side of the hillside, toward the railroad tracks. It's a good escape route."

"If you're lying, I'll find you." He tapped the point of the dagger against the hobo's cheek. "Are you sure?"

"Yes."

"Let's move, same picket line, only this time on both sides of the ditch. Alexander leads. I want it enveloped, surrounded and no noise. Only team leaders on the radios. Everyone hear that? Quiet! Move out wide, then work your way in, so they don't hear us until it's too late. When we're ready I'll flare it, we move two men into the ditch, only at one end. Alexander! Move!"

Bouman's men assembled into their assigned teams and formed two separate lines, one on his left and one on his right. Bouman centered the picket line on Alexander and jogged behind them. He reached into his pack and pulled out a second parachute flare. The men were already stringing themselves out in a moving line that crept up and over the ridge, then swung wide on either side to create a large noose of muscle and hostility, cinching itself around the storm water drain hidey hole.

"Alexander this is Bouman, take a knee about twenty yards from the ditch."

"Roger."

Moments later, Alexander slowed, stopped and then sank to one knee. Kiefer and Bouman joined him, kneeling on either side. Bouman reached down and pulled his collar up near his mouth.

"Status A team."

"A Team in place."

"Status B team." After many seconds ticked past, Bouman called again. "Status B team."

"This is B team, last man in position."

"Roger. Subject is to be detained but not harmed if possible. Otherwise use of deadly force authorized. Two unidentified white males are expendable. Alexander will clear the storm water sewer from this side." Bouman cupped his left hand over the radio Mike and clapped Alexander on the shoulder with the other. "You've got three minutes to get into position. When I pop the flare, hit the drain with your light and clear it all the way to the other end. Move."

Alexander crept to the edge of the ditch and slid down into the bed. Once his head disappeared Bouman uncovered his microphone.

"Flare in 60 seconds."

Bouman produced a second silver tube and prepared it for ignition. He checked the overhead canopy for a clear space wide enough to accommodate the flare's trajectory. After 60 seconds ticked off on his wristwatch he grasped the tube with both hands and slammed it onto the ground. The flair shot off, popped into the sky and bathed the night with day light from an alternate universe.

CHAPTER 19

THE THREE FUGITIVES RACED AWAY from the storm drain, casting long shadows and moving with relative ease over rugged terrain. Then the flare drifted below the tree line, day turned to night, and Tim's vision struggled to adjust. Before it did his foot caught on a piece of dead fall that sent him sprawling. He hit hard. The air gushed out of his lungs and he was still gasping when Yosi grabbed him under the arm pit and yanked him up.

"Run."

They eventually pushed through the last of the underbrush, then slipped down a steep hillside of loose dirt. Tim lost his footing and ended up sliding part of the way down on his rear. When he got to the bottom Yosi helped him up, grabbed his sleeve and pulled him along for a few steps before releasing him.

"What about Ari?" Tim whispered.

"He'll be along. Keep going, we still have a mile to go and we're running out of time."

Another "pop" sounded some distance behind them, but along their back trail. The sky brightened with the same harsh light as before, but like a dying star, the flare was too far away for its light to reach them.

Yosi stopped and looked back.

"I stand corrected," Yosi said. "We're not running out of time, we're out of time. They popped that flare over the storm drain. It won't take them long to figure out we're not there. As soon as they do, they'll be coming, fast."

He turned to Tim.

"Stay close, look down to your left and ahead to your right. Your night vision's better out of the corners of your eyes. Let's go."

Yosi jogged ahead, his footfalls swooshing through damp leaves. The trees and underbrush thinned out, allowing them to weave around the thick patches. Tim thought he heard someone behind them, but he couldn't be sure over the sound of his own movements. They ran until he developed a stitch in his right side. The pain increased until each gulp of air hurt. He was ready to call out when Yosi slowed, stopped and then went down on one knee. Tim knelt down alongside the Israeli.

"Keep your voice down and no moving around," Yosi said.

"What're we doing?"

"We're watching and waiting."

Tim wiped at something tickling his cheek, something wet. Without thinking, he brought his hand to his lips. Salty, sweat. He couldn't tell what Yosi was looking at, but he did hear traffic buzzing down an asphalt highway.

"It sounds like we're close to the highway." Yosi didn't say anything. "What're we watching?"

The Israeli turned and looked at him for a long moment. He moved a bit closer to Tim and pointed.

"See the clearing? Not so much a clearing as a little indentation, down there in the tree-line?"

Tim didn't see anything that looked like a clearing or indentation, but decided to keep quiet about it. Yosi turned back, maintaining his watch on the elusive indentation, so Tim switched knees to relieve the strain. He tried to look vigilant in case Yosi checked. Somewhere an owl hooted. Yosi pivoted gracefully, holding his knife up behind his ear like he might throw it. Tim heard movement in the underbrush.

Whoever it was seemed willing to sacrifice some stealth for speed. You could hear them, but they were moving quickly and not making much noise doing it. Tim squinted into the shadows but there wasn't enough moonlight to see anything.

"Yosi?"

Tim recognized Ari's voice in the harsh whisper. It came from a point far to the left of where he'd been looking, not far from where Yosi was directing his knife.

"Ari."

A man's silhouette emerged from the shadows, running and bent low to the ground. Ari crossed through the low underbrush and stopped alongside them, dropping to one knee.

"They've finished clearing the drain. I'm guessing they're trying to figure out what to do next. It won't take them long. How about the bikes?"

"Looks clear to me," Yosi said. He turned to Tim. "How about you, see anything?"

"Nope, me either." It occurred to Tim Yosi might have been teasing him.

"Let's try it, then."

"What bikes are-?"

Both men were already jogging toward the highway. Tim scurried after them, doing his best not to get tripped up. Once they got to the tree-line Tim recognized Yosi's indentation. Ari looked back.

"Come on, Tim. Once we get on the highway we've got two hours, maybe a little more. We're going to need all of it."

Tim caught up to them just as Ari reached into the underbrush and pulled back a large flap of vegetation in one big piece. He flipped whatever it was over and revealed a depression covered with canvas drop cloths. Yosi pulled the cloths back and chrome gleamed in the faint moonlight. Two motorcycles. Yosi pulled up the first bike and manhandled it out of the depression. Moments later Ari had his up and out.

"Hold this," he said to Tim.

"I don't-."

"Just hold it up!"

Tim leaned over and grabbed both ends of the handlebars, balancing the motorcycle and worrying he might drop it. He was used to the smaller dirt bikes he knew when he was a kid. Meanwhile Ari replaced the drop cloth and vegetation, which Tim now saw was woven into nylon net. Ari turned and slid between Tim and the motorcycle, taking the handle bars.

"Come on," he said nodding his head. Yosi stood a couple hundred feet away, watching them and waiting. "We'll fire up the bikes once we get close to the highway." Ari took off, trotting and pushing the motorcycle by the handlebars. This time Tim didn't have any trouble keeping up since the Israeli was muscling the motorcycle across uneven ground. Ari passed Yosi, who then fell in behind him. The buzzing of car tires rolling across damp pavement grew louder. Ari stopped.

"This is good," he said. They were standing at the bottom of a slight incline topped by a metal guard rail. "Tim, you're riding with me. Did you bring a hat," he asked.

"Yeah."

"Put it on, from a distance it might look like a helmet. You know how to ride as a passenger on a motorcycle?"

"I've done it before but I don't know-."

"Just don't do anything, relax, don't try to help me, and don't fight me. Close your eyes if you have to."

Yosi kick started his bike and it roared into life, growling and then snarling as he twisted the throttle back and forth. The next second Ari's bike joined in, sounding unnaturally loud after all the silence. Tim swallowed a face full of exhaust and looked around, like someone was going to complain about the noise.

"Get on," Ari ordered. Tim swung onto the bike and circled his arms around Ari's midsection.

"Hold on" the Israeli said.

The motorcycle leapt forward and climbed the hill. Before Tim could react they found a gap in the guard rail, bounced onto the asphalt and accelerated down the road. A cluster of lights shined in the distance.

Harrisburg.

The motorcycle picked up speed, leaving Tim initially refreshed when the wind began tugging at his face. His eyes watered and his stomach vibrated in time with the engine. Inches from his feet, foot long white lines turned into flashing dots. Tim shifted far enough in the seat to get his mouth close to Ari's ear.

"Where are we going," he shouted. The wind threw the words back into his face, rushed through his hair and reminded him he'd lost his hat somewhere. It was cold enough to make his head and ears burn.

"Other side of town," Ari shouted. "No more talking."

Before ducking behind Ari's head, Tim managed a glance at the speedometer. He almost craned his head around for another look. The red arrow wiggled between 110 and 120. Tim wasn't sure how much would be left if they hit the pavement at 110 and he didn't want to find out. He closed his eyes and tried to let every muscle in his body go to jelly, but then Ari leaned the bike into a turn.

Tim could feel the physics of the machine grasp his entire torso and push it onto the seat of the motorcycle. When he thought he could hear the asphalt he almost opened his eyes.

A good time to practice your times tables.

"Three times three is nine. Nine times three is twenty-seven. Twenty-seven times three is . . ."

Tim wouldn't have wagered a dime on the accuracy of his math but it kept him distracted. Being distracted kept him from killing himself, Ari and probably Yosi who trailed behind them no more than a couple of bike lengths.

Finally Ari eased up on the throttle and Tim risked a look. They were already into the town itself. The wind noise was considerably lower at their current speed so Tim leaned back around.

"We been in Harrisburg for a while," he said. "How fast were we going?"

Ari dropped even more speed and turned toward Tim with a grin.

"Fast, especially right before we got into town. Yosi's going to kill me. He hates motorcycles."

"Where are we going?"

"We're going to stop, get some coffee and call some friends of ours."

"Mossad?"

"Hardly," Ari said laughing over his shoulder. "Our friends' names are Guzetti and Allison. What do you think? Sound Jewish?" Ari grew serious. "We're a long way from our embassy and from home. These are two of the few people left Israel can still trust. They've got resources and expertise we don't."

"Okay, but I mean, where are we going . . . now?" Tim kept his thoughts about the name "Guzetti" to himself.

"I know a place on the other side of town, across the river. Stays open all night, good coffee and an old-fashioned pay phone. Now days a land line, or even better, a land line on a pay phone, is one of the safest ways there are to talk when you don't want someone else listening."

"What about me?"

"You're the whole point of this. Yosi and I could've gotten lost with no problem. Not you. Make no mistake; the Society has photographs of you. You need to disappear for a while. Give us some time figure out what this all means."

"How do we know the guys you're calling aren't infiltrated as well?"

"Except for my government, these guys are the only organized opposition the Society has."

"But the Society has even infiltrated the Supreme Court. What makes you so sure they haven't infiltrated this group? Especially if they're the only opposition?"

"You're just going to have to trust me."

Before Tim could say anything else, Ari downshifted and turned on his left turn signal, painting the asphalt with flashing mustard. The transmission whined with the effort of throwing off excess rpm's and pushed Tim up against the Israeli's back. Then they whipped low and around, off the highway and into the diner parking lot. Ari chugged around a steel trimmed art deco building and found a shadowy parking space in the rear. Yosi pulled up alongside them.

"Go ahead guys," he said. "I'll be there in a moment."

Ari led Tim around the front of the building and into an old-style 1950s type diner lined with windows. Three or four truckers in denim shirts and ball caps were sitting on stools at the counter, nursing cups of coffee. Two of the men were swapping tips on road conditions in voices loud enough to be heard over the clanking of porcelain plates. A waitress cleared dinnerware off of a Formica counter-top and the air smelled of fried food.

"Can I help you Sir?"

The assistant manager was dressed in a white cotton shirt and gray polyester pants. He looked to be in his mid 20's. A plastic name tag clipped to his shirt pocket said "Danny" in black block letters. Ari looked at Tim's and then his own clothing before giving the assistant manager a sheepish smile.

"Sure can, after the night we've had some coffee and sandwiches would go a long way."

Ari pulled a wad of green backs from his front pocket, about ten bills of small denominations. Tim saw fives and tens, not enough to raise any eyebrows, but enough to convince the manager they were legitimate customers and not bums. Danny saw the money and grinned at them.

"That's got to be a great story, the way you guys look. Come on let me find you a place in the back. Know what I mean?"

Ari smiled. "I wouldn't want to eat next to me unless I had to. There's another guy coming in, and he's in as bad a shape as we are."

"I'll tell him where you're at and get the coffee for you guys myself."

Danny grabbed a black rimmed pot and three laminated menus. He led Tim and Ari to a small booth alongside a window in the rear of the diner.

"Coffee coming up, boys."

Ari and Tim turned over their cups and one for Yosi. Danny filled each one.

"I'll wait for the third guy, then send your waitress back, okay?"

"He asked me to order for him, so whenever you get a chance."

"No problem."

By the time the men were finishing their first cup of coffee, a waitress was on her way. Before she got to the booth Ari looked at Tim.

"I'm going to order for everybody. Something quick. It's not a good idea for us to stay here long."

"It won't take me long, I'm starving."

The waitress sat down glasses of water, topped off their coffee and pulled out an order pad. She had a dark green mouse tattooed on the back of her hand.

"You guys know what you want?"

"What's good, but fast . . . Dorothy," Ari asked after glancing at the woman's name tag. He gave her a big smile. "We're in a hurry, got a tow truck coming."

Dorothy smiled back.

"Burgers are pretty good," she said, "and I can get 'em out in about five, six minutes. Soups good, but all we got's tomato."

"Perfect," Ari said. "How about three, and bring the ketchup and mustard on the side."

"Three burgers with side cups of soup coming up."

After she left Tim glanced at Yosi's cup which had grown cold. He took a drink of his own, sat the cup down and looked at Ari. The Israeli seemed distracted.

"Ari? What's Yosi doing?"

Ari was nonchalant about it, but Tim could tell he was wondering about his partner.

"He was supposed to call the Cardinal and then come in to get something to eat."

"Cardinal?"

"Guzetti, Thomas Guzetti." The Israeli agent was still watching the door. "He's a Cardinal in the Catholic Church and a guy you can trust."

"I know who he is, I interviewed him. He's a pretty smart guy, but I don't think he's any match for the people chasing me."

Ari looked like he was about to get up.

"There he is," the Israeli said. Tim thought he sounded relieved. Ari looked at Tim. "Cardinal Guzetti's not going to be the one coming to get you. He has people working for him, I guess working for God. Those guys are plenty tough and a match for anyone in the Society. If you knew anything about Guzetti, you'd know he is to. Where have you been?"

Yosi tapped Tim on the shoulder and then slid in alongside him. The lanky Israeli twisted around long enough to look at Tim.

"I called in and then I listened to the rest of the recording."

"He didn't have enough time," Tim said to Ari.

"I heard enough, Tim. You've done a good job just by getting here alive. No," the Israeli said, holding up a hand. "I'm not mocking you; I mean it." He whispered three or four sentences to his partner in Hebrew. Just as he finished the waitress returned with their meals.

All three men wolfed down the burgers. Except for passing around salt, mustard and ketchup, and no one had much to say. Ari finished first, reached across the booth and pulled out a handful of napkins from the metal dispenser.

"Give me the recorder," he said wiping his mouth. Yosi slid it across the table to him, but held onto it when his partner tried to pick it up.

"The part you want, it's about twenty-five minutes long. Set the tape counter to 0 then fast forward to 125."

"125," Ari said picking up the recorder and sliding out of the booth. Yosi moved out and took Ari's seat.

"Tell me what happened Tim."

Tim started telling the Israeli everything that had happened over the last two days. Yosi listened but his eyes occasionally drifted to the large window. Tim was just getting to the part where he head butted the illegal alien off the train when the Israeli stiffened. His eyes had drifted to the window once again and Tim glanced outside. No one was in the parking lot, but then he realized Yosi had been using the window as a mirror. Yosi picked up his table knife and fingered its edge. Then he reached across the table and palmed not only his own knife, but Tim's as well, adding them to Ari's.

Tim forced himself to be nonchalant as he allowed his eyes to glance past the entranceway to a wall clock mounted on the other side of the restaurant. He returned his gaze to the Israeli, forced a smile and fought to keep his voice even.

"Those two guys, just came in, standing near the cash register. They were staring at me."

"I know. It's my fault. I should've made you take Ari's seat. Heck, Ari should've made you sit here."

"These walls are all lined with windows anyway, Yosi. They probably spotted me before they even came in. What do we do now? At least they can't attack us while we're in the restaurant."

"Want to bet?"

"Don't you guys have guns?"

"Too big of a risk, remember we're posing as vagrants."

"No guns?"

"Who needs a gun? You're forgetting I've got these butter knives."

"Gee, you're a real comed-. Yosi, they're reaching into their jackets!"

"Get out of here, Tim," Yosi said. "Use the same hallway Ari used. Move!"

CHAPTER 20

THERE WAS NO ESCAPING THE distinctive jangle of a satellite phone. It woke Ted Kehr from a sound sleep thirty five thousand feet over the Atlantic Ocean. He stretched and looked around a privately owned Gulfstream Six, wondering where he'd stashed the thing. Ted's sluggishness was understandable. Only hours earlier he'd been in a jungle halfway across the world. He hadn't slept in two days. The distinctive wet odor produced by a triple canopy rain forest was still in his nostrils.

Ted Kehr was the senior Operational Leader of the Fellowship of the Essentials, a group formed only two years earlier by a coalition of rouge Christians who watched with increasing alarm as attacks on the faithful worldwide multiplied. Ted had been sent to lead a small rescue team to the African nation of Nigeria, a place where his black skin and African features served him well. Muslim terrorists captured five Christian missionaries and the Fellowship decided to intervene. Although the mission was a success, Ted was tired and headed for a well-deserved week of rest and recuperation. He fought his way through accumulated jet lag and fatigue to full consciousness. They wouldn't be calling unless it was urgent. The phone was right beside him.

"Yes sir," he croaked. He stole a glance at his watch. They were still fifteen minutes outside of LaGuardia airport.

"Ted? You sound horrible, man. Sorry if I woke you up."

"Reverend Allison."

"First, congratulations on Nigeria. It was a tough mission but . . . I'm afraid I'm about to ask worse."

Ted sat upright, rubbed his eyes and wished for a cup of coffee. Then the Gulfstream hit a thermal pocket and bobbed up in the air, tickling his stomach.

"What is it, sir?"

"Who else? Something big's happening in the States. The Cardinal got an emergency call from some of our Mossad friends."

"Oh."

For years Mossad had been dispatching operatives to help protect the United States from a terrorist attack originating south of its border. Ted always thought the Israelis had more than enough to take care of protecting themselves until a late-night conversation with a friend and Mossad agent.

"Some things you guys can't do for yourselves, for all kinds of political reasons," the Israeli said. "I think this the only country in the world with crazier domestic politics than ours. Sooner or later some Arab, posing as an illegal alien, or for all I know hiring illegal aliens is going to get a nuclear or chemical weapon into your country."

"What's it to you," Ted asked.

"First, believe it or not, most Israelis are grateful to America. This is something we can do for you guys that you won't do for yourselves, depending upon your election results. But let's face it; it's in our interest to protect the United States. If it wasn't for the U.S., Israel and the Jews would have faced a second Holocaust decades ago."

"Holocaust? Come on, that's a little extreme."

"Sure, Iran's just joking about all that stuff."

"I'm not saying Iran's joking, but the world community would never tolerate-"

"Right. Except for the United States who's going to stop it? Europe?" The Israeli started laughing. "That's one of the things Jews and Americans have in common. The only time we're popular with the rest of the world's when we're being murdered."

As soon as Reverend Allison told him Israelis had called Guzetti, the weapons of mass destruction conversation popped into his mind. Ted hunched over the phone.

"Did the Society get a device into the States?"

The Fellowship long suspected the strategy of the Society for Human Enlightenment was to try to shock the United States into isolationism. They hoped, the theory went, an attack of extreme destructive power, combined with the Society's long-standing campaign to convince Americans everything bad in the world was America's fault would shift public opinion against involvement in world affairs. Then the Society could isolate and destroy the state of Israel.

"No, that's the first thing I asked. The Cardinal said he asked the Mossad agent the same thing and he said 'nope it's something worse.'"

"What?" Ted used his free hand to rub grit out of the corners of his eyes. He was still trying to focus, but Allison rushed ahead.

"All this stuff came in over a pay phone, from an operative in the field. He said that-"

"Wait, wait, Reverend. What's the Cardinal doing taking pay phone calls? How's he even know these guys are Mossad agents?"

"Don't worry about it. Listen to me. The field operative was part of a two-man team, working along the rail lines out of New York and across the country."

"Prime transportation route to get a weapon up from the south, into one of the big population centers."

"Exactly. So, they run across this kid who's about to get mugged in a hobo camp outside of Harrisburg. That's in Pennsylvania. Young American, looks like a college kid out for a little adventure. The Israelis pull the kid out of the camp, figure they'll get a meal into him and put him on a bus home. Next thing they know the camp's surrounded by operatives from the Society."

"Harrisburg? Where's that, near Philadelphia?"

"No, it's in the center of the state. It's the state capital. Not a hot spot of Society activity, which means New York sent in a team. Why? The Israelis are telling us the kid said, 'those guys are looking for me.' He tells them he's overheard a plan to kill certain Supreme Court Justices and replace them with others to shift the balance on the Court. Justice Benjamin Kahn was the first target and the assassin was his law clerk."

"Wha-"

"Just wait. According to the kid, he overheard them Friday and the assassination was scheduled for the next day. These guys, this "Society," he says, found out he overheard the conversation and are chasing him. They're nothing to mess with, he says."

"You've got to be kidding me."

"The Israelis are pretty skeptical, so the kid tells them he's not just any kid. He says he's Tim Lewis, one of electronic journalism's rising stars. Young, handsome, protégé of Anthony Merkel, the Darth Vader of the news business."

"Come on, why Tim Lewis, why not Bill Gates?"

"They're carrying Blackberries with Internet access. They run an Internet search and find lots of pictures. Kid's a dead ringer for Tim Lewis' R.R.N. publicity photos. He produces a driver's license, credit cards, Social Security card, and press credentials, all of which say he's Tim Lewis, Special Reporting Unit for R.R.N. They search his stuff, find a recorder and listen to a random portion of it. What they heard convinced them to evacuate Lewis and call Guzetti for help. These are some pretty tough guys, Ted. They say they're worried."

"I'm getting worried too."

"It gets better. The guys on the tape are Anthony Merkel himself, head of R.R.N. news division's Special Reporting Unit and the other guy is someone named Fredrick Stueben-"

"I know him. He's the left wing law professor on TV all the time."

"Looks like they're both members of the Society. Know what else?"

"What?"

"While you were in Nigeria, Supreme Court Justice Benjamin Kahn died of a massive heart attack in his chambers. Kahn's law clerk was the only witness and Kahn died the day after the kid says he overheard the plot. Saturday."

"Suspicious, I admit, but all of those guys are old and-"

"He had his regular cardiologist visit only ten days earlier. Great prognosis. He suffered the heart attack the very next day."

"No one will ever believe him, but I guess we could exploit him for intel."

"The Israelis say the kid's got a recording."

"I can produce a recording that will sound like you and the Cardinal-"

"A digital recording, not over a phone line, from in the room. Quality's supposed to be impeccable."

Ted rubbed his eyes, trying to catch up. The traumatized missionaries, really little more than kids, he'd left behind in Nigeria. The death. Now, a digital recording. A reporter in some place called

Harrisville. Then it hit him. For the briefest second he fantasized about police and SWAT teams storming the Society headquarters building in New York. He grinned.

"That's a game changer," he said. "We can match up the voices to . . . If we can prove it, we have a shot at finally destroying these evil-"

"Ted."

"Sorry. You should've seen what I just left in Nigeria."

"I know brother, but you've got to leave that behind. We've already diverted your flight from LaGuardia to a private airfield outside of Harrisburg. That's where you're going. The two Israelis are on the run with the news guy, Lewis, Tim Lewis. Guzetti says they're on motorcycles. They're waiting for us at a local diner called "Tommy's" just outside the city limits, same side of town as your airport. We'll get you the address and you can use the GPS in your cell phone to find it. Remember, the Society already has a team in place and at least some contact within local law enforcement. The Mossad guy said one of the vehicles outside the camp was a police cruiser."

"Great. What about manpower? We're stretched awfully thin right now."

"I've got eight men, about twenty minutes outside of Harrisburg. They're driving a rental, extension van, I think."

"Wait a minute. No one's close enough to drive to the center of Pennsylvania except for-"

"They're part of the current training class."

"Trainees! Come on, Fred." Ted rarely called Fred Allison anything but Reverend Allison, and then only when they were by themselves. "I know these are good men, I helped select them. But we already trained and fielded all the guys with recent military service. The new recruits are all older, with longer periods of separation from their military service. You know what that means; they're going to be rusty, high strung-"

"We wait for an operational team to get there and it'll be too late. It's asking a lot Ted, we know that. What else is new, us asking a lot from you? I want you to land, take control of them - they'll be waiting for you at the airport."

"What about supplies?" Ted sighed.

"They're bringing their own weapons and equipment, plus gear for you. Keep your satellite phone with you and I'll try to put you into direct contact with the Israelis. Go bring this kid in. Get the recording."

"Yes sir." Ted hung up and switched the Gulfstream's intercom to the cockpit. "Al, how long till we land?"

"Harrisburg in thirty minutes Ted. We got a good tail wind."

"I'm gonna jump in the shower, so if anything happens, send Larry back to get me," Ted said, referring to the copilot. Ted clicked off and went to the rear of the aircraft. Minutes later he stepped out of the shower, drying beads of water off of a muscular, but scar covered body. When he looked in the mirror hooded eyes peered back out at him.

"Every day's an adventure," he said out loud. By the time he had changed into fresh clothes and laced his boots up he could feel the plane beginning its descent toward Harrisburg. Ted used what was left of the time to kneel alongside one of the chairs and petition the Lord in prayer. He was tired, the need was great and he wasn't sure how he was going to accomplish the mission.

"I'm in the best position I can be in," he thought with a smile. "The only way this is going to work is if the Lord does it . . ."

Ted was lost in prayer when the intercom sounded. It startled him. "Better strap in Ted. We'll be landing in five minutes." Ted rose and belted himself into a flight chair.

"Thanks."

Moments later the Gulfstream's landing gear dropped into position with a thunk. Ted looked out the window as they landed, decelerated and turned around. The plane rolled to a stop near a private hanger. When the two-man flight crew came back and flung open the door, the engines were still sorrowfully winding down.

"God bless you, brother" the pilot said.

"Keep me in prayer on this one guys," Ted said.

Without looking back he climbed down, erect and stamping his feet onto the metal stairs for effect. The small knot of men gathered below him straightened and almost stood at attention. Ted was already a bit of a legend in the Fellowship, so everyone scrutinized him as he crossed the tarmac.

◆

What happened next would remain etched in Tim's memory for what was left of his life. Yosi spun up on one knee and whipped his other leg out into the isle. Ari emerged from the hallway. Tim froze. Yosi was now facing the door, with all three table knives in his left hand. The Society men had their jackets open and were reaching for their pistols. Yosi took hold of the first knife with his right hand, cocked his arm and threw it.

Everything seemed to be moving at half speed. Yosi reached for the second knife before the first was halfway across the room. His arm moved in a blur, but the throws were accurate enough to be effective. The two men at the entrance were pawing at their exposed shoulder holsters when the first knife struck. They flinched when it cracked off the plate glass, inches from their heads and close enough to throw off the first shot, wide left.

To Tim it was almost like watching TV in slow motion. He was aware of the patrons ducking under their tables, could hear the gunshots ring out and saw the terrified face of a middle aged woman crawling across the floor, but he didn't think to move. Ari grabbed him by his sweatshirt and dragged him out of the booth. Yosi'd already thrown the second knife. Bullets stuck a nearby plate glass window. Yosi grabbed and threw the third knife, seemingly oblivious to the shower of shattering glass flying past his face and bouncing around him. The next two bullets struck Yosi in the chest. Tim looked over his shoulder as the Israeli pitched backward across the table-top, scattering the cutlery. He tried to turn back but Ari grabbed him.

"Forget it," Ari shouted, "he's dead."

Tim didn't know how or why, but he ran after Ari, down a narrow hallway and toward a steel framed glass door. A metal box with plastic lenses was bolted above it and said "Exit".

Ari pushed out the door into the cool night air.

"Around here." he said, "If we don't get to the bikes we're dead."

Tim struggled to keep up with the sprinting Israeli. Their luck held. They reached the motorcycles unmolested. Ari hopped on his and stuck in the key. Despite the itch between Tim's shoulder blades, no one was waiting for them in ambush. Ari used the electric start and the bike roared into life. Tim straddled the seat behind him. As soon as he was on, Ari pegged the accelerator. Tim grabbed hold of him just as the bike rocketed toward the two gunmen running around the corner of the restaurant.

Ari saw them and whipped the motorcycle to the right. A pistol shot cut through the air. Ari grunted as they bounced up off the asphalt, along and over an embankment and then darted between some trees at the top. Tim almost lost his seat. The motorcycle engine screamed. Tim thought he heard more gunshots behind them, but concentrated on holding on as the vegetation tore at their clothes. Finally they ripped through the last of the tangled underbrush and dropped onto a narrow alley in a residential area. Once they hit the pavement, Ari slowed up. They chugged along, past garbage cans and garages.

"Got it," Ari said, mostly to himself. He turned his head toward Tim. "Looks different on the map."

Then he sped up, rocketing down the alley, making a series of left and right turns, jumping onto empty streets and dashing back down other alleys. Tim was disoriented when they finally entered a darkened, industrial area of the town.

"Loosen up," Ari chocked out. Tim loosened his hold. One of his arms was slippery around the Israeli's torso, wet.

"You're hit," Tim said.

"Got me with the first shot in the parking lot. I don't think it's bad, but I'm losing blood. It'll catch up with me."

Ari turned off the ignition and coasted into a shadowy area between a pair of warehouses. The bike rolled to a stop. Ari put down the kick stand.

"All right," Ari said. "I heard the recording, I recognize the names and I believe it."

"I'm not sure I believe it myself."

"We're going to need someone to pick us up." Ari pulled out his Blackberry.

"Those guys you called last time may have betrayed us."

"There's no way Thomas Guzetti would betray me," Ari said.

"How do you know that's who Yosi spoke to? What if it was an assistant or something? I didn't hear you ask him."

There was just enough light for Tim to see a flash of concern cross Ari's face.

"Look, I'm bleeding to death Tim."

"I'll take you to the hospital."

"How?"

"I can ride a motorcycle, not great, but I used to ride dirt bikes when I was a kid."

"The Society has connections everywhere, including police departments and hospitals. I know they've been passing out your picture. It's what I'd do. As soon as they see your face in the ER, I'm done for."

"Do they know who you are?"

"Maybe, but they won't be passing out photos of me. It's not me they're looking for."

"I'll drop you off in front of the emergency room. I mean, in the driveway."

Ari thought about it for a minute.

"That might work," he said. "But you've got to contact Guzetti."

"Any advice on how to get out of town?"

"Tim, you'll not last long on your own. I'm telling you. You've got a point. Yosi could have talked to an assistant, but Guzetti you can trust. He's the only hope you've got."

"Maybe, but I'm not doing it here. They're all over the place. I'm getting out, out of Harrisburg and away from them. Then I can call Guzetti."

Ari seemed to think about it. Before he said anything, he swayed to one side and leaned on the bike for support.

"Your call," Ari said. "Your bag's in the saddle seat compartment. Under that's a rail schedule and map, some cash, one of those space age blankets. Here's your recorder, protect it." The Israeli took a breath. "Get the map."

The cushioned motorcycle seat popped open and swung backward on hinges mounted into the frame, revealing a narrow storage area. When they had arrived at the diner Ari had taken Tim's backpack and shoved it into the compartment. Tim pulled out the backpack, stashed the recorder inside and shrugged into the shoulder straps. Then he grabbed the cash and maps. Ari used his red light and traced a route from where they were to the hospital with his fingernail.

"Don't worry about memorizing it; I'll give you directions as we go. But once you drop me off, go straight down here, you seeing this?"

"Yeah."

"Alright, then left, this street runs under the interstate and will take you out of town. Good motorcycle terrain on either side, plenty of trees and…"

Ari stopped and waited to catch his breath.

"I'm running out of time. Follow it out of town, if cops or the Society spots you, get into the woods, then back on the road. Right here," he said pointing again, "is a train trestle. Runs over a tributary to the river. It's deep enough, push the bike in there, into the water. Hop the train; they slow down before they hit the bridge. Have to. It's the way the track's set up."

"Got it."

"Listen; make sure no one finds the motorcycle after you ditch it. The Society team knows you've got a bike, so they won't think you'll try to hop another train. But, they find the bike, especially near train tracks and they'll just follow the train."

"Ari, I'll make sure it's hidden. We've got to get you to-"

"That's enough. Let's go."

Tim swung onto the motorcycle, but Ari just stood there, swaying. Tim jumped off and helped the Israeli get his leg over the bike.

"Man, Ari!"

"Don't worry. About me. I heard the recording. I know these people. Now, listen up," he said as Tim pulled out.

Ari leaned against Tim and the young journalist could feel the man's weariness as he rested. He started speaking into Tim ear while they drove past a long line of fenced in warehouses and factories.

"You need to know what you're up against. These Society for Human Enlightenment people are just that, a Society. Also, a self-promotion club. They use their positions and power to hire other people who belong to the club. Then they use each other to leapfrog up the power ladder of important organizations. If they need someone in a position and there's no opening, they create one. False accusations, black mail, slander and whisper campaigns, physical attacks and even murder. That's the least of it."

"So what do they do it for?"

"Me? I think they figure they can do things better than anyone else. Best thing for the world is for them to get in charge and then tell everybody what to do."

"Okay." Tim stopped at the intersection to a main highway idling. "I'm going to go down this road as fast as I can. We're almost at the hospital."

"They think everyone can be the same, we can all get along, religion and race and nationality are what causes all the problems. That's why they hate Christians and Jews. Christians won't believe some conjured up religion and Jews won't stop being Jews."

"So that's why Guzetti's helping you."

"Sort of. It's more complicated than that. Look, they won't stop coming for you. Do you realize why they're taking over the Supreme Court? I always thought Guzetti was a little wacky, all that devil worship crap. Did you listen to the whole thing?"

"Not all of it."

"Listen to it and remember this. The membership of the Society for Human Enlightenment not only stretches across your country, it stretches across the globe. Its members are wealthy, they're powerful, they use parts of every country's government to do their bidding. They're killers Tim. You need help."

"This is it," Tim said.

"Find Guzetti, he's the only one who can help you and he's the only one you can trust."

"Guzetti's the only one who knew where we were Ari! How else did the Society find us?"

A brightly lit sign spelled out "Emergency Room" in large red letters, "Harrisburg Metro Hospital" underneath in smaller black letters.

"Hang on," Tim said.

Tim accelerated into a circular driveway leading around and up to the emergency room door. Two ambulances were parked along the curb, but mercifully, no police cruisers. Tim squeaked to a halt, Ari pushed off from the back of the bike, staggered, and fell backward onto the asphalt. Tim froze, indecisive. Ari looked up at him from the asphalt, gasping.

"Go! Don't forget what I told you Tim. Go!"

Tim reached down and grabbed Ari's tassel cap. He twisted the throttle, zoomed around the emergency room loop and turned onto the street, too uncertain of his driving skills to look back.

A young intern with a gambling problem stood just inside the emergency room doors. He witnessed the conversation and saw

Tim leave Ari lying in the street. Members of the Hospital staff began yelling. While the on duty Trauma Surgeon rushed outside with a nurse, two orderlies and a gurney, the intern slunk away in the confusion and found an unoccupied room down a darkened corridor.

"Tony, this is me, Doctor Stodard," he said into his cell phone. "I'm not a dead beat; I'm good for it!" Stodard lowered his voice. "I just got a little behind – wait, wait, listen. Listen, those guys you called me about turned up, yeah, on a motorcycle. One of them left the other one lying in the drive, and then took off. The guy's injured; they're treating him right now. Harrisburg General. This makes us right, doesn't it?"

"It is him!"

Stodard's face reflected the glow from his phone. In the pitch-black room, it looked like a death mask. He leaned up against the wall for balance, squeezed his eyes shut and listened.

"I'm not mistaken and I don't want to know what you're going to do to him. I'm telling you it's your man; it has to be. Listen, the Jets are playing the Cowboys this weekend . . ."

CHAPTER 21

TED KEHR SCRUTINIZED THE EIGHT men assembled before him in the late night air. All of them appeared to be in good shape, but they were older. Several were graying at the temple and three wore glasses. Ted sighed. He suspected it'd been a long time since any of them fired a weapon at another human being.

"This is the only mission briefing you're going to get, so listen up," Ted said. "We're here to rescue and extract a civilian named Tim Lewis. Evidently, Mr. Lewis stumbled onto something very important. He's wanted by the Society and barely escaped New York City alive. Allies of ours found him, brought him here and are trying to protect him, but they need help. One of the Society Operational Response Teams is in town."

Several of the men mumbled. One of the others looked up from the photos of Tim, Yosi and Ari they'd just received from Fred Allison. Ted didn't see any panic, but the men were concerned. He ignored that for the moment and kept talking.

"It looks like they have at least one contact in local law enforcement. They consider Lewis a high priority. Our job's to find our friends, secure a digital voice recorder from the civilian, then get everyone out of town and to one of our sanctuaries."

He put his hands on his hips and stared at the men. Then he addressed it, head on.

"Let's clear the air. You haven't even finished training yet and the first time out you're going head to head with a Response Team. Remember this. They put their pants on just like us and most of the time they only go up against civilians. There's no easy way to say this, so I'll just say it. It's been a long time since any of you've seen any action, so keep your heads about you. You have to shoot someone, do it, but our job is to get out of here with our people and the recorder, not to light up the bad guys. All right, brothers, after this we're operational. No conversations, discussions or debates. I lead; you follow. Any problems with that?"

Ted waited just long enough to give everyone a chance, but not long enough to drag it out.

"Bow your heads. Lord give us your favor, protection and guidance in successfully completing this mission, in Jesus' name, Amen.' Ted looked up. "Where's our transportation and where's my equipment?"

"On board the van, Sir."

"Then let's move. Who's been driving?" One of the guys raised his hand. "How long you been on the road?"

"A little over two hours, sir."

"I need someone fresh. How many people are familiar with the van besides you?"

"No one, it's a rental."

"Fresh or not, you're driving. Our destination's a Diner on Route 641 called Tommy's. Load up."

The men piled into the van and left the airport. Someone handed Ted a heavy nylon bag, which he stowed between his feet. He kept his eyes on the men and his driver, looking for warning signs someone might not be ready. Once they were on the highway he unzipped the bag and went through his equipment. The dashboard's green digital readouts provided the only light. He was still unpacking and assembling his equipment when his cell phone rang.

"Yes?"

"Is . . . this . . . uh, Ted?"

"Who's calling?"

"I'm Reverend Barry Holder and . . . oh! . . . I'm supposed to tell you Fred Allison gave me your number."

Ted placed the open cell phone on the seat beside him and pulled on his shoulder holster.

"Reverend," he said, slapping a magazine into the bottom of the pistol, "we're in a bit of a hurry here." Ted pulled the pistol's receiver back and let it slide forward with a snap.

"Of course, I'm sorry, I'm a little nervous. I think you should know I'm at Harrisburg General Hospital, visiting a member of my congregation. The poor lady has had her share of-"

"Reverend."

"Yes, of course. Sometime ago I agreed to join a group of fellows who were helping Fred on some, um, projects that-"

"Pastor, I know what you joined." Ted slowed himself down. The wear and tear from Nigeria was beginning to show. "I'm one of the guys who uses the information guys like you provide. Please try to be brief. Why are you calling?"

"Of course. I heard, from friends, a description of a small group of men being pursued by criminals and . . . they would need our help. If I saw or heard anything, I was supposed to call you. Ten or fifteen minutes ago, I was in the emergency room after having given comfort . . . some of the emergency room staff were shouting and ran outside."

"Yes?" Ted picked up his phone and gritted his teeth.

"They wheeled in a gunshot victim, someone left him lying on the driveway. Someone riding a motorcycle. Anyway, while they were wheeling him in I went back into one of the smaller rooms where I sometimes try to catch a nap."

Ted heard 'motorcycle' and became very quiet.

"It's almost always empty and I thought I could call from there. It was dark but before I opened my phone someone came in. He didn't turn on the light and didn't see me, but he made a phone call. It was one of the Doctors. He described the same men we're looking for and said 'I don't want to know what you're going to do to him.' Ted, I'm sure those criminals are planning on either killing or kidnapping that man. If someone doesn't come here soon, they'll get away with it. Should I call the police?" the Pastor ended breathlessly.

"We're not sure we can trust the police. Reverend . . . here's what I need you to do. Find out where they'll take him for surgery and where they'll take him after that. As soon as you find out, call me back. We'll meet you in the emergency room of the hospital."

The phone was silent.

"Do you understand?"

"Of course," the Reverend replied. "I'll find out where he's going and call you."

"As soon as possible, Reverend. You're right, whoever the Doctor called will send men. Reverend?"

"Yes?"

"Those men will be killers, do you understand me?

"Ya, Yes."

Ted closed his cell phone and leaned forward.

"Harrisburg General Hospital, the emergency room entrance, as fast as possible. Just don't get pulled over."

"I'm on it, Sir."

The van had the streets of Harrisburg mostly to itself. With the aid of the GPS, it didn't take long before they were near the hospital.

"Look for signs to the emergency room," the driver said.

"There," said someone in the back.

"Sir?"

"Swing around, drop me and" Ted reached around and smacked one of the other men on the shoulder. "What's your name?"

"Fred."

"Drop me and Fred off at the doors. Then park and join us inside. Most emergency rooms don't have metal detectors but let's check."

The circular drive leading to the emergency room entrance was clear, so the driver pulled up to the door. The interior of the ER was brightly lit. No metal detector. The security guard was armed with nothing but a radio.

"That's it," Ted said. "Right here." The driver stopped and one of the other men slid the side door open. "We see metal detectors, we're turning around and coming back. Wait until you see us go inside. Once we're inside, park the van and follow us in."

Ted and Fred jumped out and walked through a double set of automatic glass doors into the emergency room foyer. A Security Guard sat just inside the door at a metal desk topped with cheap brown wood veneer. A TV blared out late night talk, but otherwise the waiting room was empty and silent. Ted walked over to the Guard.

"By any chance do you know Reverend Holder or how I might be able to find him?"

The guard was a muscular, middle-aged black man with a sprinkling of gray throughout his close cropped hair. His name tag said "Armstrong." He took a moment to appraise Ted and then pointed to a set of plastic chairs.

"I know him. Take a seat and I'll see if I can find him."

Armstrong walked over to a bored looking admissions clerk, exchanged a few words with her and disappeared behind a door marked 'authorized personnel only.' By the time the guard returned, the rest of Ted's team were inside the ER and scattered throughout the waiting room. The guard pulled up short. He looked like he was about to say something, but Reverend Holder came out from behind the door first.

"Ted?"

"That's me Reverend, we've been sent by the family to look after the lad."

"What 'lad' is that," the security guard asked.

"That fellow you've got in the back, gunshot wound."

"Really? What's his name, because no one's been able to identify him so far?"

"Officer Armstrong," Ted said, after glancing down at the man's name tag, "all that can be sorted out later. I need to take one of my men into the examination room for your patient's own safety."

"What's his name?"

"For his own safety, I'm not at liberty to disclose that," Ted said. He took a step closer to the security guard. His face was a stern mask.

"Fine," Armstrong said, "but until I get permission from someone, no one's going into any un-authorized area, not you, and not any of those edgy looking white boys you got with you."

"I like cracker, not white boy," one of the team said.

"What about honkey?" asked another.

"Enough," Ted said.

Several of Ted's men had moved toward the guard. Ted held up his hand. They stopped, but continued to glare at the black security guard. Ted took another step forward, so only a couple feet separated them.

"You wouldn't want to be the one responsible for anything happening to one of your patients, would you?"

It became very quiet. Officer Armstrong took a step closer to Ted and it looked like things might spin out of control. The television set inanely promised new, improved 'fabric restore' would rejuvenate your old sheets and pillowcases. Then Reverend

Holder slipped between the two men, a pudgy white dot squeezing between two black mountains.

"Wait a minute now," he said. "I know these men are legitimate, Officer Armstrong. Ted, Officer Armstrong is just doing his job. Can we take a moment here? Mildred," Reverend Holder said, "please don't call the police."

The Reverend put one of his hands on Ted's chest and one on Armstrong's chest and gently, but insistently, pushed. Each man gave way and moved backward a couple steps.

"Okay, no problem," Armstrong said. "You've vouched for them, Reverend, but I mean what I say."

"And I mean-"

"Please, Ted. Give this a moment. Sit, please."

Ted looked at the Reverend, then took a seat in one of the orange-colored plastic chairs lining the wall. His men took other seats in strategic locations. Armstrong returned to his desk. Mildred hesitated, but hung up the phone.

Reverend Holder smiled. "Blessed are the peace makers."

Ted gritted his teeth, but Armstrong smiled half a smile, like he knew something Ted and his men didn't. Meanwhile the Reverend had a cell phone out and was mumbling into it.

"I know. I know brother, but listen to me," the little man said.

Holder walked off into a corner, whispering all the while. Armstrong watched Ted and his men. When Ted's men weren't watching Armstrong back, they were watching the driveway for car headlights or other signs of Society activity.

"Ted, would you join me and Officer Armstrong for a moment?"

Ted walked over to Armstrong's desk. The security guard stood up as the two men approached.

"We're running out of time, Reverend," Ted said.

Holder didn't reply. He held his still open cell phone out to Armstrong.

"It's Pastor Jones."

"What?"

Armstrong went from stern to perplexed in an instant.

"It's the middle of the night. Why are you-"

"Take it."

"Pastor, this is Thomas Armstrong."

While Armstrong listened to Pastor Jones, Holder turned to Ted.

"Brother Jones is Armstrong's Pastor and a friend of ours. He says Armstrong's a good man. Ted, you have to tell him the truth."

"Reverend, I can't just take the word of-"

"Considering the alternatives, what choice do you have?"

Ted looked down and saw the pasty little Pastor from a new perspective.

"If you say so."

By the time they looked up, Armstrong had hit the 'end call' button. He handed the cell phone to Holder.

"This is a little too weird for me."

"It's time to choose, Officer Armstrong."

"What?"

"My men and I are bodyguards, but the fact of the matter is we don't know the man who's lying inside your treatment room. Any moment now a group of powerful, well-connected men will come through that door. They're planning to kill your patient. It's also possible someone on your staff's helping them. We need to get back there. Now."

"Sir?"

"What!" It was a member of the Fellowship team. Armstrong gave Ted a look. Ted knew he'd let Nigeria show again.

"Headlights just swung in off the street, two sets, one after the other."

"Time to choose." Ted didn't bother to look out the window. He kept his eyes on Armstrong.

"Mildred," Armstrong said, "would you go get a Coke, please?"

"One stopped, it's idling with just its parking lights on. The other one's still coming, slow, but it'll be here in a few seconds."

"Follow me," Armstrong said.

Ted let out a gush of stale air.

"Fred, follow me," Ted said. "The rest of you, scatter around the room, back up Armstrong, whatever he says, do it."

Armstrong strode over to the treatment center door just as Mildred was returning with her Coke.

"Mildred go with Reverend Holder and this man. He's here to protect the gunshot victim."

Armstrong pulled out a key from the collection jangling at his waist, snapped the bolt and held the door open.

"Move."

Reverend Holder took Mildred's arm and dragged her, protesting, through the door. Fred followed on his heels. Ted paused long enough to whisper instructions to Fred, then hurried over to Armstrong. The security guard had positioned himself in front of the inner set of automatic doors just as they swung open.

"No entry boys," Armstrong said.

A hard looking man flanked by two others walked inside and didn't stop until he was inches from the entranceway. His men eyed the Fellowship members. The hard man and Armstrong stared at each other for a moment. Armstrong seemed to have made up his mind whose side he was on. He took an extra step closer to the hard man.

Ted nodded at a couple members of his team. They returned the nod and swung behind Armstrong, taking positions three or four feet back on either side. Ted stayed in the background. Each of his men pulled open their jackets, revealing shoulder holsters and pistol butts.

"I said no entry. I'm sorry, sir." Armstrong didn't sound like he was sorry when he said it.

"What?" the hard man said. "We've got someone in here to see."

"Who're you here for? Give me a name and I'll be glad to check it for you. You can use the main entrance; it's open now," Armstrong said, making his voice pleasant.

One of the hard man's men raised his gun hand above his waist, provoking an audible metallic pop from behind Armstrong. Armstrong stiffened like he knew what it was, one of Ted's men snapping loose the safety strap that held his pistol in the shoulder holster.

The hard man undoubtedly recognized the sound, but he never took his eyes off of Armstrong.

"Have it your way," he said. He looked at the Fellowship men arrayed behind Armstrong and then at his own two men. "Maybe we'll just come back later," he finally said. "You know, when things aren't so crowded."

Armstrong smiled. It wasn't a pretty smile. He took the final step separating him and the hard man, leaning in until their faces were only inches apart.

"I use to do some policing. Place called Baltimore, Maryland. So, I recognize a threat when I hear one. I don't have a gun, but you do." He smiled again. "Why not try to get it out?"

"Have a good evening Officer," the hard man said, turning on his heel and walking out.

"Guess it was still too crowded for him," Armstrong said.

The Fellowship team grinned at him. When Armstrong turned, Ted gestured toward the door.

"Mind?"

"Go ahead."

"Stay alert men. Listen to Armstrong."

Ted disappeared behind the treatment room door and found Fred standing near a curtained cubical. A raggedy looking man was inside, stretched out on a gurney. Everything smelled like disinfectant. A stainless steel I.V. tree stood beside the gurney, festooned with a whole blood bag, a D5W bag and clear tubing running down to his arms. Ted, who'd seen more than one gunshot wound, decided the man required surgery, but his wounds were not life threatening as long as he received blood.

"The Doc's just down the hall. We're waiting for a surgical suite," Fred said.

"I'm Ted Kehr, with the Fellowship."

"What Fellowship?" the man asked.

"Take this," Ted said, holding out his cell phone. "I bet you've memorized the number, so call him, describe me and get confirmation. We're wasting time."

The man took the cell and punched in a number.

"Cardinal Guzetti, its Ari." Ari frowned. "Could be better," he said. "Will you confirm the assignment of Ted Kehr and give me a physical description. We may be running out of time." Ari studied Ted and listened. "Thank you." The Israeli snapped the phone closed. "Tim Lewis is riding a motorcycle with about a fifteen minute head start. He's got the recorder and I've heard what's on it. It's legit. I told him to get out of town and hop another train. I'm pretty sure he'll listen, but I'm not sure where he plans to go, except he's heading West. At least for now. After that, I'm not sure."

"Fred, stay with him."

Ted rushed out of the treatment area and into the waiting room. "Back to the van," he said to his men. He turned to Armstrong. "I left one man to guard your patient. The good guys could use someone like you, so why don't you think about it? Thanks."

The Fellowship men filed out of the emergency room and into their vehicle. Ted climbed into the passenger's seat, pulled out his satellite phone and turned to his men.

"Our guy's heading west. There's only eight of us and at least twelve from the Society. Maybe more. We're not strong enough to help him, so all we can do is provide a diversion. I want us out of here, fast, like we know where we're going and I don't care about speeding tickets."

The driver punched the accelerator and the van squealed toward the street. Ted punched in Allison's number before they cleared the parking lot. He was going to need help.

Rich Bouman left the ER annoyed, but not as upset as his men probably thought. The physical description they'd received from the Doctor didn't match up with Lewis' description. Most likely the patient was one of the men Tim Lewis left the hobo camp with, not Lewis himself.

He'd done some quick calculations while confronting the rent-a-cop. He saw at least four other men backing up Armstrong, while he only had two. Besides a driver waiting in the parking lot, the rest of his team was split up, searching for Lewis. Bouman decided it wasn't worth pushing. He had a better idea.

He jumped into the empty van with one of his men and ordered the other join the driver in the second vehicle. When they rolled out of the ER parking lot, Bouman did it with roaring engines and screeching tires, ensuring his departure would be noticed by the Fellowship team.

The men Bouman saw in the ER had the look of inexperience. It wasn't something he could explain, but he thought they were excitable. Excitable, inexperienced men might make a mistake. If he waited, they might lead him right to Lewis. Bouman turned east, keyed his mike and sent the two men in the second vehicle west with instructions to keep watch for the Fellowship team. Then he found a place to watch the road and parked.

Moments later the Fellowship team's van squealed out of the parking lot and thundered down Harrisburg's still desolate streets. Bouman pulled out behind them and sped up, struggling to keep the vehicle in sight while calling the rest of the team at the same time. He finally managed to get the call out.

"They're moving, now. I'm trying to keep up. East, looks like out of town!"

CHAPTER 22

HARRISBURG WENT TO BED EARLY, so the sound of Tim's motorcycle engine echoed across empty pavement. He chugged along side streets and alleys, working his way out from the city center. Though his confidence handling the bike grew, so did his sense of unease. According to his watch, forty minutes had passed since the attack in the diner, more than enough time for Harrisburg Police to have notified the surrounding police departments of the attack. All of them would be watching for a white male riding a motorcycle. The longer he was on the road, the greater his risk.

So he sped up, slowing at intersections long enough to check for traffic and cops, then blasting through red lights and down deserted streets. Tim followed Ari's advice and used a secondary road paralleling the city's major arteries. Headlights from traffic trickling out-of-town flashed in the distance. It seemed to take hours, but the last of the commercial buildings and apartments finally thinned out and disappeared. The terrain morphed from developed to wooded, with more and more distance between isolated houses. It was cold in the late night air. The road was deserted. He was almost surprised when the first sob racked his body.

No. No way. His body shook, but he fought it down. Get hold of yourself.

When he found a good place he left the road, switched off his headlight and drove over the berm toward the tree line. The ground was soft with a slight upward slope and the back end of the motorcycle almost slid away from him. He twisted the throttle, straightened out and managed to regain control in time to weave his way into the deep shadows cast by scattered trees. When he was far enough from the road he turned off the engine, coasted up to a tree and put down the kick stand. He got off and sat on the ground alongside the bike.

It was dark there, still and quiet. He leaned against the tree. Far off traffic buzzed along, then faded. Close up, a cold wind rattled tree branches. Somewhere in the distance a dog started barking. The ground was damp and earthy, but that's not why he couldn't stop shaking.

Tim Lewis was twenty-four years old and always thought he'd experienced his share of adversity. He grew up in Pittsburgh and lost his father young. He worked a job from the time he was twelve years old and remembered when the steel mills shut down. In the aftermath, his Mom took him to the "grilled cheese sandwich" parties neighbors threw using government surplus cheese. He'd done without, worked hard and lost and won his fair share of fights with bullies. An only child, he learned how to rely upon himself alone after his Mom died. After he'd lost Angela. Now, his emotions betrayed him. It embarrassed him.

The thoughts came all at once, as if someone just blurted them into his ear.

You could turn yourself in. Everyone who could help you's dead. You can't trust Guzetti and you sure can't trust Angela, remember? All the Society wants is the recording. Give it to them and they'll leave you alone. They might even reward you. Then you can sleep, relax, go back to your life.

Tim pulled up his legs and hugged his knees. He tried to think through his next few steps, but there it was again.

Give up.

Give in.

The only time Tim ever cried was when he was alone, so he let it happen, keeping it as quiet as he could manage. Sometime later, he didn't know how long, he composed himself and threw Ari's space blanket over his head. He cupped a hand over the flashlight beam and studied the map by what little light he allowed to escape. He'd missed a turn a short distance back the road.

"One Baker fourteen, cleared for lunch, ten-four," a radio squawked.

Tim snapped off his light and looked out. The headlights of a patrol car were a few hundred feet down the road. The beam of a powerful halogen spotlight swept back and forth across the embankment. On Tim's side of the road. The car wasn't creeping, but it wasn't speeding either.

Suddenly it was obvious. The police.

Turn yourself in. They'll protect you and they'll know what to do with the recording.

But he knew the Society used police. Ari said cops helped the Society raid the hobo camp. The Society had "connections everywhere," especially in organizations like police departments. Could he trust the police?

You'll be out of it, he thought. Tim stood up.

He was drawn to the police cruiser by something akin to magnetism and could see how it would happen. He'd step outside the tree line. They'd see him. They'd take him into protective custody. They'd let him shower, give him clean clothes and a meal and let him sleep. All he had to do was turn himself in. Give them the recorder. Explain everything. Rely upon the authorities. He knew it was the smart thing, heck, it was the right thing to do. He moved toward the road. Then he stopped. He had no way of knowing if these cops were the corrupt ones or not, but he was about to risk everything, not just for himself, but for everyone else too.

Just because you're tired and want to quit.

He couldn't do it. Tim turned and walked back to the motorcycle. A fading part of him still wanted to give up, but it couldn't change who he was. For the last six years he'd lived in New York City, but he wasn't a New York boy. He wasn't from California or some other nice place. He was a WASP boy raised in Pittsburgh, a culture steeped in Steelers football, the steel worker ethic, and never, ever, giving up. Tim thought of it as saying the same thing in four different ways.

He saw Sharon's pale face on the TV screen after they'd pulled her body out of the river. He watched again while Yosi jerked as the bullets struck him. He thought about the barbed wire and crosses and huddles of people waiting their turn and knew it wasn't just a dream. Pittsburgh boys didn't hope everything worked out. They didn't wait to be rescued.

He turned back to the road with his face set in a grim mask.

You're going to have to figure out a way to stop them, he thought. Soon as you're done crying.

Then he remembered the divots. When he'd left the road, the rear wheel of the bike dug divots into the wet turf as it fish-tailed up the embankment. Even in the faint moonlight, Tim could see a line of torn turf leading from the road surface right up to his position. The Police Cruiser was less than one hundred feet away and its search light would soon illuminate the torn up embankment. The cops would investigate. Tim fought off a sense of panic, pushing it back down into his stomach. He stuffed the map and blanket into his backpack, straddled the motorcycle and waited for an idea. Meanwhile the spotlight crept ever closer to his position. He decided once they stopped he'd take off through the woods and ride without lights.

No guts, no glory.

A second set of headlights appeared at the other end of the road, moving fast. Tim held his breath and the vehicle began flicking its headlights on and off. The police cruiser killed its spotlight, then its headlights and sat idling with only parking lights for illumination. A dark colored Ford Explorer pulled alongside in the opposite lane and turned its headlights off. Both drivers rolled down their windows.

Tim was close enough to hear the men's voices, but too far away to make out the conversation. It didn't last long. After a brief exchange, both men turned on their headlights and the cop turned on his spot light. They pulled away from each other, but then the Explorer stopped. The driver stuck his head out the window and shouted back at the cruiser.

The Officer stopped and leaned out his window. Tim could hear him say "What?" but couldn't make out the reply. Whatever it was had a dramatic effect.

The cruiser, bearing Pennsylvania State Police markings, whipped around in a "U" turn, squeezed past the Explorer and took the lead position. The Officer turned on his emergency lights and drove back toward the interstate with the Explorer following behind him.

So much for turning yourself in.

Once the taillights disappeared Tim kick started the motorcycle. He decided to backtrack, pick up the side road he missed and follow it to the train tracks. He'd catch out a freight train near the trestle and river crossing Ari recommended.

He was returning to Pittsburgh and to Angela.

◆

Alan Williams flew in from New York with Carl Hardesty, then drove straight to the warehouse. The Society team was close. Williams could see the parking lights of the Christians' van on the cracked asphalt of a long abandoned parking lot.

"How long have they been here," he asked.

"Thirty minutes, sir."

"Something's wrong. He's not here," Hardesty said from the back seat.

Rich Bouman turned in his seat to glare at Hardesty. The killer stared back without blinking, his eyes flickering like a white funeral candle shining through shards of green carnival glass. Williams wondered if Hardesty was too insane to be of use.

"Mr. Williams, is this man a member of our Society?"

"Mr. Hardesty isn't a member, but he is a valued adviser of mine, Mr. Bouman."

"Valued advisor or not, we followed the Christians from the hospital to a man hiding in that warehouse. We've managed to surround the structure without being observed and as soon as Kiefer gets here we're going in. With your permission."

"Mr. Bouman, we got movement," Bouman's lookout said. The man peered at the warehouse through a set of night vision glasses.

Below the stakeout, two cars left the highway and pulled into the parking lot.

"Uh oh!"

"What?"

"The new arrivals are Cumberland County Sheriff's cruisers," the night vision guy said.

Bouman glanced sideways at Williams, but the Society Security Chief remained silent.

"This may complicate things," Bouman said.

"We'll see," Williams said.

"This is a waste of time."

It was Hardesty again. Bouman twisted around to face the serial killer and bore into his eyes with his own.

"I don't care how important you are," Bouman said. "You don't talk in that tone of voice to a member of the Society unless you belong."

Hardesty watched Bouman, but said nothing. Williams hid a smile at Bouman's displeasure.

"Do you hear me?"

"He hears you," Williams said. "Mr. Hardesty, please be so kind as to address me."

"Understood, Mr. Williams," Hardesty said.

"Both Deputies are out of the cruisers and going over to the Christians' vehicle," the lookout said. After a few moments he spoke again. "They didn't even make anyone get out. The Deputies are going back to their cruisers."

"Good," Bouman said. "We'll-"

They were interrupted by a rap on the driver's side window.

"It's Kiefer." Bouman rolled down the window allowing the trooper to lean inside with his elbows on the sill.

"Who're these guys?" he said, eyeing Hardesty.

"My boss," Bouman said, "and his, ah, assistant."

"All right. I rushed over here, but this is getting harder and harder to explain to the barrack's dispatch. You said you located him. Where?"

"Right in front of us."

"The old ball bearing warehouse?" The Trooper straightened and squinted into the night. "It looks like someone beat us to the punch."

"Worse, we're waiting for two Cumberland County Sheriff's Deputies to leave."

"I can't risk going down there and confronting other law-enforcement officers."

While the men talked, both Sheriff's cruisers turned on their parking lights. They showed no sign of leaving.

"Why not" Williams asked, speaking for the first time and sounding amused. "I think that is exactly what you should do."

"Look." The Trooper caught himself and changed his tone. "Sir, my actions tonight are unusual, but explainable. My concern is if we confront those Deputies and the Christians, my position will be endangered."

"Why? You're a member of the Pennsylvania State Police. Your jurisdiction covers the warehouse and we reported unusual activity to you. You go down; you investigate."

"Sure. Only problem is fifteen minutes ago I was on the other side of town, looking for Lewis on secondary roads. I was 'investigating.' Now, I'm on the other side of town, 'investigating' something else? I don't know if-"

"I do. Mr. Bouman, let's converge on the warehouse. Carefully of course, no gun play. Tell me your paperwork is in order," Williams said, referring to gun permits and private investigator credentials.

"Of course."

"Let's go then. Trooper Kiefer, if you would be so kind as to lead us."

Kiefer looked back and forth between Bouman and Williams. Finally he muttered "sure" and pushed off of the window sill.

Kiefer climbed into his cruiser, swung it off the berm and onto the highway. Bouman followed him down the still dark highway. When Kiefer and the Society team turned on to the access road leading to the warehouse, headlights stabbed out from 360 degrees. Sturdy off-road vehicles crept toward the decrepit parking lot.

Kiefer drove onto the lot and a Deputy Sheriff lit him up with his headlights. Once the State Police markings were illuminated, he killed the light. Kiefer rolled over to the first cruiser and lowered his window.

"Pull up; I want to hear this," Williams said. "Tell your team to close in."

"All units, circle the target and illuminate." Bouman stopped a few feet away from the two cruisers and Williams rolled down his window.

"Who're these guys, Deputy Greer?" Kiefer asked.

The Deputy stuck a bent elbow out the window and looked at Kiefer.

"Evenin to you, too, Trooper Kiefer." The Deputy leaned far enough out of the car to spit a stream of tobacco juice onto the pavement, then looked back up. "Heck, I was gonna to ask you who those guys are." Society vehicles drove up and encircled the warehouse with their headlights blazing, like spokes on a Ferris wheel at night.

"Private security working for a bail bondsman, something big out of New York. Give'm credit, they flagged me down near Thomas Run Road and ask permission. You know how some of those guys are, cowboys. These ones seem pretty straight."

"Must be a lot of money on that bond."

"Yep. What about these guys?"

"Private Detectives. Cleared by Sheriff Howard. Lookin for a runaway rich kid or somethin."

"I'm going to have to check the vehicle and warehouse," Kiefer said, throwing the gearshift into park.

"No problem Trooper, but tell those guys to stay in their vehicles."

"Come on," Kiefer said.

"You hear about the shootin in town? Couple guys go into a diner, kill one guy, shot the place up trying to get a couple more?"

"Yeah."

"We ain't having any of that here. Keep em in their trucks, okay?"

Kiefer and Greer got out of their cars, then turned at the sound of crunching gravel. Bouman nudged the vehicle closer and looked out his window. Kiefer bent down and Deputy Greer leaned against his car and watched.

"Radio your men, everyone stays where they're at," Kiefer said. "There's been a shooting in town and everyone's a little jumpy."

"Understood," Bouman said.

"I'm going to check these private detectives first. Then we'll move to the warehouse."

Kiefer walked over to Ted's van with Deputy Greer following along behind him. Greer tilted his head toward the radio mike clipped to his shoulder, mumbling as though he didn't want to be overheard. His radio unit squawked back.

"Roger, dispatch will monitor."

When Kiefer reached Ted's van, he pulled out his flashlight and shone it all around the interior. Greer stayed with him.

"These guys all PIs, Greer?"

"Yep."

"I want to take some of these bounty hunters to help me check the warehouse."

"They've already got the dang thing surrounded."

"Come on, I don't want this to take all night."

The rusting steel sided warehouse was two stories tall and an easy hundred fifty feet long. Its second story was lined with windows filled with broken panes of glass, like the cracked teeth of a giant's smile.

Greer chuckled, bent to one side and spit tobacco juice.

"Guess I can't blame you on that one. Take these guys, here," he said, gesturing to Williams's vehicle. "The rest stay put. Better for you anyhow, in case someone tries to slip out."

"Thanks."

Kiefer walked back to Williams' SUV.

"Alright, your guy's not in the van so if he's here he's in the warehouse," Kiefer said. "I want you men to come with me and help clear the place. No one else, understand?"

"Yes, Trooper," Williams said respectfully. "Again, we appreciate the cooperation local law enforcement has shown-"

"Just follow me and let's get this over with," Kiefer said.

Williams decided to overlook Kiefer's disrespect because it made things sound more authentic. When the Society men passed by the Fellowship Van, Williams eyed Ted Kehr, who eyed him back.

Kiefer led them past the Fellowship and the moment passed. They followed Kiefer down to the warehouse, jimmied a door and disappeared inside. Thirty minutes later the same group of men returned. Williams was satisfied the warehouse was empty, but certain he'd been deceived. Hardesty was right.

While they were in the warehouse the sky changed from black to gray.

"Excuse me for one minute, I think I recognize a fellow from a conference we attended," Williams said. Before anyone could object, Williams peeled off, reached Ted's door and leaned against it. Hardesty stood close behind him.

"A rather threadbare group you have here," Williams said. When Ted didn't reply he continued. "Let me guess, no time to assemble a team. You're always outgunned and over matched, always relying on tricks and ruses. It's about to catch up to you and so am I."

Ted looked over Williams shoulder at Hardesty and met his gaze. After a moment, he looked back at Williams.

"I'm sure we'll see each other again," Ted said.

"Count on it. Come along, Mr. Hardesty."

Williams watched Ted climb out and wait for the Society team to load up and leave. The vehicles surrounding the warehouse moved into a file behind Williams and the whole caravan departed.

The Society team didn't know where they were going because Williams didn't know where they were going. Once they reached the interstate, Williams told the driver to take the quickest route back to the airport. Beyond that, they had no destination.

"You've been fooled," Hardesty said from the back seat. He spoke with anger, as if Bouman was responsible for allowing a beloved pet to escape.

"Remember who you're talking to," Bouman said.

Williams watched the two men sizing each other up, amused and glad for the diversion. Bouman didn't like Hardesty. While he often dealt with dangerous, odd and even frightening characters, there was something different about the serial killer, something even a man like Bouman found unsettling. It was Hell's fire, Williams thought. It burned in Hardesty and Bouman's devotion to their master didn't render him immune from its power.

At first, Williams had wondered if the serial killer wasn't just criminally insane, which was useful, but also disoriented as to reality, which wasn't. In fact, he was neither. Williams had seen it before. On occasion, a human being was so sold out to their master that he seemed to possess a sixth sense. Hardesty was that type of man. Williams decided to tap into Hardesty's instincts.

"Regardless of who was or was not fooled, time is a matter of some concern here, Mr. Hardesty," Williams said. "Do you have any suggestions as to how we might reestablish contact with Mr. Lewis?"

"Where do frightened animals always go when they're scared, hurt, or on the run?"

Hardesty opened his mouth and his lower jaw jutted forward as he spoke. You could see his teeth. If a jackal was rendered human and could re-live the blood lust and savagery of past hunts, Hardesty's what it would look like. Williams thought he was beautiful.

"Why they run to safety, don't they?" the Society Security Chief replied in a whisper. "They go to the hole they know best; they go home." Williams smiled. "Mr. Bouman, call our pilot and let him know we'll be taking off immediately. We're going to Pittsburgh."

While Tim waited for the engine idle to level out, a wave of fatigue washed over him. He took it as a warning to get to the train bridge before his coordination and judgment were further eroded by the lack of sleep.

The missed turn looked to be only a quarter mile down the road in front of him. A calculated risk, but most likely his pursuers were heading back toward the interstate, hoping to catch him trying to make a quick dash out-of-town. He re-shouldered his backpack and eased out from under the trees. The moon and stars provided enough light for him to see without lights. He shifted to neutral, coasted down to the road, and then put the bike in gear.

It was late. Or maybe it was early. Daybreak already lightened the horizon, but Tim resisted the urge to speed up. Thirty miles an hour kept the engine gurgling at little more than an idle. Every second seemed pregnant with the threat of approaching headlights. An eternity later he reached the turn.

The same barking dog who'd serenaded him from a distance now greeted him in a frenzy. Fortunately the animal was chained, so Tim swung to the left, kept his speed constant and waited for lights to turn on and someone to shout 'stop,' or 'I'm calling the police.' The dog continued sounding the alarm, but his master's house remained dark and silent.

Once it was out of sight, Tim gave the bike more gas, then more, the engine roaring and the road flashing past, mere inches from his feet. He slowed only when overhanging trees plunged the roadway into darkness. He finally saw it, maybe a quarter mile off the road, a train bridge outlined against a brightening sky.

The road bent to the right and led him to a railroad crossing. He left the road and followed the train tracks. The outline of the bridge appeared and grew larger. When dawn broke the gathering light shone through the piles and cross beams supporting the bridge. A lazy running stream of brownish water wound closer and closer to the train track, until only a gentle slope of weeds lay between Tim and the water.

He spotted the grade Ari told him to look for. The track swung up and to the left before straightening out to cross the train bridge. He followed it until it began to curl away from the streambed.

Time to ditch the bike.

He cut the engine and coasted until the bike's momentum almost sputtered out, then leaned toward the stream and rode it down to the bottom. He stopped at the water's edge, dismounted and stood the bike up on its stand.

Tim hadn't realized how attached he was to the motorcycle. It was security, security he didn't want to give up. Then he zoned out, losing minutes just standing there. Not a good sign. Better move.

He stripped off his socks and shoes, both pair of pants and his underwear, then grabbed the handlebars. When he pushed the bike forward the stand came up and carried him half running into the stream.

He gasped as he plunged into the cold water.

Mercifully the soft stream bed squished between his toes, sparing his bare feet, but allowing the bike to shift on him. He almost lost his footing, pushed it as far as he could and then let go. The motorcycle splashed onto its side in thigh deep water.

Tim scrambled out of the stream, shivering. The world was post-dawn gray, so he risked his flashlight. The motorcycle was invisible under the dark water. Only an inch of the left hand grip jutted above the stream. From any distance it would be mistaken for a branch. Besides, he really didn't want to go back into the water.

He opened the backpack and used his last set of sweat pants as a towel. When he was dry he re-dressed as quickly as possible.

Since the sweats were only damp, he re-rolled and jammed them back into the pack, hoping to dry them later. Re-clothed and shod, the young journalist labored up the train tracks, fighting exhaustion. He found himself daydreaming as he walked. Golf ball sized rocks lined either side of the train track bed and Tim almost twisted his ankle.

Careful.

He stopped to catch his breath halfway up the hill. The track began its climb and switched back to the left. This was the point where the train would slow, both as a result of the increase in grade and so as to enable it to negotiate the sharp switchback without tipping any of the cars. The tree line was about twenty yards away from the track. Tim searched for a spot inside the tree line where he'd be hidden, but still close enough to catch the train as it passed.

It took a few minutes but he found what he wanted underneath a pine tree and some type of evergreen underbrush. It hid him from view, but allowed him a clear path to the tracks.

A train of any size would be long enough to give him plenty of time to run to the tracks and jump a car. He hoped. Tim crawled beneath the brush, then twisted limbs and arranged debris until he'd made a comfortable resting place. He munched on a package of crackers and drank one of his last bottles of water. When he was done, he curled up with Ari's space blanket, laid his head on the backpack and slept.

He heard the first train coming, but when he opened his eyes the thought of leaving his warm nest was too daunting. Instead he checked his watch. Eleven a.m. There'd be another train.

The next train surprised him and was gone before he was anything like awake. Three p.m. The day had grown warmer, so he stuffed the blanket into the pack and waited for the next train.

When Tim's eyes popped open the locomotive was already rumbling past. The first of the freight cars rattled along behind it. He crawled out, leaped to his feet and sprinted up the hill, only half awake. Somehow he still had his backpack. He struggled to swing it onto his shoulders and keep up with the train at the same time.

A brief sense of euphoria ran through him. He thought he might even be smiling.

The cars whipped by and Tim struggled to keep up. The locomotive began to slow out of respect for the sharp bend. Tim was now parallel to and keeping pace with another grainer.

Not bad, he thought.

Careful of his footing along the tracks, he angled closer. In a smooth motion he grabbed a car's handrail, left his feet and swung himself onto it. The experience seemed unreal, like watching it over your own shoulder.

Tim struggled out of his backpack and crawled underneath the grain container superstructure, amazed at the accomplishment. He leaned his head against the pack. When he woke he was in a small town just outside of Pittsburgh, in what was once the largest rail yard in the world.

CHAPTER 23

―

CONWAY YARD WAS SHROUDED IN a curtain of gray rain. Tim's locomotive crossed the fence line and crept through the yard, pulling a line of clacking freight cars in its wake. Once inside, a switch diverted the engine onto a secondary set of tracks. Powerful air brakes hissed on and off, releasing and then locking back into place with a clank. Tim squeezed into his cubby hole to avoid the drizzle and waited for a shout that would mean discovery and ruin. The train rolled along, shaking and tilting back and forth each time it switched tracks.

Riding the train all the way into the Yard involved risk, but Tim knew time now worked against him. He'd spent most of the day sleeping. Though he didn't regret the decision, the Society gained half a day to regroup and anticipate his next move. Would they expect him to do something as obvious as return to his hometown? Maybe not at first. His old friends and extended family were scattered across the country. He and Angela had split years earlier and he didn't have any family or close friends left in Conway. But, given his history of train hopping, once the Society discovered the existence of Conway Yard they would blanket the area with men. Hopping off outside the yard would have cost him valuable time, time he wasn't sure he had. He needed to contact Angela and be long gone before the Society reacted.

The train jolted to a halt. Tim slithered on his belly to the end of the car deck, stuck his head out and snuck quick looks at the locomotive and caboose. A couple guys were finishing up near the caboose, so he waited. Evening fell all at once, changing dusk to dark. The mercury vapor lights kicked on and the sky continued spitting a misty rain. The yard crew moved to the other side of the train. Tim slid off the car and lowered himself to the ground, pulling his backpack along with him. He knelt and peeked around a rail car wheel. The crew was still working near the caboose, so he jogged away from the train, toward nearby Ohio River Boulevard.

"Hey. Come back here or I'm calling the cops."

Tim laughed to himself and kept moving. The Yard always attracted hobos and the fact the guy didn't seem very excited meant he was probably okay. Moments later he climbed up to the road and vaulted a waist-high guard rail separating the yard from the highway. A passing car horn blared as it whizzed by, forcing him back against the guardrail and spraying him with road water. He waited for a gap in the traffic flow, got it, then dashed across all four lanes of traffic. Once he reached the other side he hid in the shadow cast by a highway billboard and caught his breath.

Just like the old days.

A few hundred feet ahead lay the off ramp leading from the highway down into the yard. Towering above the exit was a large, well lit sign proclaiming, "Conway Yard, Northwestern Rail, West Pittsburgh Terminal." The sign documented all the reasons Tim thought he had to leave.

Unlike most U.S. cities, Pittsburgh was a relatively small town, trapped within and spreading its steel mills along river valleys. The mills and mill towns spread out from the city to the northwest, southwest and southeast, effectively making the entire area Pittsburgh. Almost everyone from the area thought of themselves that way and in fact, they were. Their economic condition proved it. Tim remembered from his childhood when the big sign used to say "World's Largest Freight Yard." Then it said "World's Busiest Rail Yard," and then "World's Largest Push-button Rail Yard," before finally, along with Pittsburgh, relinquishing its once dominant role in American industry.

Tim hunched low and ran through the parking lot of a bar advertising "live girls dancing." He moved with confidence even though he hadn't been home in years. After his mother died and Angela ended their relationship, he found the thought of returning too painful. Nevertheless he remembered the streets and alleys of Conway, its short cuts through people's backyards, the holes in its fences and where its lights were located. As he made his way toward Angela's house the wind whipped a fine drizzle into his face. Unbidden childhood memories came to mind. His feet thoughtlessly retraced the familiar route to the home of a girl he always thought he would marry.

When he arrived he took shelter under a familiar oak tree, its sprawling branches providing him the same cover it had countless times in the past. Across the street, Angela's two-story Victorian home stood as a testament to the area's past wealth, and her father and mother's skill and determination in preserving the home. Her bedroom window was on the second floor, left-hand corner. On more than one night after a date or hours of conversation beneath the summer night sky, he'd waited under the tree, watching her light until she turned it off.

Now that he was here he was strangely reluctant to cross to her house. He knew from occasional emails from high school friends that Angela's parents died. She moved back into her childhood home. He also knew she was engaged to some local preacher. It wasn't fair to reappear in her life. It embarrassed him to reappear only to ask for help, but he knew she would help him and he knew he could trust her.

Beggars can't be choosey.

Tim slipped out from under the oak's branches, jogged across her quiet, rain splattered street and climbed familiar porch steps. He raised his fist to knock, but a wave of sadness at what could have been squeezed his heart.

He rapped on the wooden storm door. A hallway light came on, then the inside door opened. For the first time in years Tim Lewis faced the radiance of an Angela Baker smile. The smile disappeared, but her beauty didn't. She had the same dark wavy hair, golden brown eyes and full lips. It was the distinctly Angela beauty he always remembered, no make-up, little adornment, a quiet self-possession combined with a great figure and classic beauty. He blinked once or twice thinking it was the rain.

"Tim."

She already pulled the door open before seeing his face. Now she leaned against the doorframe, holding the door handle with her left-hand. A diamond engagement ring reflected the hall light back at his face.

"Angela." He took a deep breath. "I need help and there's no one else I can turn to. Please."

"Angela?" asked a deep male voice.

"I'm sorry, Tom, it . . ." she said. "Tim come in, it's just been so long. You'd never talk to me."

Angela unlatched the storm door and stood back, so he stepped inside. A well-built man in his twenties stood alongside Angela and put his arm around her shoulders. He was good looking in an unpretentious way with dark hair, dark eyes and a strong jaw line. Tim closed the door.

"Is everything okay?"

"Tom, this is Tim Lewis."

Tom stiffened for moment.

"Okay," he said relaxing, "why's he here?"

"I don't know. Tim why are you here?"

"I'm in trouble and I don't know who else I can trust. I don't know where else I can go." Tim leaned back against the door, weary in a way he'd never been.

"I'm Tom Sauer," the dark haired man said. "I hope you don't mind me saying this but you stink."

"Hi." Tim hated to admit it, but the minute he took Tom's hand he liked him and knew he could trust him.

"I'm Angela's fiancé. I'm also the youth pastor at Chapel Church Evangelical."

Angela looked up at her fiancée and took his hand.

"Tom, this is so awkward but-"

"It is awkward, but until we know what kind of trouble Tim's in the Lord would want us to at least hear him out and help him if we can."

Tim hated how Angela's eyes glowed when she looked up at him. She was still so beautiful. It almost affected him physically.

"Could I sit down somewhere, maybe a cup of coffee, something?"

"Let's go to the kitchen," Angela said. She led the two men back a familiar hallway of dark, heavily varnished wood into a comfortable sized kitchen. She hadn't done any remodeling since they were in high school. The kitchen had the same pocket door, built in cabinets, linoleum floor, and '70s era appliances. Like her parents, she kept everything in pristine condition. It almost looked like a movie set.

"Please sit down. I set up coffee for tomorrow, but we might as well drink it now. I don't think any of us will be getting a lot of sleep."

She turned on the coffee maker and re-joined the two men at a well-preserved maple kitchen table. Tim remembered spending many an hour there when he was younger.

"Look," Tom said over the gurgle and hiss of the coffee maker, "I'm a Christian and I'm pretty secure in my relationship with Angela, but you need to explain why you're here, with no advanced notice or anything." He shot a quick glance at his fiancé. "Sorry Angela, but we're engaged now."

"Don't be sorry," she said, shaking her head.

"I've been working in New York, in cable news for the last two years," Tim began. "Is the coffee done?"

Tom stood and filled everyone's cup while Tim continued.

"I was lucky enough to catch the eye of a senior producer named Merkel-"

"I've heard of him," Tom interrupted. "That guy is an anti-Christian. If you're working for him, why come to us for help?" Tom wasn't glaring, but his expression sure wasn't friendly. He looked steadily at Tim.

"He's one of the guys who's chasing me."

Tim was afraid to say, one of the guys who're trying to kill me.

"Why," Angela said.

"Angela, I don't know who else to tell or trust." Tim ignored Tom and leaned toward Angela, looking at her like he used to when he needed her to believe something. Back in the days when he knew he was going to marry her. "You're both Christians. You think Merkel's anti-Christian?" Tim laughed bitterly. "Merkel's not anti-Christian. I'm anti-Christian. Merkel's homicidal. He hates you. He belongs to some kind of club, they call themselves a Society, and they just killed Supreme Court Justice Benjamin Kahn and I can prove it."

"That's crazy Tim."

"Then why are they chasing me across the country? Angela, please."

Tim reached out and grabbed her hand. For the briefest second she struggled with him before he let her go. Tom was halfway out of his seat before sitting back down.

"Tim you're here as a guest. Don't touch my fiancée again."

"Sorry, sorry." Tim's voice broke but he maintained his composure. "I just . . ." You're losing them, he thought.

"Tim, I think you need help," Angela said. "You're not making any sense, conspiracies and–"

"You said you could prove it," Tom said in a businesslike voice. "How? Why not prove it to us, now?"

Angela looked surprised when Tom intervened. Tim knew he was. Angela seemed about to end the conversation and Tom rescued him. Maybe he'd been right about her all along.

"Tom–"

"Angela, maybe you're not thinking straight about this. If he's legit, we should help if we can. If not, I want him to leave. Otherwise we're calling the police." Angela and Tom looked at each other for a moment before Angela broke off and looked back at Tim.

"He's right Tim. If you need money for a place to stay or for a meal I'll give you some money. But this sounds crazy. Either prove it or please go get the help you need."

The last time Tim shared the tape recording with anyone else, they ended up shot. One was dead for sure and the other bleeding to death when Tim abandoned him in Harrisburg.

"Okay." Tim reached into his backpack and set the digital recorder on top of the table. "This is a recording of a conversation I overheard. Didn't overhear, over-taped, I don't, just listen, it's Merkel and another man, a guy named Fred Stueben, said they were going to kill Kahn."

"Stueben. I've heard that name too," Tom said. "All right, play the recording."

Tim reached across and reset the digital readout to zero, then looked up at the young couple holding hands across the table from him.

"I haven't heard all of this myself, not the entire thing, but I'm warning you. Do not tell anyone you heard it." He was going to say, 'at the risk of your life,' but Angela already seemed to think he was crazy, so he didn't. "The recording starts with me in Anthony Merkel's office with Merkel and Law Professor Fred Stueben." He turned on the recorder.

"You put Cardinal Thomas Guzetti on Lunch for Lunch, in a debate, with Morrie Liebowitz of all people," Merkel said.

"Mr. Merkel that's because-," said Tim's voice.

"That's you," Angela said.

"And Anthony Merkel, my boss at R.R.N."

"Shhh." Tom was bent forward, his brow furrowed.

"Did I ask you to speak, Tim?" There was a long pause. "Where'd you even get his name?"

"His office called our junior producers on four or five occasions and offered his services. He seemed qualified and-"

"And," Merkel said, "we ignored his offers because we don't want Guzetti or anyone like him appearing on television. Especially on Law for Lunch. Despite that fact you felt free to call him up and give him access to our audience. What's the purpose of modern journalism, Mr. Lewis?"

"To educate the public and provide them with an information flow-

Tom interrupted the recording.

"What about the plot to kill Justice Kahn? This sounds to me like you're in trouble for not doing your job," Tom said.

Tim reached over and hit pause on the recorder.

"That's how it started. Listen a little longer, till after I leave the room."

Tom didn't look convinced.

"Okay, I'll forward it some." Tim pushed fast forward and the LED read-out numbers sped forward. Tom's eyes never left Tim. Angela seemed perplexed.

"Let's try here," he said.

". . . and listen Mr. Lewis. This is a lecture, not a discussion. I have no doubt you 'tried' but you're not catching on so I'm going to spell-"

"That's Merkel and I'm still there, hold on." Tim forwarded further ahead.

". . . this." It was still Merkel. "Our duty is to protect the public so they're not inflamed or prejudiced by bigoted, outmoded ideas."

"Yes sir."

"Take the weekend off and come back Monday, 7:45 a.m. and wait until I call you."

"Yes, sir. I just want to say-"

"Now." Merkel yelled. "Get out of here before I change my mind."

"This is it. This is where it starts," Tim said over the recording. A door closed in the background.

"Satisfied?" Merkel said. "He practically ran out of here."

"It doesn't matter if *I'm* satisfied, Anthony"

"That's Fred Stueben, the law professor," Tim said.

"What matters is if the Board and senior membership of the Society are satisfied."

"What's this Society," Angela asked over the recording.

"It's called the Society-"

"Quiet, please," Tom said.

"I don't think the Board and senior membership appreciates the significance of our efforts."

"Wait," Tim said. He hit fast forward, then allowed the recording to resume.

"Have you ever been to Israel?" Merkel said.

"I avoid Jews like the plague. Sometimes it's inevitable," Stueben said, "like with Liebowitz, but other than that, why would I go to Israel?"

"What a politically correct answer. You maneuvering for board membership? Liebowitz." Merkel laughed again. Something made a 'clink' sound. "The only place Jews have been safe for the last three centuries is the United States. The only consistent friends they and Israel have are American Evangelicals. But, we've managed to convince some of them they'll be much safer if they destroy Evangelical political strength and undermine the public's confidence in their country."

"Is this going somewhere? I'm not Lewis and I'm in no mood to be lectured."

"I'm explaining to you why you're over reacting to Tim's little slip up this afternoon."

"Slip up?"

"Listen to me, Fred. The Holocaust Museum is in Israel. Talk about a work of art, the Nazi campaign against the Jews was flawless. The first part of the Museum is a long hallway of exhibits and you'll not find a single instance of actual persecution. It starts with framed reproductions of newspaper articles caricaturing Jews and blaming them for Germany's problems. A little further down you'll find displays of cartoon depictions and examples of plays, movies, music, books, and billboards ridiculing Jews and their beliefs. The government run, I mean public, schools began teaching children the Jews had a history of trouble making and betrayal."

"Everyone hates the Jews and we're all proud of the Holocaust," Stueben said. "So what? We're talking about here and now, the Project."

"Oh, that's horrible," Angela said.

"Wait," Tim replied. Tom looked like he had been punched in the stomach. "It gets a lot worse."

"So am I," Merkel's voice said. "Your business is the law. My business is information and the formation of perception. You want to hear this or not?"

"I want – yes."

Stueben's voice was drowned out by an "Our God is an awesome God" ring tone coming out of Tom's pocket. The young minister looked relieved as he pulled out his phone.

"Pause it for a moment, Tim," he said.

"Is it Harry?" Angela asked.

"Yeah," he said looking up from the phone. "I'm sorry Tim but I've got to take this. I admit, this is a very troubling conversation. Please wait for me."

Tom got up and walked onto the back porch, closing the kitchen door behind him. Tim and Angela could hear the muffled sounds of his phone conversation. Angela smiled to herself.

"Tom's been counseling a young guy from our church. He's fallen away from the Lord and got himself into severe depression, and . . . well, it's a mess. Tom's the only one who seems to be able to get to him." She sighed. "That recording is horrible. Mentally, you know some people hate Jews just because they're Jews, but when you confront it in real life. It's so ugly. And these are people who . . ."

"It's so good to see you." Tim couldn't help it, it just slipped out of his mouth, but he was glad. When he reached across the table to take Angela's hand, she didn't resist.

CHAPTER 24

"THAT'S MY FIANCÉ OUTSIDE. I love him. I guess," Angela said, after looking down the table for a moment, "that I wouldn't be honest if I didn't admit that even last year I still missed you. So bad. You never called; my letters came back unopened. Then, I met Tom and I'm not losing him. You coming here, it's a test, and one I'm going to pass. God's teaching me you choose to love; it's not some magic feeling. That was my mistake with you. Idolatry."

"Angela-"

"It was hard letting go of you, but I'm moving on with my life. You should too. If half of what you're telling me's true you've got enough to worry about already."

"It *is* true. Angela, we were supposed to be married, to spend our lives together. From the time we were five years old. I always knew-"

"You left." She said it flat, businesslike and Tim felt it like an ache, somewhere so deep inside he didn't even know where it hurt.

"You're the one who left," he shot back. "You turned cold to me and you wouldn't marry-"

"Quiet, keep your voice down. Cold? I stopped having sex with you when I became a Christian. I told you why and showed you in the Bible. I told you I couldn't marry you until you accepted Christ as your savior. I showed you that too. I told you I would wait one hundred years for you if that's how long it took for you to become a Christian. I didn't give up on us; you gave up on us!"

Tim needed to know why she wouldn't just tell him, then or now. It would have been hard to hear, but it would have been an act of respect for all the years they'd been together. He'd promised himself he would never lower himself to asking her why, whimpering like Sam had. Not him, no way. Now, his pride didn't seem important anymore.

"Just like Sam and Kim, right? You should have just told me Angela, I deserved that much." Tim took a deep breath. "I would never say anything to Tom."

When Angela and Tim graduated from high school their best friends were another couple from Conway. But after graduation, Sam was headed to trade school and Kim wanted more. She began dating a young married Doctor she'd met in Pittsburgh behind Sam's back, keeping Sam on a string until she knew how it would work out. She stopped sleeping with Sam and told him after going to church one week her conscious was convicted. From then on she insisted they wait until they were married. Sam believed her, until she ended up pregnant six months after they stopped being intimate.

"That's what you think? Tim, I feel sorry for you, but now more than ever I know why the Lord allowed me to lose you." She wasn't businesslike like now. "You're comparing me to Kim Karnihan?"

Tim yanked his hand back when the door opened. Why did he feel ashamed? He was the one wronged here. Angela glared at him.

"He's okay," Tom said to Angela. "We might talk later tonight if he needs to, but I think he's going to be okay." He sat alongside his fiancé and took her hand under the table.

"Give me one moment," Angela said. She took her purse and walked to a small powder room off the hallway, leaving Tim and Tom in an uneasy silence. It seemed to drag on for a long time. When Angela returned, she sat next to Tom, took his hand in hers and set them on the table with defiance.

"Everything's set," Tom said. "Let's hear the rest of it."

"Remember, Merkel and Stueben were talking about a "Project" by The Society for-"

"Come on, Tim," Tom said. "Let's just hear the tape."

"Sure." Tim clicked it on.

"The Nazi propaganda campaign used every medium of communications to present a negative, well accurate, but nevertheless negative depiction of Jews. The first step was public ridicule, fashionable bigotry. The next step had more teeth and initiated the process of isolating Jews from the larger society. For example, the Nazis passed laws, ordinances and rules excluding Jews from most professions, trades and even sports clubs."

"That's Merkel," Tim said.

"Shh," Tom and Angela said in unison.

"Like using a Doctor's or Catholic hospital's opposition to abortion to exclude them from either practicing medicine or participation in government programs and subsidies."

"Exactly. Same thing with certain small colleges and the military with the abolition of 'don't ask don't tell.' In the next step the government clandestinely encouraged certain elements of their political party apparatus and labor union allies to launch attacks against individual Jews, Jewish business, even entire neighborhoods. They blamed the Jews for most of the violence. At the same time, the government restricted the rights of Jews to vote in elections or participate in political life. The government responded to the violence it created by establishing 'Jews only' neighborhoods. The Nazis claimed it was the only way they could protect Jewish citizens from violence."

"Sure, they wanted to destroy the personal connections between average citizens and their Jewish neighbors."

"Indeed, but why? Because by the time they initiated the neighborhood relocation of Jews 'for their own safety' few ordinary Germans were affected. It wasn't as though the victims were friends and neighbors. Jews were strangers. Odd, trouble making, perhaps even treacherous strangers."

"You're making my point, Anthony. Nazis isolated the Jews by using Hitler's emergency powers. We don't have emergency powers. We need to mold public opinion if the Project is to succeed. So, I'm still waiting to find out how this little history lesson helps your friend Tim Lewis."

"What'd you think we've been doing to Christians for the last thirty years?" Merkel blurted out. "We've constantly stereotyped Christians, casting them in the most negative light possible. News reports, stand-up comedy routines, movies, TV shows. When's the last time you've seen a Christian portrayed in a positive way on a TV show or movie? How about in a best-selling novel? National news broadcast? I guarantee you two things. Tens of thousands of cases of abuse and crime occur every year and we ignore them because they're not newsworthy. But I tell you this, if a Christian is involved, we'll cover it, over and over, until the idea of Christian and abuse, Christian and extreme, Christian and dangerous, Christian and crime, Christian and weird or intolerant or stupid sinks into the public consciousness."

"Dear Lord Jesus," Angela said.

"The Catholic priesthood project made your job a lot easier," Stueben said. "Mix pedophile homosexual Catholic Priests with teenage altar boys from troubled backgrounds. It's the gift that keeps giving."

"You've got a right to be proud of your participation in that."

"It surprised me how easy it was Anthony." Stueben was regaining confidence in his ally. "We just targeted two seminaries got the door open and that's all it took. The rest of the Church had no idea what happened until it was too late."

"If we stopped everything we're doing right now, these stereotypes would still last at least a generation. We didn't and don't need to create separate neighborhoods, people don't even know their neighbors anymore. Public perception's been molded; it's too late for a couple of lost debates to change that."

"Like I've been telling you, the Board's obsessed with Pilate's Diaries, but I've got to admit, I'm surprised how successful we've been at discrediting them."

"That's a perfect example." Merkel said. "Twenty copper scrolls. Discovered by a respected archaeologist. Translated by a gifted linguist. Their authenticity attested to by a well-respected physicist after state of the art carbon dating. The Diaries of Pontius Pilate - discovered. But, they don't tell us what we want to hear. We want to hear there are many different paths to God. Pilate proved Jesus Christ rose from the dead and then claimed he was the Son of God. Oops."

"You think this is funny?" Stueben said.

"Every study ever conducted proves an early program of indoctrination influences all but the most independent minded of people for their entire life. People interpret information so it fits what they've been told. They filter out information that contradicts their world-view. The Society raised questions about the Diaries authenticity, but most people dismissed the Diaries because they contradicted what we've taught them – there are many paths to heaven. The fact is, people didn't *want* to believe the Diaries. We just gave them a reasonable sounding excuse to believe what they want to believe."

Merkel suffered through a sixty-second coughing binge.

"Your turn," Merkel said. "I know you received an invitation to Amsterdam so tell me, what's the status of the project?"

"We'll have a 5 to 4 decision within twenty-four months," Stueben replied.

"Bull," Merkel said after a long silence. "We've only got three votes, even if Anders is confirmed; you know we've only got three votes."

"That's the President's nominee to the United States Supreme Court," Tim said over the recording. "There's supposed to be a confirmation vote in the Senate this week."

"Maybe things will change, maybe opinions will change."

It was Stueben, sounding playful. The recorder was silent for a few seconds.

"A Supreme Court Justice is going to decide to change his mind," Merkel said, "and decide the Constitution prohibits Christians from voting in elections because it violates the separation of church and state? Hypocrite Christians believe in those sorts of miracles, not us."

When the conversation resumed it seemed the men moved from nearby the recorder to someplace else in the room, maybe to Merkel's desk.

"Sure, I just never saw that in the Constitution before and then it hit me," Merkel's voice said.

Both men started laughing.

"Maybe there'll be a new vacancy on the Court and maybe a sitting Justice will find a reason to change his mind," Stueben said.

"Enough cat and mouse. Tell me what's going on."

"The Anders' confirmation's in the bag. Plus, before the Senate even takes a final vote on Anders, there's going to be another opening."

"Kahn?" Merkel asked.

"That's right. Seems the old Jew's heart's going to give out on him."

"I hate that guy," Merkel said, like he was pleased with the idea of his death. Ice rattled in a glass, then someone sneezed. "Man, I'm feeling like crap."

It was still Merkel.

"Besides," Stueben continued, "Christians can still vote under the ruling, all they have to do is swear that their religious faith, allegiance and belief is secondary to the government of the United States of America. All other allegiances, secular or religious, are secondary to their citizenship."

"You shall have no other Gods before me. Deny their faith."

"Jesus." It was Angela.

"Yep. We're still working out the wording of the oath. It will be as subtle as possible, but we have to make sure no Christian can in good faith take the oath. That'll keep them from being allowed to vote. Then, after that, everything will be more straightforward as time goes by and the project picks up momentum."

"Smart," Merkel said. "What's going to happen to Kahn?"

"You know six of the Supreme Court law clerks belong to us, right?"

"No. That's fantastic."

"Keep it to yourself," Stueben's voice said, "but yeah. Our physicians recommended a certain compound, I can't even pronounce the name, but anyhow it goes into his afternoon tea and boom, massive heart attack."

"This was recorded the day before, the day before Kahn died, supposedly of a heart attack." Tim wasn't quite shouting.

"Murdering Benjamin Kahn." Merkel's voice sounded thoughtful. "We're taking one hell of a risk. Especially considering we still only have four votes."

"Wrong," Stueben said with a smile in his voice.

"You have four rock solid Catholic Christians and one rock solid conservative swing vote."

"Maybe the conservative swing vote swings in more ways than one?"

"You're kidding."

"No. Remember after his wife died?"

"Yes, but there was nothing to that. He traveled, sure, but he was with his son."

"Exactly."

"What are you saying?"

"I'm saying Thailand, underage girls and videotape of both the Justice and his son."

"No."

"Yes," Stueben said.

"Did he know they were under age?"

"Probably not, the Thais intentionally picked mature looking girls and used a lot of makeup, but does it really matter? It's not just him on the line, it's his son, his three grandkids. We are talking about serious jail time, for him and his son. In Thailand."

"He'll cave in. He'll have to, for his son's sake." Merkel was half laughing, half gasping. "It's finally going to happen. Once Christians can't vote, we'll control electoral results. When we control the electoral results we control government, we control information, even more firmly than now. No more Christian TV or Radio. Certainly no more missionaries. They'll be called home or stripped of their citizenship."

Stueben laughed and the joy was evident in his voice. "Yes. Then all the other things we've talked about, probably like you said the Nazi did to the Jews, but I don't know. You can be sure the Board has Society members studying that, writing reports, preparing contingency plans. But make no mistake, you and I will see a day when we round up every Christian hypocrite in this country and concentrate them in camps in the deserts. Somewhere far, far from the public eye. Then we'll see just how long it takes them to renounce their precious Jesus."

"What about the Jews," Merkel asked, sounding ravenous.

"Our friends the Jihadists have it backwards. First the Sunday people, then the Saturday people."

"How's it going to happen?"

"We're going to sue, of course. Five lawsuits are already drafted, waiting to be filed. The plaintiffs are chosen and we've written the complaints and supporting briefs claiming Christian suffrage is a violation of the Separation of Church and State. The Judges in each of the federal districts we'll file in are either Society members or friends. We also have enough influence to insure we get the right panel of Judges on appeal and then get expedited appeals to the Supreme Court. Like I said, twenty four months."

"It seems incredible."

"Of course the old hypocrite Guzetti was right," Stueben said, concluding his explanation. "Once we created the idea of a living constitution we could do anything we wanted, given the right Judge."

"Why wasn't there more resistance from the lawyers?"

"Never underestimate the human desire for power. A Living Constitution puts Judges and Lawyers in charge of the country. Do you remember Justice Allen? He's the one that retired right after the last election."

"Yeah. We did a two-hour special, "America out of Touch." Allen said American Courts would soon adopt foreign law; it was inevitable."

"I'll bet he did. Think about it this way. Today, when Judges decide they want to do something contrary to the law, they need precedent, an old case saying what the law is. If there is no old case, or if all the old cases say the law is the exact opposite of what they want to do, Judges end up quoting statistics, medical opinions, social worker digest's and other non-law related publications. Even the general public understands how contrived this is. But, once foreign law is accepted in U.S. Courts, Judges can truly do whatever they want and cite legal precedent. All they have to do is send out their law clerks or have so-called public interest law firms scour the world for a tribal Judge in Papua New Guinea who decided the way they wanted to. Then, they cite a tribal Judge. If they can't find one, they go to a poor Third World country, bribe a plaintiff and defendant to file a lawsuit, write the legal opinion they want, then bribe the Judge to say he wrote it. By the time the American lawsuit reaches the Supreme Court, there's a ready-made foreign law precedent to support the decision."

"Didn't Allen say well-reasoned rulings by a 'wise Indonesian Judge' could be binding on the United States Supreme Court?"

"Right. That's why mainstream lawyers called him 'Indonesian Allen.' Of course we branded them extremists, but they saw what we were trying to do."

It sounded like someone, probably Merkel was finishing the last of a drink.

"Fred, thanks for the update, but I've got to call it a day."

"I'd better go too."

Merkel was heard reaching over and pressing his intercom.

"Sharon, please call Mr. Stueben a cab.

It sounded like Stueben and Merkel stood up. Then they heard slapping sounds, like men embracing each other or slapping each other on the back.

"Soon," Merkel said.

"Soon," Stueben replied.

"This is impossible," Angela said.

CHAPTER 25

RICH BOUMAN CHECKED HIS WATCH for what might've been the hundredth time since takeoff. They'd lost the entire day trapped on the runway, waiting for permission to take off from Harrisburg regional. Airport authorities received the bomb threat and deemed it credible hours earlier, but it was next to impossible to hurry the TSA once they'd issued a "ground all aircraft" order. Williams called New York, but even the Society couldn't obtain an exemption on a weekend. By the time they received an "all clear" release and began to taxi down the runway, the late afternoon sun slid below the horizon, painting the sky scarlet.

Williams slept and Hardesty hibernated. Bouman plugged his earpiece into the aircraft intercom. The fuzzy cockpit chatter gave no indication they were nearing Pittsburgh. He was about to check his watch again.

"Mr. Bouman, Pittsburgh International's calling final approach in seventeen minutes," the pilot said via intercom.

"Roger." Bouman turned toward his boss. "Final approach to Pittsburgh International in seventeen minutes, Sir."

Alan Williams dozed in a butter soft white leather flight chair. His eyelids flickered and then opened. An exhausted Bouman looked down at the security chief with envy. Williams appeared to have slept for ten hours, not twenty minutes.

"Perfect. I suspect we will be arriving just in time."

"We've lost an entire day, Mr. Williams. Even if Hardesty's right, how do we know Lewis hasn't moved on? If he's still in the area, how're we going to find him?"

"Our network in Pittsburgh is large and well entrenched. Western Pennsylvania is still an important area of finance, medicine and technology, so, we're everywhere, political leaders, media, health care, and Universities. We're even close to the clergy."

Williams had made several phone calls from the runway while they waited for takeoff clearance. Evidently, he'd contacted the Society organization in Pittsburgh, but Bouman wasn't satisfied.

"Can we expect help from law enforcement?" he said.

"The police have proven to be a bit difficult, especially in the outlying areas. Small town parochialism, backward church goers, but don't worry, Mr. Bouman. Someone, somewhere will lead us to Lewis."

"The travel office should have an adequate number of vehicles waiting for us," Bouman said. "With your permission I'll break the team down into two-man sub units, each with their own vehicle. That'll allow us to cover more territory. If nothing else, we're more likely to have someone close by when one of our contacts spot him."

"Good thinking."

The hydraulics in the wing foils whined, sharpening the aircraft's pitch. An out of place sound caught Bouman by surprise. For a moment he thought it was an air pressure leak, but when he glanced across the aisle it was Carl Hardesty, hissing at him like a viper.

Bouman stuck his hand under his jacket and gripped the butt of his pistol before he was consciously aware of moving. For one fleeting second he intended to shoot Hardesty in the head, but worried about rupturing the aircraft skin and de-pressurizing the cabin. He decided to offset the risk by aiming for the chest. Less chance of the bullet exiting the body that way.

"Well now, that's quite enough," Williams said.

Bouman glanced sideways at Williams, then back at Hardesty, trying to make up his mind. Hardesty glared back, silent.

What the heck, kill him, Bouman thought.

He was about to shoot Hardesty and take his chances when William's phone rang, surprising them all. Williams looked amused as he answered. Hardesty looked curious.

"Yes? Is that right?" Williams chuckled for a moment then gestured toward Bouman. There was a notebook lying on a small but elegant looking table anchored to the floor. Bouman returned his pistol to its shoulder holster, then leaned over and retrieved the notebook.

"Anymore from you and I'll kill you, even if it has to be in public," Bouman said to Hardesty. He handed the notebook to Williams.

"I'll stay quiet, unless you make another mistake," Hardesty said. "If you make any more mistakes, my silence won't matter. They'll let me kill you."

"I warned you. You won't live to see me make another mistake."

"That was just as I expected," Williams said, hanging up. "Gentleman?"

"Yes," Bouman said.

"Someone very reliable has just provided us with Mr. Lewis' location. We're in luck. He's staying at a private residence in some hick town, so we won't need to concern ourselves with encountering any meaningful resistance."

"Let's get there before he leaves," Bouman said.

"No, not really a concern, although by all means let's be prompt. You see, Mr. Bouman, someone's with Mr. Lewis, someone I feel quite confident will be more than capable of keeping him there until we arrive. Get your men ready. We land in . . ." Williams checked his watch, "nine minutes."

Tim snapped off the recorder and put it in his jacket pocket. After the chilling conversation between Merkel and Stueben, the everyday smell of brewed coffee and the sight of the red and white checked tablecloth seemed out of place. Tom and Angela leaned over the table, frozen and silent. Tim took a sip of his now lukewarm joe.

"That could never happen," Angela said.

"Right, people wouldn't stand for it," Tom said. He sounded amused, almost taunting. "Same thing they said about gay adoption and marriage, zoning laws to ban churches or going around tearing down crosses that have been up for decades. They even tore the crosses off of some city seal, San Diego maybe, off the cops cars, the buildings, everything. It's going to happen."

"Tom?" Angela said.

Tim recognized the sarcasm, but the hair on his arms stood up.

"Unless we do something," Tom said.

"Any ideas," Tim said.

"We've got to get this information to someone, the newspapers," Tom said. "I know a reporter who we-"

"Are you kidding me?" Tim laughed. "They're like me. They think Christians are superstitious loons and won't believe anything you tell them, especially something like this. There's no way a newspaper's going to publish this story. I'd like to put it on the Internet; like that Archeologist did, but I-"

"I wouldn't put it on the Internet just yet, without compatible equipment or the right software; you might mess up the recording. Could I see the recorder?" Tom asked.

"Tom, at least two people already died because of this recording. It's nothing personal, but I won't let anyone else touch it until I've made up my mind what I'm going to do."

"I guess I can understand that," Angela said.

"Sure," Tom said. "Right now I don't know what to do, but think about this, Tim. Angela and I are Christians, but you're not. You're a pretty famous journalist out of New York. Plus, the guy I know is open-minded about Christians. Just think about it."

"I'll think about it," Tim said. Tom made a pretty good point, worth considering.

"Angela, Tim said something about wanting to get a shower and into some fresh clothes. Why don't you take him upstairs and get him set up for a shower. When you come down we'll pray about it."

Angela squeezed Tom's hand and smiled at him. "Good idea."

"Pray? Yeah, go ahead, it can't hurt," Tim said. He exhaled and rubbed the bridge of his nose. "A shower would be great. Just promise me you won't call the police or the media."

"That I'll promise you," Tom said.

Angela led Tim down a once familiar hallway lined with dark walnut baseboards. Cast iron heating grates were mounted into varnished hardwood floors. Cut glass shades shielded wall mounted fixtures, producing a soft, forgiving light. The classically restored home symbolized the happiest times in his life.

Tim followed Angela and before he turned the corner, Tom's cell phone burst into electronic song. Tim turned back to find Angela's shapely form in front of him, climbing the stairs. When they reached the top landing, she turned around.

"That's probably . . . the guy Tom's counseling. We're worried. He's already tried to commit suicide once. I wonder if-"

"Well, we could find out."

A smile crossed Angela's face.

"Come on." Tim grabbed her hand and pulled her into one of the bedrooms off the hallway, stopping just inside the door. They were right over one of the large heating grates. Tim held his finger over his lips like he did when they were kids, eavesdropping on Angela's parents. Tom's voice drifted out of the kitchen, up through the duct work, into the bedroom.

"That's correct. I just sent them upstairs, so Lewis can get a shower. Thirty minutes? I can keep them . . . No, there's no mistake. The recording's legitimate and those two fools laid out the entire project, every detail, including Kahn's murder."

"What's he talk-"

Tim covered Angela's mouth. When she nodded, he removed his hand and they listened.

"Extremely detailed," Tom said.

After a long moment Tim realized he wasn't breathing. Angela was quiet.

"She's my fiancé," Tom said. Then, after a pause, "I assumed she would die, but listen. She's a true believer, so we haven't been intimate. I've been working on her for a long time. As a Level Six Society member I claim property rights. Before you kill her I want some time with her, first and alone. You can turn your men loose on her after that. We'll blame it on Lewis."

"Oh."

Even through the duct work you could hear Tom's cold, merciless hunger, but all Angela allowed herself was a soft "oh." Anyone who didn't know her as well as Tim might have been surprised at her toughness. Tim wasn't surprised. She was silent, but tears rolled down her face.

For the first time since he'd been summoned to Merkel's office, Tim wasn't afraid. When he saw Angela's tears something cold and hard settled in his chest. The chill spread, numbing him to fear, flash freezing any thoughts of his own future.

You're the Prince, aren't you?

The memory flashed through his mind, the first time they'd met. They were in Brady's Run Park with their mothers. Tim was waiting for a turn at the Cowboy Bob slide when someone grabbed his hand. She was small, with those huge golden eyes, hugging a children's book to her chest with her free hand.

"What?"

She held out the book so he could see the cover. A small blonde haired boy with a crown and a sword stood between a dragon and a small girl dressed in white.

"That's me," she whispered, pointing to the girl. She pointed to the young prince. "You're the Prince, aren't you?"

"Yes."

Angela kept the presence of mind to move away from the duct so Tom wouldn't hear her sob.

"Oh, Lord Jesus, what am I going to do?"

Tim moved and stood close by, careful not to touch her.

"Look at me, Angela."

From the time he'd been five years old he'd never loved anyone else, and now he realized he'd never stopped loving her. It didn't matter what she did or didn't do when he was at college. No one would ever get "some time" with her. Not Tom, not anyone.

"I'm the Prince."

She didn't respond, she just covered her mouth and wept.

Tim dashed across the hallway, rummaged around in a bedroom serving Angela as a junk room and found an aluminum softball bat. By the time he returned she'd regained control.

"Go to the head of the stairs and call him up here," Tim said softly. "Yell, more like you're mad than anything else."

"Maybe we misunderstood–"

"He said a 'Level Six Society member with property rights?' The way he talked about that recording, about you? We misunderstood?"

Angela hesitated.

"There's no time to wait, no room for error. I had to trust you; now you have to trust me."

She sighed.

"It's okay, sweetheart, call him up here. Tell him I'm being difficult."

Angela nodded and walked to the head of the staircase, leaning down so her voice would echo downstairs and carry into the hallway. They always referred to it as the 'Angela intercom system.'

"I said I don't want to talk about it Tim! Tom! Tom? Would you please come up here for a moment?"

Tim, waiting over top of the heat duct grate, heard her strike exactly the right tone.

"It sounds like those two are bickering," Tom said. "I've got to go but they should be easy. I'll unlock the front door, come straight in."

Tim thought he heard Tom's cell phone snap close so he returned to the junk room. After all, he was a right-handed batter and it wasn't the night to take up switch-hitting.

"Coming, coming," said Tom.

Tim felt his approach through the floorboards as he pounded up the first set of carpeted stairs.

"Now what?" Angela whispered.

"As soon as he reaches the first landing walk back down the hall and motion for him to follow you. Leave the rest to me."

Angela nodded, waited and seconds later made a 'follow me' sign with her hand. Then she turned and walked down the hall. The landing groaned and squeaked under Tom's weight, allowing Tim to time his approach. As soon as he reached the top of the stairs Tim spun out of the doorway. Tom saw him, but the aluminum bat was already whizzing through the air as Tim completed his spin. Tom had good reflexes, but they weren't good enough.

Home Run.

The top four inches of the bat made solid contact with Tom's torso, just below his solar plexus. The air rushed out of him and he tumbled backward down the stairs. Tom rolled to a stop on the landing between the first and second floor. Tim straddled him almost immediately, prepared to administer a second blow. Tom gasped, choked, and struggled to suck in air.

"Good. Angela," Tim said turning.

The love of his life bounded down the stairs and kneeled beside him. She held out a cardboard box.

"Here, take one."

The box was filled with balls of yarn. Tim grabbed one, rolled Tom onto his stomach and began wrapping the yarn around his wrists. Angela took another ball and worked on his ankles.

"I always did admire your bent toward homemaking and the crafts."

"That's because you don't have any sense of style." Angela sobbed. Once.

They shared a weird, deja vu moment. Nothing was funny and he'd known his attempt at gallows humor was risky. But he knew Angela, and refused to believe she'd changed. Now it felt like two parts falling into a comfortable pattern from the past and one part, maybe, holding the promise of something in the future.

"Try to find some tape," Tim said, grinning. "I'll finish his feet."

"Right."

Tim tied off the wad of yarn binding the other man's hands and took over for Angela, working on his feet. Tom was still gasping for air when Angela returned with a roll of blue painter's tape.

"All I could find," she said.

"Angela, what are you doing?" Tom gasped. "I'm your fiancé. I'm the man who loves you."

"Shut up Shut up Shut up!" Angela's eyes were red and tears were rolling down her cheeks, but she refused to sob. "Gag this monster."

Tim took the tape, pulled a small section free and when Tom fought him grabbed his hair. Then he used his free hand to stick the tape on Tom's chin and wound it around the back of his head and over his mouth, repeating the process over and over until he ran out of tape.

"Jerk."

Tim left the last of the roll of tape dangling from the back of Tom's head. He stood up.

"Now what?" Angela said.

"Stay where you're at," Tim said to Tom. He turned to Angela. "Come on. He's not going anywhere." He took her arm and led her down the staircase to the first floor.

"A little something to make it easier for his friends," Tim said looking at her. He reached over and snapped the dead bolt on the front door back into place. "Angela I'm sorry I-."

"You didn't do anything. It was there all the time. I just didn't see it. How can I . . . How can I trust myself, that . . . I prayed about Tom, I . . . How could I be so deceived?"

"I don't know. I don't know anything anymore, but it seems to me your God made a lot of different things happen to protect you from him."

It took a moment, but Angela smiled. "Yeah." She glanced at the door and dried her eyes with her sleeve. "We'd better move."

"Where's your car?"

"In the garage."

"Wait." Tim lowered his voice and leaned close. "When they don't find us here, they'll get your car's make and model from DMV records."

"How can they-"

"They will; just trust me on that. But, they might not think to trace his car, at least not right away. They'll check yours first and, well every extra second . . ."

Tim lost his train of thought. Angela's perfume-not just her perfume-but how she smelled, looked and just was washed over and silenced him.

"Tim?"

"Sorry. He drove here didn't he?"

"Yes. Parked along the street, so people won't talk."

"They're going to be talking tonight no matter what. I'll get his keys, drive his car into the garage and-is there enough room?"

"The left stall's empty, I'm parked on the right."

"Okay, you open the garage door. We'll put him in the trunk and get out of here."

"What about money or-"

"No time. From what we heard ten, fifteen minutes may be all we've got left."

Angela opened the hall closet and went through the pockets of a man's jacket.

"Here," she said. "It's a silver Toyota. Right outside the house."

"Get the garage door."

Tim snapped the latch and walked into the drizzle, forcing himself not to rush. He found the Toyota and drove it into Angela's garage. As soon as he was inside the door rattled down and snapped into place. Tim popped the trunk, then followed Angela across a short breeze way back to the house.

He dashed ahead at the doorway, re-locked the front door latches and bounded up the steps. Tom was trying to wiggle up to the second floor. Tim caught him, grabbed the tape roll and yanked his head back.

"I told you not to move. Fine. I'm going to tell you this once,"

Tim said. "Do what I tell you to do or I'll hurt you, bad. I don't have time for you to wonder if I'm telling the truth or not."

He grabbed one of Tom's fingers and bent it backward. Tom moaned beneath the gag, but Tim kept bending until it snapped with an audible crack. Tom squealed through the tape and Angela cried out.

"Oh Lord, are you a monster too?"

"You've never acted like an idiot before Angela; don't start acting like one now." Tim returned his attention to Tom. "I'm not untying your feet. I'll pull you up and duck walk you out to the garage. If you fall down, try to yell or run or anything, I'll break another finger."

Tim hauled him down the stairs, then he and Angie pulled him up and walked him out the door and into the garage. Tim checked the trunk for sharp objects, then pushed Tom inside.

"Any noise, remember the fingers." Tim slammed the trunk and turned to Angela. "You drive," he said.

She reached into her car, grabbed a baseball cap and garage remote, then jumped into the driver's seat of Tom's car. After tucking her hair up underneath the hat, she looked over at Tim.

"Ready?"

"This guy has an awful lot keys," Tim said, handing them over.

"Most of them are for the church, the bus, youth van-."

"Youth van?"

"Yeah." Angela started the Toyota and punched the garage door remote.

"How far away's the church?" Tim asked. The door rattled upward while they waited.

"Two miles, maybe a little more. It's down Hoffman Road."

"Anything going on tonight?"

"No, Wednesday's prayer, men's group's only once a month, the kids' group is Friday. Sunday evening service is over."

"Let's go to the Church. I want the van."

Angela backed down the driveway fast enough to make the transmission whine, popped out onto the street, drifted back and shifted into drive. The garage door was already closed. She looked into the rear view mirror when they reached the end of the block.

"Get down."

Tim slithered off the seat, pulled his pack onto his lap and curled up on the floor. The floor smelled like one of those fake pine tree air fresheners. Angela stopped, waited as oncoming traffic splashed their way past, and then pulled out onto what sounded like a main artery. She glanced up at the rearview again while turning.

"They just got here." Her voiced cracked. "Stopped in front of the house. At least four vehicles, big ones, SUVs or small vans." She hesitated, then reached into her purse and came out with her cell phone.

"Angela, you can't call anyone because-"

"Tim you've never acted like an idiot before, don't start acting like one now."

Tim smiled and waited while the electronic beeps of a preprogrammed number sounded.

"Hello, Mrs. Peters?"

Tim almost laughed, but Angela silenced him with a face. Evelyn Peters, although now a widow, had been the neighborhood busy body from the time they were kids.

"No, the wedding invitations haven't gone out yet or else you would've received one, dear. Actually that's sort of why I'm calling. Tom and I are heading down to the New Brighton Hot Dog shop for a late snack and I'm afraid I left my front door unlocked. Would you be a dear and keep an eye on the house for me? Thank you so much - yes, the one in New Brighton. Tom says he doesn't care what anyone says, the other shops aren't as good as the original. Right, men. Uh uh, thanks, well listen, you're breaking up . . ."

Angela hit the end button, cutting off the call. She was crying again, but still managed a smile as she looked over at Tim.

"Well?"

"You mean you think she'll tell someone?"

They broke out laughing.

"Perfect," Tim said. "It's like putting up a 'Tim and Angela went north to New Brighton' sign, in neon letters. Get us to the church, ASAP," Tim said. "We'll stow the car in the woods and take the Van, maybe to Cranberry."

"Perfect yourself," Angela said with approval.

CHAPTER 26

Evelyn Peters watched it happen through a crack between her curtains. The last of the truck thingies roared up and slammed on its brakes in front of Angela's house. She thought they were called SRV's or something like that and wondered why people didn't drive cars and station wagons anymore. She couldn't decide what to do. Angela hadn't mentioned visitors when she called, but these people weren't acting like criminals either. What if they were out of town relatives coming in to help with the wedding? It was an awfully big group to be sneaking around, burglaring. Evelyn imagined the scene if she called the police and Angela's family ended up getting arrested. It made her nervous. She left the window, went to her phone, and pressed star 69, praying Angela would pick up and tell her what to do.

"Hi, this is Angela, I can't talk now but leave a message and I'll call you back, may the Lord bless you."

"Now what, Whiskers?"

Evelyn went to the curtains, shoved Whiskers off the back of the couch and looked out. The first of a group of large, serious looking men spilled out onto Angela's front yard. Then it hit her. She picked up the phone. It looked like the men were sneaking around the house, like one of those Traveling Irish gangs she'd heard about while watching Inside Edition. She loved that Deborah Norville.

Evelyn dialed 911 as soon as the first man went through the front door.

"Beaver County Dispatch."

"This is Mrs. Evelyn Peters at 234 Fourth Street in Conway. I think it's those Traveling Irish, breaking into Angela's house! Right across the street."

"Mama, I'm sorry but I can't hear . . ."

Evelyn realized she'd been whispering even though the men across the street couldn't hear her. "There is a break in happening at the home of Angela Baker at 248 Fourth Street in Conway."

"And who am I speaking to ma'am?"

"There's no time for this! Send the police."

"Conway police have already been dispatched ma'am. The Officer's in route, but I need to tell him who to contact. What's your name and how can he recognize-"

"Billy . . . Officer William Allmont's on duty tonight. I waved to him when I was coming home from the store earlier today. I've known him since he was four! I was his Den mother, so you just tell him Evelyn Peters-wait; there he is now, all by himself. I'm going out."

"Ma'am! Please stay in your-"

Evelyn hit the mute button on her phone, grabbed her favorite sweater, the one her granddaughter Amy bought her, and headed toward the front door.

"Whiskers, stay put," she said, pulling the door closed.

Evelyn ignored the spitting rain and hurried because Billy was alone and outnumbered by the Irish. She was halfway across the darkened street when a group of men surrounded him. The night smelled like wet asphalt.

A second group filed out of the front door, including one giant with white hair. She didn't like the looks of the men, but the giant scared her, whispering into her mind if she went back into her house maybe, probably not, but just maybe, he wouldn't come find her when she was alone and hurt her. She wouldn't die horribly. Evelyn tried without success to catch her breath, but forced herself to keep walking toward Billy. She kept trying and kept walking toward the crowd until she managed a breath. She held the cordless phone up to her ear and turned off the mute button.

"Listen, 911, send more police, there's a riot here, only it's a quiet one."

"Hey, someone get that lady," one of Irish burglars shouted.

"Billy . . . a Police Officer is surrounded by all these men and I think they're pushing him."

Evelyn thought she heard someone on the other end of the phone shout something about being "the shift supervisor" and "no lights or sirens" but she was now close enough to hear the Traveling Irish and got distracted.

"We're with Homeland Security," Evelyn heard one of the men say. He held up a wallet with a badge.

"Understood," Officer Allmont said, his voice a little shaky. "But leave the lady alone and let me see the badge so I can confirm you have jurisdiction to–"

"We don't have time." The man snapped the wallet closed. "We'll need to take the lady for question–."

"You'd better find the time," Allmont said, "and you can forget about taking the lady anywhere." He was outnumbered, surrounded and crowded, but his voice firmed up and he moved into the face of the man with the wallet. Evelyn was proud of him. Then she saw the giant again, and her heart froze.

"He's got the woman, your man and your man's car," the giant said. "They're going someplace in his car. They'll switch cars soon, but they're nearby for now. Off this pig and the biddy and let's move."

A car roared down the street, splashing through puddles, bouncing over the curb and jumping up onto Angela's poor front yard. It slid to a stop, tearing up grass as it went. The driver's door flew open and Evelyn saw "Baden Police Department" in black block letters. The uniformed officer who got out held a pump shotgun, one hand around the trigger and guard, one grasping the slide pump.

"Back off! Hey, Bill. I said, back-away-from-the-Officer!"

"Hi, Frank." Allmont's hand moved to his pistol and now rested on the butt of the weapon. The men surrounding him seemed undecided until two more cars, one marked "Beaver County Sheriff's Department" and a third one marked "Ambridge Police Department" made up their minds for them. The two cars squealed to a stop and their doors flew open. Two more uniformed men scrambled out of the cars, each carrying a shotgun. The Deputy jacked a shell into his shotgun with a loud click-clack. The Irish froze. Sirens now screamed in the distance from several points of the compass.

"Homeland Security doesn't need to justify its action to you, Officer," one of the Irish said. "Our jurisdiction covers the entire country and supersedes yours."

"Maybe, but this isn't like the rest of the country. This is Pittsburgh. Now show me the IDs," Allmont said.

Evelyn had known Billy Allmont from the time he was three years old and had never seen him like this. It scared her a little, but in a good way.

"No one goes anywhere until we sort of this out," the Deputy Sheriff said. Evelyn could tell from flashing red lights more police cars were close by.

"Thank you 911," she said, before hanging up. She fiddled with the phone for a minute. She hated new phones but her grandson Eric bought it for her so . . . then she found a listing of Angela's cell phone number and hit dial. When the stupid thing was done beeping and squeaking, the line connected, rang twice and someone answered.

"Evelyn did you call a few minutes ago? Is everything okay?" Angela said.

"No honey, I'm afraid it's-"

"Are you okay?"

"I'm fine dear, but your house has been invaded by the Traveling Irish. One of them is saying he works for Homeland Security. He's flashing a fake badge around. Deborah Norville says they specialize in that, badges like the gas man wears, like the meter reader man, even like-"

"How do you know they're flashing badges? Whatever you do, don't go outside and-"

"That's okay dear. The police are here and more are coming. I'm just going to keep an eye on your house until you get back. How long will it take you?"

"Let me ask . . . um, Tom . . . well as soon as we can, I guess."

Tim leaned forward and waved his hands to get Angela's attention. Ten fingers up once, twice, three times. She glanced over, and then nodded.

"Evelyn we're turning around now. I think we can be back in about thirty minutes. I mean, by the time we get out of town, and through the traffic lights and everything. Please tell the police and everyone else there to wait for us."

Tim leaned against the dashboard, gave her a grin and nodded his head back and forth yes.

"Yes. I'll see you then. Please, please don't provoke anyone Evelyn."

Angela handed Tim the phone and turned into the church parking lot. A yellow school bus was parked close the Church alongside a smaller white van. Both vehicles were marked "Chapel Church."

"If anything happens to her, we'll be responsible," Angela said.

"Nothing's going to happen to her. What's that, over there?"

Tim pointed to the far end of the lot. The area was dark and tree-lined.

"Just woods, slopes down a little bit and runs into brush and stuff. Then more trees."

"Pull up there. Is that the van?"

"Yes. We've also got keys for the bus."

Angela stopped at the edge of the parking lot, put the car in park and reached for the lights. It'd stopped raining, but the night air seemed to promise more was on the way.

"No, leave the lights on for a minute," Tim said as he climbed out. He walked to the end of the lot, then a few feet into the trees, peering off into the darkness. The terrain was as Angela described it. The ground was covered with brush and trees and fell away from the lot for some distance before leveling out. He returned to the car.

"Get everything we need out and leave the engine running."

Tim handed Angela his backpack, stripped the ignition key off the ring and drove to the end of the lot. When he reached the lip of the ravine he snapped off the lights, shifted into neutral and jumped out, slamming the door behind him. Gravity took over. The Toyota crunched through the underbrush toward the bottom of the ravine. It lost momentum and finally rolled into a tree.

Satisfied no one would be able to hear Tom's muffled shouts, Tim rejoined Angela and grabbed his backpack.

"Let's get the van," Tim said.

"We've got keys for the bus."

"A big yellow school bus? Little too conspicuous, Angela."

"I'm not talking about taking it, I'm talking about running it over the edge of the same ravine. Keep them guessing. You know."

"Good idea, but there's not enough room for the bus, it's too wide. It'll break down the vegetation and they'll find Tom."

"What about across the street? There's a pretty good place, a gap in the guardrail, and a steep ravine down into some woods. It's just outside the parking lot. This area's not well traveled and I can drive that bus."

"Youth group?"

"Uh-huh. I'll drive it straight out of the lot, across the road and then let it roll down the slope like you did with the car. No one will see us."

"Let's sort out the keys." They went to the van and Tim stripped its keys off the ring. He hesitated, and then handed the ring to Angela.

"You sure about this?"

"If we see lights, we just wait for them to pass. I'll leave the door open, run down the steps and jump off the platform. It won't be going fast."

"Okay."

Angela went to the passenger's side of the van, bent over and returned carrying something. A magnetic car sign. Chapel Evangelical Church. She pulled the other one off the driver's side door and tossed both signs into the back seat.

"Cheaper than having the van painted," she said. "As soon as we dump the bus we'll look like any other white van."

Before Tim could ask her again, she pushed open the bus doors and disappeared inside. A moment later the diesel engine bellowed into life and the bus crept toward the highway, crunching down gravel as it went. Tim followed in the van, waited till one lonely car drove past and watched Angela take her shot. As soon as the car's red tail lights faded from view, the bus lurched forward with a roar and picked up speed, cutting across the road, quicker than Tim anticipated. He rolled down the window and leaned out.

"Angela, slow up!"

The bus plodded across the asphalt, picking up momentum and speed. Tim swung out and behind the bus in an arc, trying to stay away from the door but now concerned Angela misjudged the bus' power. Just before its front tires left the road surface, a small figure popped out of the doorway, hit the berm and rolled. Tim stopped alongside her and jumped out. Angela was already dusting herself off and reaching the passenger's side door.

"What are you doing?" she said. "Get us out of here. Are you, nuts?"

"You're the one that's nuts."

Angela stuck her hat back on her head at an odd angle and grinned at him. Tim climbed into the driver's seat and pulled onto the highway, for a brief moment happier than he'd been in years.

CHAPTER 27

ALAN WILLIAMS WANTED TO DEFUSE the situation and extract his men, but didn't know how. They were blocked in by police cruisers parked close enough to their vehicles to prevent escape. Half a dozen Officers were out of their cars and formed up in a loose semi-circle around his men. Revolving emergency lights painted a crowd of wet, angry faces blue, then red. As additional Police units arrived, the cops were taken aside by their fellow officers, who whispered in their ears.

No doubt complaining about how we treated Allmont, Williams thought. Precious minutes were passing and with each one Lewis and the recording got further out of reach.

"The team's getting a little antsy, Mr. Williams." Bouman said. He watched everything and spoke softly. "Let's just push past-"

"No."

"They'll back down, sir."

No doubt this was a new experience for Bouman and his men, Williams thought. A Security Team for the Society for Human Enlightenment was not accustomed to interference. He took a moment to survey the police. They stared back at him and the team unblinkingly. Most cradled shotguns. Though the barrels were pointed toward the ground that was probably on account of the rain not any lack of suspicion or hostility. A small knot of Officers took Allmont aside and huddled together.

"I'm not so sure you're right about that," Williams said. "I'm afraid Mr. Hardesty's comment about 'offing' pigs and biddies didn't go over well."

When the cops brought it up, Williams, thinking fast, tried to explain that "off" meant "release" in Homeland Security jargon.

No one seemed convinced by his explanation or particularly impressed by his credentials.

"Then–"

"Enough," Williams said. "Keep a lid on your men. Mr. Hardesty, please move to a less conspicuous location."

"Yes sir."

The group of Officers around Allmont broke apart. A Pennsylvania State Police Trooper wearing Corporal stripes walked over.

"Listen up," he said, loud enough for everyone to hear. "I'm Corporal Robert McFarland of the Pennsylvania State Police, Brighton Township Barracks. We've heard a lot about Homeland Security and seen some badges flashed around, but you can't be too careful, what with terrorists and national security, you know."

The two officers beside him were smirking. Williams had a feeling what was coming next wasn't going to be good.

"So, much as we respect you and all that, I'm going to have to check everyone's credentials, picture to face, make sure you're not infiltrators or something."

Most of the cops grinned. A couple of the others on the outside ring laughed. Bouman's men were mumbling things like 'no way,' and 'bull.' Williams wanted to draw his weapon, kill the Trooper and start shooting. He fought with himself for what seemed like a long time, then held up his hand and yelled at his men.

"Quiet. Let's remember who we are and what we're about. You," he said to the Corporal, "will be sorry you interfered in a–"

"In a what? Attempt to prevent a law enforcement officer from doing his duty? An insulting and dangerous lack of professionalism and professional courtesy?"

"Fine. I'm calling my Superiors."

"No problem," the Corporal replied. "I put in my retirement papers last month after twenty-six years. Tonight's my last night and you can call whoever you want . . ."

The Trooper let his words hang in the air for a moment.

". . . as soon as you produce your badge and identification and I establish your identity to my satisfaction."

The Corporal grinned at Williams and stood a bit closer than necessary. Williams thought about refusing until he glanced around. The cops were whispering among themselves and glaring at the Society Team with open hostility. Williams pulled out his immaculate but bogus Homeland Security credentials and handed them over. McFarland squinted at the credentials, then up at Williams.

"Not a good picture of you, is it?"

Williams pursed his lips and memorized the Corporal's name for future reference.

"I guess that's you."

McFarland took a long time looking at him.

"You may go. Next man, get up here, we don't have all night."

Williams stalked off, forcing himself out of a dark fantasy staring the McFarland family, wherever they were, as unwilling participants. Then he called New York. By the time he finished establishing his identity and explaining the situation; Rich Bouman was checked out and released. Williams ended the call as he approached.

"What they'd say?" Bouman said.

"Dispatch said they'd put it right through to the Chairman. We should get some results in the next half an hour."

"Half an-"

"I know. Go keep an eye on Hardesty."

"Yes sir."

In the end, it took longer than half an hour. Finally, an Assistant Secretary of Home Land Security called, threatening to withhold federal funds designated for state and local law enforcement. Someone called the Commandant of the Pennsylvania State Police at home. Corporal McFarland pronounced himself satisfied and as the local cops left, the Society team loaded onto their vehicles.

Williams was about to climb in when Allmont's radio squawked.

"Conway police, County dispatch over."

"Dispatch, this is Conway, Allmont here, over."

"We got a call from the choir director at Chapel Church reporting the theft of a yellow school bus and a white youth group Van, recent, both vehicles were there earlier in the evening."

"Roger, Conway's on it."

Williams exchanged a look with Bouman, nodded at him, and then joined Allmont.

"Officer we're concerned that may be-"

"Mr. Williams." Bouman was out of the SUV and running toward Williams with his Blackberry.

"Excuse me, Officer." Williams went to Bouman and leaned

over his outstretched Blackberry.

"That's our guy's church," Bouman said.

"Officer Allmont, we promise not to interfere, but that's got to be our fugitive. If–"

"Follow along, but do not interfere at the crime scene, understand."

"Of course. I'm sorry about the earlier mis-under-"

"Let's go."

Allmont left with Williams and the team strung out behind him. The Conway Officer sped down a dark country road with his overhead lights rotating, but no siren. When they arrived at the church, someone had already pulled Tom Sauer out of the trunk of his car and called the paramedics. Allmont tried to interview him, but Williams signaled him to remain quiet.

"Mr. Sauer, anything you can tell us about the people who abducted you?"

"Officer, I just, confused and my head–"

"Sorry, Bill," the paramedic said to Allmont. "We've got to worry about a concussion from the head trauma. Try him again at the hospital."

Allmont left to interview the Choir Director. Before the paramedics could load Sauer into the ambulance, Williams flashed his credentials. When the paramedics turned to face him, Bouman slid behind them and bent over Sauer.

"I'm Williams, Homeland Security could you just–"

"He's a head trauma," one of the paramedics said. "Once–"

"You want to get arrested? This is a matter of national security and . . ."

Bouman signaled success to Williams, then walked away from the gurney.

"Sorry, guys, no one's getting arrested," Williams said, changing his tone. "Long day, sorry."

The paramedics loaded Sauer and pulled out. Williams waved to Allmont, who ignored him, then turned to Bouman.

"So?"

"Lewis has Angela Baker, that's Sauer's fiancé, helping him. They put him in his trunk, but he was able to crawl around and get his head up against the rear seats. They're taking Freedom Crider Road to a place called Cranberry Township. Sauer says they've got to be in one of two vehicles, either a white panel van or a big yellow school bus. Both are marked 'Chapel Church.' They've got about twenty minutes on us."

"Let's move."

They weren't far along Freedom Crider Road when Evelyn called with the news. Angela picked up and Tim could hear most of the conversation. Someone at the Church called the police to report the missing van and bus and, according to Evelyn, not only did she hear the 911 Dispatch Center's radio call to the police, so did the "Traveling Irish."

Tim didn't say anything to Angela, but he knew they'd taken too long at the Church. He accelerated until the van was flying up the rain-spattered road. Their one advantage was they didn't need to scan the driveways and side roads as their pursuers were no doubt forced to do. Tim's hands were tight on the wheel. He kept his eyes on the road, fighting the glare of lights bouncing off the wet pavement. The challenge of navigating along the treacherous road didn't detract from the intensity of his conversation with Angela.

"I've heard of him, Tim," Angela said, "and from what I know, he loves the Lord and is a man of integrity."

"Sure, just like Tom. I'm sorry. That was a cheap-"

"Whatever!" Angela's voice turned upward in pitch and volume. "What else are we going to do? If you hadn't dragged me into this in the first place-" She swallowed the next word and caught her breath. "I'm sorry too. This isn't your fault, but we don't have a choice. You've got to call him."

"Fine, but I'm not telling him anything until he answers some hard questions about what happened in Harrisburg."

"How's he going to answer that? Even if he could answer you, we - don't - have - the - time. You said those Israeli guys trusted him. If you're blaming Guzetti for these criminals finding you in Harrisburg, then how did they find you here? No one knew you were coming here, not even me."

"That doesn't mean." Tim drove on, the silence broken only by the swish of the interval wipers. "I forgot how twisty and long this dang road is." He eased up on the accelerator and risked a glance at Angela. "That's a good point, but just because I can't explain how they found me here doesn't mean someone at the Cardinal's end didn't rat me out in Harrisburg. It's a chance Angela, are you sure?"

"No! But we're gambling no matter what. It's the smart bet."

"Grab my pack." Tim gave the van more gas. "There's a front zipper compartment. His card's in there."

"Got it," she said after a minute.

"Dial the number for me. As soon as he answers ask for the Cardinal, then give me the phone."

Angela pulled out Tim's cell, flipped open the phone and squinted at Guzetti's card in the scant illumination provided by the phone's face. She punched in the numbers one by one, then waited.

"Cardinal Thomas Guzetti, please."

The phone volume was set high enough for Tim to hear Guzetti.

"I am Thomas Guzetti. This is not a number many people have and I don't recognize your voice. Who are you?"

"Hold for one moment." Angela handed the phone to Tim.

"Cardinal Guzetti, I don't know if you remember me but my name is Tim Lewis and I interviewed-"

"I remember you, Tim and even if I didn't, I remember the phone call I received from a friend while you were in Harrisburg. He is now safe but you're in danger and-"

"I know I'm in danger! Listen, I've got a digital recording of a high level R.R.N. news executive and-"

"We know all about your recording and we are certainly anxious to expose and convict those who killed Justice Kahn . . ."

Tim listened and almost missed a bend. The van dropped off the road surface and on to the berm.

"but we will have time to sort everything out once you're safe. In the meantime . . ."

"Tim!"

Tim yanked the wheel back toward the road with his free hand, but he didn't slow up. He held the cell up to his mouth. Suddenly, the weight of the last few days snapped his self-control.

"Kahn! That's the least of it," he shouted at Guzetti. "You think you've got time? Let me tell you something, Ari didn't hear the whole recording, but I did. The reason they murdered Kahn is to pack the Court."

"Please, Mr. Lewis."

"No! You listen to me. Sir."

"Tim, watch!" Angela leaned over and pushed the steering wheel toward the road. The van swayed alarmingly. Tim ignored her, mostly ignored the road and focused on the cell phone like it was Guzetti himself.

"I listened to the entire recording about an hour ago with my girl . . . an old friend of mine and her fiancé. The Society for Human Enlightenment is ready to launch some kind of pogrom."

"Tim, you're yelling," Angela said.

"I know I'm yelling! The Society for Human Enlightenment is going to launch some kind of pogrom against Christians and step one is to keep you guys from voting. They're going to use the Supreme Court, Separation of Church and State, to make you either deny Christ or else not vote. Then, they're going to elect hostile governments. Not hostile, evil."

Tim stopped talking, looked away from the phone and glanced at the road, listening to Guzetti ask him if he was sure. Then he replied.

"I'm telling you," he said. "These guys were talking about copying what the Nazi's did to the Jews!"

"Tim you sound hyster-"

"I am not hysterical!"

"Tim," Angela said.

"Okay, okay, Cardinal." Tim fought to get control of himself.

"Where are you and where can my men meet you," the Cardinal asked.

"Cranberry Township. It's an ex burb of Pittsburgh about,"

"Can we find it on a map?"

"Yeah, you'll be able to find it on a map."

"We need a place to meet."

"Ok, ok. Angela, where can we meet the Cardinal's men, some place open where we can watch and wait for them, but also see if they're being followed or-"

"There's a big Best Western on Route 19," Angela said. "I know lots of places where we can stay out of sight but still see the hotel."

Tim relayed the information to the Cardinal, then listened, focused upon the phone and the Cardinal's instructions.

"Tim!"

"Oh shoot!"

"What's happening?" Guzetti shouted.

Tim was quick and if it hadn't been raining he might have made it. But it was raining, so the road was wet and slick. When Tim dropped the phone and yanked the wheel back to the right, the tires lost traction on the slick road surface. The van fish-tailed.

The next few moments blurred. The van began spinning, whipping lose objects and papers off the top of the dash board and seats. The force threw both Tim and Angela against their tightening seatbelts. The van left the road and shot through a gap in the trees before sliding down a sloping hillside of wet turf, bushes and grass. The spinning slowed. Tim worked the steering and brakes with little effect. They continued down the embankment, losing speed, but still moving frighteningly fast. Branches, brambles and sticks clicked, snapped and broke off as the van crashed through the foliage, continuing its descent. Despite Tim's non-stop efforts, the van collided with a large tree about three quarters of the way down the slope with a loud crunch and bang of crumpling metal.

The world came to a sudden stop. Tim and Angela sat motionless in a now unnatural silence, their faces illuminated by the green glow of the van's dashboard gauges. Tim's ears hummed and his shoulder was sore, he thought from banging into the side door. He was otherwise unscathed. Rain pattered off the roof in a soothing rhythm.

"Angela?"

"Oh. Alright, I think," she said.

"Hello?"

It was Guzetti.

"I'm sorry," Tim said. "I should have been watching-"

"I wasn't watching either. I just, I knew that look of yours, concentrating, being lost in a moment."

Angela pressed her forefinger against her lips, just like she always did when she was thinking, or when she was trying not to cry.

"I wasn't paying attention," she said, "not until I saw the road out the side window instead of the windshield."

Tim reached across the seat and took her hand. Nothing more was necessary.

"Hello?"

It was Guzetti again.

Tim let go of Angela's hand, looked around, then located the glow from the still open cell phone. He leaned over and picked it off of the floor mat.

"Yeah. It's Tim Lewis. We had an accident."

"Do you need an ambulance?"

Tim started laughing, softly enough, but a little too hard. Without thinking about it, he snapped off the headlights and turned off the ignition.

"I need a tow truck, a Division of Marines and a fifth of whiskey, but no, we don't need an ambulance."

Angela laughed, but Guzetti wasn't amused.

"Get hold of yourself, young Mr. Lewis. The Society for Human Enlightenment will not stop looking for you. That means they will find you if you do not keep your wits about you. You are responsible not only for yourself, but also for the young woman with you. Do you understand me?"

Gone was the measured, pastoral tone Tim was used to hearing from the Cardinal. He sounded like a drill instructor. Tim remembered something about Guzetti being some kind of war hero and he believed it.

"I said do you understand me?"

"Yes, sir," Tim said.

"Fine, son. Now, look around and tell me if you are visible from the road."

"No. Well, maybe. I mean, sorry. We're off the road, down the side of a hill, maybe half a football field down. If someone just drives by they won't see us, but if they stop and look, they'll see us, even in the dark. Sorry. I did turn off the lights and everything though," Tim said, feeling proud about doing something he hadn't even thought about before he did it.

"Fine, good thinking. What is the name of the road you were on?"

"Freedom Crider Road."

"Do you know if you're near a major intersection or a landmark my men will be able to identify?"

"I don't. Angela, how can we let the Cardinal's men figure out where we're at? It's been years since I've been out here. What'd you think?"

"Give me a minute. I wasn't paying attention at the end but I know we passed the intersection at Route 989 so I'm thinking . . .

We're about seven miles from the intersection of Freedom Crider and Route 19 in Cranberry. That's the first main intersection."

"Could you hear that?"

"Yes," the Cardinal relied, "I'm taking notes. I see the intersection on my GPS map. Very good. This intersection with Route 19 and Freedom Crider has a red light, correct?"

"Angela?" Tim said.

"That's right, Cardinal," Angela said loud enough to be heard.

Tim handed her the phone.

"It's turned into a fairly large intersection over the years," Angela said, "but how you go depends upon which way your men will come from. Um, there's a large Denny's restaurant at the corner."

"We will work that out. Please put Tim back on the phone."

"It's Tim."

"Very well, Tim. Stay where you are, unless, of course, the Society somehow finds you. I don't think they have had time to access your cell phone records . . ."

"We're using a disposable I bought before I left New York."

"Outstanding!"

It was only when Tim heard just how relieved the Cardinal sounded that he realized how precarious he and Angela's situation was.

"We're in real trouble, aren't we? I mean your guys aren't even close."

"They are still in Harrisburg, but we have a private plane at the airport. When I get off the phone with you I am going to issue them instructions. I want you to hang up, turn off all of your phones and take the batteries out, do you understand?"

"Yes."

"Do not turn them back on unless it is literally a case of life and death. I don't think the Society team brought along the technology, but even an un-used cell emits detectable amounts of radiation. It's not worth the risk."

"I'll take the batteries out."

"Good. It will take my men at least forty-five minutes to get to you, probably more like an hour. When they arrive I will instruct them to drive down . . . Freedom Crider Road. They will drive slow and flash their high beams three times in quick succession, a pause, then flash them again, over and over as they cruise the road.

When you see the lights, turn on your headlights, then turn them right back off. Give me your cell phone number, the one you are using."

Tim read the number to him.

"I'll give my team your number. As soon as you turn on your lights, put the batteries back in the phone and turn it on. The team leader will call you immediately, over and over until he gets through. If no one calls, run, something has gone wrong."

"Great."

"Unless you have questions or there is something else you need to tell me, it's time to hang up. Is there anything else?"

"No."

"I'll be praying for you, Tim."

"Thank you sir. Tonight, you can pray for me all you want."

Tim hung up and turned to Angela.

"What did he say" she asked.

"His guys are on the way. He says he can get help here in about an hour."

"An hour?"

"I know. Normally I'd be worried, but come on, everyone's praying."

"Don't be a smart aleck."

"Tonight, I'm not sure I am being a smart aleck. The fact I've even made it this far is pretty much a long shot. We're supposed to take the batteries out of our cell phones. Do you know how to do that?"

"I can figure it out."

"Do it then. I'll leave mine on for light, then I'll take the battery out when you're done. Watch me, because this is the phone they're going to call us on. Give me the back pack."

Tim took the pack from Angela and put it on the floor between his legs. After they took the batteries out of their phones, Tim explained the Cardinal's instructions for identifying the team and why she needed to know how to put the batteries back into his phone. Angela took his phone and battery stuck them into her jacket pocket.

"Now what," she asked.

"We wait."

"I hate that part."

They were sitting together in silence, listening to the rain when it hit him. He recognized the interior of the van, the surrounding terrain and even Angela's clothes. It was from the beginning of his dream, the dream where he and Angela were running in the dark, chased, but moving too slowly, cut off and then surrounded, voices ahead, voices behind them. Tim remembered being struck from behind, plunged into blackness and his last memory was of a cry of pain, terror and worse from Angela. Then, darkest black.

"Oh."

"Tim? What's wrong?"

Tim ignored her and twisted around. The van had come to a sideways stop. The rear was still pointed up the hillside, but at an angle. He could see the road in the direction they'd been traveling.

"Tim."

Powerful headlights cut through the scattered trees and vegetation lining the roadside, rapidly closing in on their location. Then they slowed, still piercing the night, but almost motionless as they crept toward the area where Tim and Angela skidded off the road. A smaller, weaker light shone out from behind the headlights.

"Flashlight," Tim gasped.

"What?" Angela said.

"They're already here and they're going to find us. If we start running now, maybe we can get away this time."

"What are you talking about, this time? You're scaring me."

———◆———

Alan Williams leaned over the driver's shoulder for one extra second, just to make sure.

"Forget it. It's an old skid mark," he said. "Move on until we get another break in the guard rail."

CHAPTER 28

AFTER THE LAST SOCIETY VEHICLE reached the highway, Ted walked over to the Deputies.

"Appreciate it," Ted said. "I suspect this isn't your favorite way to spend the end of your shift."

"Don't know who your friends are, but anyone who can call up Sheriff Howard out of the blue and get us sent out here's got some pull." Deputy Greer bent over and spit a stream of juice. "Aw, you're welcome. I never liked Kiefer anyway. Best you stay away from him, understand?"

"I do."

"Evenin to you then."

Ted watched the two cruisers pull away, then walked back to the van.

"Where to, Boss?" the Driver said.

"Wish I knew. I wish I knew."

Ted used his Blackberry to send an email to the Fellowships' fledgling technology unit. He wanted schematics for the Harrisburg Airport.

"Take us back to the airport," Ted said. "Anyone got a demolitions background?"

One of Ted's graybeards, as he'd taken to calling them, had been an Engineer Sergeant on a Special Forces A-Team. He was an expert, not only at building things, but at blowing them up as well. Since Ted was also "ex-SF," it was only natural to turn to him for help. Once Ted's Blackberry buzzed with the response, he motioned to the Engineer. They leaned over the schematics.

"These are pretty good," the Engineer said.

"That's because they're the airport 'as builts,'" Ted replied. "As builts" were the plans the contractor submitted after actual construction to show what was really built, as opposed to how it had been planned. They were the gold standard. Reverend Allison must have brought some high level technical talent into the Fellowship, Ted thought.

"No kidding?"

"It's amazing what those guys can hack into. If you wanted to shut down the airport and cause as many fatalities as possible, where would you locate the explosives?"

"What?"

"We're not going to bomb the airport, but we don't know where Lewis went. Since we can't go anywhere, I don't want the Society to go anywhere either. Their intelligence network's a lot more extensive than ours. If they get a tip where he's headed, I don't want them to be able-"

"You're going to call in a bomb threat and close down the airport."

"Yep. Give me one of the clean phones," Ted said to the guys in the back. While someone fished out an off the rack untraceable cell, the Engineer reached for the Blackberry.

"Let me see that thing, sir."

They pulled off the road and idled in a fast food parking lot. Ted huddled with the Engineer. After the two ex-Green Berets decided upon the scariest and hardest to reach locations for bombs, Ted made three breathless calls, one to the Harrisburg Air Tower, one to a local television news broadcast and one to a Transportation Safety Administration hotline. He mentioned a number of technical details to lend credibility to the threat. After the last call he pulled the phone's memory chip and snapped it in two. One of his men tossed the phone into an outside trash bin.

"Let's go," Ted said, "we'll need a place to hole up for a while."

The driver took them down a highway crowded with pawn shops, short, run down strip malls and light industrial buildings. Ted was about to tell them to turn around when the driver pointed at the windshield.

"How about that?"

"Take it," Ted replied.

They pulled into the parking lot of a two story concrete block hotel called "Airport Rest." Red room doors dotted the sides of both levels and wrapped around the building.

"Let me off here, I'll take care of it," Ted said.

Inside the front office a bored looking clerk with chrome cheek piercings was reading a yellow cliff notes booklet. The Tempest. Ted walked to the counter but the girl never looked up.

"I need a couple rooms," Ted said.

"A couple?" She cracked her gum, but still didn't look up.

"Three in fact. I've got a work crew out there and we can't tell if we'll finish up today, tom-"

"Sure, $38.99 per room."

"I'd like rooms around back."

"In advance."

Ted reached into his pants pocket, pulled out a roll of twenties and peeled off three bills. The girl finally looked up, snatched the bills and gave him three metal keys hooked to orange plastic tabs.

"The room numbers are on them. Check outs at 11 a.m."

Ted took the keys and returned to his men. They circled the building and found the rooms around back. Ted, his driver and the Engineer took room #23. He looked at the rest of his men.

"Unload your gear but don't unpack. If we get a call, I want to be out of here in five minutes. Soon as you're unloaded, lock up the room and we'll all meet in 23."

Ted took his bag inside and dropped it on one of the beds. The driver snapped on the television and the Engineer used the bathroom. By the time he returned, local television programming was interrupted with "breaking news." The team members reassembled in Room 23 while they watched. The reaction to Ted's calls was everything they hoped for, a TSA "ground all aircraft" order, live local and national TV feeds, bomb sniffing dogs, and more. Ted assigned one of the men to take the van and find a location from where he could watch the airport runways. After checking in with the Cardinal's secretary, he decided upon a quick debriefing of his men. He'd seen something that bothered him.

"Everyone take a seat or pull up some floor," Ted said as he closed the door to the room. He gave the men enough time to get situated, then started. "It's time for a quick debrief on the work at the hospital. You've still got it," he said, looking each of the men in the eye. "You moved well, exercised just the right amount of initiative and didn't get spooked. Now, what is this with losing your cool over the 'white boy' thing by the security guard? You realize something like that could be used as diversion, right?"

No one said anything. Best way to handle warriors, Ted had learned, was to make them feel foolish.

"Are we here to do a job or promote civil rights?"

Still nothing. Ted waited, looking them over and letting the silence drag on. One of the guys looked down, another pursed his lips. Ted now knew who said what. His point made, it was time to let everyone off the hook.

"Okay, I don't want to over react. No one freaked out or threw a punch or anything. It didn't detract from your performance." Everyone started to relax. "Still, what would you think if we're working and I got in someone's face because he called me a nig–"

"You wouldn't have to get in his face Ted, I'd shoot him first."

It sounded like it just slipped out. There was a little nervous laughter until Ted let go a smile he couldn't fight back. Everyone started laughing and Ted joined them. His brothers.

"Get out of here," Ted said. "I'm going to try to get some sleep, so should you."

The team broke up and took turns napping while they awaited developments. After forty minutes of shut eye, Ted sat munching on pretzels and trying not to glance at his watch. The television droned on in the background.

"Breaking news from the Channel Fifteen news desk," a dark haired newsman said. "The Transportation Safety Administration has just issued an all clear order for the Harrisburg Airport. Earlier today a credible threat of-"

Ted cell phone rang and he hit the mute button.

"They're moving Ted. The Society jet's rolling past the tower now. It's got to be for takeoff. There's no place else to go."

"Understood," Ted said into his phone. "Get back here with the van, ASAP."

"Now what?" the Engineer said.

"Now? We pray for a break."

Ted took one of the beds and fell into a deep sleep. He still answered his cell phone on the first ring.

"This is Ted."

"It's Guzetti," the Cardinal said. "My staff tells me you're close to the airport. How close?"

"Block, block and a half away."

"Check your Blackberry."

"Just a minute." Ted looked at the Engineer. "Is Gary back with the van?"

"Yes."

"Get the team up and ready. Cardinal? I've got a local airstrip, Cranberry Township and Freedom Crider Road. Pittsburgh." Ted scrolled through the information. "What else? Downloaded maps, contact info."

"Get to the airport. I'll explain the rest when you're moving."

"We're moving now. Sir, let me call you once-"

"I'll hold," Guzetti said.

"Give me a few minutes then," Ted said before hitting the mute button. Ted made it to the door just as the other men were leaving their adjoining rooms. They met on the walkway.

"Grab your gear, close up the rooms and load up," Ted said. Moments later everyone was in the van. They stopped long enough to return the keys to an elderly night clerk.

"Get us to the airport," he said to the driver. "Now." He punched at his phone. "I'm back, Cardinal. We're loaded and moving."

"Good. The Society team's already on the ground. Get on the plane and in the air as soon as possible. Use the private gate section of the airport, Number 5."

"Just a minute. Do you guys know where the private gates are at the airport?"

"No problem, Ted," the driver said. "That's where we picked you up."

"We're good on that Cardinal. What else?"

"Someone will be waiting to escort you to the plane. The pilots are already on board."

"We're there now. Hold." Ted hit mute again.

The driver swung into a lane with an overhead sign stating, "Private Gates - Short term tie downs, Numbers 1 – 5." A small white pickup truck with a flickering light bar on the roof waited for them outside Private Gate 5. When they got closer, Ted could make out the "Harrisburg Airport Authority" markings on the side. The Authority driver leaned out his window and punched a remote at the gate. The chain link clattered as it rolled opened.

"Follow me and park behind the truck when I stop," he said.

The Fellowship team followed him to the jet, parked behind him and jumped out. Their plane's engines were roaring and the air reeked of JP8 jet fuel. Two waiting strangers took charge of the van. The team lined up and climbed into the jet.

"I'm back," Ted yelled above the roar.

"A few minutes ago I hung up on Tim Lewis, the kid from R.R.N. with the recording."

"Right, the rescue target."

"There's something else. Something I didn't want to put in an email. I even hate saying it on a scrambled phone. Ari didn't hear the entire conversation. This goes way beyond an assassination–"

The engines were howling. The tail end of the Cardinal's sentence was drowned out when the copilot pulled up the steps and slammed the aircraft door shut.

"Get strapped in Ted, we're cleared and taking off immediately," the copilot said.

"Sorry Cardinal, repeat that," Ted said, belting in.

"I said this goes way beyond an assassination designed to shift the ideological balance of the Court," Guzetti replied. "They didn't just assassinate Kahn as part of a long term strategy, its' part of something bigger, more immediate. According to Lewis, Merkel and Stueben laid out a plan to pack the United States Supreme Court. The Society already has three members or sympathizers on the Court now."

"What?'

"Listen. The current nominee, Anders, is either a member or a sympathizer. That makes four. The President has just decided on Kahn's replacement. If he's with the Society, that makes five Justices, a majority on the Court. Once the Society establishes a majority, they'll file a lawsuit in a sympathetic District Court, challenging Christian suffrage based upon the Separation of Church and State."

"Man, that's not even in the Constitution," Ted said over the whine of straining jet engines.

"Who cares! They've been putting stuff in that's not there for decades. No one's stopped them. That's how the Court's going to rule if the Society is able to stack it. They'll uphold a challenge to Christian voting based upon a violation of the 'Separation of Church and State.' They will rule that Christian suffrage tends to establish a religion. The fig leaf covering the free exercise clause is the offer of a loyalty oath. One specifically designed so that Christians can't take it without denying Christ as Lord. Take the oath and you can vote, otherwise you can't vote."

Cardinal Thomas Guzetti was one of the coolest, most level-headed men ex-Green Beret Ted Kehr had ever met, which was saying something. Although the full impact of Guzetti's words was still sinking in, Ted understood their significance. But that wasn't what scared him. It was Guzetti's tone, his loss of composure. Guzetti wasn't a man who raised his voice. He didn't say "stuff." If Thomas Guzetti was worried, even scared, Ted had every intention of working himself right up to "terrified" as soon as he hung up.

"Ted? Are you still there?"

"Yes."

"It gets worse. The idea is once they impose restrictions on our voting rights they can win a series of elections and construct an explicitly anti-Christian government. Then, no doubt after some pretext, the government will launch an anti-Christian pogrom."

"Cardinal that will never happen in United States. People won't stand for it."

"What makes you think people will know about it? Do you think mainstream media groups are going to report it?"

"I do think that, at least some. Does the recording say anything about Kahn's replacement? I mean, how could it, and unless the President is in on this, how can they be sure their man will be appointed?"

"You could be right. Maybe the Society only has one of the top candidates on the list. The President is clean; I'm willing to bet on it. But what about the people around him? Do you think the Society would murder a Supreme Court Justice if they didn't think it was worth the risk? What if they only have a one in three chance of convincing the President to appoint their nominee? Are you willing to risk it?"

"Of course not. But why are you telling me all this? I'm no lawyer, some of this is going over my head."

"Because I am ordering you to secure the recording and Lewis, regardless of the cost. I'm sorry to say this Ted, but loss of life, your life and the lives of your men are of secondary concern in this situation."

"The Society's going to fight for that recording. I got a look at their team in Harrisburg and its top notch. Alan Williams is leading it."

"Williams."

"Yeah. My guys are rusty and we're outnumbered."

Ted waited for the Cardinal to say something else.

"I'm sending you reinforcements," the Cardinal said, "but I don't know when they will arrive. A few two-man teams are doing investigative work and they're within striking distance."

"What's that mean, striking distance?"

"One was on those church fires in Ohio and the other in Northern West Virginia."

"The pastor murdered in the pulpit?"

"Right. We sent text messages telling them to report to Pittsburgh, but that's it. They're using unsecured phones and I'm not in direct contact with either team. Cell coverage in that area is spotty. I don't know when they'll arrive, but it's the best I can do. Brother, I'm sorry. This has to be done."

"What about police officers and bystanders? What do we do?"

"I don't know. Avoid them. Pray. That's what I'll be doing. Get the recording and Lewis."

"Yes sir. Anything else?"

"No, Ted. God speed."

Guzetti hung up. Ted looked out his window as the central Pennsylvania landscape rushed by 10,000 feet below him. He took Guzetti's advice and began praying.

Williams squirmed as though he could hasten Lewis' capture by an act of will. He was about to tell the driver to speed up when his cell phone went off.

"Yes."

"Mr. Williams, this is the Chairman."

"Chairman, uh, yes sir," Williams said, straightening in his seat. *This* Chairman of the Society for Human Enlightenment didn't make phone calls to field units. Period. Williams noted the effect of the call upon his men. Everyone in the SUV unconsciously leaned toward the phone. The driver eased off the accelerator, stiffening every time the wiper blade swished across the windshield.

No one knew why the Chairman was calling, but they did know their odds of a premature death had just increased.

"Have you found the fugitive and his recorder yet?"

"No sir, but we're close. My men are bracketing the area, doing sweeps of the secondary roads and-"

"I am told the same collection of Christian hypocrites who meddled with us in Harrisburg just boarded a jet headed toward the, hmm, someplace called the Butler County Airport. Our sources in Harrisburg believe the hypocrites are in contact with your fugitive and will meet him. The Board would like you to be waiting for the jet when it arrives. Follow the hypocrites to their rendezvous with Mr. Lewis and seize the recorder. Kill Lewis and everyone else."

"We're on the way to Cranberry now, that's the area where the airport's located. Chairman, it's a well-developed commercial area and if the rendezvous is in a parking lot or-"

"Those concerns are no longer relevant. I want you to listen to me closely, Mr. Williams. Are you listening?"

"Of course, sir."

"Fine, then. You're well thought of here so I am glad to be able to tell you this directly. The President reduced his so-called short list to two candidates, our man, Judge Schlack, and Harold Stossen from the Third Circuit. It took a bit of work, but we convinced Stossen to withdraw his name from consideration. The President has decided to nominate Schlack to fill the vacancy created by Benjamin Kahn's death."

"We have it!"

"No. We would have it, except for Tim Lewis. Schlack must be confirmed, a process that requires preparation. Normally, we would begin after Kahn's memorial, but this recording has forced our hand. We're speeding up the process. We've arranged for both Anders and Schlack to fly out to California with the President on Air Force One to attend Kahn's Memorial. The President has agreed to leave Washington two hours earlier than scheduled and return to Washington the same day instead of spending the night. We hope to announce the Schlack nomination right after the memorial. Mr. Williams, do you have any idea how difficult it is to change the President's schedule and add two passengers to Airforce One's manifest?"

"No sir, I-"

"It's difficult, even for us, and disruptive, and all because of this recording and our inability to capture the young man who made it."

The Chairman's tone changed. Williams winced.

"Anders and Schlack's confirmations will change the Court, this country and the World, forever. That means we cannot afford even a hint of controversy regarding any aspect of this process. Not a word, not a whisper, not an innuendo, let alone a substantiated allegation Kahn was murdered so as to allow our Society to appoint a substitute."

"Understood."

"I don't think you do. Mr. Williams, have you ever appeared before the Masters?"

You know I haven't, Williams thought. "No Sir," he said.

"As of right now, one man, barely out of his teens, is holding the entire Society for Human Enlightenment at bay. Think about that. One man, Mr. Williams. If I have to appear before the Masters to explain how that can be possible, I'm not going by myself. Do you understand me?"

"Yes, sir."

"The recording and Lewis must be destroyed, no matter what. Do you understand?"

"Yes sir."

"Mr. Williams I am ordering you, do whatever you need to do, by any means necessary. You are ordered to kill as many police, bystanders, destroy as many buildings, do whatever is necessary to get that recording, destroy it and kill Lewis. Burn Cranapple-or whatever that pathetic little village is called-to the ground, if you must. You and your men can be assured we will look after you. If you're caught, you'll be tried. If you lose, you will appeal. If you lose the appeal, you will take your case to the United States Supreme Court and they will overturn your convictions. You are immune. No matter what you do, you're immune. It's a taste of things to come, so do not fail."

Williams wasn't sure if he would be protected or not, but he knew what would happened if he let the recording slip through his grasp. Although his life on earth would be too long, and the pain too great, that time would be a mere foretaste of what would await him after he died and stood before THE Master. Williams, a man not easily shaken, suppressed a shiver.

"Rest assured, Chairman, both Lewis and the recording will be destroyed, regardless of the cost," Williams said into a disconnected phone. He snapped the phone closed and turned to his driver. "Get us to Cranberry, now!"

The Tahoe's driver stomped on the gas. The engine responded with a full-throated roar. Williams and Bouman were already calling the rest of team and issuing new orders, just as the Tahoe squealed around a corner and right past a set of fresh skid marks and torn turf alongside a gap in the guard rail.

A little more than two hundred air miles separated Harrisburg and Pittsburgh. The Gulfstream carrying Ted and his makeshift team covered the distance in less than forty minutes. Ted spent most of the flight briefing his men on the substance of his conversation with the Cardinal and possible tactical approaches to the rescue, given what they knew about the terrain. He finished with time to spare, but kept repeating or reemphasizing how different rescue scenarios might play out, as much to keep his men's mind off what was at stake as to make sure they were mentally prepared.

When the aircraft landed at a small field outside of Butler, Pennsylvania, the senior pastor and an elder of a large evangelical church in the Cranberry area were waiting for them. Both men drove their own vehicles to the airport. The pastor brought a Dodge Caravan and the elder a Ford Econo van emptied of his tools and filled with worse-for-wear looking aluminum lawn chairs.

"Hop in guys," the elder said as soon as Ted climbed off of the plane. "We'll get you to the rental lot in no time." Ted's team deplaned, loaded into the civilian vehicles and left the airport in less than ten minutes, despite a delay caused by relocating the pastor's baby car seat.

"Um, sorry about that guys," the Pastor said as they pulled out.

The churchmen took the team to a rental agency managed by a member of the Pastor's church. Two idling Ford Explorers awaited them.

"Let's move," Ted said. His men scrambled out of the churchmen's vehicles and into the Explorers. Ted kept it simple. His men were split into two equal-sized groups. Ted's was Team One; the other, Team Two. Ted waved as they pulled out, but his mind was already someplace along Freedom Crider Road.

The Explorers left the agency lot and merged into the evening traffic, heading toward Freedom Crider. Ted consulted a GPS readout.

"The intersection's three-quarters of a mile ahead on the right," he said to the driver. He looked back up at the road. "Just past the Denny's, get in the right lane."

The driver, a gulf war veteran turned practicing orthodontist first signaled, then glided into the right lane. The trailing Explorer, alerted to the maneuver in advance, followed. Ted twisted in his seat to eyeball his men. He worried the pressure of the situation might make them jumpy, but it seemed to have the opposite effect. Every now and then someone checked his weapon a second or third time, but that didn't overly concern Ted. A lot of guys did that, even when they were still on active duty. Each man on the ragamuffin team seemed to settle into himself and, at least it seemed to Ted, prepare himself to do whatever needed to be done.

"Listen up," Ted said into his radio mike. "This is Freedom Crider Road, so let's go over everything one last time. The road's long, dark and windy. There aren't a lot of houses. The targets are located approximately seven miles away, along an isolated section of the road. They're off the road, maybe fifty yards down a steep slope on our right, but who knows? Keep an eye out. Expect some houses for the first few miles, then they thin out. After four miles, we'll start flashing our high-beams. The signal is three quick flashes, a pause, then three more, over and over."

Ted looked around. No one said anything. The radio crackled with static, but was otherwise silent.

"Copy that, Team two?" Ted said.

"Roger, sir."

"When I give the order, Team Two drops back and acts as a blocker. Two, I want enough of a buffer between you and us that anyone behind you can't see what we're doing. Last thing we need is a call to the cops or something unexpected from a civilian. Team One, as soon as the targets see our lights they'll flash their headlights. That's when it gets tricky. I've got to call them and work out how we'll get them loaded. The second they're inside, we get out of Dodge. Fast."

"Understood, sir," someone in the back said.

"Questions?" Ted twisted all the way around and waited. No one spoke up.

"That's it then. Everyone except for the drivers and co-pilots watch for the target's headlights. That means Team Two especially. Remember, the targets are kids. By the time they react to Team One's flashes, we may be around a bend or something. That's it. I know your back grounds, you guys have done a lot dicier stuff than this before. Let's do this one."

Ted's driver glanced up from his odometer readout. He looked over at Ted, his face painted mustard in the dashboard light.

"We're four miles in, boss. What'd you think?"

The area was desolate, the road twisting and treacherous and the roadside sloped and wooded. There were frequent breaks in the guardrail and no houses. It was the kind of terrain Guzetti told him to look for.

"Initiate the signal, three quick flashes, a pause, then three more. Team two, drop back and watch for headlights someplace there shouldn't be any headlights."

The lead Explorer turned into a flickering, mobile strobe light. Ted monitored their progress using the dashboard odometer. After five miles he radioed Team Two.

"What's traffic like behind you guys?"

"A few trailers, but they're keeping their distance boss. No one here's seen anything."

"Look sharp. We should be running across them any minute now."

"Roger."

"There it is! Ted, there it is! Down the hillside."

Ted turned and squinted out the window. He couldn't see anything except glimpses of shadowy vegetation and inky darkness.

"I saw it too," another man said. Ted forgot his name.

"That's it, then," Ted said. He reached over and re-set the odometer mileage counter so they'd know how far to back track. Ted programmed the target's cell number into his phone when he was still in Harrisburg. He hit send and someone answered on the first ring.

"We saw your lights," the kid said in a level voice. "You just drove past us."

"We're coming back, so get ready to move. When we locate you we'll pull over and park on the berm of your side of the road. Soon as we do, kill your lights and climb up to the road. Can you do that?"

"Yes."

"When you get to us, don't wait, climb into the Explorer-"

"Explorer?"

"We're in Ford Explorers."

"Okay, I get it."

"As soon as you get to the road, climb into the back of the Explorer. Don't talk, don't look around, don't stop for anything. Get in. As soon as you're in, we move. Understand?"

"Yes."

"It'll take us a few minutes to get turned around, so keep an eye out for us. We'll be coming from the opposite direction and flashing our lights. I'm hanging up, but keep your phone turned on and call me as soon as you see our lights." Ted hung up. "Find a place to turnaround. Now." Ted keyed his radio mike. "Team Two, its Ted. We've made contact with the targets. We're looking for a place wide enough to turn around. Tighten up and follow us. When we turn, you turn. Once we reach the targets, we'll cut across the opposing lane of traffic and pull onto the berm on the other side of the road. All on my command. Team two swings ahead, stops two car lengths ahead of us and hits the flashers. Driver's side guys, get out and take positions on the other side of the guard rail, ready to engage. Passenger's side, you're sitting ducks but stay in the vehicle, windows down, ready to engage but make sure of your shots. This road gets a lot of civilian traffic. As soon as the rescues are on board we go straight to the airport, no matter what. Acknowledge, over."

"This is Team Two, acknowledged Ted."

"Let's go," Ted said to his driver. "We're going the wrong way."

"The road's too narrow for a three-point turn, forget about the traffic," the driver said.

The terrain on both sides of the road supported the driver's argument. On the left, a narrow berm gave way to a steep, rocky cliff-side through which the road was cut. On the right the guardrail was only feet away from a steep hillside.

"Then move," Ted said. "Find a turnaround ASAP."

The driver sped up and squinted ahead, looking for a wider spot. If anything the terrain became more difficult, narrowing and closing in on the road surface itself. The rain persisted, pattering off the roof and windshield, distorting the driver's vision and reducing visibility. Ted watched the odometer. A little more than a mile from the targets they emerged from another of the road's endless twists. The land on both sides flattened and widened. The guard rail on Ted's right ended, replaced by a thick set of trees.

"There," the driver said pointing with his right hand. The tree line on the right gave way to a driveway. The driveway led to a house with an open, gently sloping lawn, dotted with a few short evergreen trees.

"Team Two, tighten up," Ted said. "Let's go, let's go."

Ted's driver accelerated, and then slowed as he approached the house. He whipped the Explorer into the driveway and drove in far enough to allow Team Two to enter behind him. As soon as Team Two was in he turned to left, bounced up and over the front lawn and swung around in a circle before reaching the road. Team Two followed but misjudged the angle and ran over a three foot pine tree. Ted's driver looked both ways, then spun out of the yard and jumped back onto Freedom Crider in the opposite lane. A line of cars buzzed past in the opposing lane. Ted checked his mirror and Team Two was right behind them.

When the Fellowship's small caravan left the airport, Williams and his Society foot soldiers were waiting. They followed the hypocrites by rotating a series of vehicles in ever changing shifts. After the Fellowship team left the rental lot, William's Tahoe swung behind the second of Ted's Explorers, taking its turn in the rotation of tail vehicles.

"Here they go," Alan Williams said into his radio. "Turning back onto Freedom Crider. Good. Everyone swing in behind me. No rotations, we're following them right to Lewis. Who's tail?"

"Collins, sir. I'm last."

"When I give the order block the road, diagonally. Cover both lanes, then hit your flashers, take the keys and join the rest of us. Who's behind me, Evans?"

"Yes."

"You swing us around when I stop, block the road ahead of us diagonally, about a quarter of a mile should do it. Same drill as Collins. Remember, no restraint on tactics. If we blow this, I will not be able to protect you from the consequences."

Radio silence. Williams let it drag on a moment longer. Then a burst of static, then silence. They drove on, far enough behind the second Fellowship Explorer to avoid suspicion, but close enough to see when it sped up.

"That's it, let's do it," Williams shouted. "Red team, its Williams, initiate diversion. Everyone else, follow me."

Earlier, Collins' team had peeled off from the main group as it headed to the airport and planted a small, remotely activated incendiary device on one of the ranch houses. Now, Collins used his cell to remote activate the bomb. Williams was confident a fire as big as the one they set would divert most police units to that area.

He listened in as the last unit in the convoy dropped behind the other vehicles. As soon as they received Williams call they were to slow down, twist their vehicle diagonal so they blocked both lanes traffic and stop. While the driver jumped out of his seat and rushed back waving his arms at oncoming traffic, his passenger flipped up a cell phone and called 911.

"911, this is an emergency. You've got two cars that somehow ran into this house on Jones Street. Part of the house is on fire, I don't know what to-" He hung up on the dispatcher.

A second member of Williams' team dialed 911 and shouted a similar story into his phone before cutting the connection. They'd picked the diversion site on their way up from Conway. The site was on a road with no direct connection to Freedom Crider. Williams' plan was to isolate the cops from Freedom Crider so they couldn't interfere with the Society attack on Lewis.

"That's them," Williams' driver yelled.

Two Fellowship Explorers sped by in the other lane of traffic before anyone had a chance to react. His men exploded, but Williams remained icy.

"Keep your eyes on the road and watch your speed. They needed a place to turn and they found it. So will we, watch for it."

After they cleared the next bend, they found a driveway and house with a front lawn torn up in fresh divots.

"That's it."

Williams' driver looked across Williams at the divots and nodded. "Got it.'

"All units, it's Williams, slow down for the turn around. Stay in line. Just follow us."

Williams' driver went down the driveway far enough back to allow him to retrace the tracks of the Fellowship Explorers. The rest of Williams' caravan followed in disciplined order.

Before a now-awakened homeowner could protest, the caravan sped off, and Williams' team chased after the Fellowship as quickly as the road permitted. Williams checked his men, pleased by what he saw. They looked like freshly blooded foxhounds. When his instincts told him, he keyed his radio.

"It's Williams, block it now."

Two vehicles dropped back, slowed and then stopped. The last truck parked diagonally to block the road. Its driver turned on his flashers and jumped out, taking the keys with him. Both men sprinted to the second vehicle, got in and sped off to catch up with the remainder of the Society convoy.

CHAPTER 29

THE TAHOE DROVE PAST THEM, its lights fading and then vanishing after it cleared the bend, leaving them in darkness.

"Thank God," Tim said, without really thinking about it.

Angela Baker was next to him and he wondered if she had just smiled in the dark, invisible to all but herself and her God. They sat together in silence, listening to the rain and tensing, then relaxing, whenever traffic approached and passed by.

"Tim, we're all sinners, born with a sin nature and–"

"Angela–"

"If you ever loved me, listen to me."

"You told me this before when–"

"If you ever loved me, listen to me now."

"Go."

"We were born into sin, Tim. Adam and Eve chose to sin. From then on we were all born with a sin nature we can't resist. No matter how good you are, God's standard is perfection. Our sin and His justice require death. But He loved us so much he sent his Son, Jesus Christ, to die on a cross in our place. All we have to do is repent, accept Him, accept we are sinners, that we deserve to die and believe Jesus is the Son of God, who died for us, and is our only way to salvation. That's it."

"That was a lot quicker than last time."

"Yeah, well, I'm not sure we have as much time as we did last time."

"I'll think about what you said."

"You think, I'll pray."

Angela stayed true to her word and remained silent. Tim was abruptly and inexplicably clear headed. The tension of the last few days drained from his body and he found himself thinking about what Angela told him, the essence of the Christian faith, the faith of his fathers. It occurred to him the further America had gotten from its traditions of Christianity, the worse things got. Maybe that wasn't just coincidence. He felt odd, like they weren't alone, as though some other presence or person or something waited with them.

Tim looked over at the back of Angela's head. She was staring out the passenger's window, leaving him with his thoughts.

The rain continued its monotonous metallic patter and Tim couldn't worry about the Society, or about the recording or about Angela. All he could think of was what Angela has just told him. Sin, Jesus, the Cross. The passage of time didn't slow down or speed up, but it did seem to change.

"That's them," Tim said.

A vehicle rounded the bend with its lights flashing in three short bursts.

"Quick, you've got to—"

"Shh, we're okay, Angela."

Tim snapped his headlights on and off until the Cardinal's men passed by them. Then he picked up his phone, stuck the batteries in and turned it on. A few moments later the phone rang. Tim answered on the first ring.

"We saw your lights," Tim said, "You just drove past us."

"We're coming back, so get ready to move," Ted replied. When we locate you we'll pull over and park on the berm of your side of the road. Soon as we do, kill your lights and climb up to the road. Can you do that?"

"Yes."

"When you get to us, get right into the Explorer—"

"Explorer?"

"We're in Ford Explorers."

"Okay, I get it."

"As soon as you get to the road, climb into the back of the Explorer. Don't talk, don't look around, don't stop for anything. Get in. As soon as you're in, we move. Understand?"

"Yes."

"It'll take us a few minutes to get turned around, so keep an eye out for us. We'll be coming from the opposite direction and flashing our lights. I'm hanging up, but keep your phone turned on and call me as soon as you see our lights."

"They hung up," Tim said to Angela. "We're waiting for them to turn around. They'll pull over at the top of the hill. We're supposed to climb up and get into the back seat of the SUV with no delay."

"You're awfully nonchalant about this," Angela said. She sounded almost jealous. Tim still felt as though he wasn't alone in his own head. He reached out and took Angela's hand.

"Let's just wait," Tim said. "It's all going to work out."

A few moments later headlights re-appeared from the opposite direction, flashing in bursts of three.

"Get ready" Tim said, pulling back his hand. He called the Fellowship.

"This is Ted."

"I see you, keep coming in, keep coming."

"Tell me when to stop," Ted said. "We're going pull over on your side of the road and wait on the berm. Don't forget the recorder."

"Now!"

"Now," Ted yelled.

Tim watched the headlights slice across the oncoming lane of traffic as vehicles parallel parked off the berm of the road. The Explorers sprayed cinders and sent gravel pinging off the steel guardrail.

"Get up here, MOVE," Ted said. "Your life may depend upon it."

"Come on Angela, let's go."

Tim threw open his door, grabbed his backpack and raced around in time to get hold Angela's arm and start up the hillside. The rain turned parts of the ground muddy and even the grass and vegetation covered areas were slick.

"Tim let me go," Angela said, shaking free.

"Hurry then."

They dug their feet into the turf and leaned forward, using their legs and at times hands to scramble up toward the roadway. About halfway up Angela gasped, her feet shot out from under her and she flopped onto the loose turf.

"Tim. Tim!"

Tim watched her sliding down the hillside, reaching out, grasping at the dead fall and flailing away at the small shrubs in an effort to slow her rate of descent.

"Hurry!"

The command came from a man standing at the guardrail, back lit by powerful white halogen headlights. He cast a long, ominous shadow, like the spirit of some ancient pagan idol. The shadow motioned with its arm. "Move."

"Coming," Tim shouted. What he didn't say was 'not without Angela.'

Tim crawled, slipped and slid his way down the hillside. Angela had come to a stop in large patch of mud and couldn't get her footing. All her thrashing did was tear up the ground, create more mud and make the footing even more slippery.

"Wait. Angela wait!"

She kept trying to dig in, only to have her feet slide one way and then another.

"Stop Angela!"

"No!" She was mud covered, crying, moving almost spastically in her effort to get back on her feet.

"Angela."

"No, they'll leave me, and the others will take turns with me. They'll-"

"No! Stop. I've got the recorder and I'm not leaving without you. They're not leaving without me. I'll die before I let anything happen to you, ever. I love you."

Angela stopped flaying at the mud and sat motionless. She was still crying, but quietly now. Tim sat in the mud, a few feet away from her. He didn't move and said nothing. He just looked at her.

"What are you doing?" It was the big guy at the top of the hill again. "Get up the hillside, now. What's wrong?"

Angela sniffled and wiped her nose with a muddy jacket sleeve. She looked up at Tim with a wide swatch of mud now smeared across her cheek.

"Then what are you waiting for?" she said. "Help me get up."

———◆———

Ted Kehr was about to go down and drag Lewis up the hillside when the Societies' lead units roared around the bend and squealed to a stop a few car lengths away. Society guys spilled out of the vehicles and poorly aimed, shooting-for-the-sake-of-shooting, gunfire erupted from both sides. Ted took cover behind the heavy gage steel guard rail and post. Like all good veteran combat leaders, his perception of time slowed.

"Cease fire, cease fire! Conserve ammo and wait for clear shots," Ted yelled. His team was well armed, but no one was carrying a lot of ammunition. What little extra ammo they had was inside the SUVs's.

Alan Williams gave the same order. His team couldn't afford to waste ammunition. An extended gun battle would soon leave them with nothing to do but throw stones at the Fellowship. Since the Fellowship team just arrived Williams suspected that, although outnumbered and rusty in combat experience, they were probably better supplied with ammo than he was.

He decided to order his men to all open fire at the same time. The covering fire would allow two of his other men to hop over the guardrail, get down the hillside and move around behind the Fellowship. Then they could either get Lewis and the recording, catch the Fellowship in a surprise cross fire or both. Then his phone rang.

"What!"

"It's the trail team. Get ready Mr. Williams, someone just squeezed by us on the berm. They're flying down the road toward your position. I got a look inside when they drove by. The men are armed, looked like shotguns. They're players."

"Follow them. Get behind them, take them out or at least pin them down so they can't interfere with operations on this end. Now," he screamed to his men. Everyone opened up with a withering fusillade of gunfire, pinning Ted's men down.

"Angela, if anything happens to me, the recorder's in my inside jacket pocket. There's a zipper on it, unzip it, dig down, it's there. Take my backpack, it has money and all you'll need to get rescued."

"Tim!"

Angela was crying again and though covered with mud. Tim couldn't remember ever seeing her as beautiful.

"We're going to escape. We're being rescued," she said.

"Do you hear that gunfire? Look up; it's all coming from the other guys, the bad guys. There's an endless supply of them, they never stop coming. They know everything." A wave of despair rushed over him. He wasn't going to be given his chance with Angela. She was for someone else, not for him. Tim fought it down. "God, Jesus, it's okay with me."

"What's okay? Tim, Tim!"

"I mean it. This is bigger than me, bigger than us. If something happens. In my head, in my heart, I've done what you asked me to do. I've accepted Jesus as my Savior. Come on, through the woods."

The dream came back to him now, with more detail. Angela's cry wasn't out of fear for herself, or from pain or fright. It was grief for Tim. That was all right though. He'd been entrusted to do one great thing for his new Lord. One thing, the least he could do.

"Come on." Tim took Angela's hand and led her back down the slope, away from the gunfire, into the darkness.

They got to the bottom without much difficulty despite the slippery conditions. Tim grinned at Angela, trying to calm her.

"It's easier going down than up, isn't it?"

They reached the tree line at the bottom of the hill. Tim recognized it all. He knew what was going to happen and it didn't frighten him. It was his job to save Angela, save his Country from creatures who wanted to destroy it and be the Lord's tool to protect his brothers and sisters in the faith. Then they heard the crashing.

"I see them," Angela said under her breath. "Over there, where the bushes and trees are moving. I see them."

"Run, follow me."

Tim used his arms and legs to crash through the heavy vegetation and clear a path for the smaller Angela. They were still on a downhill slope and gravity helped Tim continue moving through the thick underbrush. "Stay close," he said over his shoulder. The crashing got closer. He sprinted.

"Run Angela, fast, now, we can lose them."

"Tim, wait, help."

He looked over his shoulder. Angela was caught in a tangle of weeds and vines. Tim was still running full out and tried to slow down, thinking the best thing to do-.

Brief but searing pain pierced his head and chest. Then there was nothing else.

———◆———

Another truck stopped after flying up Freedom Crider from Conway. It managed to reach the battle site just after the first gunshots erupted. Someone took advantage of a lull in the fusillade to yell.

"Ted! Ted Kehr."

"What?"

"We're with the Fellowship, Guzetti sent us. The Society's got some kind of makeshift roadblock back there. All the traffic's backed up. You'd better turn on the radio. Stop shooting and turn on the radio."

The reinforcements from West Virginia and Ohio or a trick?

"What're you talking about?" Ted said.

"He's right Mr. Williams, turn on the radio!"

The voice came from the Society side of the road, a new man reinforcing Williams? Ted couldn't tell, but on the north a second reinforcement team sent by Guzetti had reached the area. It and Williams' team had each other locked in a standoff. Ted peeked around the guardrail. The Society man leaned out from behind an open door and shouted again.

"We had the radio on," the man shouted, "something's happening you need to know about, Mr. Williams. Turn on the radio!"

"Cease fire," Williams shouted aloud and into his radio.

"Cease fire," Ted ordered.

"Maybe we should turn on a radio for a minute," Williams shouted. He leaned out from behind his vehicle to make eye contact with Ted.

"Maybe you're right," Ted shouted back.

One of Williams' men moved to his car door and started to reach in. Two Fellowship men raised their guns.

"Don't do it," one of them shouted.

Society operatives began shouting back, threatening the Fellowship. The situation was ready to spin out of control until Williams held up his hand, warning his men off.

"You've got to be kidding me with this," Williams shouted, looking from the Fellowship volunteer back at Ted.

"Stand down Pete! Everyone else, stay in place," Ted said. Ted pointed to William's man leaning inside the car. "Open the door and turn on the radio."

Williams motioned his permission. The Society operative opened the car door, and switched on the radio.

"Turn it up," Ted said.

Williams looked back and nodded.

". . . at 8:37 p.m. mountain time while flying to California for Justice Kahn's memorial service. Just a moment."

Empty air buzzed out of the speakers until the announcer came back on, mumbling off-mike.

The rain stopped and a cold wind whipped up, whistling through the trees. The smell of cordite was everywhere. Artificial light from the vehicle headlights lanced out in all directions, piercing the darkness and casting unearthly shadows. Ted's ears were still ringing from the gunfire.

"Debris is scattered over several miles of rugged terrain," the announcer said. "The aircraft was carrying not only the President, but also his family, Supreme Court nominee Anders and Judge Schlack, who insiders tell Fox News was the President's choice to replace Justice Kahn on the Supreme Court. Just how such a highly sophisticated aircraft as Air Force One could have crashed without any prior mechanical problems is-"

Every cell phone and pager in the area rang, beeped, buzzed or played music.

"Turn them off," Ted shouted.

The two leaders pulled out their phones, listened, and watched each other across the no-man's land separating them. Both men moved out from around cover, holding their cell phones to their ears and holding each other's eye.

"Mr. Williams, this is the Chairman. Airforce One has crashed. Everyone's dead, the President, his family, and both of our Supreme Court Nominees. The police have recovered from the diversion you've set and are now responding to some sort of incident along Freedom Crider Road."

"What should-"

"Get your team out of there," the Chairman said. "Immediately. Any violence will only lend credence to the allegations the hypocrites will make against us."

"What about the recording?" Williams said.

"We've already provided the media with fraudulent psychiatric records of impeccable quality for Merkel and Stueben. They go back decades in the case of one man and since childhood in the case of the other," the Chairman said. "I'm told not only do those records detail their paranoid fantasies and history of hallucinations, they almost predicted the tragic murder suicide that just took place."

The Society killed both Merkel and Stueben and framed them. Williams wondered who was next. The Chairman continued.

"Any record of their insane ramblings will make a spectacular, but temporary, splash in the national consciousness. Just get out without incident."

"Understood, sir."

Williams put away his phone and watched Ted Kehr.

Ted watched him back. Guzetti had confirmed the crash and probable death of the President and two Supreme Court nominees, but he wasn't quite as certain. The Society still had better intelligence than the Fellowship. Before Ted could decide how to respond to a fluid situation Williams called out to him.

"If you don't interfere, I'll pull my men out," Williams shouted to Ted. "Your two rescues and recording are nothing more than a National Esquire story now. Interfere with our departure and you'll all die."

"Don't be so sure."

"Of course," Williams sneered. "You've got nothing but the best backing you up, right?"

The news reports on the radio cut away from the national announcers as one of the broadcasters brought in a local reporter.

"Craig, we've got a local reporter on site."

"Please, go ahead; we understand a cell phone caller from the crash scene is coming in on our "You make the News" eyewitness line. This is Craig Howard on World News Radio, go ahead."

For a moment the airwaves were filled by a woman's sobs, then, "Yes, my name's Ainsley Dunlap, I live nearby here and was coming back from-"

"Tell us what you can see from your vantage point?"

"It's Airforce One, I mean a part of it, you can see it says 'United States of Amer' and then it's cut off. All the metal, like a big can opener." Dunlap sobbed. "I mean there are just pieces left. Nothing."

"What about survivors, Ainsley?"

"No. You have to see this, there's fire and pieces and hunks of the plane, nothing I can see bigger than a car, maybe one piece is as big as our double wide, but it's all on fire."

"So load up then," Ted said.

Williams motioned and his men backed up, one by one climbing into their vehicles, then leaning out the windows with their weapons at the ready, covering their teammates.

Two men climbed up the hill and over the guardrail a bit further down from Ted's position. On the Fellowship side of the road. It struck Ted, Williams had almost flanked him. No, not almost, *had* flanked him. Williams out maneuvered him and only the Lord saved him, his men, the rescues and the now useless recording. The Society men scrambled into the back of one of the waiting vehicles.

Williams waited until the last of his men boarded, then backed up while keeping his eyes locked onto Ted's. The Fellowship leader didn't blink.

Finally, Williams stood alongside his door, holstered his gun, and then pointed his empty left hand at Ted's face, finger straight out, thumb up, like a pistol. After a long moment, he let his thumb fall down in a shooting motion, like the pistol's hammer.

"See you around, hypocrite."

Then he jumped into the SUV and roared off, his caravan of killers following along behind him.

"See you around," Ted whispered after the fading tail lights.

CHAPTER 30

Ted waited until the last set of tail lights disappeared before calling Guzetti.

"Yes?"

"Cardinal, no time to talk. I'm going to evacuate everyone including the West Virginia and Ohio guys by air. We'll get to the airport, but you need to do the rest."

"Understood. The plane and pilots will be ready."

Ted turned to his men.

"Anyone hit?"

"Me, shoulder."

Everyone else was standing, but the wounded man was sitting in the gravel, leaning against a guardrail post.

"Blood type?" Ted said.

"O positive."

"Someone get the kit and deal with that," Ted said. There was an M-5 medical bag in the Explorer. "Cardinal? We've got one wounded. Nothing critical but he's losing blood. He's O positive."

"We'll work on it."

"That's it then." Ted hung up. "Eyes on me," he said in a loud voice. "We know the Society created a diversion, but we have no idea how long it will delay the police. The clock's ticking."

Ted took a flashlight out of his Explorer and slammed the door shut. He pointed at the two newly arrived teams.

"You're leaving with us by air. I want the West Virginia team to recon the road to Cranberry. Are the Society vehicles still blocking the road? Any police check points? Any backed up traffic? Leave your weapons here and swap cell numbers with us. Call in as soon as you know. Everyone else, split up with the Ohio guys, equal distribution in the vehicles. Leave a hole in the Explorers for four people, two and two. Pete and I are going after the two rescues. When I get back, I want to be moving the second I close the door. Let's go."

Ted high stepped over the guardrail and began a slip sliding descent to the van. When he reached it he turned on his flashlight and swept the area. Lewis had left a clear path of beaten down vegetation. It started raining again.

"Pete?"

"Yeah."

Pete was huffing a bit.

"Over there," Ted said, pointing with his flashlight. The beam cut through the night and glistened off of wet, autumn colored plant life.

"I see it."

"I think the Society cleared out but who knows? Keep your pistol drawn, just don't shoot the rescues."

Ted followed the path Lewis created and worried about the time. He pushed through a heavy patch of underbrush and looked up. A short distance ahead someone was sitting on the ground beside a prone figure.

"We're from Guzetti and the Fellowship," Ted shouted, flashing his beam on the couple. He could sense Pete closing the distance and picked up his own pace. A lovely, mud covered young woman sat with Tim Lewis' head cradled in her lap. She was crying.

"Will he live," she asked as he reached them.

Ted pulled Lewis' eyelids back with his thumb and forefinger, flashed the light in his eyes, then checked his ears for blood. That's when he felt it. One side of Lewis' chest was sticky with blood.

"He ran into that tree and hit his head, really hard," the woman said. "Is he going to be okay?"

Ted shone his light on the tree. Somehow one of its chest high branches had been broken off. A sharp three or four inch stub jutted out, smeared with blood.

"He has a concussion, but that's not the problem." He impaled himself on that tree, that's the problem, Ted thought. "What's your name?"

"Angela. But is Tim going to be–"

"This could still–"

"Ted?"

Ted looked up. Pete holstered his pistol and tapped the face of his watch with a finger. Ted grabbed Lewis by the front of the shirt and pulled him into a sitting position.

"This could still turn out badly Angela, so do exactly what I say, as quickly as you can. Understand?"

"Yes."

"Pete, fireman's carry. Angela, follow us."

The woman got to her feet and waited. Ted and Pete each took one of Tim's legs, locked arms behind his back and then stood, lifting him. Once they got their balance Ted said, "Let's go." They half jogged, half hobbled back to the van.

"Put him down," Ted said.

"How are you-"

"Quiet Angela."

"I'm thinking we drag him," Ted said.

"Then let's carry him over there. The grass is wet, but not torn up. He'll slide," Pete replied.

"Right."

They carried Lewis a few dozen feet further, then laid him in the grass. Each man grabbed an armpit and pulled, slipped and scrambled, dragging Lewis' dead weight toward the top of the hill. Two men were waiting at the guardrail.

"West Virginia says the SUV is still blocking the road," one of them said. "There's no sign of cops, but some of the civilians are squeezing around the barricade. So far, all's still clear."

Ted didn't bother grunting back until they got to the top. When they neared the guardrail two team members took over.

"Tell Doc he's got a puncture wound in the chest," Ted said. The men picked up Lewis and put him into one of the Explorers. Ted gestured to the other Explorer.

"Come on Angela."

She followed without complaint, impressing Ted. The woman knew when to keep quiet and didn't lose her head when separated from Lewis. Ted pushed Angela into the Explorer and climbed in behind her. As soon as the door closed the driver took off. The SUV's closed ranks and sped up until the first of the civilian vehicles flashed by them.

"Easy," Ted said. His driver let up on the gas. The number of cars in the opposite lane increased from a dribble to blocks of two and three cars at a time. Someone's phone rang.

"Ted?"

"Yeah?"

"The West Virginia team parked at that Denny's in Cranberry. Four police cars just blew past them, sirens, lights, the whole she-bang."

Ted's driver looked over. "I'd feel a lot better if we were past the SUV barricade by the time-"

"Do it."

The driver accelerated, dodged a car drifting over the center lane and maintained his speed for about five minutes. They rounded a final bend and closed on the Society SUV. It was parked cross way in the road, its four-ways flashing. A cherry red Chevy Impala was creeping between the grill of the SUV and the hillside.

"There," the driver said pointing, "but that guy's trying to sneak-"

"Take the other side."

"Ted, there's not enough room."

"Do it."

"Yes sir."

The driver swerved into the opposite lane, straightened the Explorer's approach and looked for the best angle to squeeze between the Society SUV's bumper, the guard rail and a very steep hillside. There didn't appear to be enough room. Committed, the driver didn't hesitate. After a few minute corrections as he approached the gap, he slowed, then accelerated. The Explorer scraped the SUV's bumper and guardrail, but cleared both. The others followed them.

A line of backed up traffic prevented them from re-crossing to their side of the road. The Explorer tip toed along the edge of the hillside, spraying cinders and gravel into the wheel wells as it went. A few car lengths down they found a gap between an already slowing Ford Taurus and a Volvo Wagon. A wide mouthed platinum blonde jumped on the Volvo's brakes. Ted's driver twisted the wheel and shot through the gap behind her. Ted glanced down at a weirdly spelled "Coexist" sticker on the Volvo's bumper.

"Try telling *them* that, Buffy," he muttered under his breath.

"What's that Boss?"

"Slow up until the others get clear," Ted said.

"I've already got two sets of head lights in my rear view," the driver said after a minute.

"Go," Ted replied. "Everyone in the back, get down below the window sills until I give you an all clear. Call the other men and pass that on. It's an order. Angela, you okay back there?"

"Yes."

"This is almost–"

"Ted."

Ted swiveled around to find multiple sets of fast approaching emergency lights.

"Act normal. Slow down, move to the right and make as much room for them as you can. Watch them as they go by, like we're rubber necking. Everyone else get way down."

They slowed and inched toward the right side berm. The first police car flashed by, followed by another, then a third. None of them gave the Explorer a second look. Ted watched the police whizz past the other Fellowship teams.

"That's it, fast, but not too fast," Ted said to his driver. "Everyone else, keep your heads down. I know it's uncomfortable but a loaded SUV attracts attention, especially when it's loaded with guys who look like us. Probably another twenty minutes to the airport."

Ted's phone rang. "Ted."

"It's Doc. Tom's shoulder's stable, but Lewis' becoming a problem, boss." All present or former Special Forces medics were forever called "Doc," even if, like Doc, they were now ophthalmologists in civilian life.

"Tell me."

"That puncture wound in his chest must have nicked something arterial. I've got him plugged up, but he's still leaking some. He's lost a lot of blood, Ted. I'd guess he's right between a Class Three and Class Four Hemorrhage. I just took off the BP cuff and his pressure's dropping. Fast. Unless we do something, it won't be long until he goes into shock."

A Class III Hemorrhage meant the kid had lost at least 30 percent of his circulating blood volume. At that point, your blood pressure drops, heart rate increases, and you either pass out or become delusional. When you lose more than 40 percent of blood, a so-called Class Four Hemorrhage, you die.

"Angela, do you know Tim's blood-"

"It's A positive," Doc said before she could reply. "Kid's a blood donor. Got a Red Cross card in his wallet."

"Never mind," Ted said to Angela. "How long do we have?"

"Fifteen, twenty minutes," Doc replied.

"I'll call you back."

Ted punched Guzetti's number.

"This is Guzetti."

"Cardinal, the rescue's bleeding out. Besides the O positive we'll need A positive whole blood waiting-"

"Negative on the blood Ted. We'll be ready for you at the retreat, but not on the plane. Too short a notice."

"He won't make it."

"I'm sorry but we couldn't get any-"

"Gotta go." Ted hung up. No blood and they didn't have plasma either. The hospitals showed up as symbols on his Blackberry and they were all too far away to help. Right after a big drop in blood pressure came shock. After shock came death. The Lewis kid was barely done with acne.

Ted punched in Doc's number. They were going to have to do a direct blood transfusion - man to man. No one did "man to man" anymore, not only because of technical progress, but because of the danger the procedure entailed for both donor and recipient. No one did it. No one, that is, except for deep insertion Army Special Forces detachments. SF used it because after they were inserted hundreds of miles behind enemy lines, they were on their own. There was no whole blood, no plasma and no refrigeration, let alone a hospital. SF often relied upon techniques for survival that other westerners hadn't used in half a century or more. Someone picked up.

"It's Doc."

"You've got an M-5 bag, what about a man to man transfusion?"

"I was afraid you'd say that so I asked around. Nobody here is A pos-"

"I'm not sure we could make it to the plane in time, even if we had blood, and we don't."

"No blood? Then we've got to get him to a-"

"Not enough time. I checked the hospital and they're too far way. This happens now or not at all. Is everything in the bag?"

Doc would need Inter-venous or IV line, two catheters or IV needles, and specially formulated anticoagulant tablets. Of course a hand pump would be nice too, but not necessary. One of the greatest dangers in blood transfusion was the tendency for the blood to clot, blocking the lines or catheters connected to the recipient. Even though it was dangerous for the donor, the answer was to give the donor anticoagulant drugs that retarded blog clotting.

"I've got everything I need, Boss."

"Anybody here A positive?" Ted didn't wait for an answer. "What about universals?" There are eight types of blood, counting positives and negatives. So called Universal Donors, both Os for plasma, O negatives for whole blood, were the gold standard. They could donate blood to almost anyone without causing an immediate transfusion rejection and death.

"This is going to be hard enough going A to A, Ted," Doc said over the phone. "O negative to A positive with no cross matching and–"

"Tough. Get–"

"I'm A positive."

It was Angela. Great, Ted thought. In the first place, women only had about five pints of blood to a man's seven. Next, under normal circumstances, an anticoagulant like warfarin takes four to seven days to work. SF used a specifically designed anticoagulant that started to work in minutes, but carried risks so severe that the FDA banned it for all but limited emergency room uses. Several hundred recipients of Anstar-X, as the drug was called, died. SF used it on some of the most physically resilient men on earth, and then only grudgingly. Angela was about 5'4" tall and if she weighed more than 120 pounds, it was when she was soaking wet.

"We're going to hook an IV line between Tim and another person to transfuse blood. To do that, we have to give you a powerful drug that starts thinning your blood almost–"

"I'll do it. He's the Prince."

"What?"

"I'll do it. I'm in good shape, I don't have any health problems and I love him."

"Doc?" Ted sighed into the phone. "You hear all that?"

"Yeah. They don't make many like her anymore. Ted, it's as much how your body reacts to the drug as it is your size or strength." Doc lowered his voice so it wouldn't carry. "Don't tell her, but I'll control the blood flow and cut it off if she gets in trouble."

"When we get to Denny's, pull in," Ted said to his driver. "Doc, call everyone else and tell them we're stopping at the Denny's. Swap one of your guys for Angela and start to transfuse right away. Use a lot of line so we can move them to the plane without–"

"I'm doing this, not you," Doc said. "If we use a lot of line we increase the likelihood of clots, backflow–"

"Do it your way. We're here. Angela? When I tell you, get out and swap seats with a guy from the other Explorer."

"Tell me when."

Ted's driver signaled, then cut across traffic and pulled into the Denny's lot. The West Virginia team flashed their lights once, signaling where to park. The last two Fellowship vehicles pulled in and parked nearby.

"Go now."

The guy next to Angela threw his door open. Someone from the other Explorer climbed out and Angela didn't hesitate. She got out, walked toward Doc's Explorer and laughed as the Fellowship operative drew near to her. She held out her hand in a high five sign.

"They couldn't take me anymore, Jimmy," she said laughing.

"Jimmy?" Ted's driver said.

"Very cool," Ted said with a smile. Angela made the whole thing look like a family or group of friends traveling together and changing seats.

The Fellowship man may have been surprised but he slapped her hand as they crossed paths. Both climbed into the other Explorer without incident.

"Smart kid," the Fellowship man said as he got into Ted's Explorer.

"Go," Ted said. "How's Lewis," he asked as they pulled out.

"Not good. Sir, I'd leave Doc alone for a while. He's already got Lewis cathed and was going to dose the girl as soon as she got in. He's probably cathing her now," he said. Ted's driver turned left at the light and headed north, retracing their earlier route to the town of Butler and its small airport. Ted turned in his seat and watched the other three Fellowship vehicles make the turn and fall in behind them.

"Just stay in the right lane," Ted said.

Only two heads were visible inside the closest SUV, so they were maintaining discipline. Ted couldn't imagine how Doc was doing his job, but he hadn't detected movement from the back of the other Explorer either. The caravan slowed, then came to a stop while several vehicles made right hand turns. The delay caused them to miss the light and all the lights in Cranberry seemed to be maddeningly long. Ted's driver gripped the wheel with white knuckles, but otherwise didn't respond. The light finally turned green and Ted's phone rang.

"It's Ted."

"Doc told me to give you an update, Ted."

"Go." Ted watched out his window as they passed by a Wal-Mart and Best Buy. Traffic thinned and so did the commercial development.

"Doc has them both cathed and Lewis is getting blood. The girl seems to be doing okay so far and . . . Docs says to tell you Lewis' pressure has stabilized, but's still too low. He's using a hand pump between two sections of line. That's slowing things down but keeping blood flow smooth. That girl Angela's a trooper, she's . . . what? I've got to help Doc. Ted, Doc says the sooner we're on the plane the better."

"Got it."

It took them another ten minutes to reach the small county airport. When they arrived, a Dodge Caravan and Ford Econo Van were parked close to their plane. Four men were standing nearby, the same Pastor and Elder who'd greeted them when they landed and two other men Ted didn't recognize. He jumped out and heard Doc shouting orders. He turned to his driver.

"Get everything and everyone out of the vehicles and onto the plane. Give Doc whatever he wants."

The Fellowship team hustled over to Doc. Ted joined the four civilians. He didn't bother to shake hands.

"Thank you. There's blood in the back of one of the Explorers. I've got to go."

Doc had split them into teams. Four guys cut out the cargo netting from both Explorers and use it as a litter for Lewis. As they slid him out, two other men picked up Angela in a fireman's carry.

Doc protected the IV line and hissed insults at his teammates for "carelessness." Angela looked pale. Lewis looked like he was dying. The other men ran between the vehicles and the plane, loading up their gear and weapons.

Ted helped his men finish loading the gear, checked the vehicles one last time, then jogged up the metal boarding stairs. The co-pilot yanked up the stairs, slammed the fuselage door behind him and rushed to the cockpit. They were already rolling by the time Ted made it up front. Doc had Angela and Tim on blankets, lying on the floor. He sat between them with his legs spread wide for stability, watching the IV line and working the hand pump. The plane whined hard, rolled fast, then began to till upward. Ted threw himself into one of the chairs, reached out and put a steadying hand on Doc's shoulder. A few moments later the whining eased and the plane leveled off.

"How are you?" Ted asked Angela. She was pale and seemed confused.

"I'm good."

"You're lying."

"How's Tim?"

Ted looked at Doc and nodded.

"He's stabilizing, but not stable." Doc leaned toward Ted and lowered his voice.

"Hey," Angela said.

"I'm using the pump to regulate blood flow," he said to Ted. "She's given him a little over half a pint, but she only has five. I can't give him more than thirty percent of her blood without endangering her. I'll check her blood pressure-"

"Quit whispering," Angela said. "Look at him, he's dying. I feel fine. You can give him more."

"He's not dying. I'll keep the flow steady." Doc looked at Ted and lowered his voice again. "They're taking us to a sanctuary in West Virginia, not far from Wheeling Jesuit College. The co-pilot says it'll take about twenty five minutes with good winds. They've got blood, a small field hospital and honest to gosh Doctors. All we have to do is get there before Angela runs out of blood."

CHAPTER 31

AT FIRST, TIM THOUGHT HE was dreaming. Then he decided he was in heaven. He'd been lost down some deep hole, but managed to climb most of the way out. He was very sleepy, but it was a good, "you want to give in to it," kind of sleepy. Everything around him was soft and it felt like someone was massaging him. When he came close to the top of the hole, his chest and head hurt. Bad. He opened his eyes and there was Angela. She was lying beside him, watching a television mounted in the wall. When she sensed he was awake she turned her head.

"Where are we?" Tim said. "What's going on?"

"You're sucking the life blood out of me," Angela said. She smiled. Tim wanted to cry but didn't.

"Tim, we're together and we're safe."

"I've got to go." His chest hurt so bad.

"Don't go. I love you."

"Okay then, I'll come back later."

He thought it was a nightmare, like before, when he dreamed they were murdering Justice Kahn. It was only the television. When Tim opened his eyes, Angela was still beside him, but staring ahead and upward.

A familiar voice said, "The already gruesome murder suicide of Law Professor Fredrick Stueben and Real Reliable News' Director of Special Reporting, Anthony Merkel, has taken yet another bizarre turn." It was a Fox News announcer. Fox. Merkel hated Fox and now they were talking about him. Pretty funny. He giggled.

"Tim?"

Wait, Merkel dead? Wasn't Kahn dead? Was it a dream? He was

on a soft white cloud, or was it one of those fuzzy white blankets like they give you on airplanes? It sounded like a choir was humming in the distance. The announcer continued.

"Yesterday, elite Manhattan Media, Business and Social Circles, already staggered by the death of the President and the loss of much of our government on Airforce One, were rocked yet again. The mutilated bodies of Frederick Stueben and Anthony Merkel, two of the most respected and influential media personalities in the nation, were discovered by R.R.N. Security in Merkel's Fiftieth Floor Office in R.R.N. Tower.

"Now, Fox News has learned both individuals were undergoing psychiatric treatment. Merkel heard voices at times and Stueben had grandiose delusions. According to our sources, the two men became convinced they were the only people standing in the way of a world-wide conspiracy set to overthrow constitutional government in the United States. Another source close to the investigation tells Fox that a rambling note written in Merkel's hand was discovered next to the decapitated body of Frederick Stueben. In the note Merkel claimed responsibility for murdering Supreme Court Justice Benjamin Kahn and assassinating President John F. Kennedy. Justice Kahn recently died of a heart attack in his chambers and President Kennedy was, of course, assassinated in 1963 when Merkel was a young child.

"According to law enforcement and other sources, both men had long psychiatric histories, dating back to their childhoods. Colleagues, who wish to remain anonymous, have confirmed to Fox that in the last few weeks both men's behavior had become increasingly erratic. Some say they fed upon each other's illnesses until a certain paranoid critical mass was reached that exploded into violence."

"That's the real tragedy," said newly appointed R.R.N. Executive Vice President for Security and Internal Safety, Carl Hardesty. "If they'd never met, perhaps each would have sought out the help both so desperately needed. This tragedy could have been prevented if government offered better mental health coverage under the Affordable Care Act."

Unnamed sources are claiming authorities have uncovered evidence implicating both Merkel and Stueben in the rape and murder of R.R.N. receptionists Sharon Adams and Amy Delray.

A tight lipped Hardesty would only reply "no comment" to those rumors, but NYPD Detectives confirm that the investigation is ongoing. In Washington . . ."

Tim closed his eyes and dropped off. When he awoke he was in a queen sized bed with fresh white sheets. Soft morning light poured into the room through a nearby window. His chest hurt, but with a vague, faraway sort of pain that reminded him a tooth ache after taking Percocet.

Angela was curled up in a nearby chair, laughing quietly along with an attractive looking couple seated beside her. The couple looked familiar, but Tim couldn't place them. He didn't move. A long red IV line ran from Angela's arm up to a bag of blood hanging from a stainless steel tree.

"I think someone's awake," the man said.

"You look familiar," Tim said.

"Hi," Angela said.

"Hi," Tim said. "Where are we?"

"Someplace safe. Cardinal Guzetti and his men flew us here. There are armed guards everywhere."

"And these guys?"

"I'm Kevin Elliott," said the man.

He was a good looking sort of fellow who seemed a bit oblivious to his surroundings. The woman was pretty, with short blond hair and fascinating blue eyes. She watched him for a moment before responding.

"I'm Jill Elliott," she said.

"The archeologists. You said you discovered The Diaries of-"

"We *did* discover them," Kevin said.

He doesn't seem oblivious now, Tim thought.

"Cardinal Gazetti suggested it might help if had a chance to talk," Jill said. "Kind of help you get your bearings. You can't tell just anyone you were chased by a satanic conspiracy and have them understand."

Tim smiled.

"It's really helped me a lot, talking to them," Angela said.

"Most of what Jill and I went through, at least we went through it together," Kevin said. "We've been talking to Angela and according to her, most of what happened to you happened when you were on your own. It's hard to imagine how you did it."

"It's not hard when you realize they were planning on hanging people off of crosses, hanging Angela on a cross."

"Well," Kevin said, "I'd really like to hear about it."

"I'll tell you all about it," Tim said. "But first I want to know about you and the Diaries."

"Deal," Kevin said.

"Do you want anything?" Angela said. "Ice Chips? I don't know whether you're allowed to have water or eat anything or not. I know you're still getting nutrients and painkillers through the IV."

"Yeah, I can tell. I'm sleepy again. I'll talk later."

The next time Tim opened his eyes the sun was sinking behind the horizon. Kevin Elliott sat in an institutional looking side chair, reading a book.

"Classic Latin to English?" Tim asked. The IV was gone and he felt a lot more like himself.

Kevin looked up. "Yeah. It's kind of embarrassing to admit when you're an archaeologist concentrating on the Mediterranean and Middle East, but my Latin has always been weak. The person I relied upon for translation work died. I decided I better brush up on it."

"Professor Pearl Jeske, right," Tim asked.

"That's right. You've got a pretty good memory," Kevin said. "She was one of my best friends - more like a sister or maybe even a mom. Funny, I used to hate Latin but now, reading it reminds me of her. Almost makes me feel like I'm talking to her." Elliott closed the book and set it on a serving table.

"Where are the girls?" Tim asked.

"Dinner. They might go to the Chapel for devotions afterward."

"I just realized I'm starving." Tim slowly worked his way up to a sitting position in the bed. "Can I get some food?"

"Be careful. You've got some stitches in your chest. The wound's a couple inches deep and it nicked an artery."

"Do you know if I'm allowed up?"

"Actually I do. Your Doctor stopped in right before Jill and Angela left. He said when you woke up it might not be a bad idea for you to move around a bit."

"Where'd they go to eat? You bust me out of here and I'll buy."

"They're not far." Kevin grinned. "This place is technically a Catholic Retreat, but it's really kind of a compound. There's a cafeteria one floor down, at the end of the hall. The Doc did say you should move around . . ."

"You'll have a friend for life."

"Your clothes are in that closet. If you can get your clothes and get dressed without any problem, I'll talk you past the guard."

Tim threw off the blankets, but took his time rolling into an upward position. The IV painkillers had long worn off, so he was well aware of the tenderness in his upper chest.

"Kevin, do you know what happened to the recording?"

"I'm not sure. I can tell you it's not important anymore."

"'Not import-'," Tim sat down as quickly as he'd risen. Big mistake. It felt like someone stuck a fiery poker in his chest. Kevin jumped up and rushed over. Tim gasped.

"Just hope you didn't re-open that wound," Kevin said. "Sit for a minute. If the bandage starts to stain, I'm calling the Doctor."

Tim, still gasping at the pain, waved Kevin back to his seat. Kevin didn't move and it was an uncomfortable position, half on half off the bed.

"Right. How about a hand with the legs then," Tim said.

Kevin bent over and slowly raised Tim's legs so he could slide into an upright sitting position in the bed. Kevin returned to his chair.

"Those two Supreme Court nominees, Anders and Schlack, are dead. So is the President."

"I thought I dreamt Airforce One crashed and everyone on board died. I guess-"

"No dream Tim."

"Then it was all for nothing."

"That's not what Allison and Guzetti think. According to them you forced the Society's hand. If you hadn't made that recording-"

"Making that recording was sheer luck."

"If Jill were here she'd say 'sure it was Tim.' Just like you escaping from the most powerful organization on the face of the earth. From what I've seen of Angela, I'll bet she'd say the same thing."

"True. That's true. They'd be right, wouldn't they? I've just become a Christian so I'm still wrapping my head around all this stuff."

"Guzetti and Allison are convinced you forced the Society to move up their timetable for confirming the two nominees in the

Senate. They were splitting the difference. On the one hand, they were trying to catch you. On the other, they were working to keep you on the move, cold, tired and distracted. Not sure who to trust. They hoped if they could delay you and speed up the confirmation process, they'd beat you to the finish line. After the two nominees were confirmed to the Supreme Court, it wouldn't matter what happened with the recording. It'd be too late. So, if you hadn't managed to hold them off, the two nominees would have never been on that plane when it crashed and neither would the President. They would have been confirmed to the Court."

"How'd the plane crash?"

"Yeah. Guzetti and Allison get into that every now and then, free will, God's sovereignty. Who knows?"

"What do you think?"

"I think if you hadn't done what you did we'd be on our way to a dictatorship. The rest? I'm still working on some of this Christian stuff so I'm not the best person to ask."

Kevin looked uncomfortable so Tim grabbed the remote from the bed stand and turned on R.R.N. A flustered looking anchor ran a hand through her hair, looked off stage and then back at the camera.

"We're interrupting our news special, 'Losing a President' for breaking news. R.R.N. has just learned three fugitives have seized a laboratory building in the Physics department of Gulf University near Coden, Alabama. Reports are sketchy, but according to police sources . . . wait a minute, we're taking you right now to . . . Eric are we switching? . . . Yes folks, please be patient. We're sending you now, live to a police briefing on the Gulf University campus with the Coden and Gulf Campus police departments."

The screen cut away from the anchor, first to an RRN logo and then to an auditorium full of reporters. A uniformed police officer appeared to be in the middle of a press briefing.

". . . three men wanted in connection with the slaying of two Coden undercover police officers, as well as four Mexican nationals, yesterday afternoon during a drug deal. The suspects' names are Jamall Harris, Lionel "Lucky D" Ellis and DaShaw "T-Bone" Thomas. After killing the officers, the three men apparently car jacked a young women near the crime scene and escaped apprehension. Early this morning, they entered the Gulf University campus, going–"

"Where were they last night?"

"I'm giving you the information we have ladies and gentlemen. They went to the foreign language department and forced," the officer looked down at a slip of paper, "Professor Arnold Hartel to accompany them to a nearby laboratory building associated with the physics department."

"How does this fit in with their claim they have, in their possession, the copper scrolls that Dr. Kevin Elliot claimed contains the Diaries of Pontius Pilate?"

The police officer frowned at the reporter and turned to consult with a colleague. Another man joined them and after a few moments of fevered whispering, the officer returned to the podium.

"First, be sure that when I find out who leaked that informa–"

"Jamall Harris called into the newsroom and told us."

"Here's what we know," the officer said. "Someone identifying himself as Jamall Harris called the Campus Police Department and told us he and his accomplices had barricaded themselves in the physics lab. He said they were holding hostages. After warning us not to try to force our way in, he said he stole two backpacks of copper scrolls from Doctor Kevin Elliot and now had the scrolls with him. He said the scientists he kidnapped have confirmed Elliot's assertion as to the scrolls age and the subject matter of what's written on them."

The entire auditorium exploded with questions.

"Wait, wait, this Jamall Harris is saying he has The Diaries of Pontius Pilate? They're real?"

"How could they know that?" someone else said

"It turns out," the Officer replied, "that the portion of the building the criminals have taken over is where, among other things, carbon dating is conducted."

"Carbon dating," one of the reporters yelled out.

"Carbon dating. And, I suppose it's only fair to tell you that Arnold Hartel is a Professor of Ancient Latin."

"Nice to meet you," Kevin said. Before Tim could say anything, Kevin was out the door and gone.

ABOUT THE AUTHOR

JOSEPH MAX LEWIS SERVED AS A member of an Operational Detachment in the U.S. Army's Seventh Special Forces Group, the storied Green Berets. During his service Lewis received antiterrorist training and his detachment was tasked to "Special Projects." Afterward, he served as an instructor at the Special Forces Qualification Course. Lewis attended the Pennsylvania State University, where he was elected to Phi Beta Kappa, the University of Tel Aviv in Israel, and the University of Pittsburgh, receiving degrees in International Politics and Law while being certified in Middle East Studies.

After living and studying abroad, first in the Middle East and then Southeast Asia, Lewis returned home to practice law. He's a columnist in the New Bethlehem Leader-Vindicator and currently lives, writes, and practices law in and around Pittsburgh, Pennsylvania.

Find Joseph at *www.josephmaxlewis.com*

Made in the USA
Middletown, DE
03 July 2019